TORI CARRINGTON

Multi-award-winning, bestselling authors Lori Schlachter Karayianni and Tony Karayianni are the power behind the pen name Tori Carrington. Their more than forty-five titles include numerous Harlequin Blaze miniseries, as well as the ongoing Sofie Metropolis comedic mystery series with another publisher. Visit www.toricarrington.net and www.sofiemetro.com for more information on the duo and their titles.

KIMBERLY RAYE

Bestselling author Kimberly Raye started her first novel in high school and has been writing ever since. To date, she's published more than fifty novels, two of them prestigious RITA® Award nominees. She's also been nominated by *RT Book Reviews* for several Reviewers' Choice awards, as well as a Career Achievement award. Currently, she is writing a romantic vampire mystery series for Ballantine Books that is in development with ABC for a television pilot. She also writes steamy contemporary reads for the Harlequin Blaze line. Kim lives deep in the heart of the Texas Hill Country with her very own cowboy, Curt, and their young children. She's an avid reader who loves Diet Dr. Pepper, chocolate, Toby Keith, chocolate, alpha males (*especially* vampires) and chocolate. Kim also loves to hear from readers. You can visit her online at www.kimberlyraye.com.

Bestselling Author

TORI CARRINGTON

Private Investigations

USA TODAY Bestselling Author

KIMBERLY RAYE

Breathless

TORONTO NEW YORK LONDON
AMSTERDAM PARIS SYDNEY HAMBURG
STOCKHOLM ATHENS TOKYO MILAN MADRID
PRAGUE WARSAW BUDAPEST AUCKLAND

Recycling programs
for this product may
not exist in your area.

ISBN-13: 978-0-373-68829-6

PRIVATE INVESTIGATIONS & BREATHLESS

Copyright © 2011 by Harlequin Books S.A.

The publisher acknowledges the copyright holders
of the individual works as follows:

PRIVATE INVESTIGATIONS
Copyright © 2002 by Lori & Toni Karayianni

BREATHLESS
Copyright © 1999 by Kimberly Groff

TABLE OF CONTENTS

PRIVATE INVESTIGATIONS

Tori Carrington

This one's for all our online buds at Writerspace.com,
NovelTalk, R.E.A.D., Writers Club Romance Group,
Cata Romance, Compuserve, Romance and Friends,
The Romance Journal and, last but definitely not least,
RomEx. Thanks for keeping it real.

CHAPTER ONE

SLICK FINGERS SLID DOWN the length of the long, hard surface then back up again. Moist heat swirled up and around, dampening her skin, making her long for something that was taking far too long to achieve. She gave a good squeeze, gauging the liquid ready to ooze out, then rested her cheek against the familiar object she'd been longing to get her fingers around all day.

Ripley Logan finally judged the bathtub water deep enough, uncapped the bottle of bubble bath in her hand and upended it. She watched, mesmerized, as the contents mixed with the rapidly falling water. She couldn't wait to sink in and soak away the weariness that had built up through the long day.

Okay, she admitted, maybe she'd made more informed decisions in her life. Sitting on the side of the hotel room bathtub, she took a deep breath, allowing the smell of peaches to wash away some of her exhaustion. Who would have thought being a private investigator would be so grueling? Exciting, yes. That was the whole reason she'd learned how to handle a firearm, taken six months worth of specialized classes and studied up on the finer points of surveillance equipment. But her first case, and second day on the job, and she was wondering why no one had told her about the long hours, the countless people who wouldn't talk to her even if she threatened Chinese torture treatment and, well, the plain loneliness of the job. Turning the nearly empty bottle upright, she capped it then stretched to her feet. Muscles she'd forgotten she had hurt. If the reason for her tired state had been interesting, that would be one thing. Pounding the pavement looking for a woman who didn't want to be found was quite another.

She glanced at the time, then took off her watch and laid it on the sink. After midnight, and she was no closer to finding out anything more about a certain missing person, Nicole Bennett, than she had been twelve hours ago, roughly the time her plane set down at Memphis International Airport.

Ripley could practically hear her mother saying, "Maybe they'll take you back at your old job, honey. You do have six years in there. And you're a reliable and skilled worker. I'm sure they'll understand that you've had a change of heart."

Merely imagining the conversation with her mother was enough to snap Ripley's spine straight. The company she'd worked for had been bought out by another company, and a good third of the employees had been offered early retirement or attractive severance packages. She'd been the first in line to take one of the latter. Of course, the part she'd never tell her mother was that she'd seen the offer as a sign that she should stop chomping at the bit and run full out. The perfect opportunity to do something more exciting with her life. Something that didn't involve carrying an extra pair of nylons in her purse and hours shopping for dress shoes that wouldn't kill her.

Not that she expected her mother—or her father

either, for that matter—to understand her recent decision. Vivian Logan had been forty-five when she and Fred had given up trying to have a child of their own and adopted Ripley. They'd always been out of step with her friends' younger parents. While classmates were having cool birthday parties with roller-skating or movie themes, she had suffered through Kool-Aid and cupcake get-togethers with games of pin the tail on the donkey—or worse, piñatas. It wouldn't have been so bad when she was five. But she'd been fifteen.

After the last humiliating experience, when her mother had introduced crazy string to the party and emptied an entire can on top of Jason McCaffee's handsome blond head, she'd talked her parents into the notion that she was an adult and no longer needed parties, and her birthdays were marked with a quiet dinner out with her parents.

Yes, she knew her latest career move would worry the hell out of them. But the thought of continuing with her blah life the way it was scared the hell out of *her*. It would be one thing if she actually made her parents happy by leading her life the way she thought they wanted her to. The problem was that they seemed ceaselessly exasperated by her decisions, especially during her very brief but frequent streaks of rebellion that neither began nor ended with adolescence. Rather, Ripley had come to suspect that the alter ego behind those streaks was the real her. And she'd found it was fun finally letting her out to play.

She unstrapped her brand-spanking-new nickel-plated 9mm from her shoulder holster and weighed the two and a half pounds of steel in her hands. Despite how many times she held it, she couldn't get used to seeing herself holding the firearm. She felt like a kid playing cowboys and was ceaselessly filled with the urge to point it and mouth, "Pow, pow!" Only if she did it now, the pow would put a very real hole in something or someone.

The pad of her index finger easily slid to rest against the trigger. Her thumb checked the safety. It was all she could do not to hold it out, close one eye and aim at an imaginary tobacco-chewing cowboy. Instead, she pushed the cartridge release, caught the magazine, then thrust it into place, shivering at the metallic clicks and scratches. She let the powerful firearm drop to her side, then placed it on the sink beside her watch. The way things were going, the only shooting action she'd ever see was at the range. She twisted her lips. Not that she thought she could shoot anyone if the situation called for it. There was a big difference between a black-and-white outline of an individual and an actual flesh-and-blood human being. But just the thought that she could if there was absolutely no other choice made her smile.

And to think, only last week her biggest physical risk had been getting a paper cut.

The problem was that right now she'd be downright ecstatic with a paper cut.

Ripley sighed and pushed her auburn curls from her face. Okay, so today hadn't been as thrilling as she'd hoped. But that didn't mean things wouldn't liven up tomorrow. If foul play was involved in Nicole Bennett's disappearance, then Ripley was going to uncover it. All she needed was a nice long bath and a good night's sleep. Things couldn't possibly look as bad in the morning.

Suds flooded over the side of the tub to pool at her

feet. Ripley rushed to shut off the faucet. The water level was midtub. Perfect. She stripped out of her slacks, shirt and panties, then gingerly stepped into the tub. As she stood there, growing accustomed to the heat of the water, she glanced in the bathroom mirror, then did a double take. What was it about hotels that they had to position every mirror so that you had a view of every corner of the place, much less of your personal self? Choosing to ignore the bit of cellulite that begged for exercise on her right thigh, she noted that the bathroom mirror reflected the mirror on the bathroom door that in turn reflected off the mirror in the bedroom, which then revealed a view of the sitting room. She supposed some guests found comfort in seeing their surroundings—and perhaps even their stubborn cellulite. For Ripley it only served as a reminder that she was alone in one of the best hotel suites Memphis had to offer.

She reached out and pushed the door to close it. Only it didn't close all the way. As she sank into the silky bubbles she still had a sliver of a view of the rest of the suite. She closed her eyes, blocking it out.

Bubbles tickled her nose. She wiped them away with a bubble-laden hand. *Well, that worked, didn't it?* She grabbed for a towel and cleaned away the fragrant bubbles, then lay back and relaxed again. Her feet felt as if she'd just run the Boston Marathon. Either that or walked the entire distance between her home city of St. Louis to Memphis. Her body felt like she'd swum the Mississippi, which was visible just beyond the open balcony doors of her bedroom. What she wouldn't give for a thorough massage right now.

As far as she was concerned, massage was a highly

underrated skill when it came to choosing members of the opposite sex. Out of the three guys she'd dated in the past five years, a total of zero had known what to do with his hands. She groaned, finding her mood going from bad to worse. After the last dating disaster, she'd given up trying to find that one guy for her, that soul mate magazines touted, the storybook prince little girls dreamed about. She'd gotten to the point where she'd accept companionship. The problem was none of the guys she had dated had been interested in that, either. So she'd decided that her entire life in general needed some livening up. Her friend Nelson Polk had made the fateful mistake of agreeing with her.

"Never found a woman who lived up to my idea of one, you know?" Nelson had said, the steel-wool-like tufts of hair above each ear not stirring as he shook his head and considered his next chess move. The late autumn weather had been mild, the St. Louis park teeming with people out to store up memories to see them through the winter ahead. "Took me three divorces and two bankruptcies to figure that one out. Don't let the same happen to you, Ripley."

That conversation had taken place seven months, two days and ten hours ago. Ripley could pinpoint the exact moment because it had been the only time Nelson had revealed a clue to what had led to his hanging up his P.I. hat and ultimately calling a homeless shelter home and the park his backyard. That moment would be forever locked in her mind because she could envision her life turning out just like his if she didn't do something about it…now.

She had immediately voiced her thoughts to Nelson,

expecting objections or arguments or even exasperation. Attempts to talk her out of her silly idea. Instead, he had smiled, neither encouraging her nor discouraging her. And she remembered thinking that if one day she ever did become a mother, that's the type of parent she would be. She wouldn't try to stuff her child into a mold. She would give her son or daughter the freedom to make his or her own decisions.

That conversation had opened an irreparable and irresistible crack in the mold she'd felt suffocated by her entire life, and she'd stepped right through it. She'd looked up shooting ranges in the phone book and held a gun in her hand for the very first time. A life-altering experience. Not because she harbored any secret desire to go around blasting people to kingdom come. That couldn't have been further from her mind. Rather the act of standing there with her feet planted at shoulder width pointing a .22 at the target a mere five yards away shined a spotlight on her and her life. In that one moment she'd known she was solely in charge of the direction she was going. That if she continued going with the flow, making as few waves as possible, she'd end washed up on shore somewhere wondering how in the hell she'd gotten there. She'd been a secretary because… She frowned into the bubbles. It seemed so long ago even she could hardly remember. Her degree was in computer science. But she'd signed up with a temporary agency to get a feel for various companies and ended up staying a secretary.

Going with the flow.

A brief knock sounded on the hotel room door. Ripley snapped open her eyes. Room service forgot something, maybe? The bathroom mirror revealed her chef's salad still on the table in the sitting room, untouched, the requisite glass of water, side order of dressing and bread sticks all there. She reluctantly began sitting up when she heard what sounded suspiciously like a room key being slid into the lock mechanism, then an ominous click she was afraid had allowed entrance.

Someone was coming into her room.

Ripley stared wide-eyed into the mirror even as she slowly sank lower in the tub. The first thing she saw was two hands holding a nasty-looking gun. One that made her 9mm look like a toy.

This didn't make any sense. She'd spent all day beating the bushes, hoping for some sort of revealing reaction to her questions about Nicole Bennett's where-abouts. The most exciting response she'd gotten was a belch from the pawnshop owner whose coffee cup probably hadn't held coffee. At least she thought she hadn't caused any interesting reactions. She'd have to go back over her notes on reading people. Obviously she must have brushed past that section. And now there was one—now two…and three—gunmen slinking into her room.

Speaking of guns…

Sloshing as little as possible, Ripley reached out and grabbed hers from the sink. Then disappeared com-pletely under the bubbles.

Talk about being in over her head….

OH, BOY, WAS THIS EVER a night to remember.

Joe Pruitt tossed the shoe catalog to the hotel room floor then switched off the bedside light and lay back, folding his hands behind his head. Pale moonlight streamed in from the open balcony doors, reminding him of the overly bright sliver of moon he'd seen earlier. A moon made for lovers, he remembered thinking. He grimaced. Lovers. Yeah, right. For the past ten years his only lover had been his athletic-shoe company, Sole Survivor, Inc. Well, okay, maybe he wasn't being completely honest. There had been Tiffany in Texas. Nanette in North Dakota. Wendy in Washington. He just now realized the correlation between the names and the states, and his grimace deepened. Anyway, his relations with each of the women had lasted no more than a couple of weeks. Long enough for them to figure out that his company came first and everything else a very distant second, and for him to discover that once sex was out of the way, he had very little in common with any of the women. Not that it made much difference. He'd figured out a while ago that settling down wasn't in his blood.

Home base was in Minneapolis, but he had a house in San Francisco, an apartment in Chicago and a condo in New Jersey, and he probably couldn't recite the phone numbers of any of them. His cell phone. Now that was the important number.

Although recently an altogether different number had begun resonating through his brain. The number one. The Three Dog Night song of the same name had been playing right along with it. Where one had been more than okay with him before, now it seemed to be emerging the loneliest number, indeed. He noticed it during his last trip to New Mexico, when he'd landed the big deal with Shoes You Use. Deals like that one always planted a grin on his face. But for some reason, the three months of courting the account, wining and dining the company's reps, then the bigwigs, had felt anticlimactic somehow.

Anticlimactic. Now there was a word. Yeah, well, if he'd paid more attention to the girls at the strip joint earlier, maybe even now he'd be experiencing some real climactic moments. Instead, he'd spent the four hours at the men's club staring at the dancers' feet, fixated on his plans to expand his collection of sports shoes to include daily wear. It was then he knew something was really wrong with him. Here were fantastically sculpted women with perfectly bare breasts, and he was fascinated with their feet.

Joe shifted uncomfortably. He was reasonably sure that the account reps he'd been schmoozing hadn't noticed his distraction. Then again, why should they have? They'd been doing all the things normal men did when a naked woman was shaking her wares in their faces. Namely hooting, hollering and stuffing sweaty bills into barely there bikini bottoms.

Maybe he'd just been to one too many strip joints, he reasoned. There was nothing wrong with him. It was normal to encounter the odd rough patch, wasn't it? Times when things didn't make much sense? When a guy stopped cold in his tracks and asked himself just what it was all about, anyway?

Yeah? Well, then, why had he never experienced one before?

He'd always been happy with his bachelor status. Very happy. A jock of all sports throughout high school, he hadn't allowed his physical capabilities to get in the way of his education and he'd graduated in the top ten percent of his class. An injury while playing college

basketball had left him facing a long recovery period.
But rather than wallowing in self-pity, he'd traced his
injury back to the shoes he'd been wearing and had
designed the first of what would be many pairs. He'd
graduated, was featured in Forbes at age twenty-five and
for all intents and purposes was one of the most successful bachelors on either side of the Mississippi. He'd even
finally managed to earn his father's stamp of approval a
couple years back when he'd finagled a sponsorship deal
with a top player with the Minnesota Timberwolves. A
basketball fan from way back, his retired Army colonel
father had grinned from the courtside seat the entire
season. It was the first time Joe had ever seen tears in
his father's eyes, the day when the entire team had posed
for a picture with the old man in center court.

Joe found himself grinning. Yes, that had definitely
been a highlight. And his actions had earned him an
ally against his mother whenever she launched one of
her "I want grandchildren" attacks.

Joe figured he'd had it pretty good. An only child.
A successful entrepreneur. A relatively problem-free
existence.

Then why in hell did he suddenly feel like he was
missing the point? That there was something he just
wasn't getting?

A shadow fell across his bed from the direction of
the open balcony doors. Probably a cloud. He rolled
over, away from the balcony, and folded the pillow
under his head. He had a full day on tap for tomorrow.
Another tour through the target company's inventory
warehouse. A look at charts and graphs of how their

other products were doing. Another night spent playing the good old boy.

The sheet around his midsection stirred. He grimaced and looked at it. What the hell?

His thoughts stopped completely when a slender female hand circled his waist from behind. Simultaneously, he felt a hot, wet body slide against his back. A very naked, hot, damp body.

Had he fallen asleep? Was this a wet dream, like the ones he used to have when he was seventeen?

The hand rested against his abs between his ribs and his navel. His stomach automatically tightened. The smell of peaches teased his nose. The details seemed very real to him. And if he was asleep, he wanted to get a glimpse of this dream girl.

He moved to turn around.

"No, don't!" a female voice whispered, the arm tightening around his waist, the hand slipping a little lower.

Joe swallowed hard. Definitely not a dream.

Sounds of footsteps on the balcony, and more shadows fell across his bed. Then suddenly, where he'd been pinned in place moments ago, the same arm was flattening him on his back and the woman was straddling him.

Breasts. Bare breasts. That's the first thing Joe saw as firm thighs squeezed his hips. The same type of breasts that hadn't moved him one iota at the strip joint earlier but now made his mouth water, the stiff, peaked tips swaying a mere inch or so away.

The woman bent forward. "Stay still," she quietly ordered.

What did she mean? He *was* still.

Oh. Well, maybe there was one part of him that wasn't completely obeying.

The sound of the balcony doors being slid open, then the woman was kissing him.

No, she wasn't kissing him. She was on the brink of devouring him. The instant her lips pressed against his, her tongue darted shamelessly inside his mouth, along the length of his, then around the interior like it was a hot, dark cave she was determined to map out.

Joe stared at her, bug-eyed in the dim yellow light. Lots of dark curly hair, wide, dark eyes—her tongue dipped again, flicking against his—and a hotly decadent mouth.

He groaned against the mattress and lifted his hands, burying his fingers in the mass of damp fragrant curls tickling his face.

Sweet Jesus, but this was better than any dream. Forgotten were the strangers on his balcony, the identity of the woman straddling him, the bizarre notion that he didn't have any idea what was happening. All he could think about was the rush of heat to his groin, the *thunk thunk* of his heartbeat in his chest, the taste of the mouth even now plundering his, the feel of soft curls clasped in his fingers.

Then she moved.

Oh, God, she moved.

Joe had to break contact with that incredible mouth and groan as his erection pressed into the V of her thighs. He grasped her bare hips and held her still, his hips jutting upward against her.

Somewhere in the back of his mind, he realized the shadows were no longer at the balcony doors.

The dream nymph on top of him moved again. But this time it was away.

Joe reached for the shadowy silhouette but missed as she padded toward the balcony. A dull click, a rasp of fabric, then the light next to his bedside table was switched on.

Joe blinked at the woman standing in front of the backdrop of the closed balcony doors and heavy maroon curtains, finding her visually every inch as delectable as she had felt. Wild, curly auburn hair framed her oval face, contrasting against her pale skin, the length brushing her shoulders. Breasts full and pouty stood high on her chest, shadowing the slender waist below. The triangle of fleecy curls between her toned thighs was just a shade darker than her hair and seemed to point toward her legs—wondrously long, shapely legs that ended in a pair of sexy feet.

But it was her eyes, almond shaped, brown and large as chestnuts, that told him what had just happened was an aberration.

"I need your help," she said, her voice void of the sexy whisper of moments ago and filled with what he could only equate with panic.

CHAPTER TWO

WELL, THIS WAS NEW.

Ripley stared through the peephole in the door. Two of the three gunmen left her room then strode down the hall, obviously minus one of their buddies. Had he stayed behind in her room in case she returned? She jumped when the gruesome twosome seemed to look directly at her before stepping into the elevator. But that was ridiculous—they couldn't see her through the peephole. She drew her head back. Could they?

She turned, her hands flat against the thick metal door. The only problem was that the new view offered another unfamiliar man who also made her want to jump. But for altogether different reasons.

Peering at him through the open door to the bedroom, she saw him lying on his side against the crisp white bed linens, one elbow propping him up, the top sheet draped across his bare waist. Ripley's heart felt like it might beat straight out of her chest. When she'd formulated her plan in her bathtub, she hadn't thought beyond getting out of her hotel room—stat. She lay under cover of the bubbles for as long as she could, avoided a probing with what she thought looked suspiciously like a silencer, but the instant the men left the bathroom and were in the sitting area, she'd hightailed it out of the bath and straight through the open balcony doors. Of course she hadn't stopped to consider that she was as naked as the day she was born or that her room was two floors from the ground. She'd merely clutched her 9mm for dear life, eyed her neighbor's balcony some two feet away and acted.

She swallowed hard. She supposed she should be glad her neighbor wasn't some middle-aged, pudgy salesman. But she wasn't convinced that this guy was better. She stared at the *Playgirl* poster material staring back at her. He had tousled deep blond hair with the slightest of coppery tints, a handsome cowlick over his forehead making him look even more devastating. Blue, blue eyes that tempted every last clichéd comparison to the sea, with a fringe of dark lashes. She knew from visual confirmation as well as touch that he was one hundred percent lean, hard muscle. And he was…long. When she'd straddled him, it had taken a bit of a stretch to reach his mouth, a kiss the best she could do at the time to keep him from reacting as the gunmen appeared at the balcony doors. Well, at least she had prevented him from reacting to *them*. To her…well, he'd been a more than welcoming host.

Ripley realized her breath still came in rapid, shallow gasps and fought to control it. The problem wasn't that the guy was handsome. It was that, despite her predicament, for a minute there she'd actually enjoyed the kiss. Enjoyed it? She'd damn near inhaled him when a simple closed-mouth peck would have done.

In fact it had taken the shock of feeling just how thorough his reaction to her had been through his knit boxers to snap her out of it.

She'd never been so fiendishly unabashed in her life.

It didn't matter that three ugly guys toting guns had been the motivation. They didn't explain the genuine hunger that had filled her lying on top of a hot, anonymous guy in a dark hotel room.

"I'm, uh, what I mean is…" She faltered, not quite sure what to say to him now that the immediate danger had passed. She rolled her eyes to stare at the ceiling. *You're a P.I., for God's sake. An independent woman in charge of your own destiny.* She blew out a breath. Yeah, right.

"Thanks," she finally, lamely offered, waving her hand in his general direction.

The rasp of sheets. She blinked to see that he had thrown back the top sheet to reveal the other half of the mattress. "Well, don't you think you should give me a chance to give you something to thank me for?"

Ripley stared at him as if he'd gone insane. Then his suggestive, heat-filled perusal of her person left her mind resonating with one undeniable fact—she was still naked.

"Oh, my God." She slapped one arm across her breasts and her other hand over her…oh, my God. It wasn't that she was overly modest by any means. Her mother had always had to remind her to keep her legs crossed when she wore a skirt, or put her robe on over her pj's. But this definitely didn't fall into the same category. She looked first this way, then the other, visually searching the room for something to put on. Against her better judgment, she stepped into the bedroom. The closet door was ajar.

"Wow, the rear view is just as amazing as the front."

Ripley started, then turned slightly, giving him a side view. Awkwardly positioning her leg so nothing showed, she reached in and grabbed a blue oxford shirt from a hanger, pulling the hanger with it. It took some doing but, with her back still to him, she finally managed to shrug into the soft cotton with what she hoped was a modicum of dignity. At least until she realized that the mirror on the sliding closet door allowed the man behind her a full view of the open front of the shirt. And judging by the grin on his face, he was enjoying every moment of it.

She made a face at him. Just what kind of man didn't blink at a strange, naked woman climbing into his hotel bed in the middle of the night? She shakily buttoned the shirt. Scratch that. She didn't want to know. The truth was, she'd come across one too many just like him. Well, okay, maybe not as drop-dead gorgeous, but externals didn't matter in this case. What did is that he was probably just like every other guy she'd ever dated. "Forget the small talk, babe, and let's get down to business."

Hadn't guys figured out yet that a woman needed more?

Then again, she couldn't blame him. Hey, when a naked woman sneaks into your bed in the middle of the night, what do you do? Kick her out? No. You make the best of the situation, right?

She crossed to the bed, noticing his grin grow wider. She grabbed the sheet and gave it a yank. He moved over to make room for her. She smiled and reached toward his crotch.

"Now that's more like it," he said, patting the spot beside him.

She withdrew her 9mm revolver from under the sheet and weighed it in her hand. She was gratified by the vanishing of all amusement from his face.

"Whoa," he said, holding his hands up almost comically. "You climbed into my bed, remember?"

Ripley smiled and sat on the edge of the mattress. "Yes. And it's a good thing you're used to such events, isn't it? Or else neither one of us might be here now."

She didn't think she'd ever seen a person move quite so fast. One minute he was in a reclining position, looking like temptation incarnate, the next he was standing next to the bed, clutching the sheet to his chest like he'd been violated. Which, she decided, was how he should have looked when she crawled into bed with him. "Let me get this straight," he said. "You're not a…gift from one of my colleagues."

Ripley's brows moved up on her forehead. She polished the nickel-plated gun with the corner of the sheet. "Do you often get gifts of that nature?"

"Never."

"No, I'm not a gift from one of your colleagues. And I'm not housekeeping looking to make your bed while you're still in it. Or room service, wanting to redefine the meaning of the term." She waved the revolver. "Don't worry, I pushed the wrong button and the clip fell out in the bathtub anyway." She put the handgun on the bedside table closest to her, then leaned across the bed, her hand extended. "Hi. I'm Ripley Logan, P.I."

Oh, how she'd always longed to say that. Some of the patina had worn off during her daylong search for answers, since not one person had seemed impressed by the badge she'd ordered from a magazine. But this guy's reaction made all those blank, unimpressed stares worth it. Even if his expression was probably due more to the gun he kept staring at. While the people she'd encountered all day had gone out of their way to see that she didn't get what she was looking for, this one had wanted to give her everything she was looking for. Er, everything she *wasn't* looking for.

A surprising shiver shimmied along her arms then down her back as she remembered the texture of his tongue against hers and the hot, hair-peppered skin of his chest whispering against her hardened nipples. God, but the guy could kiss. She'd give him that. It had been a good long while since someone had made her toes curl.

She watched him, waiting for him to snap to. Only when he did, she immediately wanted the other guy back. This one…well, the amused glint in his blue eyes warned her to prepare herself. "P.I., huh?"

Just as she thought. She finished buttoning the borrowed shirt, her damp hair falling over her face. "Do you have a name?"

"Uh-huh."

She slid a glance at him. "Are you going to share it with me?"

"Depends," he said, looking to where he still grasped the sheet. He dropped the linen then widened his stance, planting his fists on his hips. For a guy in nothing more than clingy cotton knit boxers he managed to look sexier than all get out.

"On what?"

"On whether or not there's a camera crew ready to

spring through the door and tell me this is a practical joke."

"Don't I wish," Ripley said quietly, then added while stabbing a thumb toward the hall, "be my guest."

He stood still for half a heartbeat, then strode to the door in the other room.

Oh, boy. Talk about the back looking just as great as the front. He had a pair of buns a girl could dig her fingers into. And thighs that hinted at an endurance level beyond anything she was used to. He peeked through the peephole then turned, catching the direction of her attention. She quickly looked away and reached toward the bedside table where a wallet lay. She flipped it open. "Joseph Albert Pruitt." She closed the fragrant, faded leather and put it back where she found it. "Nice to meet you, Joseph."

"Joe."

She smiled. Joe. She liked that. Where he could have easily pulled off a name like Fabio, Adonis or Romeo, he had a simple, everyday name. But he was far from your everyday average Joe.

She watched as he took a pair of jeans from a chair and easily stepped into them. She swallowed. Of course he was the type to leave the top button open, revealing where the dark V of hair trailing from his navel disappeared into the waistband.

"So," he said. "The way I see it, we have two options." His suggestive grin should have sent her packing. Instead it made her stomach dip to somewhere in the vicinity of her ankles. "Either we both climb back into that bed...together."

Ripley couldn't believe she found the idea very, very

tempting. For crying out loud, she didn't know the guy from...well, from Joe. "And the second option?"

Joe ran his right hand over his tousled hair and shrugged. "You tell me what's going on."

AN HOUR LATER JOE SAT across the sitting room table from one very hungry Ripley Logan, P.I., trying not to think that under the shirt she wore, *his* shirt, was nothing but a precious expanse of flawless skin and shadowy crevices. She had one knee pulled up to her chest, leaving him to wonder what the view looked like under the table as she popped another French fry into her mouth and chewed. Part of the deal she'd made with him included ordering up room service. Only after the meal arrived would she tell him what he wanted to hear.

Well, not exactly what he wanted to hear, he amended. If he had it his way, she'd be making those quiet little throaty sounds she was making as she ate, but she'd be making them in the bed in the other room.

"I can't believe how hungry I am," she said, digging into a burger the size of a plate, then licking ketchup from the corner of her mouth. "When I got back to my room earlier I couldn't even think of food. Amazing what a little action can do, huh?"

Joe sat up straighter. He wished she were referring to the type of action he was interested in. The sight of her pink little tongue sweeping her lips just about undid him. "Yes, I suppose running from armed men will do that to a person."

She stopped chewing and blinked at him. Then a twinkle entered her cognac-colored eyes. She was enjoying this, he realized. Not the meal. Not his company.

Not what had happened between the two of them in that perfectly good, imperfectly empty bed in the other room. No, she had enjoyed being pursued by gunmen—one of whom could still be camped out in her room, if he bought what she was telling him.

"I guess," she said, waving the burger.

"The funny thing is, I haven't a clue who they are or what they're after, even though I know they have to be involved in this missing persons case I'm working on, but considering all the dead ends I hit today, and I mean not one person would—"

Joe took that as his cue that no further participation was required by him for the time being and tuned out. The way she was going, he figured he had a good five minutes before she ran out of steam and expected a response from him. He sat back and crossed his arms, enjoying watching her. He'd never seen a woman eat and talk at the same time. His mother would have been absolutely horrified. His father would have probably made one of those sounds of disapproval deep in his military throat. But all Joe could think about was how damn sexy the action was. If she approached food and conversation with such vigor and passion, he could only imagine what she would really be like in bed. Ravenous. Insatiable.

Joe rubbed his chin with his index finger. He didn't quite know what it was about Ripley Logan that captured his attention. Yes, she had Julia Roberts's girl-next-door good looks, but compared to the women at the strip club earlier in the evening, she didn't begin to scream bedroom material. But that's exactly where he wanted to get her—in his bed. Take up right where they'd left off.

The top few buttons of the oxford she filched had been left undone, and as she leaned forward to take a French fry from his untouched plate, the shirt bowed open, revealing more than a healthy stretch of soft skin. He nearly groaned, remembering all too vividly how it had felt to have the rounded flesh of her breasts pressed against his chest.

He started coughing and reached for his water glass only to find she'd already drained it.

"Sorry," she said. She wiped her hand on her napkin, then held out her cola. "I guess I was thirsty, too."

So was he, but he wasn't about to say for what. He gulped the rest of the cola then held out the glass. She narrowed her eyes and took it back.

Brushing her hands together, she said, still chewing, "So that's it. What I know, you now know."

Joe sat back. Well, that had ended quicker than he'd thought. He'd entirely missed all the cues women usually gave when they were reaching the end of their monologues. Which caught him off guard. "Well, that's... interesting."

"Exciting," she said, and that twinkle entered her eyes, making him wonder all over again what put it there. "At least after the bath part."

"Hmm. The bath."

She laughed, and he had the distinct impression it was at him. "You didn't hear a single word I said, did you?"

His brows rose high on his forehead. Women were usually offended when they figured out he wasn't paying attention. She appeared amused. He scratched his head. Go figure.

"Sure I did. I heard every word," he said, feeling required to make at least the token objection.

She pushed her plate away and rested her elbows on the table, then crossed her arms. "So tell me what I said."

Now this he was used to. All he had to do was choose a few words he'd picked up during the past half hour and he'd convince her he had been listening. "There's the missing person...the bath...the gunmen."

Her full lips quirked. "And?"

"And..." He was surprised at his own laugh. "Okay, you're right, I wasn't listening."

Now why had he gone and admitted it? He'd never done that before.

Ripley waved her hand. "That's okay. I don't think I made much sense even to myself. I probably won't until I figure out who those guys are and what they wanted." She looked to her left, then her right, then leaned forward to peer into the bedroom. "Is it nearly two already?"

She began to get up, and he caught her wrist. "What did you say?"

She blinked at him. "Is it two already?"

He shook his head. "No. The other part."

"What? That I'm going to figure out what those guys wanted?"

Yes, that was it. Now that his mind was functioning at least seminormally, an obvious thought emerged. "Don't you think it would be a good idea if you reported them to the police first?"

"Police? Why would I call the police?"

She glanced at where his hand rested against her

slender wrist. He swore he could feel the thrum of her pulse there. He removed his hand. "Oh, I don't know. Call me stupid, but if three armed men were pursuing me, and one was still possibly camping out in my room, the police would be the first people I'd call."

She reached out and grasped his shoulder, bringing her face mere inches from his. He caught a brief whiff of peaches. "Don't worry, Joe. I think I can handle a couple of armed men all by my lonesome. That's part of what being a P.I. is all about."

"Uh-huh," he said slowly. "Has anyone ever told you that you're one scary woman?"

She was insane. It was as simple as that. And if he knew what was good for him, he would be picking up the phone right now and calling the police himself.

She smiled, then turned from him, allowing an unobstructed view of her from behind. Okay, maybe he'd call in a minute. The shirt she wore was creased at her waist on one side, revealing just a glimpse of a curved cheek. He cleared his throat.

"Besides, what do you think the police would say?" she offered along with the fantastic view. But he'd bet she didn't have a clue what she was doing. "'Do you know who the men were, Miss Logan?' No. 'Do you know why anyone would want to hurt you, Miss Logan?' No. Then they'd flick their little notepads closed and tell me to call them if anything else happens." She waved her right hand, hiking up the shirt even more as she walked away from him. It was all Joe could do not to slump in the chair and groan.

She tossed him a glance over her shoulder. "By the way, you're not married, are you?"

"Married?" He all but croaked the word.

She smiled. "I'll take that as a no. Good. I wouldn't want anyone getting jealous over my staying here."

"Jealous?"

"Yeah, you know. Wives tend to get a little crazy when they find other women staying in their husbands' rooms."

"Yeah, um, crazy." Talk about the pot calling the kettle black. "What do you mean by staying? What—here?"

She frowned. "Why, yes. Where else would I stay so long as one of those mean, nasty men is still in my room?"

Mean? Nasty? Joe scratched his head. Did those words come straight from the P.I. academy?

He didn't get a chance to ask. Ripley waggled her fingers at him, then disappeared into the bedroom, not even the view she'd offered enough to take his mind from the situation at hand. "Good night, Joe. Oh, and thanks again."

She closed the door.

Huh.

Joe sat there for long, silent moments staring at the white enamel of the door, trying to convince himself that what had just happened had, in fact, happened. Had she really locked him out of his own bedroom? He slowly shook his head. This was nuts. In fact, not much of what had happened tonight made much sense. First a naked woman smelling of peaches climbs into his bed buck naked and plants a wet one on him, awakening all sorts of reactions he had just been wondering if he'd grown immune to. Then she virtually takes over his hotel room, wearing his clothes and ordering room service on his tab. Now she'd just told him she was taking over his bed…without him in it.

The same woman who claimed to be a P.I. but struck him as anything but.

Making that phone call to the police was looking more and more appealing.

"Oh, no, you don't."

He got to his feet, made it to the closed bedroom door in five strides and opened it. "I think you and I need to have a…"

His words drifted off along with his thoughts. Lying flat on her back, her mouth slightly open, one certain sexy, mystifying Ripley Logan was fast asleep in the exact spot he'd been lying in when they'd, um, first met. Slowly he neared the bed. Although why he was being quiet he couldn't be sure. He *wanted* to wake her up. Didn't he? He grimaced. Okay, maybe he didn't. Well, not to kick her out of bed, anyway.

The top sheet was bunched around her knees. He reached for it to pull it up then caught himself. Since when had he developed protective instincts? If she was cold, let her cover her own damn self up. He crossed his arms over his chest and stood stoically for a whole two seconds then sighed and reached for the sheet again. Only something else caught his attention. Namely the soft cotton of her—his—shirt. She must have moved around a bit trying to find a comfortable spot. Her squirming had caused the sheet to come off and the shirt to ride up. The hem brushed her upper thighs, mere inches from the area that had driven him crazy ever since she'd covered it. He could imagine the springy curls just under the soft material. Joe swallowed, the sound loud in the quiet room.

There was something decidedly decadent about standing there like that, watching her without her knowledge. Imagining her slick, swollen flesh just under the soft cotton.

Get a grip, guy.

Joe shook his head and turned toward the door to head for the couch in the other room. Suddenly, he stopped. Ripley lay on the far side of the bed. That still left three quarters of the king-size mattress free. He ran a hand through his hair. They were both adults, weren't they? Certainly they were capable of sharing a bed without sex being a factor. There was plenty of room. They wouldn't even have to touch. Unless, of course, they wanted to.

Ripley shifted in her sleep, rolling onto her side and bending her leg at the knee. The movement caused the shirt to pull tight across her shapely little bottom.

Without sex being a factor? Yeah, right.

He left the room and softly closed the door behind him.

CHAPTER THREE

"THIS IS THE CHART SHOWING our fiscal growth over the past three years during our contract with your competitor."

Joe sat in the cramped Shoes Plus conference room with the great view of the Mississippi that no one was looking at, trying like hell to concentrate on what the company sales rep was saying. If only the peaks and valleys on the graph didn't remind him of a certain someone's peaks and valleys, he'd probably be having an easier time of it. Unfortunately, the distractedness he'd noticed yesterday, even before one certifiably insane Ripley Logan had thought about climbing into his bed, was doubly worse today. He pinched the bridge of his nose and glanced at his expensively produced graph showing his projections for the next two years if Shoes Plus decided to contract with his company. But he couldn't seem to summon up the energy to do as he planned, which was to use his graph to cover the one the rep was droning on about.

No, he hadn't gotten much sleep the night before. Call him an idiot, but he hadn't called the police. He hadn't been able to do anything more than lie on that uncomfortable, scratchy couch not even trusting himself to go into the bedroom to get the spare linens from the closet. Instead he'd tossed and turned on the narrow sofa, fallen off the sucker no fewer than two times and spent a perfectly miserable night fantasizing what would have happened had he been able to convince the delectable Miss Logan to finish what she had so skillfully started earlier in the night.

Finally, the sales rep put down his pointer and wrapped up his spiel. Ten sets of eyes turned in Joe's direction in unison. He blinked at them, having completely forgotten where he was.

He discreetly cleared his throat, then smiled. "If you'll excuse me for a minute…"

He pushed from his chair and stepped from the room, closing the door against the open mouths that followed his progress. He pulled out his cell phone and moved toward the farthest corner of the waiting area, nodding at a woman waiting there. He punched a number, asked to be put through to someone, then waited. And waited. He waited for a full eight rings before a decidedly sleepy, infinitely sexy voice answered.

"What are you doing answering the phone?" he asked in a fake chastising voice.

He heard a soft gasp, then sheets rustle. "Who is this?" Ripley finally responded.

"Who do you think it is?" Joe turned away from the woman watching him curiously. "The guy you threw out of his own bed this morning."

"Joe?"

"Unless there's someone else you evicted from their room."

"Where are you?"

He glanced toward the closed door to the conference room. He was supposed to be working. "In a meeting."

A long, protracted yawn. "I didn't even hear you leave."

Which was a wonder, because he'd gone out of his way to make as much noise as possible two hours ago, slamming doors, opening and closing drawers, after the sounds he'd made showering and getting ready hadn't broken the rhythm of her soft snoring. He'd come out of the bathroom with her smack dab in the same position he'd left her in the night before.

"Isn't sleeping so soundly a job hazard?" he asked. "Especially after what happened last night?"

A pause. "I wasn't in any danger after I got to your room."

"How would you know that?"

"Because…because, well, I have a sixth sense about these things, that's why."

"Ah, something else you learned from the private investigator's handbook?"

A soft laugh. Joe found himself smiling.

"Is there something in particular you wanted, Mr. Pruitt, or did you just call to annoy me?"

Joe realized that there really hadn't been a reason for his call beyond seeing if she was still there. And his relief that she was proved a little off-putting. He thought of the display case on the conference table in the other room and asked if Ripley saw it around the hotel room anywhere. She told him to hang on and he waited while she looked.

He supposed he should tell her that he'd spotted the guy left behind in her room leaving at the same time he did. In fact, he'd shared an elevator with him. But that might mean she'd leave the minute they hung up.

Joe glanced at his watch and called himself a moron. A moment later she was back on the line. "Nope. Nothing of that description around here."

"Damn. I must have left it in the car," he said.

"Is that all?"

He grimaced, drawing a blank for other reasons to keep her on the line. Well, aside from the guy. "Yep. That's it."

"Okay. Well, bye then."

"Yes, bye—wait."

He was afraid she'd hung up, then she sighed and mumbled a distracted, "What?"

"Don't answer the phone again. You, um, never know who might be calling."

"I thought you said you weren't married."

"I didn't say I was a monk."

"Oh. Okay."

Joe disconnected the line, waited a heartbeat, then pressed redial. As expected, Ripley picked up on the first ring.

"I thought I asked you not to pick up the phone."

"Well, then, quit calling me."

Joe disconnected again and chuckled as he headed to the conference room, ready to face the suits in there.

RIPLEY REACHED OVER TO REPLACE the receiver on the nightstand, then collapsed against the pillows, smiling. And he thought *she* was weird. What kind of person called to tell her not to answer the phone, then called back and checked to see if she would? She stretched. The kind of guy with a sense of humor, that's what.

She settled her head more comfortably against the pillows. How long had it been since she'd dated someone with a sense of humor? A while. Maybe never, even. At least not a guy with the same wicked, inventive sense of humor Joe had. Of course, she and Joe weren't dating. They'd just slept together. In the same hotel room.

She pushed up to her elbows. A hotel room she should be at least thinking about getting out of.

She caught a glimpse of a note next to the phone and reached over to pluck it up.

"Call the police," was written in large block letters. It was signed, "Joe."

She put the paper down and glanced at the clock then leaped off the bed. Was it really nine-thirty already? She'd meant to get up early and try to follow the third guy when he left her room. Assuming, of course, that he *had* left her room.

She crossed to the wall and pressed her ear against it, although common sense told her one person waiting for another to return probably wouldn't make all that much noise. She sighed then eyed the phone. A person waiting for another probably wouldn't answer the phone in that room, either.

She placed an order for room service to deliver to her room. As soon as she broke the connection, she rushed into the bathroom for a quick shower, only after toweling off realizing she didn't have anything to wear. She stood in the doorway to the bedroom and eyed the drawers. Well, she'd already borrowed the guy's bed. A pair of underwear wouldn't be completely out of line, would it? She put Joe's shirt on, fished a pair of those clingy cotton boxers out of the top drawer, then a pair of socks from the next. Not exactly the epitome of fashion, but it would do. Then she hurried to the door to stand watch for room service, wishing she had thought to have something sent to Joe's room when her stomach growled.

Five minutes later she watched the elevator open and a white uniformed guy roll a cart in the direction of her room. She followed it as far as the peephole would allow, then with the security block securely in place, cracked the door open so she could listen.

A brief, determined knock next door. "Room service."

Ripley smiled. She couldn't help thinking that Nelson Polk would be proud of her little ruse. She resisted the urge to open the door the rest of the way and poke her head out, deciding that wouldn't be very smart. The way her luck was running, the guy would spot her when she was trying to determine if he was still there.

Another knock and a more strident call.

Ripley gave in to temptation and her screaming stomach and opened the door. The room service guy was just beginning to turn away from the door to her room when she waved at him, hurrying down the hall.

"Oh, I'm so sorry! I locked myself out of my room."

He eyed her skeptically. "Ma'am?"

"I'm Ripley Logan. This is my room."

He didn't say anything.

"You don't believe me. Okay. I'll tell you exactly what I ordered then." As she told him, he silently read the order. "Convinced?"

He grimaced while she cautiously eyed the door to

her room. Was the guy in there even now, watching her? Attaching a silencer to his gun? She shuddered and stepped a little closer to the wall where she couldn't be seen from the peephole. She'd seen a movie once where someone was shot through the peephole. Even if the logistics didn't make much sense, a little caution never hurt anybody.

The delivery guy called to a maid cleaning a room down the hall. Within minutes she was unlocking the door. Ripley hung back, trying to see beyond the small crack.

"Ma'am?" the delivery guy asked.

"What? Oh, of course."

She swallowed the wad of wool in her throat and tentatively pushed the door open, smiling her nervous thanks to the maid. If the guy was in there, she wanted to be sure she could make a clean run for it. Besides, the room service guy was pretty hefty. He would jump in to protect a damsel in distress, wouldn't he? She eyed him more closely. More likely he'd be running down the hall right after her.

Nothing in the living area.

Ripley tiptoed into the room, craning her neck to make out the bedroom. Remembering the mirrors, she glanced behind her. From the living room, into the bedroom, into the bathroom, she saw no scary shadows. She stepped into the bedroom and closed the balcony doors. Whew. He was gone.

THE WOMAN WAS AN EGO BOOSTER.

Joe grinned at the conference room full of sales reps and company bigwigs, confident that after a sluggish start, he'd made a successful comeback and had just given one of his strongest finishes ever. Jackpot. This contract was as good as in the bag.

"Gotta tell you, Joe, you had me worried there for a while," VP John Gerard said, pumping Joe's hand after he took down his chart and slid it into its carrying case.

"Don't tell anyone, but I had myself worried there, too."

John chuckled and moved away. Joe straightened to shake hands with the remainder of his colleagues, easily moving from speaker to greeter. His secretary, Gloria Malden, once told him she loved to watch him work. That no one could work a room the way he could. It was a good thing Gloria was fifty and a grandmother or else he might have thought she was coming on to him. Instead, he'd taken her words as a rare compliment. Lord knew he'd had so few of them growing up. And while he'd like to think he'd grown beyond the shallow desire for praise, he reasoned that it wasn't hurting anyone to acknowledge it when the occasional bit did come his way.

"Dinner tonight, right?" Percy said quietly, leaning closer to him in a conspiratorial way.

Percy had been the biggest tipper at the strip joint last night. Joe was surprised he had money left to slip in any more G-strings.

Joe thought of the sexily provocative Ripley Logan and wondered if she was still in his room and whether or not she'd still be requiring his…services when he finished here. He grimaced. Even if she was and did, he had too much riding on this deal to chuck it all in exchange for some amateur sleuthing with someone who was so wet behind the ears she squeaked.

"Mr. Pruitt?"

Joe told Percy they were on, then glanced toward the door through which most occupants of the room had already exited. His smile froze on his face when he saw the guy he had shared the elevator with that morning, the one who had chased Ripley from her room and into his bed, standing squarely in the doorway. His body—as wide as it was tall—effectively blocked the exit, and two guys with the exact same build and height stood behind him.

Damn.

RIPLEY REACHED ACROSS THE TABLE and plucked a strawberry from the nearly empty service tray in her room, then turned over the picture she was staring at. Dressed in dark blue jeans and a purple T-shirt, she felt much better now that she had regained possession of her room and there were no armed gunmen hiding in the shadows. Her chewing slowed as she eyed the security lock on her door. Of course, it probably wasn't a good idea to stick around too long, lest they figure everything out and make a return appearance.

She brushed her fingers on her jeans then turned the photograph right side up again. The black-and-white shot was of a dark-haired woman of about her age who could have been a double for Angelina Jolie, except that her hairstyle was different. But it wasn't so much the woman in the picture that caused questions. Rather it was the picture itself.

Ripley ran her thumb along the length of the photo. It

wasn't on traditional stock paper. Rather it appeared to have been run off a printer. And the grainy quality and downward angle of the shot made it look like something from one of those low-end security cameras. Which really didn't make any sense considering she'd gotten the picture from Nicole Bennett's sister, Clarise.

She glanced over the information again. Nicole Bennett. Twenty-eight years of age. Dark brown hair, gray eyes. No noted employment. She'd been visiting her sister one day when she just up and disappeared with the family silver. The pieces, bearing the recognizable initials ZRD, had popped up at a Memphis pawnshop two days ago.

"She does it all the time," Clarise Bennett had said in response to Ripley's questioning stare. "One Christmas she took antique ornaments from the tree."

No, she hadn't reported the episode to the police. This was a family matter. And all Clarise was really interested in was retrieving her silverware and making sure Nicole was all right.

As to the initials, Clarise had said she'd inherited the set from her maternal grandmother.

Ripley propped her chin on her palm and stared at the photo again. What type of person stole from her own sister to finance a trip to Memphis? Allowing, of course, that that's the reason she'd stolen the items. Was she on drugs? Clarise had assured her she wasn't, but Ripley wasn't convinced. Especially when she'd visited Nicole's apartment in East St. Louis and found that it was little more than a room in a flophouse, a furnished room with a sink in the corner that could technically be listed as an apartment but was little more than a closet with running water. She hadn't found anything there to give her a clue about the woman she was looking for.

She reached for another strawberry only to discover they were all gone. As were the eggs Benedict, the two pieces of toast, a side of bacon and an extra large helping of hash browns and fruit. She glanced at the front of her jeans and groaned. If she wasn't careful, she would need a whole new wardrobe in a larger size by the time this woman hunt was over.

She reached for the phone to call Clarise and give her a status report. Asking for a better picture of her sister probably wouldn't hurt, either. She consulted the file then dialed the number. A moment later the sound of a recording telling her the number was no longer in service couldn't have surprised her more. She pressed disconnect and tried again, only to get the same result.

Well, that didn't make any sense. The number had worked just fine yesterday when she'd called to tell Clarise she was on her way to Memphis. She tried one more time then finally dropped the phone into its cradle, drumming her fingers against the cold plastic, before putting in a call to her own answering machine. Nothing. Not even a call from her mother reminding her to come for dinner Sunday night.

She hated when there were no messages.

A dull, muffled sound came from the direction of the hall.

Ripley nearly catapulted from the chair and fell on her face, given the way she was sitting with her leg bent under her. But that was nothing compared to the way her heart thunked in her chest. She tiptoed toward the door, her hand resting against her chest as if to keep the rowdy organ still.

She knew she shouldn't have hung around as long as she had. She should have gathered her belongings and hightailed it right out of there the instant she knew the gunmen had left. But no. She'd had to sample the room service tray. And while she was doing that, she thought she might as well review the case file, too. No sense wasting any time.

Right.

Another sound.

Ripley scrambled for the bedroom, hoping she wasn't in for a replay of the night before.

WHAT IN HELL WAS HE getting himself into?

Even as Joe asked himself the question, he knew that whatever it was, it was sure to be a whole hell of a lot more interesting than his life had been of late. He got off the hotel elevator on his floor and strode purposefully toward his room. He'd called there no fewer than four times after Larry, Curly and Moe had left him at Shoes Plus twenty minutes ago. No answer.

Which was essentially what he'd given the three men who had introduced themselves as FBI agents. No answer.

Oh, he'd spoken with them, all right. Only he suspected he hadn't given the responses they had been banking on. Instead, he'd asked them how they'd known where he was. The first guy had said they had gotten his name from the hotel, then put a call into his secretary in Minneapolis.

Great. They probably knew more about him than any of the women he'd dated in the past five years.

No, he'd told them, he didn't know the person in the hotel room next to him. And for good measure asked what the guy was wanted for. Yes, he'd had a female visitor last night. A little Memphis treat from his, um, colleagues. Did he know how to contact her? Well, they might try the Kitty Kat Lounge, but he really couldn't give them any more than her stage name.

After talking around in circles like that for fifteen minutes, Joe had somehow gotten away with not even telling them what that stage name was. If it had come down to it, though, he probably would have made up a name. Like Naughty Nelly or something. Over the past ten years, building his own company, he'd gotten good at staving off disaster. He'd never had to lie, really. He'd merely stretched the truth now and then.

Of course he had lied to the FBI agents. Blatantly. Which meant he'd be in deep doo-doo if they figured that out and caught up with him.

After giving a brief knock on the door, he slid in his card key, then opened the barrier. No sign of Ripley, not that he expected one. The fact that the security block hadn't been on the door was a pretty good indication she wasn't in there. Still, he walked to the bedroom. Either housekeeping had already visited or his surprise visitor was a neat freak. The bed was made. The room service tray from the night before was in the hall. He looked in the bathroom. All the discarded towels sat in a neat pile in the corner.

Neat freak. What kind of woman cleaned up a room at a hotel?

He backtracked to the living area, plucked up the phone and dialed the room next to his, although he'd tried it, along with his number several times earlier. No answer.

Great. The FBI was on his tail for Lord knew what reason. And the woman who was the reason for it had as good as disappeared.

Or at least she wanted to make it appear as though she had.

Joe stalked to the balcony and pulled first the curtains, then the doors open wide. He looked from the left to the right then strode toward what would be Ripley's balcony. He hiked his brows up. There was a good two feet between the railings, and a two-story drop. Had she really climbed over, naked, last night?

The question was, was he ready to climb across, fully clothed, in the light of day?

He gripped the railing and looked over the side. An Olympic-size pool sat in a courtyard surrounded by trees. People milled about, but no one seemed to notice the man staring down at them. All it would have taken was one glance and he'd have scrapped any idea of climbing over. He'd been athletic throughout high school and college. Heights were the only thing that had ever gotten to him.

He gritted his teeth and tried to see into her balcony doors, which wasn't going to work from this vantage point. So much for that idea.

The only way to do something difficult was just to do it.

He gripped the railing tightly and vaulted to the other balcony then stood straight up, brushing his hands together in a show of great pride. Hey, what do you know? It hadn't been half as difficult as he'd thought it would be.

He stepped to the balcony door, expecting to find it locked. Instead, it slid easily open.

Damn. Not a good sign. If Ripley was in there, he highly doubted she'd left the balcony doors unlocked.

The white filmy curtain sheers billowed out and hit him in the face. He yanked them out of the way. The bedroom was just a little too quiet for his liking. Then again, Ripley might have hightailed it out of the hotel altogether the instant after they'd hung up earlier. Maybe she'd gone to the police, as his note to her suggested.

Yeah, right.

He hesitantly stepped inside, not knowing what to expect. At least he was fairly sure The Three Stooges couldn't have beat him to the hotel. Then again, who was to say that there were only the three of them?

He grimaced and looked around the bedroom for any sign that Ripley might still be there.

Well, at least the fact that she wasn't a neat freak was reassuring. Whereas she'd straightened up his room, this place was a mess. In the bathroom he made out discarded clothes on the floor. If he stood staring at the red lacy bikini underwear a little longer than he should have, he wasn't going to admit it. He crossed into the living room where a room service tray sat, not a crumb in sight to indicate what it had held. He stepped to it and smiled. The girl had an appetite, he'd give her that much. He leaned beyond the tray to the table. Papers were strewn across it. He frowned. He was fairly certain they were her papers. But had she left them there the night before, or had she been in the room recently?

He backtracked to the bedroom and stood silently in the doorway, gripping the doorjamb speculatively. The closet door was open, revealing no one was in there. The shower curtain was wide, showing an empty tub. He rubbed his chin, then crossed to the bed. Reaching blindly underneath, he groped around a bit. He heard a gasp at the same time his fingers wrapped around a warm, slender ankle. He gave a good tug, and Ripley Logan lay staring at him as if she expected Jack the Ripper.

He grinned.

RIPLEY KICKED AT JOE'S SHINS, muttering every last curse word she'd ever learned, heard or sounded like it fit the occasion. "For God's sake, Pruitt, why didn't you say anything when you came in here? I thought you were one of them."

She got to her feet and stood glaring at him, completely humiliated at having been caught skulking under the hotel room bed. And given his expression, she didn't think he was going to make it any easier on her.

"Don't tell me. Rule number two in the P.I.'s handbook. If you hear an intruder, hide under the bed."

She told him to do something that was physically impossible then strode toward the living area. Yes, this might be her first case. And yes, she was probably making a first-class mess of it. But that didn't mean she had to put up with Joe's wiseass remarks at every misstep.

"Where's your gun?" he asked, following her.

She lifted the lid that had kept her eggs warm and snatched the 9mm. She'd put it there thinking that if she was interrupted during breakfast, it would be close at hand.

Of course, the minute she'd needed it, she'd forgotten it. Out of sight, out of mind, or so the saying went. She took some pride in that the clip was firmly in place. At least this time it had been loaded. She chose to ignore the rest for the time being.

"What are you doing here, anyway?" she asked as she swung around.

"Whoa, there."

Ripley found him standing closer than she thought he would be, and the muzzle of the gun nearly pressed against his solar plexus. He carefully pushed the gun and her hand aside.

"Don't worry. It's on safety," she told him.

"Tell me why that doesn't make me feel any better."

She smiled at him. She'd forgotten how enticingly handsome he was. Her gaze caught on his mouth, and she leisurely licked her lips.

"Ripley?"

"Hmm?"

"Don't look at me that way." She watched a swallow work its way down his throat. "You might not like what happens as a result."

For all intents and purposes last night marked their first kiss. But given the circumstances, Ripley hadn't enjoyed it to the extent she would have normally. Gunmen probably had that effect on a woman. But right here, right now, there was nothing to stop her from thoroughly exploring Joe's smart, sexy mouth. She stepped forward, her gaze firmly on his lips. He caught her by the shoulders.

"Sorry, Ripley. Some men might find a woman with a gun attractive. Me? Frankly, it scares the shit out of me."

She realized she still held the 9mm in her right hand and sighed. "Party pooper."

His grin could have coaxed seedlings into full-grown plants. "You had your chance last night."

"Last night I didn't know you."

"You don't know me all that much better now."

She twisted her lips to rid them of the itching. "Maybe. Maybe not."

He glanced at his watch. "And of course you would pick now to change your mind."

"Of course."

He sighed. "I'm supposed to be in a meeting right now. A very important meeting that could have a very important impact on my company."

"Uh-huh." She could tell by the way his gaze kept drifting to the front of her T-shirt and her mouth that the idea of her kissing him was looking better by the second. She leaned in until their lips were almost touching.

"Which, um, brings me to the reason I'm here," he murmured.

"You mean you didn't come back just to pull me out from under the bed?" But before he could answer, Ripley softly pressed her lips against his.

Joe groaned, his left hand going for her right and the gun. He held it still while his right hand skimmed under the hem of her T-shirt to grasp her breast. She dipped her tongue and tasted his lips. Coffee. Something sweet.

A doughnut? She worked her tongue into his mouth. Vanilla. Definitely a doughnut. Bavarian cream.

He quietly cleared his throat, flicking the pad of his thumb over her erect nipple. "What I have in mind takes place on top of the bed, not under it…."

CHAPTER FOUR

OH, GOD...

Joe had never considered himself a particularly religious man, but standing there kissing Ripley while holding her gun still with one hand, the fingers of his other stroking her bare breast under her T-shirt was the closest to heaven he'd ever come. A heart-pounding mixture of denial and raw need exploded in his groin until he took the gun out of her hand and put it on the table, then backed up until he plunked down in a chair and she tumbled after him. Much maneuvering ensued, and what he had hoped for happened as Ripley put her legs on either side of the chair and straddled him. Preferable would be if she was minus a pair of jeans, but when her pelvis made solid contact with his he forgot about logistics and delved his tongue deeper into her mouth.

In one smooth move her T-shirt was up and over her head, tousling her auburn hair so it fell wild and curly around her face. He hungrily grasped her breasts in both hands. Not too big, not too small, she fit in his palms perfectly. He fastened his mouth over an engorged nipple and generously laved it with his tongue, reveling in the deep sound she made in her throat and the digging of her fingers into his shoulders. He skimmed his hands around her rib cage to her back, then dove toward her lush bottom, dipping his fingers into the waist of her jeans. She felt so softly decadent, so sinfully sweet. He pressed her more tightly against him, filling his mouth with her flesh and bringing his erection more fully against her.

Ripley thrust her hands into his hair and pulled him back and away from her breasts so she could launch a fresh attack on his mouth. "This...is...so...crazy," she said between kisses.

Joe completely agreed. Crazy was exactly the word he'd use to describe every moment of the twelve hours since she first slipped between his sheets and into his bed.

He ran his fingers up and down the hot silk of her back, then plunged them under her bottom as she pushed his jacket back, and fumbled for the buttons to his shirt.

Joe thought he heard a sound in the hall. Still kissing Ripley, he slanted a gaze toward the door. The security latch was securely in place. But when it came down to it, how much security would it actually provide, especially against those three guys?

All too quickly the reason he'd run out on his lunch meeting with a couple of sales representatives and re-turned to the hotel to see her came rushing back.

"Ripley," he whispered, trying to tear his mouth from hers.

She made a low sound in her throat as she tugged the tails of his shirt from his slacks.

He caught her hands in his and pulled his head back as far as he could without giving himself whiplash. He nearly cursed at the sheer desire he saw reflected in her brown eyes.

"Ripley, we need to talk."

The instant the words were out, the unmistakable sound of a card key being inserted into the lock came from the door.

In a flash she was off his lap and diving for the bedroom.

Joe began to follow, nearly colliding with her when she backtracked to retrieve her gun and myriad papers from the table. Her hands shook as she grasped all of it and sought safety.

He wrapped his fingers around hers, pulling her to a stop. Maybe it wasn't such a good idea to run with her, or help her run, not considering what he knew. "Ripley, those guys—the ones from last night—they tracked me down to talk to me this morning."

She blinked at him, apparently not understanding at first, then her eyes widened.

"I don't know what you've gotten yourself into, Ripley, or how deeply you're in it, but they identified themselves as FBI."

The lock mechanism clicked. The hell with grappling between right and wrong. He grasped her by the shoulders and thrust her into the bedroom, closing the door behind him just as he heard the outer door get caught on the security latch.

Christ. Joe closed his eyes and cursed. What were the laws concerning harboring a fugitive?

He glanced at Ripley and the panicked expression on her beautiful face. Aw, hell, who was he kidding? He'd bet his belt and his business that she wasn't any more a fugitive than he was. While half a day wasn't a lot of time in which to get to know someone, he doubted

Ripley could even bring herself to jaywalk. The woman had made his bed, for God's sake.

The sound of a body being thrown against the outer door filtered through to them.

Ripley gasped then wriggled from his grasp. He watched, frozen, as she stuffed the gun into her jeans and covered it with her T-shirt, then grabbed a duffel bag from the bed. She stuffed the papers into it. "FBI my behind." She rushed toward the balcony.

Joe followed her, the sweet bottom in question looking damn fine in those close-fitting jeans.

"Ripley, I don't think it's a good idea for you to be going to my room right now. They know about me, remember?"

"How much?" she asked, searching his face.

"What do you mean, how much?"

She stared at him.

"They know I'm your next-door neighbor. No, they don't know you stayed in my room last night, but I think they suspect it. Strongly."

"So who did you say you were with then?"

He cleared his throat. "A stripper."

She surprised him by kissing him full on the mouth.

"What was that for?"

"A thank-you. You lied to protect me."

That, he had. And he was beginning to hope he wouldn't live to regret doing so.

He watched her throw her bag over the side of the balcony and had the sinking sensation that he indeed *was* going to live to regret it. He looked over the side with her. Her bag was caught in one of the lower branches of a tree next to the pool. He swallowed hard and took a step back, taking her with him.

"What in the hell are you doing?" he asked in a hushed voice.

She frowned at him. "I'm going to climb down to the ground. What did you think I was going to do?"

"Climb down to the ground."

She wriggled out of his grip. Something she was getting good at. Before he could move she had swung her feet over the railing and was crouching to grab the lower bar of the wrought iron.

Joe closed his eyes and cursed again.

She laughed. "What's the matter, Joe? You're not afraid of heights, are you?"

"No. It's you I'm afraid of."

He gripped the railing and watched her let go and hang from the bottom part. Her feet swayed for several seconds, then she gained a foothold on the railing on the balcony below.

Oh, God...

The irony that those were the same words he'd mentally uttered only a few minutes ago when they started kissing wasn't lost on him. He feverishly rubbed the back of his neck, wondering why he and God were getting so well acquainted all of a sudden, and knowing it was because of the sexy little demon now dropping from the next railing...and straight into the pool.

Joe grinned as she broke the surface of the water, sputtering, and gave her a little wave. Then it hit him— the sound of the door about to give way in the room behind him. And there was Ripley down below pulling herself from the side of the pool. In two seconds flat he and Ripley would be separated for what could possibly be forever.

Then where would she be? Whose bed would she crawl into in the middle of the night? What other imbecile would she shock the hell out of with her recklessness?

Before he could talk himself out of it, he gripped the railing and followed Ripley's lead. When he was on the balcony below, he aimed for the cement patio beside the pool. Too late he figured out that a guy didn't have the most accurate aim when he was shaking clear down to his bones. He landed smack dab in the middle of the pool.

RIPLEY'S NECK SNAPPED BACK as Joe maneuvered his late-model sedan from the hotel parking lot. Even as she twisted the water from her T-shirt and onto the floor, she glanced around the car, which could have been a twin to the one her parents owned, a four-door Lincoln that had old fogey stamped all over it. Either that or pimp. She gazed at Joe through half-lidded eyes. No. He didn't look like a pimp. Despite the power he seemed to wield over her body, she didn't think he intended to use that same body to make money for himself.

She glanced in the back seat.

"What are those?" she asked, staring at about eight shoe boxes.

"Shoes."

She stared at him. "I meant what are you doing with them?"

He glanced at her. "I'm a sports shoe maker."

"A salesman?"

He crooked his neck as if trying to work out a few kinks. "For the purpose of this trip, yes, I suppose you could say that."

Ripley recalled climbing into his bed the night before and being thankful he wasn't a pudgy salesman. Little did she know. He *was* a salesman. Though, thankfully, not a pudgy one. There wasn't an ounce of fat on Joe's long, lean body. He had the physique of a top-rung baseball player. And a completely decadent one-track mind. Just thinking about his searing kisses, both to her mouth and her breasts, made her hot all over, despite the coolness of the water soaking her clothes.

She slid the 9mm from the waist of her jeans and laid it on the seat beside her, then pawed through her duffel bag, thankful it hadn't landed in the pool along with her. She didn't say anything when Joe took the firearm and put it on the floor under the seat. She pulled out a fresh, dry T-shirt and a pair of khaki shorts. With a quick yank, she peeled the wet material from her torso.

The car swerved, throwing her against the passenger door. "What in the hell are you doing?"

She readied the fresh T-shirt to put on. "What do you mean?"

His eyeballs looked ready to pop straight out of his head as he drew to a stop at a red light. "You're..."

She followed his gaze to her bare breasts, shocked right alongside him. She quickly put on the T-shirt, yanking it down farther than she should have. His hot gaze told her that wasn't much better. She glanced to find her pebbled nipples standing out in clear relief against the soft cotton.

She'd been so preoccupied with their flight, she

hadn't thought twice about trading her wet shirt for a dry one, completely oblivious to the fact that they were in a moving vehicle in the middle of the day. She glanced out the side window and found an elderly man grinning at her, gums and all, from a bus stop bench. Oh, boy.

Still, Joe's knee-jerk reaction thrilled her straight to her toes.

She longingly eyed the dry shorts she held, then looked at the heavy, damp denim weighing down her legs.

"Don't even think about it," Joe warned.

She smiled. "What?"

"Changing your shorts in here."

"Why?" She batted her eyelashes at him, something she had never done in her life but that felt strangely natural right now. "You wouldn't want me to catch cold, would you, Joe Pruitt? A cold could lead to a nasty respiratory infection. A nasty respiratory infection can lead to full-blown pneumonia. And you can die from pneumonia."

"We can die if I drive the car into a telephone pole, too."

She shrugged and eased the top button of her jeans open. "You don't have to look."

"I don't have to breathe, either."

She laughed. "You aren't really putting me into the same category as breathing, are you?"

"I'm putting looking at a naked woman into the same category as breathing. They both happen automatically. There's no way I'm going to be able to act like you're not doing anything over there."

"Then I'd suggest you pull the car over," she said,

and with one wrenching, skin-chafing yank, pulled her wet jeans off.

The car swerved again, then screeched to a halt in the parking lot of a small grocer. Ripley wriggled the shorts halfway up her thighs and was about to pull them the rest of the way when Joe beaned her in the head with a cardboard windshield shade he retrieved from the back seat.

"What are you doing?" she asked, rubbing the back of her head.

He was staring at her lap. "Are those my underwear?"

She grinned sheepishly. "Yeah."

He muttered something under his breath, then nearly decapitated her with the shade.

"Would you stop?" she said.

"Somebody has to save you from yourself," he said, spreading the shade so it blocked part of her from outside eyes.

Ripley bristled at his words. While they appeared innocent on the surface, she suspected a much deeper meaning lurked just beneath. Only because she'd spent a lifetime listening to similar words from her parents. "Trust us. We know best, sweetheart," her mother had told her when she'd come home with a battered dirt bike at age fourteen, bought with money she'd made babysitting and doing lawn work for neighbors in a ten-block area. Her parents had taken the bike away, promising her they'd reconsider getting her another one when she was a little older. Back then, she'd been slow to realize that "reconsider" basically meant "not in this lifetime."

She hated when people tried to take care of her. Her parents she had to put up with. Joe…

She finished dressing then maneuvered to do the zipper. "No need. I'm done."

"Thank God for small favors."

She ducked as the shade made another pass overhead until it was once again in the back seat.

She squinted at him in the bright midday light streaming through the windows. "Aren't you going to change?"

He backed the car out of the lot, nearly getting rear-ended for his efforts. "I would, but I'm afraid I wouldn't be able to get my pants off."

"Your pants should be easier to get off than mine."

He stared at her as if she weren't only missing the point, but the entire paragraph. She glanced at the front of his brown trousers and saw immediately what he was talking about. "Oh."

"Oh? Oh?" He whipped the steering wheel around quicker than he needed to and was forced to make a correction. "You nearly get us both killed by playing Sally Striptease and all you have to say is oh?"

She tucked her T-shirt into her shorts, then gathered her wet garments. "I would have thought you'd know how to handle yourself around strippers."

WELL, JUST WHAT IN THE HELL was that supposed to mean?

Joe dragged in a deep breath and slowly let it out, still not entirely convinced Ripley had just did what she had. What was she thinking, stripping down to her skivvies, *his* skivvies, right there in the car? He didn't mind so much that he was around to see. But he could have done without the old geezer nearly smashing his stubble-dotted face against the passenger window to get a better look.

The slow, even breathing exercise wasn't working. He was still as aroused as he'd been two minutes ago. And his mood wasn't improving considering he'd just as good as admitted he'd been angry that someone other than himself had gawked at what he wanted all to himself.

He felt remarkably possessive. As though Ripley was his and his alone to look at. Nude. Naked. Bare as the day she was born. Her rosy nipples pert and puckered in the middle of her swaying breasts.

All this and he hadn't even slept with the woman yet.

Yet? He ran his hand restlessly through his damp hair, then reached across her lap to the glove compartment where he always kept a clean golf towel. If he had a brain in his head, he wouldn't even consider slipping between Ripley Logan's deliciously toned thighs, much less be so obsessed with the idea that he could barely think of anything else. Including the three beefy FBI agents that not only were hunting for her, but obviously already suspected he was linked to her in some way.

He grimaced. If they'd had any doubts before, they certainly didn't now—not with both their hotel room doors securely bolted from the inside, but no one inside.

He pulled out the golf towel and ran it over his face and hair, then offered it to Ripley. She passed on it, saying she was pretty much dry enough already. He was glad somebody was. He felt like he was sitting in a warm puddle. Or like he *was* a warm puddle...of lust.

She shifted on the seat next to him. Joe was almost afraid to look for fear she'd changed her mind about her choice of clothing and was stripping yet again.

What was with him when it came to her, anyway? For three hours last night he'd been in the company of some of the finest-looking ladies Memphis had to offer and spent the entire time staring at their feet. Meanwhile, Ripley had him so hot and bothered that his wet clothes and the blasted air-conditioning weren't enough to cool him down.

He put the wet towel on the seat next to him then made the mistake of looking in her direction. "I was thinking—"

The words got lost somewhere between his brain and his mouth. Ripley was bending over the seat, doing Lord only knew what in the back, her bottom stuck high in the air. The hem of the shorts was fine when she was sitting, but when she was positioned like that...

Whatever ground Joe had managed to recover in the past few minutes disappeared altogether. He nearly ran off the road again. The blare of a horn behind him made his ears stop ringing but did nothing to put out the fire raging through his bloodstream.

"What are you doing now?" he said between gritted teeth, his fingers gripping the steering wheel so tightly he was afraid he might snap it off its mounting.

Mounting. He shifted uncomfortably then slid another glance at her round, well-shaped bottom.

She glanced at him, that same damn innocent look in her eyes. "I'm spreading out my clothes to dry." She finally turned to sit down, though Joe couldn't really say he was relieved.

He had no idea where he was going, but he figured it was good enough just to be heading away from the hotel. He hadn't spotted anyone tailing him, but that didn't tell him much. He didn't trust his abilities to spot someone if they were following him.

Minutes passed. Joe grew increasingly aware that Ripley hadn't said anything for a while. And he suspected she was staring at him. A glance verified his suspicions.

"What?" he asked, not sure he liked the deep furrow between her dark brows or the contemplative way she considered him.

"What did you mean when you said that someone had to save me from myself?"

He loosened the tie around his neck, then glanced down to find he'd never attended to the buttons she'd undone. He pulled the tie over his head and began shrugging out of his shirt. He started to protest when she reached to help. He didn't think it was such a good idea to have her hands anywhere near him right about now. Her fingers slid down his arms, following his shirt-sleeves. After she'd freed the soaked material from his body, he was left with his cotton tank top underneath. He drew in a ragged breath when she began to tug it from the waist of his slacks.

"I asked you a question. Are you going to answer me?" she asked, the backs of her fingers grazing his stomach, robbing him of breath before she stripped the tank top off.

Joe swallowed, catching her hands when she aimed for the zipper to his pants. "Not...a good idea."

She stared at him then shrugged and sat back in her seat, crossing her arms over her chest.

Uh-oh. He got the definite impression he'd upset her.

"I didn't mean anything by it," he said, inexplicably irritated that she was irritated with him.

"I think you did," she disagreed. "I think what you meant is that you think I'm incapable of taking care of myself."

He grimaced. "Well, I have to tell you, Ripley, judging from what I've seen so far, I'm beginning to wonder."

She reached for the revolver on the floor by his feet.

"What are you doing now?"

"Pull over," she said.

He looked between her and the gun. "Not until you tell me what you're going to do."

She gave an exasperated sigh, which, coming from her, was almost humorous. Almost. If she hadn't been checking her gun, it probably would have been laugh material. "I'm going to get out."

She slid the gun into her duffel bag, then raised onto her knees, presumably to collect her clothes from the back seat. Joe caught her leg before she could offer him a primo view of her bottom again. "I don't think that's a good idea." He felt her shiver under his touch and snatched his hand back. "Your getting out, I mean. Of course."

"Well, it's a good thing I didn't ask for your opinion then, isn't it?" she said, bending over.

He blew out a long, slow breath as people...

Joe briefly closed his eyes and said a little prayer, then kept his gaze steadfastly focused out the windshield and on the road beyond until she was sitting again.

"Tell me something, Ripley. What would you do if I let you out? Where would you go?"

She shifted on the seat. "What's it to you?"

He backtracked over what had happened in the past few minutes to change the atmosphere between them. He'd grown up as an only child in a house where the only person who had talked had been him. He'd had all his hopes of pursuing a sports career ripped away from him when he was nineteen. He'd gone on to build his own business from scratch and had done a damn good job of it if he did say so himself. After all that, he considered himself quite proficient at problem solving. But when it came to Ripley he drew a complete blank. "Look, that didn't quite come out the way I intended."

"Oh?" she asked with a raised brow that said something along the lines of, "You could have fooled me, but I'm listening."

He ran his hand through his hair again, then glanced in the rearview mirror to find the red-gold strands sticking straight out at different angles. He finger combed it. "Obviously some things have happened over the past day that have given me the wrong impression about you."

"Obviously."

"I'll be the first to admit, I don't know very much about you. So any impression I have is superficial at best."

She nodded, indicating that he was going to have to find his own way out of this.

He blew out a long breath. "What I propose is this,"

he said. The road he was on was about to dead end near the Mississippi River. He flicked on the left blinker, deciding to drive around until one or the other of them figured out what in hell they were going to do from there…*if* he talked her into staying in the car. "We go back to square one and start over from scratch."

She narrowed her eyes. "How do you mean?"

He slid his gaze over her, then he offered a grin along with his right hand. "Hi. My name's Joe Pruitt, creator and owner of Sole Survivor, Inc. Nice to meet you."

She stared at his hand, then warily put her hand inside it and gave a brief squeeze. He was astounded by how slender her fingers were, how delicate, but forced himself not to let on to his reaction, reminding himself that she knew how to handle a gun.

Then she smiled, the brightness of it, the guilelessness, hitting him both above and below the belt. "Ripley Logan, private investigator," she said, taking her hand back.

Joe stared unblinkingly at the road. Okay, that was easy enough. But since making her angry had been equally effortless, he figured he'd better watch his step from here on out.

Only now that he wasn't preoccupied with the source of her anger and his irrational desire to keep her in his car, he questioned both at length.

The FBI was looking for her, for crying out loud. And they were probably now looking for him.

It was impossible to believe that just last night he lay in his hotel room bed alone, wishing something would happen to liven up his life. Had he known this was what lay ahead, he would have thought twice about the careless desire—would have nixed it altogether.

"So, Ripley Logan, private investigator. What did you do before you became a P.I.?"

Her smile disappeared, and she turned her head toward the window, away from him. "I was a secretary."

Joe nearly choked.

She glared at him, then said, "Up until two weeks ago."

"Don't tell me. You just up and quit your job one day and hung out your P.I. shingle."

She made a face. "I knew this wouldn't work."

"What?" he asked, trying not to sound too judgmental. "I'm just trying to make conversation."

"No, what you're doing is making me sound like an idiot."

He grimaced. She fell silent again.

"You didn't ask what I used to do," he said quietly.

She blinked at him.

"Before I got into sports shoe designing."

Wariness entered her eyes, but she apparently decided to humor him. She cleared her throat. "So, Joe Pruitt, what did you do before you became a shoe salesman?"

"I played sports."

Her gaze dropped to his chest. "Nice."

He wasn't sure if she was commenting on his answer or his chest, so he cleared his throat. "I was working toward signing with the pros when my knee imploded."

Her gaze shifted to his face. "Which sport?"

"Basketball."

She nodded, as if that was what she'd guessed.

He shifted in the seat, wondering why he'd offered that information. Not many women asked about what he'd done before. Ripley hadn't, either. It was that he'd offered it that surprised him.

"I thought I saw a scar last night," she said, reaching out to rest her left hand on his right knee.

Talk about your knee-jerk reactions. She took her hand back, and he tried to laugh off the violent twitch of his leg.

He stretched his neck. Not many commented on that, either. His scar. It ran up the inside of his kneecap, a whopping eight inches long and a quarter inch wide. Even now when he looked at it, he was almost surprised to find it there. The doctors had told him he was lucky to be walking on the knee. Of course that hadn't meant a whole lot to him at the time, not when his entire life had revolved around sports.

"That must have been hard on you," Ripley said quietly. "Having your dreams ripped out from under you like that."

"Yeah, it pretty much sucked."

She sat and quietly contemplated him for a long moment. "It looks like you're doing all right for yourself, though. Not everyone can do that, you know. Recover from such a blow. I have a cousin in St. Louis, twice removed on my mother's side, who got into a car accident the night before final negotiations with the Cardinals. He pretty much exists on welfare, beer and Springsteen. Not a pretty picture."

Joe looked at her, really looked at her, hearing what

she was saying and what lay behind her words. "I don't suppose being a secretary was your dream when you were a little girl."

Her smile nearly swallowed her face. "No."

"So was Nancy Drew your heroine?"

She stared blankly at him for a moment, then finally shook her head. "Not exactly. I'm a computer programmer by training." She shifted slightly away from him. "Turn left here."

He got the distinct impression that she wasn't going to offer any more. "Why should I turn here?"

She smiled at him, but her expression was determined. "If you're going to question everything I ask, Joe, then you might as well pull over and let me out now. Because this isn't going to work."

"What? Don't you think I have a right to know where we're going? Or would you like me to put a blindfold on?"

Her eyes darkened as her gaze flicked slowly, suggestively over his face. "That's a thought."

Indeed, it was. Only he didn't want to be behind the wheel of a car when it happened. He'd prefer to be in a bed with his hands tied to the posts and Ripley straddling him.

"We're going to check the pawnshop I went to yesterday. The woman I'm looking for…she sold the guy a couple of items the day before yesterday."

"And you think she'll come back?"

She nodded.

"Why?"

Her gaze snapped up.

"Sorry," he said, raising his hands. "Just please tell me it's not women's intuition."

She smiled. "It's women's intuition."

He groaned.

She laughed. "She told the owner she might return today to sell him a couple more items."

He glared at her.

"Gotcha."

That, she did, indeed. Have him. Right by the short hairs. The problem was, he wasn't in a hurry for her to let them go, no matter how painful the experience was proving to be.

She directed him to turn right at another corner a couple of blocks up. It was an area around Beale Street, not as well kept as the infamous street and in need of some tender loving care it probably wasn't going to get anytime soon. A group of black men on a corner stopped talking and turned to watch them drive by. Ripley told him to slow down on the next block.

"Oh, boy," she muttered.

But before Joe could ask her what was wrong, she was burying her head in the crotch of his slacks.

CHAPTER FIVE

"I'D ASK WHAT YOU'RE doing down there," Ripley heard Joe say as she burrowed her head into his lap. "But I'm afraid you'll stop doing whatever you have in mind if I do."

Ripley rolled her eyes. "Car at noon. Dark four-door sedan. Anyone look familiar to you?"

She didn't hear anything for a long moment, then Joe's car sped up to what she guessed was the speed limit.

"Damn," Joe said, then repeated the word a couple of times for good measure, his thighs growing tense under her cheek.

Ripley tried to ignore the heat radiating through his damp slacks, and the fact that a certain part of his anatomy was mere millimeters away from her mouth. She swallowed hard. "Is it safe to come up?"

"What?" Joe sounded distracted, then sighed. "Yes. Seeing as the reason you're down there isn't the one I hoped."

Ripley sat up in the passenger seat and smoothed her hair from her face, her heart hiccupping. They were two blocks from the pawnshop. Directly across the street sat a dark sedan not all that dissimilar to Joe's. She watched as one of the World Wrestling Federation wannabes got out of the back of the car, looked both ways, then crossed to the pawnshop. She twisted her lips.

"How in the hell did they beat us here?" Joe asked, though Ripley was pretty sure it was a rhetorical question, since there was no way she could know the answer.

"If you hadn't stopped in the parking lot back there to protect my modesty, they wouldn't have," she said.

He stared at her.

She shrugged. "What? It's the truth. It looks like they just got here, which means they beat us by a couple of minutes."

He grimaced. "Yeah, well, if I hadn't stopped, they would have caught you inside the shop." He rubbed his chin. "Besides, given the reason for my stopping, I probably would have gotten into an accident had I continued on, anyway. Then where would we be?"

Ripley couldn't help but smile. His reaction to her changing in front of him had been humorous, yes, but in some strange way, it had also been touching. It wasn't so much that he was trying to save her honor or something equally chivalrous. No, she suspected that one very stuffy Joe Pruitt had wanted to keep anyone else from gazing at her the same way he apparently enjoyed doing.

She turned to stare out the window. Joe had driven toward the Mississippi. The muddy brown water sparkled in the midday sun as a barge, choked with different-colored containers sluggishly made its way toward the gulf.

She couldn't put her finger on it, but for some reason she seemed to be tuned into the same channel Joe was.

She instinctively knew when he was looking at her. And it didn't take a woman more experienced than she was to know what he had in mind when he was looking at her. She seemed aware of him on every level. Knew when he thought she was completely nuts...and when he wanted her so bad it made *her* ache.

She glanced at him. At the way his blond hair lay tousled against his forehead, giving him a sexy, boyish look. His bare chest was broad and toned and made her mouth water with the desire to drag her tongue across his skin for a forbidden taste. Which, of course, was the completely last thing she should be thinking right now.

"Something's going on here I don't know about," she said to herself, reaching for her duffel. She took out the crumpled file and smoothed it against her legs before opening it.

"Where should I go?" Joe asked.

"What do you mean?"

"Well, I can't exactly keep driving without a destination."

She hadn't thought of that.

In fact, it appeared she was incapable of thinking about a lot when she was around Joe. She wondered if that's the way it worked with couples. You had to set aside a part of your brain to devote solely to them—for the consideration of the other person's feelings, thoughts, intentions—leaving you less equipped to do things the way you normally would.

Of course, she and Joe weren't a couple. He was just some poor innocent fool who'd gotten into trouble because of her. That he looked anything but an innocent wasn't his fault.

"I don't know," she said softly.

His jaw tensed at her words.

She closed the file. "Look, Joe, I've already told you that you don't have to do this. If you want the truth, I don't seem to function all that well around you, anyway."

He glanced at her, a skeptical glint in his blue eyes.

"And I don't want to get you into any more trouble than I already have. Whatever that trouble is." She sighed and squeezed the file against her chest. "I think it would be better for both of us if you just took me back to the hotel and dropped me off. I'll get my rental car and…"

"And?" he prompted.

"And what?"

"What do you do from there?"

She shrugged. "I'll figure something out. In fact, I wouldn't be surprised if the answer came to me the instant you're out of the picture."

His lips twitched upward in the beginnings of a smile.

"What?" she asked, inexplicably irritated all over again.

"So you don't function well when I'm around, huh?"

She looked away and waved her hand. "You…mess with my mental wiring, or something."

"Hmm. Or something."

She shifted until her leg was bent against the seat

and she was facing him more fully. "What would you suggest it is?"

"Simple," he said, the smile a stomach-tickling grin. "You want me. Bad."

Her laugh was spontaneous, but a tension resonated through her, making it sound husky and sexy.

He looked in the rearview mirror then changed lanes to go into the city. "I have a suggestion if you'd like to hear it."

"Does it include me naked and a bed?"

"Maybe."

"Then I don't want to hear it."

He gave a mock frown. "Okay, then, it doesn't involve either." He glanced at her. "For now."

The promise in his voice sent shivers skittering all over her. She didn't say anything for a moment. Then she said, "Tell me."

"Well, since we've already established that we're in this together for as long as it takes you to find your missing person—"

"Nicole Bennett."

"Yeah, this Bennett person, I suggest we stop at the next diner and have some lunch."

"And this helps us find Nicole how, exactly?"

"It doesn't. It stops the growling in my stomach." He glanced at her. "And gives me a chance to call my secretary in Minneapolis and have her make reservations for us at another hotel. Under another name. Nothing that can lead the FBI—"

"They're not the FBI."

"Okay, then, those guys to us."

"Then?"

He blinked at her. "Then what?"

"What happens after that?"

His gaze swept over her, dark suggestion in his eyes. "Do you want to hear what I hope will happen or what I think will happen?"

Her nipples tightened against the soft cotton of her T-shirt. "The, um, second."

He shrugged and looked at the road. "You call the shots from there. I'm not sure you know a lot about what you're doing, but I can say I know zip about being a private investigator. So I'll get us the safe place to stay, and you'll tell me how I can help you from there."

"Okay."

"Fine."

"Perfect."

"Do you always have to get in the last word?"

Ripley stared at him, realizing that's exactly what she had been doing. A behavior that used to be completely out of character for her. For as long as she could remember, she had been more likely to nod and acquiesce than risk rocking the boat. It had begun with her parents, whom she had yearned to please, then continued with every other person she met, be it through work or in her personal relationships. It was...liberating, somehow, to feel the competitive fire kindling in her belly, making her want to question and challenge everything, consequences be damned.

She grinned at Joe. "Always."

"HERE."

Joe sat back in the diner booth, staring at the cell phone Ripley held out to him. At her request, they'd chosen a diner near enough to the pawnshop to watch people go in and out and far enough away that if the three stooges returned, they'd be safe. Right after they'd placed their orders, Ripley had told him she had an errand to run and disappeared through the door. He'd thought she was going to go to the pawnshop, but she'd headed in the other direction.

She tried to hand him a scratched and dented wireless phone he wasn't sure he wanted to touch.

"What's this?"

"A cell phone."

"I can see that." He took it, and she slid in the booth across from him. The waitress popped up with their orders.

"Oh, good. I'm starved," Ripley said, licking her lips as her barbecued beef sandwich and fries were put in front of her. Joe made a face at his bland-looking chicken salad.

"Whose is it?" He waved the cell phone to catch her attention, which was focused on her meal.

She took a bite of her sandwich, her tongue dipping out to lick a dot of sauce from the corner of her mouth. An average, everyday movement that had everything but an average, everyday effect on him. She shrugged. "I don't know. I guess it's mine now."

He ordered himself to stop staring at her.

"I bought it from one of those guys on the corner." She stabbed her thumb over her shoulder. "So it's my guess it's hot."

"Hot. As in stolen?"

She smiled. "Yep. I thought that if our new friends

were tracing your calls, this would cause them a little pain."

Pain. Why was Joe getting the feeling he was the only one who was going to be experiencing any pain when this was all over?

"And if they're tapping the phone on the other end?" he asked.

She slowed her chewing then swallowed. "That's the line I'm talking about. What did you think I meant? Your cell phone?" She shook her head. "Just be careful what you say. I bought the phone so they'd have trouble tracking you back to where you are now."

He stared at the receiver then cautiously punched out the number for his office in Minneapolis. Gloria answered on the first ring. If she was concerned or curious about his suggestion that she make hotel arrangements under a different name and have all charges billed to her personal account—for which he promised to reimburse her double—she didn't let on.

It was when he asked her to cancel his afternoon, in fact, cancel everything involved with Shoes Plus, that she went silent.

"Pardon me?" she asked after a few moments.

Joe rubbed his face, his salad not looking all that appealing, while Ripley's meal appeared far more appetizing. Of course, Ripley devouring her BBQ was most enticing of all. "Tell them I came down with a bug."

Ripley wrinkled her nose. "Original."

"Gloria, scratch that. Tell them I have a family emergency and had to return to Minneapolis on the first flight out." A roll of Ripley's eyes. "No, no. Make my apologies and pass on that I fell from the second-floor balcony at my hotel and am on the mend."

That got a smile of approval from Ripley, a smile that made his stomach tighten. He pushed his salad away.

"Joe?" Gloria asked, clearly confused.

"What is it?"

"It's just that, well, in the five years I've worked for you, you've never canceled an appointment."

Joe frowned. Could that possibly be true? What about when he'd come down with the flu last winter? Or when his aunt had died a few months before that? He absently rubbed the back of his neck. He realized that neither occasion had caused him to cancel anything related to work. He'd merely worked around the incidents.

Incidents. Is that what his personal life boiled down to? A series of incidents to work around?

He grimaced and said to Gloria, "Well, then, don't you think it's past time I started?"

A soft laugh filtered over the line. "I think it's long past time. But far be it from me to tell you that."

Joe was surprised at his secretary.

They spoke for a couple more minutes, then he disconnected the line. Ripley held out her hand palm up. Joe placed the hot cell phone into it, wondering how long bacteria could survive on plastic.

"What are you going to do with it now?"

"Throw it out."

Joe stared at her, then his food, and forced himself to pick up his fork. Then he changed his mind and waved the waitress over. "Take this back and give me what she's having."

"You're still going to have to pay for this."

"Big deal." He leaned forward, ignoring the waitress as he considered Ripley. "So tell me about this missing person."

Her chewing slowed, giving him little to concentrate on but her mouth until she finally swallowed. He found himself swallowing right along with her. An empty action that made him feel even more drawn to the woman across from him.

"There's not much to tell, really." She dunked one of her French fries first into BBQ sauce then into ketchup. "Her sister called me the day before yesterday and set up an appointment." She smiled. "I'd just placed my ad in the paper, and she was my first call. Well, technically she was my second, but the first doesn't count because I didn't take the case."

"What was it?"

"A man wanted someone to set up his wife with."

"I'm not following you."

She sighed and waved the French fry. "He suspected she was having an affair...with another woman. He wanted to hire me to play bait. Contingent on his getting a good look at me first, to see if I made the grade."

"You're kidding?"

She popped the French fry into her mouth. "Nope." She wiped her hand on her napkin. "Anyway, the second call was from Clarise, Nicole Bennett's sister. She'd asked to come to my office, but since my office is my apartment until I can afford to rent space, I proposed we meet at her house. She'd said something about her husband not knowing about this, and we settled on a coffee place." She tucked her hair behind her ear. "She gave me a picture, gave me Nicole's most recent address and said that during a recent visit Nicole had stolen a few objects from her."

"What did she steal?"

"Silverware—and jewelry, too, though the silver is all she's sold so far. Yes, I know, I was surprised, too. I mean what kind of world is it when you can't trust your own sister, right? Anyway, she told me that, unfortunately, Nicole has always had sticky fingers and that Clarise wasn't so concerned about the stolen objects, she just wanted to make sure her sister was all right."

The waitress delivered his plate, and Joe rubbed his hands together, then dug in.

"I went to Nicole's apartment, but it really wasn't an apartment at all—more like a nightly or weekly room rental. And it hadn't looked like she had been there long."

"Drugs?"

"That's what I asked. But the sister told me she'd never known Nicole to take drugs. And the people I questioned in the building said she'd been quiet and never looked stoned, so…" She shrugged.

Joe considered her around a mouth full of some of the best-tasting beef he'd had in a long time. Probably because it was the only beef he'd had in a long time. "How did you manage to track her here?" he asked.

"That's what Nelson would call a fluke. He says if you're lucky they happen more often than not, but that you can't count on them."

"Who's Nelson?"

Was it him, or had her cheeks just reddened? "That doesn't matter." She waved his question off. "I did the usual. You know, checked the airport, the train station, the car rental places—she didn't have her own car—and came up with a big fat zero. It wasn't until I was at the airport and accidentally ran into an airline attendant not averse to a little cash falling into her hand that I hit pay dirt." Her smile was brilliant. "She recognized a picture I have of Nicole and told me she sold her a ticket to Memphis and personally saw her get on the plane for here the night before.

"So I came here, found the hotel she was staying at and checked into the same room she'd vacated—though I didn't find anything useful in it. Either housekeeping had already cleared all clues, or more likely, given the clean state of the room in St. Louis, Nicole had cleared it herself. Then I started pounding the pavement. The pawnshop—" she jabbed her thumb in that direction "—was my third stop when I got into town."

Joe watched as a taxi pulled up in front of the pawnshop in question. A dark-haired woman got out, paid the driver through the front window, then walked toward the establishment, a brown bag in her right hand.

"You got a picture of the woman?" he asked.

Ripley nodded, then fished a copy out of the file lying next to her on the table.

Joe glanced at it, then the woman walking into the pawnshop. "Don't look now, but your girl just arrived."

THIS IS BETTER THAN SEX.

Ripley's mind paused as she raced through the diner door, her heart beating a million miles a minute. Well, okay, maybe it was just as good as sex, at least the type she was used to having. But she couldn't really think about that now because she was busy closing in on her first missing person.

She should have signed up for this a long time ago, she thought, even if she couldn't quite bring herself to believe her luck. Could Joe have been mistaken? Could the woman going into the pawnshop have just looked like Nicole Bennett? After all, a good hundred feet separated the diner from the shop. Maybe he hadn't gotten a good look.

Or…

Or else he was toying with her. She'd bolted from the table so quickly, she hadn't stopped to consider that option. She glanced behind her to find Joe being tackled by the waitress, likely to pay their bill, and was relieved. She'd have gone into murder mode had she found him still sitting in the booth grinning at her.

The sound of her feet against the pavement. The feel of her hair flying behind her. The burning of her lungs, which revealed how little exercise she usually got. All of it combined to make her feel…well, pretty damn good.

Near the pawnshop, she slowed, her hand clutching her side. She really needed to get into shape. As inconspicuously as possible, she poked her head around and peered through the grimy glass, then pulled back. She smiled so wide, her face hurt. Definitely one very wily, sticky-fingered Nicole Bennett.

She'd been given strict instructions on what she was to do when she tracked down Nicole. Namely follow her to find out where she was staying, then contact her sister in St. Louis.

She frowned. But the last time she'd tried calling

Nicole's sister, she'd received a recording telling her the line had been disconnected.

She briefly closed her eyes. So what did she do?

The clang of a cowbell found her springing from the side of the building next door. She stared as Nicole Bennett came out of the pawnshop, minus one shopping bag and tucking money into the pocket of her jacket.

"Freeze," Ripley said.

Freeze? Had she really just yelled freeze? Good Lord, she wasn't a cop. She wasn't even supposed to approach Nicole. Nicole wasn't even supposed to know Ripley was following her.

Her first case, and she'd already royally messed it up.

Nicole's gray eyes widened in surprise. Then she looked at Ripley's hands, which were obviously minus a weapon, and took off running in the opposite direction.

Ripley took off after her. She didn't know what she was going to do once she caught up with her, but she was trusting she'd figure that one out when the time came.

"Is that her?"

Joe's voice so close to her ear made Ripley scream. Then, before she could stop herself, she lost her running rhythm and started a headlong dive for the hard pavement. The only thing that stopped her from getting pavement burn was Joe's fast thinking. He grabbed the back of her T-shirt, holding her suspended in midair. Ripley jerked her head up, watching as Nicole darted around the corner and out of sight.

She awkwardly regained her footing, straightened

her T-shirt, then stomped squarely on Joe's foot. His resulting *yeow* only dented her disappointment.

"What was that for?" he asked, hopping on one foot.

"For making me lose my first missing person."

The only problem was that the person she was working for to find a missing person had also recently joined ranks with those already on the missing persons list. Which left her exactly…where?

She glanced in the direction Nicole went, stepped that way, then stopped and started walking toward the diner. Only the instant she did, she spotted the dark sedan carrying the three bozos claiming to be with the FBI.

Oh, boy.

CHAPTER SIX

RIPLEY KNOCKED BRIEFLY ON the hotel room door, then reminded herself to stand squarely in front of the peephole. A moment later the door opened, and she stood staring at Joe, who was freshly showered, a towel slung low on his slender hips, his abs standing out in glorious relief. God, but he was magnificent. A true thing of beauty in all the confusion swirling around her.

"Are you coming in or what?" he asked quietly, gripping her wrist then tugging her inside. He looked both ways down the hall, then closed the door.

Ripley grimaced at him, hating that he could stop her dead in her tracks with very little effort. Actually, with no effort. He hadn't done anything but stand there looking like dessert, and her brain completely zonked. All she'd been able to do was stand there gaping at him.

She strode across the room to the king-size bed and flopped down on it, letting her duffel fall to the floor at her feet. Feet that ached from all the running she'd done in the past half hour—first after Nicole Bennett, then from the three goons hot on her trail for God only knew what reason.

Thankfully, she had seen them before they saw her, giving her a good head start. And she'd taken complete advantage of it, ducking inside the antique shop next to the pawnshop and taking Joe with her. They'd pretended to be out-of-town browsers interested in the splotches of red and black paint that somebody called art, waiting until the three men sitting in the car moved on.

After fifteen minutes they had. Then Joe had driven them to the hotel that would be their new digs. She'd insisted on getting out of the car at the corner so they wouldn't be seen together any more than they had to be, gave him a chance to check in and get to the room, then called him using the hot cell phone she bought from the guys on the street corner. Joe told her what room number, and here she was.

She rubbed the skin between her brows, feeling the beginnings of a whopper of a headache coming on. "Are you sure no one can connect your name to the one on the room?"

"Completely."

She blinked at him. He grinned.

"You probably don't want to hear this now, but you could probably run better if you had the right pair of shoes."

Ripley rolled her eyes to stare at the ceiling. "Oh, great, now he's trying to sell me shoes."

He shrugged. "It's what I do. So shoot me."

"Don't tempt me," she muttered under her breath.

Actually, she was more in a mind to shoot herself. *Freeze.* She cringed, still unable to believe she'd yelled that when she'd spotted Nicole outside the pawnshop. The incident played out in her mind like every apprehension scene she'd seen in every television cop show she'd ever seen a rerun of. Who did she think she was, Police

Woman? Or worse, Wonder Woman, with her invisible plane and golden lasso? While she was on the topic, why had Wonder Woman carried a lasso, anyway? Anyone who could pull off and pilot an invisible plane certainly deserved a weapon more potent than a wimpy lasso. She couldn't remember why, and that irked her more.

She flopped on the bed and groaned. Here she had probably just blown her first case, and she was thinking about a woman who wore a red-white-and-blue bustier.

Maybe her mother was right. Maybe they would still take her back at her old job. If she offered them the money from the employee package she'd taken and crawled to them on hands and knees, maybe they'd hire her back, no questions asked. Of course, she supposed it didn't help that she'd already spent the money in question, and that she'd said a few unkind words to her immediate supervisor on her last day. Her own rendition of take this job and shove it.

No. Returning to her old job was definitely not an option.

She felt hands on her feet. Hot, probing hands. She shot to a sitting position and gaped at Joe, who was crouched beside the bed. "What are you doing?" she whispered. It wasn't supposed to be a whisper. But that's what it ended up being as he took one of her sandals off and ran a fingertip along her overly sensitive arch.

He offered a grin, then dragged his fingers along the length of her size-eight foot. Ripley gasped as a shiver wound up and around her, seeming to touch every one of her nerve endings.

"What's the matter, Ripley? Are you ticklish?"

In all honesty, she couldn't have said. No one had tried to tickle her before. Her parents hadn't been the touchy-feely type. And certainly none of her boyfriends had ever gone near her feet. But given her response to Joe's touch, she'd have to say that she definitely was ticklish, even if laughing was the furthest thing from her mind right then.

She swallowed hard. "Half the grime from Memphis's streets is down there. Doesn't that, um, bother you?"

He slid her other sandal off and worked her foot around and around. "What's a little grime between friends?"

"Friends?"

"Yeah. I'd like to think you're my friend."

Friends.

Ripley sat completely still, staring at him, mesmerized. "Aren't you, um, going to make another crack about what happened back there?" she asked, not liking the thickness of her voice. She sounded too near to tears for her liking. And the last thing she wanted to do was cry. So, all right, she'd mucked up her first case as a private detective. That didn't mean she should throw in the towel, did it?

Or maybe this was one of those signs, like the ones she'd used to change her life around to where it was now. Her meeting Nelson Polk in the park and lapping up his stories about what his life had been like as a P.I. The flyer for a gun range she'd found stuck under her car's windshield wiper. The offering of employee severance packages where she worked. She'd grabbed onto all those signs tightly, telling herself that she was meant to be a private investigator and this was the Fates' way of telling her that.

So what were the Fates trying to tell her now?

"You're wound up tighter than a shoestring," Joe murmured.

"You would be, too, if you just found the person you'd been looking for then lost her again."

She stared into his eyes, finding them bluer than she remembered, darker, somehow, now that they weren't full of irritation or amusement or both. "At least you found her."

She nodded. Yes, she supposed that much was true. She had found Nicole Bennett.

A bit of Nelson Polk wisdom echoed in her mind. "Missing persons cases are the toughest, especially if the missing person doesn't want to be found. Accept that you're lucky to find half of the people you go after. And make sure you get paid up front."

Ripley smiled. If someone as successful as Polk had a fifty percent average, then she supposed she wasn't doing too badly. The smile slowly vanished. Of course, she'd been so excited about landing her first real case that she hadn't followed his second piece of advice. Yes, she'd gotten a two-hundred-dollar retainer, and one fifty toward travel expenses. But the way this case was going, she would be in the hole in no time. And seeing she had no means to contact her client, there was little hope she'd ever see more money. In fact, it was looking like she no longer had a case.

She swallowed hard. "Who am I kidding? I'm not meant for this. I should just pack it all in and go home."

"Home?" Joe asked.

Ripley blinked at him, only then realizing she'd said her thoughts aloud.

"Where's home?"

"St. Louis." She cleared her throat and slid her foot from his grasp, not comfortable with showing him her weak side, even if he did work miracles on her feet. "And you?" she said, trying to steer the conversation away from herself, afraid that if she discussed the possibility of her returning home—giving up before she'd really started—it might become reality.

"Minneapolis," Joe said.

Well, that was a revealing scrap of information, wasn't it? Ripley pulled her bare feet on top of the mattress and wrapped her arms around her knees. Joe sat back against the bed, still on the floor.

"Do you really want to give in?" he asked. "Go home?"

She shrugged, not really sure what she wanted to do just then. And despite her fears, she found she needed to talk about the situation. "It seems the only reasonable, logical thing to do. I mean, the woman who hired me to find a missing person has gone missing herself. Meaning that if I can't find her, too, there's no money…and no client, for that matter." She laid her cheek against her knees, gazing at him. "Then there's the tiny fact that I have no personal interest in finding Nicole Bennett. I mean, even if I had caught her outside the pawnshop, what would I have done with her?"

"Good point."

"Yeah, but not very satisfying." She sighed, then turned her head the other way, away from him, and closed her eyes. "I don't know. Maybe this whole thing, my becoming a P.I., is just pie in the sky. Every day I'm getting closer to the big three-oh. The only thing I know how to do with any amount of success is answer phones and type others' expense reports. My computer science education is probably even obsolete now." She caught her lip between her teeth and bit down hard. "What was I thinking?"

She felt the mattress shift and guessed that Joe had sat on the bed next to her. "Interesting that you should use the word satisfying," he said quietly.

Ripley didn't move, didn't say anything, merely sat there staring at the hotel room wall, trying to ignore that there was a gorgeous, nearly naked man sitting next to her.

"Recently I've been thinking I haven't been getting a lot of satisfaction from my own life."

Fingers slid onto her shoulders. Ripley shivered, realizing he was not beside her, he was behind her. And he was touching her.

"I don't know. I suppose I've been charging full steam ahead for so long that I never stopped to ask myself whether or not I was happy."

She nodded slightly, knowing exactly where he was coming from. That kind of talk was what had gotten her into so much trouble to begin with.

The fingers slid from her shoulders to her back where they kneaded her muscles through her T-shirt. "Mmm, that feels good," she murmured, and closed her eyes.

He didn't respond to her comment, merely continued working his magic with his hands. "I know I've made some cracks here and there about your abilities as a P.I.,

Ripley," he said quietly, gently moving her hair out of the way and pressing his thumbs to the base of her neck. "But the truth is I admire what you're doing."

She twisted her lips. "Yeah, right. I've done a lot for you to admire. What is it that did it for you? When you caught me hiding under the bed? Or when I practically swallowed a good chunk of pavement when I tripped over my own feet?"

He squeezed her shoulders, and she said, "Ouch."

"Just be quiet and let me finish, will you?" he murmured, his mouth close to her ear.

Air was suddenly at a premium. "Okay."

He continued working the kinks from her muscles. But while the tension eased from certain areas, a different kind of tension began to wind low in her belly.

"Think about it, Ripley. You've done something that a lot of people would never have the guts to do. You took a look at your life midstream, found it lacking, then completely shifted tracks. You quit your old job—"

She made a sound. "I was offered a severance package."

He squeezed a little too hard again, earning a yelp. "I'm talking here, remember?"

She nodded and bit her tongue to keep herself from offering further comment.

"You quit your job—" he paused, waiting to see if she was going to say anything "—and followed your heart."

Yes, she supposed that she had.

"You did something I would never have had the balls to do."

Ripley's heart tripped into a higher gear. She turned

her head so she could watch him from the corner of her eye. His expression was thoughtful, intense as he continued his massage. She squinted at him. "But you're successful in what you do—very, if I'm not mistaken."

He grimaced. "Successful doesn't equal happy."

She let go of her legs and sat up. "Do you mind if I take off my T-shirt?" she asked, then went ahead and did it before he could respond.

She was very aware that she wasn't wearing a bra underneath. She wore the torturous contraptions as seldom as she dared. Of course she'd had no way of knowing that while she was reviewing her case in her old hotel room she would be taking a dip in the pool soon. She drew her knees up and waited. After a moment, she felt Joe's fingertips on her exposed flesh. She shivered at the heat of his touch.

"So, tell me, Joe Pruitt," she said, her voice soft, "what would be the one thing you would do if you could choose anything in the world?"

No immediate response except for the hesitation in his hands. "Is that the question you asked yourself?"

"Uh-huh."

"Dangerous question."

She smiled. "Yeah. I'm proof positive of that."

He didn't respond with words, but his hands seemed somehow hotter, more probing, rubbing her muscles with the skill of a pro, working away the last of her tension and making her feel far too relaxed. Far too turned on.

"So?" she murmured.

His fingers grazed her back then slid to tickle the underside of her breasts. Ripley caught her breath, suppressing a whimper of protest when he returned to her back.

"I don't know," he said finally, thoughtfully. "I'm past my prime for sports to be an option. If they were. And they're not. Not with this knee."

"And I'd like to be a model but, gee, I haven't worn a size two since I *was* two."

His chuckle tickled her skin.

She felt something wet and hot against her back and realized he was kissing her there, right in the middle near her spine. He drew back and blew on the area he'd kissed. She shuddered, and her nipples hardened where she had them pressed against her knees.

"I can tell you what I'd like to do now. Right this minute."

Ripley found her voice. "What?" she asked, though she was pretty sure she already knew the answer.

"Order up room service. I didn't get a chance to finish my lunch."

Ripley threw her head back and laughed so hard she nearly fell off the bed. Joe caught her around the middle, turned her and pressed her into the mattress. Ripley instantly stopped laughing. Her heart thudded unevenly in her chest. The tension in her belly had moved lower, making her throb with want for this man who made her feel like hitting him one minute and kissing him the next.

"Liar," she said.

He stretched out next to her, propping his head on his hand. "Not a liar. A wiseass. There's a difference."

"Oh?" Her gaze slid to the towel he still wore, then her bare midriff. She thought about covering herself with her arms, then stretched her arms out above her head instead, arching her back. She watched his eyes darken as his gaze slid from her eyes to her neck, then finally rested on her bare breasts.

He reached out with his free hand and caught the very tip of her nipple between his thumb and forefinger. He rolled the sensitive stiff flesh then gave a gentle tug. Ripley's back came off the mattress as a rush of heat flooded her inner thighs. He moved his hand to her other breast, using the same massaging technique he'd used on her muscles to bring her nipple even more erect. Then he caught the tip of the breast closest to him in his mouth, and Ripley was sure she had died and gone to heaven.

Suddenly it wasn't enough to be receiving. She wanted to take. Hectic energy filled her to overflowing as she caught his shoulders and pinned him to the bed, straddling his hips. She kissed him restlessly, her hands fumbling for the towel that covered the area she was most interested in.

Joe chuckled softly. "This would work a lot better without the shorts."

Ripley rolled off him, stripped off the shorts in question and followed with the borrowed briefs while he did a search for something on the nightstand table. His wallet for a condom, she realized, her heartbeat kicking up.

This was really going to happen. Here. Now. She was going to have sex with Joe Pruitt. The mere idea was enough to send her lunging for him again.

Since the first moment they met, skin against skin in his hotel bed, she'd felt an electrical shock of attraction. The kind of pull that drew people to rubberneck at car accidents or stare at dead bodies. A dangerous appeal that made you stick around just to see what happened next. Usually nothing did. But Ripley got the distinct impression that something very definitely was going to happen here. And it was going to be damn good.

"Dear Lord," Joe murmured, dragging his mouth from hers and gulping deeply. Ripley felt a thrill that his reaction was due completely, totally, one hundred percent to her.

She smiled at him. "Do what you gotta do, because I'm not waiting anymore."

He squinted at her, the action making his eyes even darker, then scrambled to put on the condom. But when Ripley would have slid down over him, he rolled her over instead so that her back pressed into the soft mattress and his erection pulsed against her slick, swollen flesh.

Oh, boy. Ripley wasn't quite ready for the gaping need that opened in her lower abdomen. A burning ache that begged, yearned to be filled, that she feared might never go away. She wriggled against him restlessly. He smiled at her, spreading her thighs with his knees, then finding the source of her agitation with his fingers. Ripley instantly stopped moving, the breath rushing from her body with that one simple, beautiful move.

"God, are you hot," Joe murmured, running his open mouth down her neck and to her shoulder.

He flicked the hooded bit of flesh at the apex of her thighs with his thumb, and Ripley gasped, automatically thrusting her hips up, seeking a firmer, more satisfying touch.

"Lie still."

That was like waving a tenderloin in front of a hungry lion and telling him to sit. Ripley reached for his hips, wanting to have him inside her...*now*. Needing him to satisfy the ache growing with every leap of her pulse.

"Stop it," he murmured, nipping her ear.

She shuddered and tried to turn her head into his kiss. He grinned and pulled back to gaze into her face.

"You're cruel," she whispered.

"You're hot."

She slid her hand between them and grasped his erection, marveling at the length and width of it. "You're... big."

She'd meant to say that he was hot, too, but the other word slipped out. He kissed her then, deeply, hungrily. "You're good for the ego, you know?"

"Shut up and let's have sex."

He chuckled, and Ripley laughed, then gasped as he slid two fingers deep inside her. He kissed her open mouth, dipping his tongue inside. "Wow. You're so... warm. So tight."

Ripley caught her bottom lip between her teeth and bit hard, trying to keep herself from flying apart right then. "Joe, if you don't—"

Then he was inside her. All of him. Filling every last inch of the emptiness she'd felt a moment before. "Oh," she murmured, although the word came out as a long moan.

Then he moved. Slowly. Deliciously. As if afraid he might lose the control she was even now frantically holding onto with her fingernails. The friction of his flesh inside hers made her tremble all over, made her thrust her hips up to meet his rather than allow him escape.

He groaned and sank deep into her again, robbing her of breath, of movement, rendering her incapable of anything but feeling the sheer ecstasy pounding through her veins, skittering over her skin, hardening her nipples. She curved her legs around his hips and squeezed, holding him tight against her, not caring about the world beyond the bed or the really crappy state of her life right now, only wanting the feelings raging inside her to stay there forever.

Then he withdrew nearly all the way and rocked against her again and the emotions expanded to the tenth power. The next time he withdrew, she let him go without resistance, deciding that, boy, did he know what he was doing. He rolled into her again…and again… and Ripley found his rhythm, clenching her leg muscles then unclenching them, her fingers digging into the taut muscles of his shoulders, her mouth mindlessly seeking and finding his as his arousal reached pleasure spots she didn't know were there.

"So…good," she whispered against his mouth, the tips of her nipples brushing his chest.

Then he murmured something, curses, she thought, and he increased the speed of his thrusts. Ripley gasped and grabbed the blanket on either side of her with both hands, seeking an equilibrium she was quickly losing, trying to stop the world from spinning.

Too late. The explosion in her belly was so overwhelming, so beautiful, her back came up off the mattress, meeting Joe's suddenly still form, straining against him.

Minutes later, Ripley's heart still felt as if it might beat straight out of her chest. She tested her legs by tightening them around Joe's waist, gasping as another spasm ripped through her. He lifted his head where it was buried in the pillow beside her. His grin was all too enticing.

She cleared her throat. "Had I known that was what I was missing, I would have let you have your way the first time I crawled into your bed."

He kissed her. "No, you wouldn't have."

"You're right. I wouldn't." She ran her fingers lazily up and down his back. "But it's nice to think about, isn't it?"

She felt his erection twitch inside her, and his grin told her it wasn't involuntary. "Oh, I think actually doing it blows that one right out of the water."

Ripley threaded her fingers through the damp hair on his head and ground her hips against him. His eyes darkened, all laughter gone. She smiled. "I think you're right."

He tilted his head and kissed one side of her mouth, then the other. "I knew you'd come around to my way of thinking sooner or later." He began to withdraw, and she thrust upward again. "Am I ever glad it was sooner...."

CHAPTER SEVEN

JOE LAY BACK, CAUGHT in that state between sleep and wakefulness, taking more comfort than he probably should in the warm, female body curving against his. Early evening sunlight filtered through the white sheers at the window. No balcony this time. He'd made doubly sure of that when he'd called Gloria to reserve a room. If she'd been puzzled by his request, she didn't indicate. Her hands-off approach was exactly the reason he'd hired her. His mother's wanting to run his personal life was enough to handle. He enjoyed that Gloria stuck to strictly professional, although she wasn't above shocking him with an occasional off-color joke.

Ripley shifted beside him. Joe lazily turned his head, watching her through half-lidded eyes as she carefully, very slowly slid away from him and off the bed. In one sweep, her T-shirt covered her delectable back. But her round bottom was all his to covet as she gathered her shorts and her duffel and made her way toward the bathroom.

"Going somewhere?"

Ripley nearly hit the ceiling, she jumped so high. She turned to face him. "Must you do that?"

"Do what?" he asked, quirking a brow.

"Scare the daylights out of me every chance you get?"

His grin widened. "Every chance I get."

She murmured something under her breath then closed the bathroom door after herself. Joe lay there listening to her taking a shower and tried like hell not to let the afternoon's events completely occupy his thoughts. But it was impossible. Not when he was even now contemplating crawling into the shower with her. If he were convinced she hadn't locked the bathroom door, he'd have made the effort. But though he'd coaxed a sexual openness from her, he was beginning to suspect that a more emotional connection with Ripley would take a little time and a great deal more effort. Call him dumb, but when she'd turned her back and gone silent on him moments after their third mind-blowing bout of sex, he'd considered that an emotional wall.

He pulled the pillow she'd used across his face and breathed in her scent. He detected a bit of chlorine from their dip in the pool earlier, but beneath that lay the peachy scent he was coming to associate solely with her.

He told himself he was a sorry bastard and forced himself to put the pillow on the other side of the bed, just in time to find her staring at him from the bathroom door.

"What are you doing?" she asked, the brush she was using on her wet hair hovering above her head.

"Trying to smother myself. Why? You have a problem with that?"

A quirk of her lips indicated she was about to smile. Good. That was good. At least he hadn't totally spooked her.

He ran his hand over his face. "What is it about

women that they always go into this silent, contemplative mode after sex?"

Ripley gaped at him, the brush again in her hair, where it stayed as she apparently tried to find a response to fit the emotions drifting across her pretty face. "What is it about men that they have to lump every woman they've ever slept with together after sex?" She walked into the bathroom, and a moment later he heard a hair dryer switch on.

"Shit," Joe murmured, throwing the sheet off. He supposed he deserved that. Had she compared him to anyone else, especially after they'd just had sex, he'd have been injured, too.

He pulled on a pair of jeans he always kept stashed in the trunk of his car to change into when he found himself going straight from work to a more casual event. Then he stepped, barefoot, to the door of the bathroom. He leaned against the jamb and watched her declare war on all that glorious auburn hair.

"Sorry," he said.

She notched up the speed of the dryer. "Huh?" She shook her head. "I can't hear you."

He pulled the hand holding the dryer away from her ear and yelled, "I said I'm sorry."

She made a face at him. "You can say that again."

He grimaced and crossed his arms, watching her until she nearly fried her hair to a crisp. Finally, she had to shut the damn thing off. Not that she acknowledged him as she slipped the pistol into the holder. Instead she turned and went to battle with the unruly curls surrounding her face.

"Do you plan on talking to me ever again?"

She shrugged almost petulantly, and he felt his grin beg for a return. "I haven't decided yet."

Joe swiped the brush from her hand. He moved to stand next to her and began brushing his hair.

She snatched the brush back, but even the irritated reaction was better than none at all. "You've probably got dandruff or something."

"Considering that all my stuff is at the other hotel, I figure you getting my dandruff is the least you can do for me."

"No, thanks."

She tried to pass him, but he blocked the door. She rolled her eyes then stared at him. He realized she'd exchanged her T-shirt and shorts for a clingy red dress that hugged her in all the right places and made him wonder what she did or didn't have on underneath the short skirt.

"Where are you going?" he asked, twirling an errant curl around his index finger.

She avidly watched the movement, then licked her lips. "Out."

He chuckled. "I guessed that. Where?"

She ducked under his arm and away from him. He turned and followed her into the room. She sat on the bed and rifled through her duffel bag, pulling out first one strappy sandal, then a second. Another pair of shoes that would torture her feet.

"I thought I'd go back to the pawnshop. I never did get to see what Nicole was doing in there earlier."

"They're closed."

She glanced at him. "They're open till eight." She smiled. "Nice try, though."

He shrugged, did up his jeans, then reached for the polo shirt he always kept with the jeans. Her movements as she laced up the sandals slowed, and he knew she watched him as he pulled the cotton over his head, then tucked it into the waist of his jeans. It was comforting that she felt the same way about him as he did about her. Basically he wanted to jump back into that bed and continue where they'd left off.

"I'll come with you."

She pushed from the bed, tested the sandals, then grabbed her purse. He grimaced as she worked to fit her 9mm into the small clutch purse that obviously carried very little, the gun a huge, obvious bulge inside the black leather. "Is that such a good idea? Um, you wouldn't want that thing to accidentally go off or anything."

She smiled at him and breezed on by. "Don't worry. If it goes off, and you get hit, it'll be completely on purpose." She opened the door and leaned against it. "So are you coming, or what?"

RIPLEY STOOD AT THE DUSTY counter of the pawnshop, her gaze flicking every now and again to the grimy window and the empty street beyond. Dusk had fallen, painting the shabbier part of town with edge-smoothing hazy purples and yellows, covering the smaller scars and lending a mystical, almost sentimental quality to some of the larger ones.

She glanced at Joe, who was gawking at men's watches at a counter behind her. "It's a Rolex," she heard him mutter. "A real one."

"That it is, my man. You want a closer look?" a voice from the back said.

Ripley shifted restlessly from foot to foot as the owner she'd met on her previous visit came out and made his way toward Joe instead of her. She drummed her fingertips on the scratched glass countertop and waited. It took far longer than it should have, considering they'd come here for information, not to shop for high-end timepieces. She sighed and tucked her hair behind her ear, about to say something, when Joe turned, something other than a watch in his hand.

She crossed to stand in front of him, staring at the ornately decorated box he held. Measuring about nine by four by four, the exterior was covered in plush red velvet, semiprecious jewels secured like upholstery pins in a pretty pattern along the sides and top. He popped open the lid.

"Is this it?" Ripley asked, looking at what lay inside. "Is this what Nicole sold?"

The guy behind the counter crossed his arms. "Along with the other two-bit pieces of silverware you saw yesterday. Nobody wants silverware with someone else's initials on it. I haven't had time to inventory and appraise this stuff yet, so what you see is exactly the way she left it."

Ripley fingered a necklace that looked suspiciously like large diamonds mounted in gold, then pulled it out. She wasn't a pro at this, not yet, but she found it odd that Nicole had chosen the pawnshop for loot of this sort. Wouldn't a jeweler be more appropriate?

"Oh they're real, all right," the owner pointed out. "One hundred percent, top of the line zirc."

Cubic zirconia.

Ripley's cheeks went hot. "Oh."

Joe handed her the box and turned toward the owner to barter the price of the lot. Ripley absently stepped to where she'd been standing before, glancing through the box's contents. There were several pieces nestled inside the red velvet, each piece prettier than the one before it. She hadn't been aware they made such quality knock-offs. She glanced through the window, realizing that she and Joe were clearly outlined in the bright interior light. A cab pulled to a stop at the opposite curb, and the back door opened. Ripley stepped nearer the window as a woman's leg appeared, then the rest of her.

Her heart skipped a beat. Nicole's sister.

Gripping the box, she started for the door, then stopped, her gaze colliding with Clarise Bennett's. Thank God she was here. Now that Ripley had recovered the goods Nicole had filched and could report on having seen Nicole in the flesh, maybe she'd get paid.

But rather than head toward her, as was expected, seeing as she'd hired her to do a job a couple days ago, Clarise scrambled into the cab, and the car screeched away from the curb.

"Oh, boy."

Ripley rushed outside, saw the cab turn the first corner, then hurried inside to find Joe still haggling with the pawnshop owner over the price of the box. "Come on!"

She grabbed his arm and tried to tow him toward the door. "Hurry!"

"Hey. You're not going anywhere until you cough up the box or the money," the owner said.

Joe took a handful of bills out of his back pocket and slapped them on the counter, nearly missing it as Ripley dragged him toward the door, then through it. "Keep pulling on me like that, and you'll turn around to find yourself holding an arm with nothing attached."

Ripley glanced at him. "At least it would be moving faster than you are. Come on, Pruitt, get the lead out."

Finally they were in his car and with a jolt and a roll they were taking the same corner as the cab. Joe stared at her. "Do you have any idea how much I had to pay that guy in there?"

"Never mind that," she said. "My client is…" She stared down each of the streets they passed. "There! Back up, back up! Turn there."

"Your client?"

She nodded emphatically, clutching the box in her hands for dear life.

Joe sighed next to her, jammed on the brakes, slammed the car into reverse then made the turn. "Don't tell me. She's running from you, too?"

She spared him an exasperated glance. "Save the gibes for later, will you? We have to catch her."

"And what do we do when we do?"

She blinked at him, her plans not having gone that far. "Why, ask her why she's running from me, of course."

"And get the money I just dropped on that worthless piece of crap you're holding."

Ripley glanced at the item in question. She ran her fingers over the top of it, then opened the lid again. Why would Clarise Bennett go through all this trouble to find a boxful of costume jewelry? And what did the FBI—allowing that they were, indeed, FBI—want with it?

"I don't like this." Joe muttered the words she was

thinking. "Something smells very fishy. And it has nothing to do with the Mississippi looming ahead."

Ripley snapped her gaze up to find that they were, indeed, near the Mississippi. The cab made a quick right.

"Hurry! Don't lose her!"

He cursed under his breath, then made the turn. Ripley blinked and stared at the giant glass pyramid they were nearing, the sun's last rays reflecting off the structure like it was some sort of mystical aberration nestled between the banks of the Mississippi and the city's modern skyline. "God, she's going to the Pyramid."

"A little late to take in the Egyptian exhibit, don't you think?" Joe asked quietly.

"Public place. Nelson told me they always head for a public place. Much easier to get lost in a sea of other people." She scanned the stairs leading to the front entrance as Joe followed the taxi up the drive. The ground-level exit doors on the side of the Pyramid Arena opened, and people began spilling out.

"Who in the hell is Nelson?" Joe asked.

"Huh?"

"You just said Nelson told you they always head for a public place."

She snapped the box closed and waved her hand. "Nelson Polk. He's, um, he's a friend." Now was not the time or the place to go into detail about who Polk was and why he had given her advice. "The cab's stopped."

But, unfortunately, they weren't anywhere near it. Ripley was on the edge of her seat as Joe maneuvered around a stopped vehicle, then another, trying to catch up to the taxi while Ripley glued her gaze to the woman hurrying from the back. She tucked the curious box under the passenger seat then reached for her door handle. She glanced at what she was wearing. *Figures.* One of the few times she decided to wear heels and a dress, and she had to chase someone. Not that it mattered. She was in shorts and a T-shirt earlier and tripped over her own feet.

She only wished she knew why the woman who had hired her was running from her.

Joe pulled into the spot the taxi just vacated, and Ripley hit the pavement, running after Clarise with all the speed her four-inch heels would allow her. Which, it turned out, wasn't very fast at all. She bumped into one person then another, exiting the building, as she made her way to the door Clarise had disappeared into. Puffing for air, she glanced back to find Joe arguing with a guard. She rushed headlong into someone and nearly knocked the other woman right to the ground.

"Sorry, excuse me," she said, continuing her mazelike route for the entrance that only seemed to get farther away.

She finally reached the door and tried to duck inside. A guard caught her by the arm. "The Pyramid is closing," he said, staring at her.

Ripley caught her balance, staring at him in breathless exasperation. "I left my purse inside," she offered by way of explanation. "Please. It will only take a second. I know right where I left it."

The excuse was working. Well, at least until he caught

a glimpse of the bag she was trying to hide behind her back.

He grinned at her. "Nice try, lady. Look, you're just going to have to hold it until you get home. I can't let you in."

Ripley ridiculously felt like stomping her feet and throwing a tantrum. Clarise had gone in there not two minutes ago and didn't appear to have a problem. Why was she being singled out?

"Problem?" Joe appeared at her elbow, eyeing the guard who still held her arm.

The guard released her. "No entrance."

Ripley watched Joe's chest puff out, even though the guard had at least a hundred pounds on him. She grasped his arm and smiled at the guard. "Oh, well. I guess I'll just have to wait until we get to the restaurant to use the rest room, won't I, pooh bear?"

Joe cocked a brow at her. Pooh bear? Okay, it had been the best she could do at the moment. She tugged on his arm, pulling him to the side before they got trampled by the exiting hordes. Either that or shot by the guard. She looked at Hulk Hogan and wondered if he was carrying. He had stepped into the shadows to allow a larger exit, so she couldn't tell.

"Are you sure you saw her going inside?" Joe asked, his chest still puffed out.

Ripley smiled at him, unable to suppress the urge to smooth her hand down that magnificent chest barreled in prime confrontation mode just for her. "Positive."

He glanced at her fingers, that dark energy she'd seen so much of that afternoon looming large as life in his blue, blue eyes. "So, um, what do we do now?"

She dropped her hand to her purse and straightened it. "I guess we wait for Clarise to either come out or get kicked out."

"Some plan."

"You got a better one?"

He shook his head. "Nope."

She stood back and scanned the morphing crowd. Now she knew why people eluding capture or being tracked targeted such gatherings. There were so many people, colors and sizes seemed to blend together, making it difficult to spot a relative much less a woman she'd seen only once. Well, aside from the glimpse outside the pawnshop. And then she hadn't noticed anything more than that Clarise had been wearing a black dress. She squinted at the horizon where the sun had slipped silently down and twisted her lips. This wasn't looking very good. She glanced in the direction of the access road, and her eyes widened.

"Oh, boy."

"What? What is it?" Joe asked, trying to follow her line of vision. "Did you spot her?"

She swallowed. "That guard you were talking to when you parked—what did he say?"

"That he'd have me towed if I left the car there. Why?"

She pointed at a tow truck pulling away from the curb. "I think he just made good on his threat."

Joe stared, then sprung into action, sprinting after the departing truck with the speed of a man who ran regularly. Not that he could have caught up with the vehicle in any case. The battered truck towing his car had gotten the jump on him.

Ripley slipped a pad and pen from her purse, careful not to disturb the gun, and copied the number on the side of the truck. She used to think towing operators put their contact information there for advertising purposes. Now she suspected it was for moments like these.

She stuffed the pad into her purse and pretended an intense interest in her shoes as Joe dragged himself back to stand next to her.

"They towed my car," he said unnecessarily.

"I got the number. We'll call when we get back to the hotel and see where it is."

Joe paced away from her, then back.

"Don't worry," she said, finally looking at the tense expression on his face. "I'll cover everything."

He stopped pacing. "There's one little problem with that scenario, Ripley."

She straightened.

"If those goons this morning really are the FBI, they'll be all over the car."

"Right," she said absently. Then she was pacing alongside Joe, muttering under her breath the same way he was. Forget that they no longer had wheels. The box Nicole had sold to the pawnshop was in the car. A box that possibly held the key to unlock the mess Ripley was currently smack dab in the middle of. A box that she had hoped to dangle in front of Clarise's eyes to get her to spill what was really going on. A box that was sitting under the seat of the car being towed out of the parking lot.

"Damn, damn, damn," she whispered, missing the turn as she paced with Joe and nearly colliding with him when she finally did pivot.

She blinked into his eyes, her nose filled with the manly scent of him. Every sexy minute of the past few hours rushed back to her. She licked her lips, and he followed the movement, making her mouth dryer still.

"Pardon me," she murmured.

"Sorry," he said at the same time.

Ripley watched as he rounded her and continued pacing. She gave up and leaned against the building, crossing her arms over her stomach.

Could anything else possibly go wrong during the course of this case? She'd nearly been snowed under with the hopelessness of it all earlier. Then she'd found her legs again after incredible sex with Joe, and now here she stood, right back at square one.

Twenty minutes later, darkness completely cloaked the area in which they stood, and the ceaseless column of people...well, ceased. Ripley stared, unsurprised, when the large door was closed with a dull clang and a key was turned in the lock. Joe had stopped pacing and was standing next to her, his arms crossed over his chest in the same way hers were. A few cars remained in the gargantuan, well-lit parking lot, probably belonging to the maintenance and security crew. Otherwise the place was completely deserted.

Ripley tucked her hair behind her ear. "She must have gotten past us."

"Yeah," Joe muttered. He glanced at her, clearly irritated. "So now what do you suggest?"

She dropped her gaze. "I don't know."

He sighed, then ran his hand over his face. He looked at her. "Don't even think about busting into that place and checking the rest rooms."

She smiled. "The thought hadn't even crossed my mind."

"Good."

"Fine."

"Perfect."

"Wonderful."

His grimace turned into a half smile. "Do you always have to get in the last word?"

"Always."

His gaze flicked over her face, lingering on her mouth.

Ripley ignored the instant fire that ignited in her belly and rolled her eyes. "I'm not even going to ask what your suggestion is."

"What? That we go back to the hotel room, forget about your missing person and missing client and become reacquainted with the bed?"

She pointed a finger at him and pushed from the wall. "Why did I know you'd say that?"

"Because you're thinking the same thing?"

Maybe. But she wasn't going to tell him that. She liked his handsome head the size it was. She turned toward the hulking pyramid and started walking on the off chance that Clarise was even now slinking from one of the other exits. She turned the corner and stopped dead in her tracks.

"Why are you following me?" a female voice asked, two hands holding a gun pointed directly at Ripley's stomach.

CHAPTER EIGHT

NICOLE BENNETT.

Ripley stared directly into the face of the very woman she'd been sent to find but who instead had found her, trying to ignore the size and nearness of the gun Nicole held tightly in both hands.

Yet another first in what was adding up to a whole series of them.

"I'll repeat, just in case you didn't hear me. Why are you following me?" Nicole took a step back when Joe rounded the corner at full throttle.

Ripley put her arm out to stop him, and he held up his hands and said, "Whoa."

Ripley wondered how long it would take to get her gun out of her bag. Judging that it had taken her five minutes to get the sucker in there, it would probably take at least that long to get it out. And somehow she didn't think pointing her black leather bag at Nicole and yelling, "Freeze," was going to work, either.

"We're not following you," Ripley said. She shifted, agitated. "I mean, I am…was looking for you, but I'm not now."

Nicole Bennett was prettier than the grainy picture Clarise had given her. With long dark, almost black hair, and wide gray eyes, she was strikingly beautiful and very dangerous. The fact that she had a gun pointed at

Ripley could very well have a lot to do with the latter description.

"Say that again?" Nicole asked.

Ripley tucked her hair behind her ear. "Look, I'm a P.I. from St. Louis. I was hired to find you by someone concerned for your welfare."

Nicole's expression was clearly skeptical, but she nodded. "Go on. I'm listening."

Ripley nodded. "Your sister. She wanted me to find you, and the things you, um, borrowed from her."

Nicole narrowed her eyes, but the gun never budged. "Interesting. My sister is in a sanitarium."

Ripley blinked at her. "Well, then, she was released. Because I met her. She gave me a picture of you, told me you have a habit of lifting things from her house, but that she never pressed charges, and asked me to find you." She frowned. "Your name is Nicole Bennett, isn't it? And your sister is Clarise Bennett."

The other woman was not looking very sociable. "Describe the woman who hired you to find me."

Joe leaned closer to Ripley. "Remember that fishy feeling I had earlier?"

Ripley elbowed him in the ribs. "She, um, has blond hair. About your height. No, a little taller. Slender. Kind of a Grace Kelly look-alike with an edge."

The gun dropped to the woman's side, and she shocked the hell out of Ripley by smiling. "That's what I thought," she said. She opened her black trench coat and slid the revolver into the waist of an equally dark pair of slacks, then covered the gun with the hem of her black mock turtleneck. "Did you find the stuff?"

"By stuff, I'm assuming you mean the box you sold to the pawnshop?"

"That's it."

"Yes, I retrieved it." Ripley stared at Joe, warning him not to say the same box was on its way to a holding lot even as they spoke.

"Good." She glanced one way, then the other. "Give it to…my sister."

Ripley grimaced at her. "Well, that's the problem. It seems your sister is now also running from me. In fact, we followed her here."

"Here?" Nicole looked suddenly antsy and mumbled something under her breath.

"Yes. That's what I meant when I said we weren't following you. We were following her. Here."

Nicole began backing away, her expression wary as she scanned the area surrounding them. "Just make sure she gets that box."

She turned and began hurrying away.

Ripley grabbed her purse, reaching for the gun in it, and started after her. "Hey, wait a minute!" she called. She supposed she should be glad she hadn't yelled, "freeze," although in her book, "Wait a minute" ranked right up there alongside it.

Joe grasped her wrist. "What are you doing?"

"Going to get some answers, of course."

Joe shook his head. "I don't think that's a very good idea."

"That's funny, did you hear anyone asking for your opinion? I didn't." Ripley had just had a gun held on her by a woman she had been searching for but who had found her instead, and Joe wanted her to pass up the opportunity to get answers to the questions mounting in her brain?

He released her.

She turned. Only to find that Nicole Bennett had disappeared into thin air.

THE FOLLOWING MORNING RIPLEY pored over the contents of the too-thin case folder strewn across the bed in front of her, staring at the photo of Nicole Bennett, checking out the information Clarise Bennett had given her and trying to piece it together with what had gone down so far. She sighed and collapsed against the pillows, suddenly all too aware that the king-size hotel bed seemed big and awfully empty without Joe in it.

She poked a sheet of paper aside with her toe and reprimanded herself. She and Joe were not a couple. She didn't even want a relationship right now, much less one with an uptight and overbearing albeit super sexy shoe salesman who had sex on the brain.

She turned her head to stare at his pillow. They'd had more of that great sex last night after getting back from the Pyramid. Well, not directly afterward. There had been the hour-long period where she tried to fit the puzzle pieces together and he questioned her sanity, but the instant she'd climbed into bed and turned her back, he was right in there alongside her. And the more she told herself she was not going to have sex with him again, the more her body rebelled, responding to the feel of his hot body pressing against her. She'd eventually given in and arched into him, and that had clinched it. They'd had sweaty, hot, wild monkey sex all night long.

Ripley rubbed her fingertips against her forehead and stared at the door he'd disappeared through. He had said he was going to scare up some doughnuts. She didn't need four days of detective experience to figure out it didn't take nearly an hour and half to get them.

She supposed that when all was said and done, Joe was being a pretty good sport about all of this. After all, it wasn't every day that you woke up to find a strange naked woman in your bed, got chased from your second-story hotel room and dropped into a pool, had your car towed, then, as if all that wasn't enough, had a gun pulled on you by the very woman you had been looking for, but hadn't been looking for that minute.

Then again, she supposed it could be the sex.

But a guy like Joe…well, he could pretty much have any woman he wanted. He had it going on and then some in the looks department. And his sense of humor had her smiling even if she did want to sock him one when that acerbic wit was turned on her.

And what about her? Why was she hanging around with Joe when she should be concentrating on her new career and figuring out what had gone wrong with her first case?

She smiled. "Very definitely the sex."

She sat up and hung her legs over the side of the bed. She'd always thought the intimate act highly overrated. She'd dated and had sex with three men before Joe. First had been Jack Basset in the back seat of his father's Chevy after the senior prom, when she'd been left deflated and unfulfilled while he got out, his sky-blue suit pants hanging open as he cheered from the hood of his car. Number two had been Terry Sheen in college. He hadn't owned a Chevy, but he had been a quick finisher. So fast, in fact, she wondered if what they'd had was really sex or more like a series of hit-and-run episodes, with more running involved than hitting.

Then, of course, there was the guy behind door number three. She should have had Monty Hall close the door on him and opted for the lifetime supply of laundry detergent instead. Whoever said size didn't matter? Well, they'd never slept with Tiny Tim Bensen. And here she had thought they jokingly called him Tiny because he was six foot four, two hundred pounds. Little did she know.

Ripley laughed, unable to believe she was thinking of her sex life in such a lighthearted manner. It wasn't so long ago—two days, in fact—that she had questioned her own sexuality as a result of those same three men, thinking it was her fault she had never achieved orgasm during sex. She'd never even imagined that the problem had been the guys, that they hadn't been able to keep up with her.

Then came Joe.

She got hot just thinking about him. Was it ever nice to know that sex's reputation was well deserved. While she suspected even former jock Joe might have the urge to climb onto the rooftop with his jeans open and shout the news of their great sex to the entire population of Memphis, he stuck around to make sure she was having at least as much fun as he was. And oh, boy, was she ever. Places were sore that she hadn't even known could get sore. And every time she took a step, she was prompted to wonder if there might be such a thing as too much great sex.

Naw...

She gathered her papers, straightened them, then put them into the plain manila folder. Well, that was productive, wasn't it? She'd sat down to figure out the case and instead ended up thinking about Joe. She'd suspected there had to be some drawbacks to what was happening between her and Joe. But for some reason she hadn't equated a very good sex life with a sucky professional one.

Of course, she couldn't help but realize that both Joe and the case had a time clock ticking on them. There was only so long she could continue to pursue a case that she was now officially paying out of pocket to solve instead of the other way around. And Joe...well, as soon as she went home to St. Louis, he was—

The lock on the door clicked. Ripley stared at it. She started when someone tried to open it, stopped by the security latch.

"Ripley, it's me," Joe said, knocking.

She let out the nervous breath she was holding and padded to the door. A moment later he stood inside, the latch firmly in place, grinning at her like he'd been gone days instead of ninety minutes...and like he was very happy to see her.

He held up a bag, and Ripley snatched it from him, opening it before she even returned to the bed.

"A thank-you would be nice."

She fished out a whipped-cream-filled éclair and wrapped her mouth around it, humming with approval. "Thank you," she said with her mouth full.

Joe shook his head and put another bag on the table. "Just save me one, will you?"

Ripley looked in the bag. Five éclairs left. She didn't know if she'd have the strength to leave him any.

"Better yet, give me one now." He stood next to the bed and held his hand out. She put the bag in it, then changed her mind, took it back and handed him one éclair instead. She smiled at him, dipping her tongue out to lap cream from her bottom lip.

Joe very obviously had a difficult time swallowing. "Maybe this wasn't such a good idea."

"It was a great idea." She moved the file then patted the bed beside her. "So tell me."

"Tell you what?" He did a move that left him bouncing on the mattress, legs crossed. Ripley saved the file from falling to the floor.

She swallowed and reached for the coffee he was handing her from the night table. "I know it doesn't take that long to get a couple of doughnuts, Joe."

He grinned at her. "Did you miss me?"

More than you'll know. "Nope."

He leaned over and pressed a kiss to her bare knee. "Liar."

She laughed and wriggled away from him, heat blazing up the inside of her thigh straight to the area that would like to be kissed. "Never come between a woman and her doughnuts. You're risking serious injury." She took another bite. "So give."

He ate his doughnut first. Very slowly. Ripley fidgeted as she dug into her second éclair. Okay, so the guy had been raised with manners. But she didn't think talking with his mouth full was what he was worried about right now.

"I went to the tow yard."

She raised her brows.

"Yeah. The car's stored behind eight-foot fences with two very hungry-looking dogs running around loose inside." He frowned and took a slug of coffee from her cup, then handed it back to her. "And another familiar car full of stooges sitting outside."

Ripley had trouble swallowing. "They were there?"

"Yep. All three of them."

"Great." She collapsed against the pillows and sank down, not really thinking about the fact that she wore nothing but a T-shirt and panties. At least until Joe's gaze caught on the patch of cotton between her legs.

"Hmm. Yeah…great."

Ripley tugged on the hem of her T-shirt and covered the area in question. She didn't want to be distracted by sex right now, no matter how much her body responded to his simple suggestive words. "Did anyone ever tell you that you have a one-track mind?"

He grinned at her. "Yeah. You."

"Besides me."

He thought for a minute, then crossed his fingers over his flat, cotton-covered stomach. "Nope. You're the first."

Ripley's stomach tingled. "You're lying."

"And you're beautiful." He reached over her for the bag of doughnuts. She moved it out of the way and smiled at him around another mouthful.

"You're not really thinking about eating all those?"

She swallowed. "Why not?"

"Because you'll get fat."

She whacked him in the arm then tossed him the bag. "One more. That's it."

He grinned and took out another one. "Okay, have it your way. But I think we're going to have to come up with some inventive ways to burn off those calories."

Ripley licked her fingers then wiped her hands on the napkin he supplied. "I think we already did."

"Doesn't count. You have to exercise after the, um, calories." His gaze had drifted suggestively to the hem of her shirt again. She smiled and pushed from the bed.

"Nice try."

She picked up the file from the bed and went to the table, away from temptation in the shape of Joe Pruitt. She opened the folder and fanned the documents.

He sighed in exaggerated exasperation. "Well, since sex is not in my immediate future, you mind tossing me that bag next to you?"

She absently grabbed the bag he'd left on the table when he came in and threw it to the bed, then sat down to concentrate on the case. She ignored the rustle of plastic coming from the bed and her curiosity about what else Joe had bought and stared at the closed file. There had to be something she was missing. What was it?

First off, she was reasonably convinced that there was no blood connection between Nicole and Clarise. She questioned if Bennett was their real name. When she'd arrived in Memphis, the first hotel attendant she'd dropped a twenty on had told her Nicole had checked in under the name Kidman. *Har, har,* she remembered thinking at the time. But if she was going around using false names, then it was possible that Bennett wasn't her real name, either.

She picked up the phone and put a call through to

her cousin three times removed on her father's side who worked at the phone company in St. Louis. Janet was two years younger than she was and wasn't the brightest, but they'd always gotten along. After the normal amount of chitchat, she asked Janet to check and see if there was a listing for a Clarise Bennett in the St. Louis or surrounding area. Shocker of shockers, there wasn't. Then she asked her cousin whose name was connected to the number Clarise had given her that was now out of service. Janet seemed a little put off by that one.

"Geez, Ripley, you know I can't do that. That's illegal."

Ripley bit her tongue, stopping herself from saying that's exactly the reason she had called her instead of Information. Ripley rested her chin in her palm, trying to think up an inventive story that would get her what she was looking for. She found one. She told Janet she was going out with this guy, and that was the number he had given her, but he suddenly up and disappeared. The kicker was, she was afraid he was married.

Boy, was she ever going to hear it from her mother once that news made it back to her.

"The name on that account is Christine Bowman," Janet said a moment later. "Only after the initial installation two months ago, she never paid her bill, and the company cut off service a couple of days ago." She made a low sound, then read off the address. Ripley wrote it down. "Swanky. Funny how she could afford a place like that but couldn't make the phone payment." Her voice lowered. "You think that's the wife?"

"Wife?"

Oh, yeah. She'd forgotten her story. "Just as I expected. The no-good, low-down rodent."

She thanked her cousin, then hung up. Was Clarise Bennett really Christine Bowman? She'd bet she was. But why go through all the trouble of giving a false name?

She thought about the story she'd just fed to her cousin. She realized Clarise, aka Christine, had probably fed the sister story to her in order to find Nicole Bennett. But why?

She picked up the photo of Nicole and squinted at it. She wondered at the odd angle again, and the grainy quality. While she'd questioned why it looked like it had been taken from a security camera before, now, armed with the suspicion that Nicole and Christine, aka Clarise, weren't related at all, she was convinced it *had* been taken from a security camera. She leaned closer, examining the surroundings. The shot had been taken on the front steps of a house with white columns flanking the steps and a brick sidewalk snaking beyond them. Nicole wore a simple light-colored dress—it was difficult to tell what color because the shot was in black and white—that looked more like a uniform than your run-of-the-mill dress.

Ripley sat back, thinking.

Okay, so Nicole wasn't Clarise's sister. And Nicole hadn't been at Clarise's house for a regular family visit, either. Ripley suspected Nicole had been working at the house, and not for very long, at that, if Clarise had just moved in a couple months before. Then Nicole had stolen the box….

She crossed her legs. But why then wouldn't Clarise

have called the police and reported the items stolen? Why, instead, did she hire Ripley to find Nicole and recover what appeared to be nothing but a boxful of worthless costume jewelry?

She took a deep breath then let it out, the answers she found only sprouting more questions.

"I need that box," she said aloud.

She looked at Joe who lay across the bed, reading a book he had open on his washboard stomach. She ignored the little skip her heart gave then crossed to sit on the bed next to him. "What are the chances of our getting into the car without anyone noticing us?"

He laid the book, cover down, on his stomach and glanced at her. "Oh, about zero to none."

"Not the answer I was looking for."

"Unfortunately it's the only one I've got for you."

She snuggled a little more comfortably against the pillows and fingered the pages of the book. "What are you reading?"

She found it hard to believe he would be reading a novel in the midst of all this. But the truth was she didn't know Joe very well. Maybe he read when he was nervous or in trouble. Lord knew others did far stranger things to calm their nerves. Her mother scrubbed the walls in the entire house when she was worried about something. Ripley eyed the hotel room walls, thinking she'd prefer to read.

He held the book up so she could see the cover.

How to Become a P.I. In Ten Quick, Simple Steps.

She gaped at him. "You're kidding."

He grinned. "Nope."

She snatched the book out of his hands and glanced

at the back cover. She was familiar with the book. She'd checked a copy of it out of the St. Louis main library a month ago. But what was he doing with it?

She tossed it back to him and sighed. "What are you doing, Joe?"

He closed the book and put it on the nightstand. "I figured I needed something to do when we weren't having sex."

"And your becoming a P.I. is what you came up with?"

He shook his head, his grin making her thighs quiver. "Nope. You're the P.I. I just thought reading up on the subject would make me more of a help than a hindrance."

She lolled her head on the pillow, not sure if she should be touched or insulted. She opted for touched and tried to ignore the other. "So does this mean I have to read up on shoes now?"

He chuckled. "Not unless you want to."

He leaned closer to her, his index finger finding its way to the hem of her T-shirt. "You know, we could skip all the P.I. and shoes stuff and go straight to the sex part."

A thrill raced up her skin, hardening her breasts and making her blood start to simmer. "Hmm," she said, watching as he lifted the hem of her T-shirt and revealed her plain white panties.

"You ever hear of Victoria's Secret?"

She tried to move his hand away. "You ever hear of tact?"

The finger worked its way under the elastic of her panties and lightly stroked her. Ripley gasped, surprised by the instant awakening of all sorts of hot feelings up and down her body.

He withdrew the finger from the bottom of the panties and moved to the top, tugging the cotton down her hips. "We could always eliminate the topic of underwear altogether."

Ripley swallowed hard. "We could."

Down and off went the panties. But instead of coming right back up, Joe took one of her feet in his hands. He did something to her toes that made her nipples ache. Then his long fingers rubbed her instep, sending shivers up her arms and down her back.

"Do you have a thing for feet?" She'd meant the comment as a mild crack, but her voice sounded raspy even to her, betraying how very much she liked what he was doing.

He grinned and ran a fingertip from heel to toe, eliciting a shallow gasp. "Feet are my business."

She caught her bottom lip between her teeth. "Some men are breast men. Others leg men. Just my luck that I'd pick a guy with a foot fetish."

His chuckle tickled the sensitive skin on her leg, making her realize he'd graduated from her feet and was making his way up her body.

Ripley settled a little more firmly on the mattress, stretching her neck when his fingers found her magic button and began stroking it.

"God, you're so hot," Joe murmured, the air from the words stirring the hair between her legs.

Ripley cracked open her eyes just as his mouth pressed against her heated core, his thumbs holding her swollen flesh open to his attentions. She gasped, caught between needing to push him away and wanting him to do exactly what he was doing.

Her back arched violently, shamelessly pushing her against him as he laved her with his tongue. She restlessly licked her lips, thinking a girl could definitely get used to this. He sucked her most sensitive piece of flesh, and she shuddered. Oh, yeah…definitely.

Up and up she soared. She was teetering on the precipice…when Joe removed his mouth.

"No!" she cried, trying to force him back down.

He chuckled, and a moment later her protests left her when his mouth was replaced by his arousal, thick and hard and pulsing between her legs. She thrust her hips against his.

"Impatient this morning, aren't we?" he murmured, nipping the flesh at the base of her neck.

"Just shut up and give it to me."

He ran his shaft the length of her flesh then back again. "Give you what, Ripley? I want to hear you say it."

She blinked her eyes open to stare at him, her breath rushing from her lungs at the raw, undiluted need on his face.

She reached down and gripped his length in her fingers, giving a squeeze for good measure, and finding him sheathed in a condom. She fit the knob of his arousal against her opening, then thrust her hips quickly upward. "This…oh, yes, this…"

CHAPTER NINE

THE MORE SEX THEY HAD, the more sex Joe wanted.

Ripley wriggled beneath him, and he rocked into her to the hilt, taking great pleasure in her shudders, the sway of her breasts, the bowing of her lips as she pulled in quick, shallow breaths. He claimed her mouth, running his tongue along the length of her lips, then thrust again.

Who knew it could be this good?

The emotions raging through him were both familiar and foreign. He'd had sex with his share of women, but the burning need that always invaded his groin roared through his entire body when he was getting sweaty with Ripley. He stopped short of thinking they were a perfect fit, but when her slick muscles contracted around him, he felt like the most important man on earth. Like this was the place he was meant to be, and he never wanted to leave it. Before…well, he had been after only one thing—his own gratification. And it wasn't simply that he was concerned with Ripley's pleasure, it was also that he didn't want their physical coming together to end. And pleasuring her helped ensure that it wouldn't.

He ran his fingers over her breasts, then between the two globes of flesh, wondering at the dampness there, then moved his hands beneath her to cup her bottom, fitting her to him even more closely. She protested the lack of freedom, and he kissed her words away, reluctantly sliding his hands from her bottom and down her thighs, curving her legs until they were bent between them. When he thrust this time, she called out his name and shattered beneath him. He watched the myriad expressions cross her face as she climaxed.

He tried to hold back, to enjoy merely watching her. But just seeing her experience so much pleasure, knowing he could take credit for it, made him explode right along with her.

Moments later, his mouth pressed to Ripley's sweat-dampened neck, he felt a moment of what he was pretty sure was fear. Not fear that he hadn't performed well. Or that his weight was too much for her. Fear that what was happening between them wouldn't last.

Ripley gave a low, husky laugh. "You know, at some point we're going to have to get out of this bed."

He pulled back to gaze into her face, taking in the humor in her eyes, the flushed state of her skin. "Why?"

She took his head in her hands and kissed him fully on the mouth. "Because I have a case to solve."

He couldn't help his grimace. And what happened when she did solve that case? Would she go back to St. Louis? Where would that leave things between them?

For the first time in his memory, probably ever, Joe thought he'd gained an insight into what went through the minds of those women who desperately tried to cling to him after sex. And it wasn't a pretty picture.

Ripley pushed at his shoulders, and he reluctantly rolled off her, watching as she headed for the bathroom and the shower.

Joe rubbed both hands against his face, breathing in the sweet scent of her that lingered there and trying like hell not to feel like an idiot.

He'd spent some time with a woman in Dallas. Once, after they'd had sex and he lay almost indifferent on the other side of the bed, she had told him that one of these days he was going to meet that one person who would make him feel what she was feeling. He'd stopped himself from scoffing at her and listened patiently, but he'd been thinking he was immune to whatever it was that made women turn from perfectly good bed buddies into demanding, commitment-hungry monsters.

He glanced toward the open bathroom door. Unfortunately, he thought he was finding out that not only wasn't he immune, he was feeling whatever that feeling was in spades.

He rolled out of bed, discarded the used condom, then began pacing the length of the room. This wasn't good. This wasn't good at all. This wasn't supposed to happen to *him*.

He caught himself. *Okay, get a grip, guy. So you like having sex with this woman. And you don't want that sex to end just yet.* There was nothing wrong with that. It didn't mean he was falling into the big one. That he'd stuck his foot right in the middle of it.

Love.

No. No. There was a difference between sex and love. He'd learned that in sex ed classes.

And that was exactly the reason he was afraid he was coming to know the other side a little too well.

Ripley came out of the bathroom freshly scrubbed,

her auburn curls somewhat tamed. She was dressed in khaki shorts and a white blouse with a white tank top underneath. And she couldn't have looked sexier to him had she been in one of those sheer, body-hugging getups he saw in the Victoria's Secret catalogues that were delivered to his house.

Holy shit, I am in love with her, he realized with a breath-robbing gulp.

"Ready?" she asked.

No. Hell, no. He wasn't anywhere near ready. In fact, he'd never be ready. What was he going to do? Where was he going to go? She was watching him. What was he going to say?

"For what?" he forced himself to ask.

"To get the box from the car, of course."

"Of course," he repeated, pacing from one end of the room to the other. He forced himself to stop, to try to gain some perspective, but all he could think of was the terrifying "L" word.

He finally forced himself to put on his clothes, more to distract himself from his thoughts than as a response. Then her words sank in, and he turned to face her even as he tucked his shirt into his jeans. "What did you just say?"

She glanced at him guilelessly from where she was putting her file together. "What? That we're going to get the box from your car?"

"Yes, that's it." He crossed his arms over his chest and tried to ignore how much he wanted to tackle her back to the bed. "Are you insane? There's no way we're getting into that place without those goons seeing us." Or the dogs. He wasn't sure which was worse.

She slung her purse over her shoulder, tucked the file under her arm and headed for the door. "Exactly."

Joe caught the door with his hand, pushing it closed. He eyed the damp tendrils of hair that clung to her finely curved neck. "What do you mean, exactly?"

She shrugged and held the file against her chest. "Nelson told me that there are times when it's wise to make friends out of your enemies."

That Nelson Polk again. Joe sighed.

She smiled. "I think it's time you and I found out who our new friends really are, and what, exactly, they're after."

OKAY, JOE WAS ACTING DECIDEDLY weird. Ripley pulled her hair off her neck then fastened it into a loose twist at the top of her head. She'd come out of the shower to find him looking at her in a way she could only describe as shell-shocked. And that seemed to be the general way he'd looked at her since. No wiseass remarks. No trying to get into her underpants. Instead, he appeared ready to bolt in the other direction if she so much as said boo to him.

She smiled, tempted to do just that.

In the back of the taxi she'd called to pick them up, Joe couldn't have sat farther away from her had he tried. And she got the distinct impression he was trying. He all but had the side of his face smashed against the window in his effort to stay away from her.

So she did the natural thing. She reached out and touched him.

He started, and she laughed.

"Am I missing something here?" she asked. She

began to remove her hand from his arm, then changed her mind, deciding she liked him being a little ill at ease. At her mercy, so to speak.

She watched him swallow hard then shake his head. "It's just that I don't know if this is such a good idea."

She smoothed her hand up his arm, then over his chest, her fingers seeking and finding the opening of his shirt and slipping inside to tease the fine, crisp hair there. The tension that practically radiated from him was of the anxious variety. She smiled and dipped her fingers down to roll over one of his flat nipples.

He caught her hand. "Would you cut it out? I'm serious here."

That was the thing. He was a little too serious.

Could it be that all this was finally getting to him? That the source of his anxiety stemmed from the three goons they were about to face off with? After all, she could only guess at what had happened when he'd gone head-to-head with them alone.

"There's nothing to worry about, Joe," she said, sitting back on her side of the seat and watching as he collapsed against his side in almost comical relief. "If they are FBI, then we're safe because neither of us has done anything wrong." She hoped. "If they're not…well, it's the middle of the day. What do you think they're going to do? Shoot us?"

"The thought has crossed my mind."

"Well, then, we'll shoot them back." She patted the bag that held her gun for emphasis.

"Gee, that's reassuring." A return of the old Joe, but the words didn't hold half the energy they usually did.

She'd told the driver to let her know when they were

getting close. He spoke. She requested he drop them off at the corner opposite the towing yard then gave him a nice tip for his efforts.

She got out of the car and held the door open. "Are you coming?" she asked. Joe didn't seem to be aware the cab had stopped.

He grimaced then climbed out to stand next to her, smoothing his already smooth shirt. The cab drove off, and they both watched it, wrapped up in their own thoughts.

Ripley took his arm and began walking toward the holding lot. There. The sedan holding the three goons sat parked at the curb on the opposite side of the street. Ripley crossed, heading straight for the garage next to the towing lot that probably held the office.

"Where are we going?" Joe asked, blinking at her.

"To get your car back."

"Fine. It's your ass."

He seemed to consider the body part in question as she walked slightly in front of him. She tugged him so he walked even with her. "I don't have a thing to worry about." *I hope.*

With barely a glance at the dark blue sedan, she and Joe entered through the door of the garage, the interior dim and cluttered and looking pretty much like every other garage she'd been in. The only difference was that normally her heart didn't threaten to pound a hole through her chest, and she usually didn't have three goons following her.

Joe stepped up to a caged office where a guy smoking a cigar sat reading the sports section of the newspaper.

She supposed he needed protection. Most people didn't take kindly to having their cars towed.

Joe took his license from his wallet, put it in front of the guy and launched into his spiel, while Ripley stood to the side, slipping her hand into her purse. Her fingers met with the cold, unyielding metal of her gun as she watched the door. She quickly snatched her hand out. Who was she kidding? She couldn't shoot a rabid dog if it were charging her. Well, okay, maybe she could. But she wasn't in a hurry to find out. She only hoped these guys weren't foaming at the mouth.

Joe's voice rose, and Ripley blinked to find him arguing with the attendant who stared at him indifferently and shifted the cigar in his mouth with his tongue. She realized the cage was also necessary to enable the occupant to get away with highway robbery.

Joe finally counted out bills one by one and flicked them at the attendant. Ripley calculated the amount, adding it to the running tab she already owed Joe. The sum was starting to eat into a good chunk of her savings, but the guy hadn't breathed one word to her about all he'd given up for her so far. Besides, she owed him more than money.

The door to the outside finally opened, and Ripley wasn't ready for it. She jumped and turned toward it, only to see a woman she didn't recognize step to the cage. Another towing victim? She'd venture a yes. Ripley stepped closer to the door and opened it a crack to peek at the sedan. Still there. Men still inside. She frowned and let the door close again.

"Over there," the smirking attendant said, pointing to

another door to the side that probably led to the towing yard. "Just give me a minute to call the dogs in."

Joe said something to him Ripley wasn't sure she wanted to hear, then led the way to the door the attendant had motioned to.

"Hey!" the woman who had come in called after the attendant. "I've got appointments."

"Yeah, well, now you gotta wait," he shouted.

Ripley didn't have to wonder why he'd taken the job. Obviously he enjoyed it.

Joe leaned in closer to her. "Where are our friends?"

"Still outside."

He grimaced.

Her thoughts exactly.

"So what's the plan now?"

She tapped her finger against her lips, considering the situation. She pulled her bag closer to her side, reassured by the weight of it. "Pull the car out on the street and wait for me."

She began to walk away, only to be towed back by the collar of her blouse. "Uh-uh. Not an option."

She wriggled free from his grasp. "That's not for you to say."

"So long as I'm with you, it is."

Ripley scanned Joe's handsome, irritated face, finding the frustration from dealing with the attendant gone and the seriousness back. Then it dawned on her what may be behind the change. "You're worried about me, aren't you?" she asked wonderingly.

She'd never had anyone outside her parents worry about her before. And it felt pretty good. Not that she had given her parents much to worry about. Up until now she'd always done things exactly the way they wanted her to. She figured she must have saved up her bad-girl points and was cashing them all in on this one case.

"No, I'm worried about me," Joe said, though she could see it wasn't true. If he was truly worried about only himself, he would have dumped her a long time ago.

"Uh-huh." She glanced toward where someone rapped on the other side of the door. Joe opened it to stare at the attendant. "In a minute." He closed the door again.

Ripley smiled at him. "You know, he may decide to keep the car if you keep doing things like that."

"Let him." He narrowed his gaze. "What are you going to do?"

She shrugged and glanced at the woman drumming her orange acrylic nails against the counter in front of the cage. "I'm going to walk up to the car and ask them what they want with me."

She thought of Nicole Bennett confronting her and Joe the night before and felt a stab of envy. What she wouldn't give for guts like those. Then again, there was a big difference between a green P.I. with a guy along for the ride and the three goombahs sitting outside.

Joe grasped her hand and tugged her toward the door. "We'll confront them together. Right after I get my car out of this godforsaken lot."

She stumbled through the door after him, a protest on her lips. A protest that died right there when Johnny the attendant pressed a button and the gates opened to reveal the three men in question standing there with their arms crossed over their chests.

RIPLEY SAT IN THE BACK SEAT of the plain blue sedan, one of the goons sitting next to her while another sat in the front seat watching her through the rearview mirror. She bit her tongue to keep from asking them what they ate. Whatever it was, it couldn't be healthy. It wasn't normal for guys to be this big.

She peered out the window to where the third guy was talking to Joe near the front of the car.

She sighed and sat back. "Are you guys really FBI?" she asked, staring at first one then the other.

The one in the front seat reached inside his jacket, then flipped open a wallet over the seat, all without turning. She eyed his identification, wondering if he'd ordered it from the same catalog she'd gotten her P.I. badge from.

He flipped the wallet closed and put it away.

"I've never seen agents that look like you." Of course, she'd never really seen an FBI agent up close and this personal before, period, but they didn't have to know that.

Neither of them said anything.

Ripley sighed again and rolled her eyes. Apparently the only one capable of speech was talking to Joe, leaving her here with Harpo and his clone on steroids. All they needed were handheld horns to blow to indicate yes or no, and they could take their act out on the road.

"You look more like Mob to me," she said, then nearly bit her tongue in two. Neither man moved, but she felt the driver's stare intensify on her via the mirror, something she could only sense because all three of them wore mirrored sunglasses. She crossed her arms over her chest. "Then again, if you were Mob, I don't think you'd be flashing FBI IDs around, would you?" she thought aloud. "You wouldn't have to. The mere suggestion of Mob affiliation would be enough, wouldn't it?"

Someone rapped on her window, and she jumped. She looked up to see goon number three motioning for the door to open. The automatic locks sounded, and he pulled the door open.

"You're free to go, ma'am."

She squinted at him. A Mob guy wouldn't call her ma'am, would he? "Are you sure?"

Did she really just ask that? When someone like him said that you were free to go, you went.

A smile tilted the sides of his mouth then vanished. "Not unless you don't want to."

She couldn't have scrambled from the car faster had she been pushed.

Ripley stood in the middle of the street, gaping as the guy rounded the rear of the car and got into the front seat alongside Tweedledum. Then the sedan drove away from the curb and down the street, turning at the next corner.

Joe came to stand next to her. "Come on, let's go get lunch."

JOE SAT ACROSS FROM RIPLEY in a rib joint on the edge of Beale Street and grinned at her sudden loss of appetite. He'd had to order for her, because she hadn't said a word since he'd stuffed her stiff body into his car and driven the short way to the infamous street.

They sat in the corner of a bar decorated with old posters of blues legends, donated musical instruments and autographs written directly on the wall. The three-piece band set up near the door played without a singer.

Ripley finally blinked out of her shock-induced coma. "You're telling me he let you go because he's from Minneapolis and remembered you from your college basketball days?"

Joe leaned his forearms on the table. "Yep." Seldom was he reminded of the time he'd spent with the University of Minnesota Golden Gophers. But if he could have chosen a moment, this would definitely have been one of them.

She rolled her eyes and flopped back in her chair.

"Well, that, and I told him everything I knew about you and the case you're working on." He straightened his napkin.

Her eyes widened.

"And here I thought you'd be happy to find out that you're not in any trouble."

"I already knew that. Sort of. I haven't done anything wrong."

He stared at her. "You wouldn't happen to know a Christine Bowman, would you?"

She blinked at him. "Christine Bowman is Clarise Bennett."

He cocked a brow.

"I found that out this morning when I called to check whose name the contact number Clarise had given me belonged to." She chugged down the water in the glass in front of her, her gaze constantly darting through the window. "So it's Nicole that they want, isn't it?" She looked squarely at him, her chocolate brown eyes wide and wondering. "What did she do?"

"As far as they're concerned, nothing."

"Nothing?"

"It's not her they're after. It's Christine Bowman."

"The woman who hired me?"

He nodded.

"Did they say what they want her for?"

He chuckled and leaned back so the waitress could take his plate. She reached to take Ripley's, as well, but she slapped her hand down on the edge and said she wasn't done, when in truth she had yet to touch it. Joe guessed that her appetite had made a comeback. "It wasn't exactly a give-and-take kind of conversation, Ripley. I did most of the giving, and Agent Miller did most of the taking."

"So they want Christine…" She broke off a rib from the small rack in front of her and rolled an end into a bowl of barbecue sauce. Her gaze suddenly flew to his face. "You didn't tell them about the box, did you?"

He motioned for her to lean forward, and he slowly cleaned a drop of sauce from the side of her mouth with his napkin. He groaned when her tongue dipped out to finish the job.

"No, I didn't tell them about the box," he said, sitting solidly back and out of touching distance.

She seemed to notice his body language, and the tiniest of smiles played around her lush mouth.

He took a business card from his back pocket and held it out to her. "I did, however, promise that we'd contact them if we get any information on either Christine or Nicole."

"Why Nicole?"

"I'm guessing because she might lead them to Christine."

He sat back and watched her dig into her ribs with a vengeance, obviously determined to make up for lost time. He shifted uncomfortably when she made soft, sexy sounds in the back of her throat, the same kind of sounds she made during sex.

"These are the best ribs I've ever had," she murmured before launching another attack on the plate in front of her.

Judging from her slender frame, he'd guess they were some of the few ribs she'd ever had.

"So that's it then?" she asked, finishing in no time flat. Joe glanced around, wondering if they posted a record anywhere. "We don't have to worry about them anymore?"

"We don't need to be jumping from any more balconies, if that's what you mean." He leaned forward and rubbed the back of his neck. "In fact, we can go to the old hotel...you know, if we want."

She stared at him as the waitress removed her plate. "That's good, right? All your stuff's there."

"Yeah," he said. What he didn't say was that returning to the old hotel also meant separate rooms and that there would no longer be a need for them to pretend to be a couple for the purposes of evading the three goons they now knew were with the FBI.

She looked as disappointed as he felt while she cleaned her hands with the wet towelette next to her napkin. The prospect of her thinking with sadness about them parting pleased him.

She balled up the towelette and tossed it toward the ashtray. "Well, that was a little anticlimactic, wasn't it? The FBI, I mean. Here I thought I'd done something even I didn't know about."

Joe grimaced. He should have known she was thinking about the case.

She stared at him. "But why would they come into my room with their guns drawn?"

He shrugged. "They said they weren't entirely certain of your connection to Christine and thought it was a pretty good bet that she might be rooming with you."

"Oh."

He couldn't believe it. She was disappointed the FBI hadn't been after her. Go figure.

She scooted her chair back and got up. He quickly followed.

"Where to now?"

"Back to our old hotel, I guess. And to try to figure out what, exactly, is in that box that both Christine and the FBI are interested in."

CHAPTER TEN

RIPLEY SAT CROSS-LEGGED ON the bed in her original hotel room, the contents of the mysterious box spilled across the sheets in front of her. Hours of fingering the fake jewels, examining the clasps and the larger gems, holding them up to the lamplight and jingling them left her no closer to the truth than she'd been before.

She sighed and leaned back on her elbows, her gaze automatically drifting to the empty pillow beside her, then the wall her room shared with Joe's room.

When they'd returned to the hotel, she'd automatically assumed he would come to her room with her. But he hadn't. Instead he'd said something about contacting his home office and trying to work some sort of damage control and left her in her room, alone.

She straightened the watch on her wrist. That had been several hours ago. And he hadn't tried to contact her since.

She wasn't sure what she was supposed to think. Since the threat of the FBI wasn't hovering over them, and since Joe had already gotten her between the sheets, there was no longer a reason for them to be stuck together. She made a face, hating to describe their time together in that way. But it was accurate, wasn't it? She thought of his long, hard body and the many, many hours they had spent stuck together. Her stomach tightened with desire despite the dull sensation of feeling used that spread through her.

She dragged the free pillow over her head and groaned loudly, mostly because she couldn't quite bring herself to believe it had just been about the sex, no matter how phenomenal that had been. Joe had gone out on a limb for her in more ways than one. And people didn't do that for a roll in the hay.

But if he hadn't been with her merely for the sex, where was he?

She threw the pillow aside and sat up, pushing her hair from her eyes. She really shouldn't be thinking about that now. She should be trying to figure out what was in this box and why so many people were after it.

She picked up the box and fingered the semiprecious jewels dotting the side and lid. A soft knock on the door, and her intentions to solve the mystery flew straight out the balcony door.

She pulled the door open to find Joe standing there looking good enough to eat. "Hi," he said.

Gone were the jeans and casual shirt and back were the starched shirt, tie and dress slacks. She yanked on the tie, pulling him into the room. The door whooshed shut behind him.

He chuckled. "So you missed me, huh?"

She had. Bad.

"Here," he said, holding out a box to her. This one was a cardboard box similar to the ones that had littered the back seat of his car. "These are for you."

"You shouldn't have." She popped open the lid and stared at the athletic shoes inside. She fished one out and held it up. "Are we going somewhere?"

"I thought we might go for a walk."

"A walk." She considered him long and hard, then her eyes widened in awareness. "Are you asking me for a date, Joe Pruitt?"

His immediate grimace spoke volumes.

"You are, aren't you?" she asked.

He cleared his throat, getting that ill-at-ease look again. He glanced at his watch. "I just got back from the company I'm trying to contract with and figured it was feeding time."

He glanced at the rumpled bed behind her, and Ripley waited for him to try to get her into it. Instead, he looked at her and asked, "Any luck with the box?"

She frowned and glanced at her shorts and shirt. There was no discernable difference that she could detect. But he had yet to make one suggestive remark or look at her breasts.

Not good.

"Okay. We'll go for a walk," she said carefully. "Just let me get dressed first."

JOE WALKED BESIDE RIPLEY, trying not to notice how well the red dress she'd changed into fit her, or how her breasts threatened to spill out of the top of it, making his mouth water for just a taste of the smooth, warm flesh. He swallowed hard, nodding at some lame comment she made on the history of Sun Studio and Elvis Presley.

Since she was obviously not going to wear the shoes he'd given her, he'd driven them to Beale Street, and instead of the walk he'd planned, they were walking the length of it. The sound of various blues bands filtered onto the street from the doorways they passed, the music sometimes slow and seductive, other times fast and lush. Even though the sun was sliding over the horizon, it was hotter than it had been at any other time of the day, a result of the asphalt beneath their feet having absorbed much of the sun's heat. Of course, Ripley's sexy attire wasn't helping in the heat area much, either, but Joe was trying not to notice that.

He sighed and wished he had changed into something more comfortable, cooler. He'd rolled his shirt sleeves to his elbows, loosened his tie and undid the first few buttons of his shirt, but he was sure he was sweating through the back of the crisp cotton.

A kid ran past them then launched into a series of flips the length of the sidewalk, then back again. Joe reached into his pocket, but Ripley caught his arm. "Let me."

She gave the preteen a couple of bills then tucked her hand easily into the crook of Joe's arm where he had stuffed his hands into his pockets. He felt his spine immediately snap straight and something akin to pride puff out his chest. She angled a smile at him, and he was sure she knew what had just happened. But rather than worry about her powers of observation, he merely smiled at her.

She laid her head briefly against his shoulder then lifted it. "So, tell me," she said quietly, "what's life like being Joe Pruitt?"

Pretty damn dull, he thought. At least until recently. He shrugged. "I don't know. The usual, I guess."

"Define the usual."

He squinted at her. "Are you hungry?"

"Not yet." She squeezed his arm through his shirt.

"Since this was your idea, then you're going to have to start answering some of my questions."

"Define the usual," he repeated, slowing to allow another couple to pass in front of them. "I get up at six in the morning, go for a five-mile run if weather permits. In the office by eight. Out at five." He shrugged again. "The usual."

She hummed. "Except when you're traveling."

"Except when I'm traveling," he agreed.

"And how often do you do that?"

He made the necessary calculations. "Last year, I was on the road nearly thirty-two weeks."

"That much? That makes two-thirds of the time."

He nodded.

"So you travel as much as a rock star."

He chuckled. "Yes, as much as rock star. Just with different hours." And no groupies.

Trust Ripley to make his job sound more interesting than it was.

He caught himself. He'd never really thought of running his company as a job before. It was his career. His way of life. Never merely a job that he had to do to pay the bills.

"And you used to be a secretary," he said, unable to bring himself to compare her to Gloria. He couldn't imagine Ripley sitting still for more than five minutes at a time. Aside from the fact that she'd be damn distracting taking dictation.

Then again, if he had a secretary like Ripley, he probably wouldn't go out on the road as much as he did. He had four other low-level salesmen on the payroll who could take up much of the slack. But even when he'd hired them, he hadn't considered cutting back his travel hours.

"I was a secretary for six years," Ripley said quietly, as if the reality surprised her as much as him.

They walked in silence for another block, Ripley lingering in front of the glass fronts of nightclubs, watching the bands inside. Joe stared at his feet and felt pretty miserable, although he couldn't understand why.

When he'd left her alone at the hotel earlier, he'd decided to try to regain a hold on his life. He'd contacted Gloria and retrieved his messages and told her how he could be contacted. Then he put a call in to the company reps he had been wooing to set things in motion, only he didn't know how successful he'd been after an afternoon full of meetings he hadn't wanted to be in, his mind steadfastly on what kind of trouble Ripley was or wasn't getting herself into while he was away.

But he couldn't place the blame on her for his distracted state. Not completely, anyway. He was coming to realize that beyond his incurable lust for Ripley, and the bizarre, dreamlike quality of the past couple of days, what he was feeling for his job—it certainly wasn't an adventure—had been slowly lifting to the surface for the past few months. Landing distribution contracts, launching promotional campaigns and signing sports heroes to wear his products just weren't doing it for him anymore.

The problem was that beyond Ripley, he didn't know what *would* do it for him.

Then there was the little detail that soon not even Ripley would be in his life to distract him.

There was a tug on his arm. He looked to find her

watching him curiously. "You know, I'm starting to worry about you," she said. "You haven't looked at my breasts once."

His gaze automatically drifted to the top of her dress and the soft, smooth skin there. "Yes, I have. You just haven't seen me do it."

Her smile was one hundred percent pure Ripley.

"Besides," he said. "I thought you hated that I had a one-track mind."

She seemed to consider his words. "One track is better than no track. Ever since this afternoon I feel like I've lost you."

That makes two of us, Joe thought.

Her hand slowly dropped to his, then she crossed in front of him, pulling him forward. "Tell me, what do you want to do? Name it. Anything, and we'll do it."

He wanted the world to start making sense again. But he didn't think that was going to happen anytime soon.

"Joe?"

"Hmm?" He blinked to stare into her face.

She stopped next to a lamppost, a decidedly suggestive smile curving her mouth. "Kiss me."

A groan started somewhere in the vicinity of his groin and twisted its way into his throat. Right that second, taking in her big brown eyes, pouty lips and suggestive expression, he couldn't name anything he'd rather do more.

Curving his fingers around her neck, feeling the throb of her pulse at the base, he slowly backed her against the lamppost, taking first one step, then another. Her eyes darkened as her gaze slid from his mouth to meet his gaze. Her tongue made a command performance, dragging across her full bottom lip, then dipping inside the slick depths of her mouth. Her back met with the post, and she reached to steady herself. Only Joe had no intention of allowing her to regain her equilibrium. He put his other hand on the pole above her head then bent and brushed his lips against hers.

Soft and sweet and heady. Joe closed his eyes and rested his forehead against hers, pulling his mouth mere millimeters away, their breath mingling between them. For an incredible moment, he wondered if he was going to survive her. And the question had nothing to do with the FBI, runaway clients or gun-pointing missing persons. Or even Ripley's penchant for finding trouble where none previously existed. No, his fear grew from knowing the woman herself. Watching her eyes brighten as she thought about her new career, the wrinkle between her eyebrows as she tried to figure out her case, her enthusiasm when she attacked a plate of ribs. He stroked his finger along her cheek and delicate jaw. There was also a lot to be said about the curve of her back as she strained against him during climax. The soft sounds she made when he thrust madly into her. The feel of her soft mouth covering his erection, giving him the complete attention she gave to everything else in her life.

Ripley stood staring at him, her whiskey-brown eyes full of questions. Then she tilted her mouth and pressed her lips more urgently against his.

Joe couldn't help but respond in kind.

The bustling street around them vanished, the world

shrinking to include only Ripley where she stood in the pool of lamplight. As she dipped her tongue into his mouth, he couldn't help thinking she had crawled completely inside him over the past few days. He moved. He felt her right there under his skin even when they weren't together. His first waking thought was of her and where she was and how quickly he could sink into her silken, hot flesh. His last thought was to hold her to him as closely as possible to keep her from vanishing in the same mist that had brought her into his life.

The damnable part about the whole thing was that he didn't have a clue how she felt about him.

Ripley pulled away from the kiss, her soft, sexy laugh doing things to him that hands could never do. "Well, that was, um, nice."

He rolled an auburn curl between his fingers. "Nice?" he asked with a cocked brow.

"Very." She smiled then curled her hands into the open edges of his shirt. "Come on. I think we'd better go get something to eat before we get arrested for indecent exposure."

"We still have our clothes on."

"Exactly."

RIPLEY UNLOCKED THE DOOR to her room while still kissing Joe. In all honesty, she was afraid to stop kissing him for fear that he would get that serious expression on his face again and find an excuse to go to his own room. She pushed the door open with her hip, loving the taste of beer on his tongue, the feel of heat in his hands as he captured one of her breasts, pinching her tight nipple through the fabric of her dress. She let the strap of her purse slide off her shoulder, and the bag dropped to the floor with the weight of all it held.

Somehow she'd made it through dinner without diving straight into his lap and kissing that adorable but alarming expression from his face. She wished she knew what he was thinking, but she'd asked once, and he hadn't answered. She'd silently vowed not to hound him about it, too afraid she'd sound like her mother, who had a tendency to sound like a broken record when you weren't in a talking mood. Either that, or what you were thinking wasn't suitable to share with your mother.

She closed the door and pushed Joe against it, tugging his shirt from the waist of his slacks, then digging her fingers into the smooth, rippled flesh of his stomach. Maybe what Joe was thinking he couldn't share. While she didn't think he would lie to her about being married, it wasn't beyond the realm that he had a woman somewhere, a girlfriend maybe.

She didn't like the direction of her thoughts, so she stopped thinking altogether and concentrated on feeling.

And oh, boy, were there lots of feelings to be felt.

The instant they were in the privacy of her room, Joe thrust his hands up the short skirt of her dress, palming her bottom in that way that made her shiver with anticipation. Before she could get his shirt halfway unbuttoned, he'd stripped her of her panties. She gave up on the buttons and yanked the shirt off over his head, pressing her breasts against the solid wall of his chest. She sighed, loving the way he felt against her—her breasts smashed against his chest—his arousal hot and hard against her stomach.

He backed her toward the bed as he worked the zipper of her dress down. She tripped over something on the floor and he caught her, the incident affecting their mood not at all. They continued their blind search for the bed, and Ripley tripped over something else, this time something that sounded breakable. Her eyes flew open, and her mouth froze against Joe's.

"I hate to say it, but that doesn't sound good." He ground out the words between ragged gasps.

She agreed.

He kissed her hard again then reached to switch on the lamp. Only there was no lamp to be turned on.

"Wait here," he said.

Ripley groaned, reluctantly letting go of him so he could backtrack to the foyer and the switch there. Instantly, the room was awash in light. And Ripley didn't much like what she was seeing.

Joe let rip a string of ripe curses that Ripley wished she could have mouthed, if she were capable of speech at all.

The place was a mess. The lamp Joe had tried to turn on was the source of the glass sound. It lay on the floor, the bulb shattered, the bottom pulled off as if the something that someone had been looking for was inside the body of it. The mattress was slashed to shreds, pieces of stuffing and springs popping out at odd angles, and the pillows had been completely defeathered. Ripley hugged her arms around herself, noticing that not even her clothes had survived the search. Articles were strewn around the room. She picked up a T-shirt, eyeing the rip down the middle.

She shivered, but this time it had nothing to do with Joe's hands on her bottom.

"I knew we should have gone to my room," he said under his breath.

AN HOUR LATER RIPLEY SAT ON the destroyed bed holding the card Agent Miller had given to Joe. There was nothing but a simple number printed in the middle. No name. Nothing to indicate if he or the other two men were, indeed, FBI.

After Joe had verified that his room had been left untouched, they'd called the hotel manager, who had called the police. They'd told the officials as much as they had to, considering that they didn't know much themselves. Joe was seeing the hotel manager out, assuring him that Ripley didn't need another room, that she would be staying with him but that that information wasn't for public knowledge. Should anyone call, hotel personnel were to say she had checked out.

Ripley cleared her throat. "Wait a minute."

Joe turned to face her from the door along with the manager.

"If anyone calls, I want them put straight through to Mr. Pruitt's room," she said.

Joe frowned at her.

She couldn't argue with him about staying in his room. The truth was, she didn't even want to contemplate sleeping alone tonight. Not when the person who had ripped her room apart had done such a thorough job of it. The police officers hadn't found the item used to rip apart the mattress, but they were fairly certain it had been a razor. Probably a straight edge, and a long one, at that.

Joe closed the door after the manager then came to sit on the destroyed bed next to her. She was grateful for the feel of his heat, although for an entirely different reason than before.

"What are you thinking?" he asked.

She glanced at him. "I don't know." She rolled everything around in her mind. Clarise Bennett, aka Christine Bowman. Nicole Bennett, whose name may or may not be Bennett at all. The FBI. The pawnshop....

Her heart did the equivalent of a tire skid across her chest.

"What is it?" Joe asked, watching as she got up and scrambled toward the door. She plucked up her purse then made her way to the bed. But rather than sitting again, she emptied the contents of her bag on the spread. She pushed aside her gun, her makeup bag, a pamphlet from the hotel, then found the item she wanted hiding under a wad of tissues.

The jewelry box.

"You had it with you?" Joe asked.

She nodded. "I stuck it into my bag right before we left, you know, thinking that if something occurred to me, I wanted to have it with me so I could go through it again."

She flipped the lid open and stared at the fake jewels inside.

Was it possible that they weren't fake? How much did the pawnshop owner really know about jewels? Could Nicole have told him they were fake, thinking they were, too, and he hadn't questioned it?

"So you know anything about jewelry?" she asked Joe.

He shook his head. "Not a thing."

"Me, either."

"You're not thinking what I think you're thinking, are you?"

"What, that they're real?"

"Yes."

"Then, yes, I am."

She crossed the room and picked up the phone, staring at the card still in her hand, then dialing the number there. "Only one surefire way to find out."

JOE STEPPED OUT OF THE SHOWER, having finished in record time. "Ripley?" he called.

"What?" Her head popped into the doorway.

He grinned at her. "Nothing."

She rolled her eyes then walked into the other room.

Shortly after the phone call Ripley placed to Agent Miller to arrange for a meeting first thing in the morning, they'd gone to Joe's room. Not only was the security latch in place, he had moved a low bureau in front of the door, and he hoped like hell that Ripley would remain the only person ever to sneak into his bedroom via the balcony doors.

He hadn't wanted to leave her alone long enough to take a shower, but he'd been in dire need of one after their walk down Beale Street. He felt better now, not only because he'd had one, but because he was out again.

He draped a thick white towel around his hips and

stepped into the other room where Ripley sat on the floor cross-legged, the box and its contents spread out, the television turned on low in front of her. ESPN? A girl after his own heart.

"Anything?" he asked.

She shook her head. "They still look fake to me."

He sat on the edge of the bed, drying his hair with another towel. "Maybe it's not the jewelry they were after."

She twisted her lips and looked at him. "What else could there be?"

He picked up the box. "The box itself, perhaps?"

He turned it around and around in his hands, looking inside, then out, then turning it upright. It didn't look like anything special to him. But what did he know?

"Wait," Ripley said softly, reaching to still his hands.

She positioned her head so she was staring under the box. Either that, or she was trying to sneak a peak under his towel. He was hoping it might be the latter. Unfortunately, it proved to be the former.

She steadied the box with one hand, then tugged on something with another. He watched an orange-tabbed key drop to the floor.

"Oh, boy," Ripley whispered, plucking the key and holding it for him to see.

He turned the box over and stared at the fake bottom. Actually, it was more like a small compartment in the corner. Very easily missed, as both of them could attest to.

Ripley turned the key over in her hand.

"Looks like a locker key," Joe said. "One of those you find in an airport or something."

"Or a bus station, or a train station, or even a health spa."

He held his hand palm out, and she dropped the key into his palm. No identifying marks to indicate exactly where it was from, only the locker number, 401.

Ripley pulled her knees to her chest and rested her arms against them. "The locker could be anywhere from here to St. Louis and beyond."

He grimaced. "You weren't actually thinking to open it if you did know where it was, were you?"

She shrugged her slender shoulders. "Sure. The contents would probably help to explain a lot."

He reluctantly handed her the key then put the box on the bed next to him. "Judging by how things have gone down so far, I'd recommend against it."

She blinked at him. "And what would you recommend?"

"I say you should give the box and its contents to the FBI tomorrow, including the key."

She frowned, curling her toes against the carpeting. She had sexy toes. Slender, fingerlike, the nails painted a metallic pink. "Then we might never find out what's really going on."

"Fine by me."

Her brown eyes narrowed as she considered him. "Really? I mean, you can just walk away without knowing who Christine Bowman is, what Nicole's relationship is to her and what's in this locker to explain why the FBI's involved?"

"Walk away isn't the way I'd put it. Run would probably cover it more accurately."

She turned to stare at the key resting in the middle of her palm.

She just didn't get it, did she? He didn't care about Nicole Bennett, Christine Bowman or that damn key she held. All he cared about was her. And the only mystery he wanted to uncover was whether or not they had a future together.

CHAPTER ELEVEN

RIPLEY SAT FACING THE THREE goons with FBI IDs who were squashed into the booth opposite her. She was concentrating on her breakfast. The middle goon elbowed the one on the end, and he nearly fell out of the bench and onto the floor, reminding her of an old Three Stooges episode.

The rejected agent stumbled to his feet, then stood, his mirrored sunglasses reflecting the table and its occupants but nothing about what was going on inside his head.

"Sir," a waitress said, trying to pass. "I'm going to have to ask you to sit down."

Not a flicker of emotion passed over his stone face as he gave their table a once-over, then moved to sit at the counter some fifteen feet away, positioning his stool so he could keep an eye on them.

"Where's the box?"

Ripley smothered jam on a half piece of toast. Ever since meeting in the lobby of the hotel half an hour ago, she'd been delaying giving the agents what they were after. There were a few things she wanted from them first. And she wasn't going to get what she wanted if she rolled over and played dead.

Okay, she'd had to concede to Joe that maybe trekking through every plane, train and bus station from

Memphis to St. Louis wasn't a very good idea, even if she was chomping at the bit to see with her own two eyes what lay in the locker the key opened. So she'd offered a compromise. She'd hand the key over to her new friends here, but only when they shared some information with her.

She wiped her hands on her napkin then fished the box from her purse, the back of her hand grazing Joe's side where he sat beside her. His eyes held a mixture of amusement and exasperation.

"Here," she said, setting the box in the middle of the table.

Agent Miller glanced around the restaurant then plucked the box up while Ripley picked up her toast and took a bite.

A moment later, he stared at her. "Where's the rest?"

She squinted at him, pretending not to understand. "Can you take off your sunglasses, please? I don't much like talking to my own reflection."

He whipped them off so fast she was surprised he didn't put an eye out. He gave her a steely gaze that half tempted her to tell him to put the glasses back on. "Ms. Logan, I'd suggest you put your cards on the table now before I take you into protective custody and order a body search."

Obviously he'd used the threat before. And even she had to admit that the imagery wasn't particularly pleasant. "That would be a waste of time. It's not on me."

What went unsaid was that *it* was the key. The same key she'd sealed in an envelope and put in the hotel safe early that morning, long before the agents showed up for their meeting.

"Are you sure you don't want something to eat?" she asked.

They stared at her.

She shrugged and leisurely finished her breakfast, letting them chew on the information they already had—that she had the key and knew that they wanted it.

Joe shifted uncomfortably next to her. The waitress tried to refill his cup, and he put his hand over the rim to stop her. "Decaf, please."

Ripley accepted the full octane, then added four sugar packets and heavy cream. She looked Agent Miller full in the face. "I need you to fill in some missing gaps for me."

"What do you want to know?'

"What relationship does Nicole Bennett have to Christine Bowman, aka Clarise Bennett?"

For a long moment, it appeared he might not answer. Then finally he said in a short, clipped voice, "Bennett hired on as Bowman's housekeeper and cook a week ago."

Ripley raised her eyebrows. "Referred? Through an agency?"

"Cold interview as a result of an ad in a newspaper."

"Then she took off with the box."

"Yes."

"Which is why Christine followed Nicole here to Memphis."

He narrowed his eyes. Ripley shivered then stiffened her shoulders. "You've seen Christine Bowman?" the agent asked.

Joe leaned close to her. "I, um, left out the details of our little Clarise hunt the other night. Of course, I didn't know Clarise Bennett was Christine Bowman at the time, either."

God, but he smelled good. "Ah," she said slowly.

The agent leaned closer. "I need to know the details."

"Tell me what's in the locker first."

He went silent.

Ripley sighed, much as she would have had she been talking to a stubborn five-year-old. "Okay. But what I'm about to tell you I'm only offering as a good-faith gesture. With or without you, I am going to find out what's in the locker the key opens."

Silence again.

She launched into her explanation. "When we were making arrangements with the pawnshop owner to purchase the box and its contents, I noticed Christine getting out of a cab on the street outside. When I started to approach her she got back into the cab and took off. We followed her to the Pyramid, where we lost her. But we ran into an armed Nicole Bennett."

Agent Miller glanced at the agent next to him.

Ripley sighed. "I don't much like having my client run from me or having a gun held on me, so you can see why I'm interested in finding out what this is about."

Miller stared at her. "The pawnshop owner is dead."

Ripley nearly choked on her coffee.

Dead? The pawnshop owner was dead? She rested her head against her hands, trying to stop the spinning of the room. The problem lay in that the room wasn't spinning, she was.

"Define dead," Joe said quietly next to her.

Ripley looked up. Could Agent Miller have meant, "He's dead," as in, "I'm going to kill him for selling the box to you?" Figuratively speaking?

Miller motioned for the waitress to fill his cup when she came with Joe's decaf. "His body was found late last night, stuffed inside one of his own display cases."

Nope, there was no figuratively in that equation.

Every last trace of bravado seeped from Ripley's muscles. She sank against the red plastic of the booth, wishing herself one with it. Images of her ransacked hotel room, her torn clothing, her shredded mattress chased the air from her lungs.

"Christine?" Joe asked.

The agent nodded. "We're guessing that right before she swung by your room with her straight edge, she made that visit to the pawnshop that she had aborted when you happened across her. I don't think she liked what the owner had to say. Clean shot straight to the head, execution style." He made a gun with his hand and pressed his index finger between his eyes. Ripley started when he made a *pow* sound.

"Oh, boy," she whispered, not for the first time feeling way out of her league here.

She'd never had direct contact with a known killer before. Clarise…Christine had seemed so normal. Just your average, everyday, run-of-the-mill woman concerned about her sister's welfare.

"Who *is* this person?" she asked.

"If we told you, we'd have to kill you."

Ripley nearly dropped her coffee cup. He cracked a small smile.

"Ha, ha. Agent humor. I get it."

The smile disappeared. "The only thing you need to know is that she's a dangerous woman. We've been trailing her for over ten months now, trying to get the drop on her, and she's always been one step ahead of us."

"Until Nicole, who I'm guessing is a thief, unwittingly targeted Christine's house."

"Right."

"Do you know where the locker is?" Joe asked.

The agent didn't blink, didn't say anything.

Ripley swallowed. "I'll take that as a yes."

"Ms. Logan, I can't emphasize enough how important it is that you give us that key. So long as you have it, you remain a target."

"A target for what?"

He really didn't have to answer that, and thankfully he didn't.

Joe slid his arm around the back of the booth then pulled her to rest against his side. She was glad for his closeness and warmth. Suddenly, she felt cold.

"Explain something. How does your gaining possession of the key help me?" she asked. "As far as you know, Christine doesn't know of your involvement. So if I hand over to you what she wants, then she's going to think I still have it anyway."

"She already suspects we're onto her."

"Maybe so, but how does she know I handed over the key? Unless…"

"Unless you tell her that," Joe finished for her.

Ripley sat bolt straight. "Call me stupid, but I'd prefer it if I didn't have to come within spitting distance of Christine Bowman again, at least not in this lifetime."

Everyone at the table went eerily silent. Ripley stared at the empty plates that had held her super breakfast, wondering if it had been a mistake to eat all she had. Of course, when she'd thought she'd get one over on the agents, she hadn't known murder was included anywhere in the picture. The waitress cleared her plates away, and she was left with nothing to stare at but the other men at the table. After flicking a gaze at the two agents across from her, she looked at Joe, and felt sanity slowly return.

So Nicole Bennett was a thief who had cased and targeted Christine Bowman's house, stealing from someone who was already on the wrong side of the law, eliminating any risk of Christine reporting the theft to the police. She'd brought the goods to Memphis, unloaded them at the pawnshop and…

But that didn't explain why she didn't leave after the sale. Why had she been at the Pyramid?

Ripley shook her head. Wrong avenue. This wasn't about Nicole, it was about Christine.

Then it occurred to her. A plan that would take care of Christine, keep her and Joe safe and, she hoped, give her the answers she was looking for.

"Tell me what's in the locker, and I'll tell you how we're going to handle this," she said stoically.

JOE WAS RUNNING ON BORROWED time. He'd pretty much figured that out over breakfast with Ripley and the three agents. Hell, he'd worked out that much one day into his bizarre, sexy relationship with her. But now that their plane had touched down in St. Louis, and he and Ripley were in her ancient Ford Mustang—which might have been a classic had the previous owner or owners taken care of it—chugging toward her apartment, he could hear the clock ticking on the time he had left with Ripley.

"Diamonds," Ripley whispered next to him, kicking the windshield wipers into action to combat the rapidly falling rain.

Heavy gray clouds choked the sky, seeming to crowd around the car as she negotiated the slippery streets to her place. It was just after noon, but the storm overhead made it look more like dusk. There was a burst of lightning on the horizon, then a crack of thunder seemed to shake the already shaky vehicle. What Joe wouldn't do for his own car, which was sitting in a parking lot at Memphis International Airport.

Diamonds. That's what Agent Miller had finally told Ripley was in the storage locker. Ten months ago someone hit a wholesale jeweler in New York, making off with a bag of flawless, uncut white diamonds. That person was Christine Bowman. The catch was that they hadn't had much luck in proving the priceless gems were in Christine's custody, thus the reason she had yet to be arrested. Then Nicole Bennett had entered the picture and had thrown everything into a tailspin.

That connection between Christine and the diamonds was what Ripley had promised to give the agents.

"Do you think they told us the truth?" Ripley asked him, taking her eyes from the road.

"Whoa," he said, grabbing the dashboard. "Can we

talk about this when we get to your place?" *And off this slippery road in this poor excuse for a car.*

She waved off his comment. "I drive in this stuff all the time. Have to, or else I'd be housebound now, wouldn't I? Besides, we're not going to my place. Not yet." She looked directly at him. "Anyway, I'm still waiting for an answer to my question."

"I'd feel better if this old thing had a passenger-side air bag." He glanced at her. "And what do you mean we're not going to your place?"

She smiled.

He released a long breath. "Why wouldn't they tell you the truth?"

"I don't know. Call me cynical, but everything connected with this case hasn't been what it seems."

Everything? Joe looked at her, wondering if that comment extended to them and their tentative relationship.

He ran a hand through his damp hair. "Back to the not going to your place part…"

The plan Ripley had worked out with Miller included her returning to St. Louis, going straight to her apartment and waiting for Christine Bowman to contact her. The minute she did, Ripley was to arrange for a public meeting in which she would ask for what remained on her fee and then pass the box, including the key, to Christine. Pretend she'd never been contacted by the FBI. That she didn't know Christine was indeed Christine. And act like she had no idea the pawnshop owner had been stuffed in his own display case. Ripley was a simple P.I. who had performed a simple task. She'd tracked down Nicole, recovered the stolen items her client directed her to, and was returning those items. Nothing more, nothing less.

And Joe liked absolutely nothing about this.

He glanced over his shoulder at the road behind them. He was pretty sure that agents were tailing them, but he'd be damned if he could make them out. "You know, they're not going to like this very much."

"Tough." She glanced at him. "Besides, where I'm going will only take a few minutes."

"And that is?"

"The park."

"Hmm. The park." The response should have surprised him, but it didn't. Only Ripley knew how Ripley's mind worked. Like always, he was just along for the ride.

She rubbed her palms over the steering wheel. "You see, while we know what the locker holds, we still don't know its location."

"And that affects us how?"

She looked at him. "I want to be there when Christine goes after those diamonds."

Joe stared at it her. Had she gone completely insane? Forget that they were talking about a woman who didn't hesitate to whack those who didn't cooperate with her. There was no telling what she would do if she spotted Ripley anywhere within a hundred-mile radius of that locker.

"I think it's safe to assume it's here in St. Louis," she said, appearing to think aloud. "Miller would never have asked us to return here if it weren't. Besides, this is where Christine started out. The only reason we ended up in Memphis in the first place was—"

"Because of Nicole Bennett."

Joe didn't know what concerned him more. That he was in tune enough with her to finish her sentences or that he was nodding in agreement.

He cleared his throat. "So how do you propose we find out where this locker is?" He glanced out the back window again. "I think our friends will be suspicious if we start hitting bus and train stations." He jabbed a thumb toward the back seat. "And we just left the airport and didn't check there."

"How?" Her smile made something go thump in his chest. "You'll see."

"I was afraid you were going to say that."

A few minutes later Joe pretty much thought he had their tail pegged. It was a late model SUV with a woman driving, though there was a baby seat in the back—empty—and the guy wearing a ball cap in the passenger's seat appeared somehow too relaxed. But when Joe suspected Ripley didn't make an expected turn, the guy sat up, instantly alert.

He glanced at Ripley. God, but even now he found her the most attractive woman he'd ever been around. It was more than physical beauty. A buzzing kind of energy seemed to emanate from her, a thirst for life that made him hum just being next to her. Made him question things he wasn't so sure he wanted to question. Made him want her beyond anything having to do with sex. Well, okay, sex, too. But he was increasingly wanting more, while she appeared happy with the way things were.

She pulled to the side of the road and parked at the curb, throwing the car into park. She glanced at him, the telltale way she worried her bottom lip making his stomach tighten. "Um, I think it would be a good idea, you know, if you waited here."

"Not a chance in hell."

She grabbed his arm when he moved to climb out. "Please, Joe."

A great pair of breasts and pleading. A lethal combination. And two things he could never resist. At least not in Ripley.

"Fine," he said, feeling anything but fine.

He watched her get out of the car and visually followed her form as she walked toward the park. The SUV slowly passed, and Joe watched it, wanting to throw his hands in the air in exasperation.

BY THE TIME RIPLEY PULLED UP next to the park located on the banks of the Mississippi, the Arch visible just over the rise, it had stopped raining. Although judging from Joe's stormy expression, she was surprised it hadn't started pouring *inside* the car.

Unfortunately, she didn't think his countenance was going to change anytime soon.

Not many knew of her friendship with Nelson Polk beyond the boundaries of the park. She didn't think her mother would be very happy if Ripley brought him home to dinner, although she had thought about inviting him a couple of times. She'd settled, instead, for buying him a bite or two or three at a nearby diner. It wasn't that she was ashamed of him, exactly. She knew others might not understand her bond with this fifty-something washed-up private investigator for whom a bottle of cheap red wine comprised his entire food intake.

And it looked like he'd had a little too much to eat today.

"Nelson, I need a favor from you." A big favor. A humongous favor. Although she was afraid it was going to take an act of God to get anything from the man slumped in his chair, his chess set closed on the table in front of him, his mouth hanging open in mid-snore.

Ripley glanced uneasily toward her car some hundred yards away, a car for which she'd traded in her two-year-old Taurus with three years of payments left in order to lower her overhead. She moved so she blocked Joe's view of Nelson, then crouched next to her friend.

"Oh, please, don't do this to me now, Nelson," she whispered, closing her eyes.

At that moment it was hard to recognize the sloshed, barely conscious man next to her as the guy who shared so many words of wisdom over a competitive game of chess. She'd never seen him this far gone and wondered what had caused him to drink himself into such a state. She reached out and rested her warm hand over his cold one.

"Ripley? Is that you?" he slurred, without opening his eyes.

Her heart did a little drumbeat. "Yes, Nelson, it is."

He smiled, making his two-day-old gray stubble stick out all the more. "Thought so."

"Nelson...I need your help."

The smile vanished. "Help. A lot of people asking for help these days. Unfortunately it seems to be in short supply."

Ripley squinted at him, wondering who else had asked him for help, and in what form it had come. "Actually, I think this kind of help is right up your alley." She looked toward the churning waters of the Mississippi, then at the sky, which looked moments away from opening up again. But Nelson was dry. Either he had just made his way to the park bench or the tree overhead had protected him from the worst of the previous downpour. "You remember when I told you about that first case I took on?"

His eyelids cracked open, and brown eyes peered at her. "Uh-huh."

She smiled overly brightly. "Well, guess who needs some information and you're the only guy she can get it from?"

He didn't say anything for a long moment. But his eyes remained semiopen, and he appeared to be considering her long and hard. Either that or he could sleep with his eyes open. "So," he said finally, making her jump, "that's why you haven't been to see me lately. This case."

"I've been in Memphis."

He struggled to sit up, only whatever he'd drunk wasn't cooperating.

"Nelson, how about I treat you to some coffee?"

He grinned at her. "I'd love a cup."

"NELSON, I'M SORRY TO SAY THIS, but I think you're going to be spending the next two days in the bathroom," Ripley said, stepping to the diner table with two extra-large cups of coffee. She slid them in front of the tattered old man, then slid into the booth next to Joe.

This was the guy who had inspired Ripley to become a private investigator? Joe stared, astounded, at Nelson's gnarled hands as he pushed aside the cup he'd just drained then reached for one of the others. He rubbed the back of his neck and glanced out the window, where the SUV was stopped across the street, the agents inside pretending to consult a map.

That's what Joe could use right about now—a map to find his way out of the mess he was sitting in the middle of.

"How are you feeling?" Ripley asked.

Joe glanced at her, but she hadn't directed the question to him. Instead, she was gazing at Nelson Polk as if he was Moses, seeming unaffected by the ripe smell coming from him and his unwashed clothes.

Polk nodded. "Better." He turned unfocused eyes on her. "At least now I know that I'm not seeing double, and the guy next to you must be a friend."

Ripley smiled. "Nelson, this is Joe Pruitt. He's a shoe salesman."

Nelson's bushy white brows moved upward on his ruddy face. "A shoe salesman. A respectable position."

"I suppose you could say that." Joe grimaced, not up to correcting the description. He was a whole hell of a lot more than a shoe salesman. Well, at least he was before he met one sexy, insane Ripley Logan.

Nelson quickly drained the second cup of coffee, obviously familiar with the routine. Color began returning to his face, and he sat a little straighter in the booth.

"So tell me about your case, Rip," he asked even as he popped the lid off the third cup, this time adding a good portion of sugar and cream to it before bringing it to his lips.

Ripley told him, from first being hired by Clarise Bennett—information Joe suspected Polk already knew—then finding out she was really Christine Bowman, to where they were sitting across from the old man in the diner.

Joe glanced at his watch. All within five minutes. And if he didn't know better, he'd say that Polk had not only followed every word of the explanation, but understood them. Which put him way ahead of Joe. Joe still wasn't convinced he understood what was going on.

"Where's the key?" Polk asked.

Ripley glanced toward the window and the SUV parked on the opposite side of the street. She reached into the pocket of her jeans, palming the key, then holding her hand palm down for Polk to take.

"Be careful that our friends don't see what you're doing," she said.

"I wondered whose friends they were. For a minute I was afraid they were mine," Polk said, adding pocket change to his hand then cupping it and pretending to be counting out the price of the coffees. "Got yourself in mighty deep first case out of the gate, didn't you?" The smile he gave her was affectionate, and now that he no longer looked like he was going to fall face first to the tile and start snoring, Joe noticed he appeared shrewd.

Great, that's all they needed. A homeless Colombo.

Polk held his hand out to Ripley, dumping the contents into it. It didn't appear he'd glanced at the key long enough to make a determination. Joe fully expected him to say he didn't have a clue.

"The bus station."

Joe blinked.

"The bus station? Are you sure?"

"Positive." Polk sipped leisurely at his coffee. "Which makes sense considering the traffic around there lately."

"What traffic?" Joe found himself asking.

Ripley and Polk stared at him. He shrugged, acting like he'd been involved in the conversation from the onset.

Polk subtly motioned toward the window. "More of your friends hanging around there. Brooklyn Bob was complaining about the lack of prime bench space there this morning. They've had the place under surveillance for at least the past month, but traffic picked up considerably over the past couple of days."

Ripley leaned across the table and gave Polk a sound kiss on the cheek. Joe cringed. Polk beamed.

"You're a prince among men, Nelson."

No comment, Joe thought.

CHAPTER TWELVE

TWENTY MINUTES AND A MEAL fit for a prince later, Joe watched Ripley pull up to a curb on a downtown street and maneuver her way into a spot that didn't appear large enough to hold a golf cart. Amazingly she squeezed into it without incident, while the driver of the SUV drove past them as if she hadn't a care in the world. And, Joe guessed, she probably didn't. Additional agents were probably already set up around the area to keep an eye out for Ripley and to throw off anyone else who might be watching her.

"You ready?" she asked, grabbing an old newspaper from the back seat and spreading it, presumably to shield her head from the pounding rain that had picked up again after they left the diner.

Ready? Hell no, he wasn't ready. But the alternative was sitting in the car alone for an unspecified amount of time. He watched her get out of the car and run around it toward the sidewalk to his right. He opened the door and sprinted after her.

The building was an older brick construction, four stories high, four apartments to each floor. The wet paper plastered to her head, Ripley unlocked the outer door, then quickly ushered him inside. Another key and they had access to the hall and the stairs.

She peeled the paper from the side of her face and

offered a sheepish smile. "I used to have a nice place in a newer subdivision in the suburbs, but I thought an apartment downtown could serve double duty as an office. You know, until I can afford to rent commercial space."

She was apologizing for where she lived, he realized. "I've lived in worse places," he said.

She looked at him skeptically.

"Okay, no, I haven't. But I don't see anything wrong with this place."

"You haven't seen the apartment yet."

He didn't say anything as she led the way up the stairs. And up. And up again. Now he knew how she kept that tidy little figure despite how much she put away at the dinner table. She stepped to the first door to the right and opened it, flipping a switch just inside. She stood aside for him to enter.

SOMEHOW THE TINY APARTMENT seemed even smaller with Joe Pruitt's huge frame standing in the middle of the combination living and dining area. Ripley watched his face for his reaction, then looked around the place herself. The furniture wasn't bad. She'd bought it all when she'd had a nice condo just outside the city, so she wasn't concerned about that. It was the water stains on the ceiling that no amount of repainting had been able to get rid of. The chipped sink visible in the small kitchen off to the left. The scarred floor that had been under the green shag carpeting she had pulled up her first day in the apartment, thinking anything had to be better than the rug. She'd been right, but just barely. And her area rugs didn't nearly cover the surface.

She put her hands on his shoulders. He started then turned to stare at her. She gave a nervous laugh. "Looks like we're going to be here for a while. I, um, thought maybe you'd like to take your jacket off until then, especially since it's dripping on my floor."

"Oh." He shrugged out of his suit jacket. She shook it on the rug near the door then draped it over the radiator in the dining room. The top of the one in the living area was filled to overflowing with plants meant to cover it.

A punch to her answering machine revealed three messages. The first two were from her mother, inviting her to dinner. The last one was nothing but air. The machine said it was left a half hour ago. She shivered, then stepped to the front window where she'd closed the curtains before she'd left for Memphis. She peeked from the side, staring at the street below.

The plan was that she would come to her apartment with the hope that Christine Bowman would contact her here in search of the key. Of course, Ripley wasn't supposed to let on that she even knew of its existence. Instead, when Christine made contact, Ripley would give her the entire box.

"Are they out there?" Joe whispered.

His breath disturbed the damp hair near her ear, making her shiver. He was referring to the FBI, who had promised to have someone watching her, just in case Christine decided to do to her what she'd done to her mattress last night. Agent Miller had offered to have one of his agents trade places with Joe as an extra precaution. Ripley had passed, feeling far safer with Joe than she would with a hundred agents.

"I don't see anyone."

She remained at the window, though her sight had turned inward, her every nerve ending aware of where Joe stood so close yet not touching her.

Last night after the break-in, she'd crawled into his bed, expecting him to follow her, to take up where they'd left off before she'd nearly tripped over the broken lamp in her room. But he hadn't joined her. Instead, she'd jerked awake at some point during the night to find him sleeping at an awkward angle on the couch, his position allowing him a view of the room door, the balcony doors and the bed. The big lug had been protecting her. The least she could do was get him a pillow and a blanket. And she had, even though she'd mostly wanted to wake him and drag him into bed with her.

Since then he'd been…distant somehow. Preoccupied. He'd barely said a word to her on the plane ride home. Then again, she'd been so consumed with what she'd learned that morning, creeped out by the knowledge that the pawn shop owner had been killed, that she probably hadn't been very good company herself. In fact, she knew she hadn't.

"What if she pulls a gun on me?" she murmured, referring to Christine.

Finally she felt him touch her…of all places, on her feet.

Positioning his shoulder to balance her, he lifted first one leg, then the other, slipping off her shoes and massaging the pads of her feet. She moaned, thinking that this was definitely something she could get used to, this thing Joe had for her feet.

In fact, Joe was something she could find herself

getting used to. No matter where they were or what was happening, all he had to do was touch her, and every last thought vanished from her head, leaving her with nothing but longing.

He put her right foot on the floor then stood so he was behind her. His hand curved around her waist then came to rest against her stomach. A small tug left her back flush with his front. "I'll be there, right alongside you."

She covered his hand with hers, reveling in the feel of him against her. "Somehow the thought of you buying it along with me isn't very reassuring, but thanks anyway."

He skimmed his lips over her right ear. "Well, then, we'll have to make sure she never gets a chance to squeeze off a shot, won't we?"

And that was the plan. If Christine called, Ripley was going to give her directions to her apartment…if she didn't already know the way. Ripley would instruct Christine to slip the recovery fee into her mailbox downstairs, then exit the building to stand on the sidewalk across the street where Ripley could see her. Ripley would retrieve the money and put the box between the two security doors, propping open the outer door before hightailing it up the steps to safety.

The click of her thick swallow sounded awfully loud in the quiet apartment.

"Nervous?" Joe asked.

She nodded.

"Good. That means you are human, after all."

She turned in his arms, bringing her chest-to-chest with him. The brushing of her erect nipples against his hard chest nearly made her forget what she was going to say. "I don't know if this is such a good idea. Maybe we should change the meeting place to somewhere public."

His gaze swept over her face. "You *are* scared."

She glued herself more tightly to him, resting her cheek against his shoulder and squeezing her arms around him so hard she was pretty sure he was having difficulty breathing.

His hands hesitated on her back, then slid up and down, cupping her bottom in his palms and pressing her against him. "You know, there are things we could do to keep ourselves occupied until she calls."

She smiled against his shoulder. "Yes, that there are."

Only she wasn't sure she would be such good company. Her mind was so packed full of information it felt like it might explode. And her nerves were stretched to the breaking point.

One of Joe's hands slipped between them and fit around her breast. She caught her breath, amazed by how quickly every last bit of that information zapped from her head and how loudly her nerves started clamoring for the release they knew he could give her.

She hugged him tighter, trapping his hand between them. She honestly didn't know what she would have done if she hadn't made the mistake of crawling into bed with him on that fateful night. He made her laugh, sometimes want to scream in exasperation, more often cry out in such exquisite passion that she had begun not to recognize herself in the mirror. A transformation begun when she'd switched professions but completed when she invited Joe Pruitt between her thighs. He awakened emotions in her she couldn't begin to identify. Emotions that demanded merely to be felt, rather than analyzed. Lived and breathed rather than denied.

"Thank you for this," she whispered, rubbing her cheek against the crisp cotton of his shirt.

"For what?"

She pulled back to look into his overwhelmingly handsome face. "Oh, I don't know. For not saying anything when I hopped into your bed, maybe. Or for not bolting in the other direction even when you were sure I didn't have a clue about what I was doing." Her gaze dropped to his mouth. His hot, generous mouth. "For, um, coming back here with me when it would have been easier for you to leave me at the Memphis airport."

"You act like I had a choice," he murmured.

She tried to step away, but he wouldn't allow her the freedom.

"You don't understand what I mean by that, do you?"

She stared at him, spellbound, afraid to ask for fear he might say she'd railroaded him into coming along.

He freed the hand trapped between them and ran his fingers through her hair, pulling it back and holding it there. "You have no idea how I feel about you, do you, Ripley Logan?"

She blinked. She felt evidence of how he felt growing thick and hard between them. She pressed her hips into his and smiled. "Oh, I think I have an idea."

His eyes darkened, but she wasn't convinced desire was completely to blame. "I don't think you do."

His gaze flitted to her lips, her ear, her hair where he

held it, then to her eyes. "Sure, I'll be the first to admit that when you popped into my bed that night, all that was on my mind was sex." He smiled faintly. "I am only human, you know." His fingers lowered to rest at the base of her neck. "Then I got to know you. Spent some time with you. You asked me questions I would never have dared ask myself. Made me take a closer look at my life, at what I was doing with it. Or, rather, what I wasn't doing with it."

"Joe, I—"

"Shh." He pressed his fingers against her lips, appearing to have a difficult time not kissing her. "I'm trying to be serious here."

"That's what's scaring me," she whispered.

He frowned at her.

She dropped her gaze to his chest, pretending a phenomenal interest in the whiteness of his shirt. "There's so much going on now…happening… Joe, I don't know which end's up."

He stared at her long and hard. "Then I think I should show you."

He launched an all-out assault on her mouth that left her knees buckling under her and her body screaming in sheer pleasure. Even as her mind called out, *no, no!* her limbs melted against his and her heart countered with an even louder, *yes, yes!* His erection pressed hard and insistent against her stomach, and a need to have it pressing inside of her, pushing everything else from her mind, overwhelmed her. Her fingers were in his hair, on his chest, over his tight rear, as her mouth fought to keep up with his.

"Where's the bedroom?" he asked, his hand up her

blouse and under her bra and stroking her nipple to aching hardness.

She licked her lips, then kissed him again. "Behind you. To your left."

She fumbled for his belt, pulling it loose as he backed them toward the closed bedroom door.

Closed...

The word rang in her passion-filled mind, but she couldn't seem to grasp the importance of it. Not when there were other more pressing needs clamoring for attention.

Joe reached for the handle and opened the door, and she reached for his zipper, then an ominous metallic click told them they weren't alone.

RIPLEY HAD NEVER FELT so violated, so helpless. Just a short while ago she'd been questioning the wisdom of arranging a meeting at her apartment for the simple reason that she wasn't comfortable with Christine Bowman knowing where she lived. Suppose something went wrong? Suppose the FBI didn't catch Christine with the diamonds red-handed and she got away? Suppose she blamed Ripley for the close call and came back looking for revenge?

Of course as Ripley sat with her hands tied behind her back, Joe sitting next to her, none of that made a bit of difference. Christine had been in her apartment all along, waiting for them, probably even before their plane had touched down at Lambert Airport.

They should have come up with a way to alert the FBI when they were in trouble. Another moot point because Ripley couldn't have moved if she'd tried.

Seeming satisfied with her handiwork, Christine pulled a dining room chair out and sat down, looking at them where she'd tied them up on the tiny kitchen floor. Heat seemed to radiate from Joe. She glanced to find his jaw flexing angrily, his eyes steadfastly on Christine. She nudged his leg with hers. Anger wouldn't get them anywhere but dead.

"Where's the box?" Christine asked, looking directly at Ripley.

The other woman wore black leather pants, a black Lycra tank top and black leather gloves. Her blond hair was pulled into a twist, and the gun looked right at home in her hands.

Why hadn't Ripley noticed what a con artist she was when they first met? It could have been the plain flowered dress. The fluffy blond hair that looked like she'd just come from the hairdressers. Her horror at having nicked a nail while hiring Ripley.

Now she looked like she could play the starring role in a vampire flick, right down to her blood-red lipstick.

Ripley purposely cleared her throat. "Clarise, what are you doing? I don't understand—"

"Cut the crap, Logan," Christine said, sighing. "I know you're on to me. I also know about your new little friends sitting outside your apartment right now."

Interesting how everyone kept referring to the FBI as her friends when they were anything but. Any law enforcement friends worth their salt would never have let this woman gain access to her apartment.

"You know, if you hadn't run from us outside the

pawnshop, we probably never would have figured it out," Joe said.

"Then there's the little matter of your phone being disconnected," Ripley added.

Christine lifted a finely penciled brow. "Who are you kidding? Neither of you would have figured out anything if not for the Feds." She cocked the gun, a 9mm similar to Ripley's, except in gunmetal black. "The box."

Ripley had never wanted to hit, really hit, anyone before. But oh, boy, did she want to sock it right to Christine Bowman in her red-painted mouth.

Then she remembered that the box didn't hold the key Christine was looking for. The key was in Ripley's back pocket.

"Over there," Ripley said. "In the bag near the door."

Christine stared at her for a long moment.

"What?" Ripley asked. "I'm tied up, remember?"

Christine pushed from the chair, trying to keep them in sight as she went to the door and rifled through Ripley's duffel. Unfortunately for her, and fortunately for Ripley, Christine had picked the one blind spot in the apartment to tie them up.

Awkwardly maneuvering her hands, Ripley slid the locker key out of her back pocket and began working the jagged edge against the thin rope that bound her wrists together. She winced when the rope cut into her flesh.

"What are you doing?" Joe whispered harshly.

She glanced at him, then at Christine, who had her back to them trying to find the box, which Ripley had wound in clothing and tucked way at the bottom of the bag for safekeeping.

"Shh." She hushed him.

The damn key wasn't accomplishing anything. But her movements trying to saw the rope had. Somehow she'd managed to work the ropes a little looser. She winced as the binding cut into her wrists again. There. All she had to do—

Christine found the box.

Ripley urgently leaned over and slid the key into Joe's front pants pocket. He stared at her.

"The key." Christine appeared in the kitchen doorway, such as it was, the gun at her side, her expression clearly exasperated.

"You know, when I picked your name out of the paper, I really never saw you getting this far." She smiled, her teeth white against her red lips. "No, the other two overpaid idiots were the ones who were supposed to get the job done. But surprise of surprises, you're the one who came through. Good thing I'm a woman who likes to cover her bases, isn't it?"

Ripley didn't know if she should feel complimented or insulted. She decided on insulted.

"The key," she repeated.

"In my pocket," Joe said. "The left one."

Ripley glanced at him, not missing the message he was trying to send her not to do anything.

Christine stood stock-still, then motioned for Joe to scoot forward. He did. She reached into his pocket and took out the key, then waved her gun for him to back up.

The grin that spread across her face would have been attractive, if only Ripley didn't know she was a murderer. "Bingo."

Ripley swallowed hard. "What about my fee?"

Christine stared at her as if she were speaking a foreign language.

"You still owe me money, whether you're Christine or Clarise," Ripley said. "Do you have any idea how much I lost tracking down that box?"

Christine laughed so hard she nearly dropped her gun. Nearly, but unfortunately not quite.

"Oh, you're priceless." She tossed the key in the air then caught it. "But not nearly worth as much as what's in this locker."

Ripley opened her mouth to say something when Christine cocked the 9mm and stepped forward to settle the muzzle against Ripley's forehead. The strangled cry that filled the kitchen very definitely came from her throat.

Joe jerked next to her. "You got what you wanted." He ground out the words. "Now why don't you just get the fuck out of here?"

Christine glanced at him.

"We're tied up. Just what do you think we're going to do? Scoot on our asses and follow you?"

She appeared to consider that as Ripley stared beyond the barrel of the gun, the metal cold against her skin. A crazy prayer wound around and around her mind. *Please, please don't let her shoot me and get gray matter all over Joe's nice white shirt.*

Christine stepped back, taking her gun with her. Ripley nearly dissolved into a puddle of relief at her feet.

"You're right," Christine said. "I'll be long gone before either one of you has the chance to tell anyone what went down here." She smiled. "Besides, I suppose I do owe Ripley, here, for getting back my property."

"Does that mean I'm going to get paid?"

Not even Ripley could believe she'd uttered the words as Christine and Joe stared at her.

"You know, in another lifetime, you and I might have been friends." Christine laughed, then turned and was gone, the apartment door clicking closed behind her.

Ripley refused to give in to the incredible desire to close her eyes and instead tried to come to terms with all that had just happened. It wasn't every day someone held a gun to your head, threatening to kill you for a job you did right. Of course, she didn't think very many people got that type of reaction for messing up, either, but that was neither here nor there.

Instead, she scrambled to her knees as she shrugged her way out of her bindings. In no time flat she had Joe freed, as well. She scrambled to the phone and called the number Miller had given her.

"She's got the key. Christine Bowman's got the key."

CHAPTER THIRTEEN

JOE DIDN'T LIKE THIS. Everything felt...wrong.

"Come on," Ripley said, getting out of her Mustang and running across the street, her raincoat blowing behind her like a cape. Joe shook his head, not liking the superhero imagery that came to mind at the vision.

Of course, it didn't help matters that he hadn't been able to get down a decent swallow since Christine Bowman had stood with that damn gun pressed against Ripley's flawless forehead. Within a blink of an eye, it seemed that everything important to him was about to be taken away. Both the realization that Ripley had grown to be so important to him and the fear that he'd never get to tell her that was enough to knock any guy's legs out from under him.

Add to that Ripley's need to go to the bus station to see Christine's capture, despite what had happened at her apartment, and he was operating solely on autopilot. Half of him wanted to pin her down with his body weight and make her admit what she felt for him was more than sexual, while the other half was filled with the desire to tie her up again and leave her to sit in her apartment, alone, until all this was over with.

The rain came down in a torrent, an all-out summer shower that turned dusk to midnight. He rushed after Ripley across the street and to the bus station entrance, earning himself a honk from a driver coming from his left.

How did you like that for discreet?

The instant Ripley had placed the call to Miller, they'd watched through her apartment window as two cars pulled from parked positions on either side of the street and roared away, obviously positioning themselves for Christine's arrest. Of course, had they been doing their jobs right, Christine would never have gotten into Ripley's apartment in the first place. But right now, that was neither here nor there, was it?

Ripley ducked to the side of the bus station door. Joe sidled up next to her, uncomfortable in the T-shirt she'd given him to wear—something purple with a picture of Winnie the Pooh on it, and a Cardinals ball cap—while she wore a floppy beige rain cap that covered the hair she'd tied into a knot on top of her head, and a trench coat that made her look like the detective she was.

"You know, we could both just go back to your place, order up some pizza and read about this in tomorrow's paper," he said.

She gave him a long-suffering look and led the way inside. Well, he thought, it was worth one last try, anyway.

They paused just inside the door. The station was bustling with the traffic Polk had told them about. Joe kept his head down as he scanned the stark interior of the station. In fact, Polk himself had taken up residence on one of the benches, a brief wink all the acknowledgment he gave Ripley.

"I knew he wouldn't be able to pass this one up," she said to Joe, yanking her collar up.

"What in the hell are you doing here?"

A homeless man had come up behind them. Joe eyed him, noticing he didn't smell the way Polk did. Then he realized it wasn't a homeless man at all, but Agent Miller. He glanced around them, then held his hand out and asked for a dollar for a cup of coffee, speaking with a slurred voice slightly louder than the one he'd first addressed them with.

Joe began digging in his pockets as Ripley looked around.

"I want…no, I'm ordering you to turn around and go right back out the way you came in," Miller fairly growled. "Bowman spots you, this is all over with before it starts."

Joe looked at Ripley hopefully. Pizza and her were sounding mighty good right about now.

"No way," she whispered harshly, that stubborn look on her face. "I'm in this till the end."

"End being the operative word, Ms. Logan," Miller said. "Look, I don't know how in the hell you found out where the locker was—" Ripley flashed him a smile "—but I want you out of here. Now. If you don't leave willingly, I'll see to it that a couple of men will—discreetly, of course—escort you out."

Joe placed a dollar in the agent's hand to go toward the change for coffee he'd asked for, and Miller stuffed it immediately into his pocket. He began to say something more when another guy dressed as a street person who was probably an agent motioned to him. Miller looked distracted, then with a dark scowl in Ripley's direction, he ambled toward the other man.

Between the real street people and the FBI disguised as the same, the place was abundant with odor and color. Joe had to give the agents credit. He couldn't tell them from the real deal, the baggy clothing allowing for plenty of room to hide weapons without telltale bulges. And the rain was certainly working in their favor. Had it been a nice day, it would have been a little difficult to pull off so many homeless men in one area at the same time.

"Looks like Polk spread the word," Joe murmured, steering Ripley toward the ticket window.

She stared at him. "At least we know Christine hasn't shown up yet. If she had, Miller wouldn't still be here."

Joe grimaced, not finding that bit of info the good news she obviously did.

He honestly didn't know what she hoped to accomplish here. But the fact that she wanted to do something only emphasized the differences between them. The longer he was around her, the more distanced he became from his own life. While that appealed to him on various levels and for various reasons in the beginning, now he felt more like a freshwater fish swimming in an unfamiliar sea. And he was starting to view Ripley as leading him straight into a school of sharks.

Somehow he'd never imagined when he eventually found someone to fall in love with that he would have to compromise. He'd always figured it would be the other way around. He had the successful company. He had the assets, the houses, the cars. He'd assumed the woman he'd want to spend the rest of his life with would have to compromise to be with him.

Instead, he was finding that everything he'd ever held dear was at risk. And he didn't know how he felt about that.

Yes, he did. He didn't feel very good about it at all. It was happening too fast. He felt like he was on an endless roller coaster that kept building up speed, going faster and faster, swinging through loops and careening around corners and shooting down slopes that left him gripping the bar in front of him for dear life. Never mind that he'd left his stomach somewhere in Memphis. All he wanted was for it to end so he could get off the sucker.

And the difference between him and Ripley was that she had her hands up in the air and was demanding that the ride go on and on....

THE LOCKER WAS TO THE RIGHT, second from the end and two rows from the floor. In the block of lockers closest to the side exit.

In the minute Joe had taken to give a dollar to Miller, Ripley had completely scoped out everything and everyone and was pretty sure she knew who was who in the crowded station. Miller she'd pegged immediately, even before he'd swooped down on them. He looked too healthy to be homeless. Too...hulky.

She stood behind a guy in line for tickets, trying to ignore the buzz of blood through her veins, fear and excitement a very heady mix.

Joe, on the other hand, looked ready to bolt for the door.

She squashed a smile. He looked so adorably sexy it was all she could do not to thread her fingers under that too small hat, then run them down the front of the only

T-shirt she'd found that would fit him—a gift for Christmas from her parents that she wore as a nightshirt.

The man in front of her moved, and she stepped forward, scanning the schedule on the wall behind the attendant.

"I'm going to go get a newspaper," Joe grumbled beside her.

She smiled at him. "I'll be right here."

As she watched him walk away, she had to remind herself to tear her gaze away from his nicely shaped tush and give the station another once-over.

"God, I thought he'd never leave," a voice said from the other side of her. "No, don't look at me. Just casually turn to the attendant and ask for two tickets to Detroit."

Christine Bowman. Ripley didn't have to look to know it was her. It also didn't take much to figure out that she'd probably been in the bus station since before Ripley came in and that not one single agent had identified her.

Figured. Ripley had been having too much fun for something not to go wrong.

She did as Christine requested, then slid a glance toward the woman in question.

Christine had the audacity to smile at her. "I knew you wouldn't be able to resist coming here. Now, move casually, normally, toward the women's rest room. There, to the right."

Christine was decked out in full call-girl mode. Curly red wig. Bright red lipstick. Scarlet red dress that hugged her in all the right places. And a small black handbag that very obviously held the gun Ripley was far more familiar with than she wanted to be.

Oh, sure, Christine garnered the expected leers from every guy in the joint, agent or otherwise, but not a one of them seemed to put together that she was Christine Bowman.

Oh, boy.

"You know," Christine said, steering her toward the ladies' room. "I didn't have a clue how I was going to get inside that locker what with all the G-men crowding the place." She nudged Ripley with her bag, the unmistakable metal jabbing into her side. "Then I saw you come in thinking you were going to fool me with that getup, and I knew I was saved."

Ripley smiled at Polk, trying to do a head tilt toward Christine, but Polk seemed too interested in checking out Christine's wares than in Ripley's subtle gestures.

The door to the ladies' room closed with an ominous click behind them. Christine checked inside the stalls, making sure they were empty, then threw the lock on the door, likely there to keep people from coming in while the room was cleaned.

"Strip."

Ripley blinked at her. "What?"

The handbag moved. "You heard me. Take off every last piece of clothing you've got on." She wrinkled her nose. "Except for your underwear. That, I can do without."

"Gee, thanks for small favors."

Ripley shrugged out of her coat, took off her hat, then her jeans and T-shirt, laying each over a nearby sink. The coat was an impulse buy last fall, an expensive designer name. But it was having to give up the shoes Joe had given her that annoyed her most.

"You know, you're never going to get out of here with those diamonds," she couldn't resist saying.

Christine's brows shot up as she kept her purse aimed with one hand and wiped off the loads of makeup she had caked on with the other. "So you know."

"Yes, I know. And I also know that a smart woman would wait a day or two for things to calm down before trying to get them."

Christine slanted a look at her as she pulled off the wig. "That's what I said to myself two months ago. And look where that's gotten me." She blew out a long breath, carefully maneuvering the purse as she slipped out of her dress. She bent to pluck off one of her shoes.

Ripley shot forward, her intention to catch the woman off balance and grab her purse.

Christine instantly straightened and thrust the gun into Ripley's stomach. "I knew you'd do that." She pushed harder. "Get back."

Ripley did as she was ordered, hating that she'd left her gun at the apartment. *Don't worry,* she'd told herself, *there'll be enough firepower there to stop a horse.*

Only that horse had been wearing a slinky red dress and appeared to have a price tag stamped on her back.

A female agent would never have fallen for the getup.

"Put on the dress."

Ripley stared at her. "What?"

"You heard me." Christine slipped into the jeans, T-shirt and sneakers, all the while keeping the purse on

Ripley. Ripley was only slightly mollified that the other woman couldn't do up the top button of the jeans.

Within moments, the two had completely swapped clothing and Ripley finished applying the lipstick Christine handed to her. She turned her head this way and that. She didn't look half bad as a redhead.

"Come on," Christine said, handing her the locker key then jabbing the purse into her side again.

"Would you stop? You're going to give me a bruise."

"You'll be lucky if a bruise is all you come away with. Now get a move on." She unlocked the door and motioned for Ripley to precede her out. "I want you to head straight for the locker. Do not pass go, do not collect two hundred dollars. Got it?"

Ripley whipped her arm away. "You know, this probably all would have gone much smoother if you'd just paid me what was due."

"Move it."

And Ripley did. Straight to the locker. It wouldn't do any good to try to signal anyone. They would probably think she was looking for some business, given her new attire.

Except for Joe. Joe would certainly know that Christine wasn't her. Wouldn't he?

She glanced to find him leaning against the wall, pretending to read the business section of the newspaper, Agent Miller giving him an earful of what were undoubtedly threats. Neither one of them was looking in her direction.

Great. Just great.

She reached the lockers far more quickly than she would have thought, and her heart started beating double

time in her chest. Things were definitely not looking
good for her. She had little doubt of Christine's intentions once she had the diamonds in hand. Namely pull
the trigger on the gun poking into her side and make a
run for it. While Ripley didn't think the other woman's
chances for escape were good, the chances Ripley would
get out of the station without a little extra lead looked
dim, indeed.

"Open it," Christine whispered, pretending an interest
in the locker two up from the one in question. She put
what looked like her lipstick in it, then added the coins
that would release the key. Out of the corner of her eye,
Ripley noticed Miller part from Joe then loom a little
closer, probably wondering what the hell she was up
to.

Ripley slid the key to the locker in and popped open
the door. Only it was yawningly empty. Oh, boy.

"Give it to me!" Christine ordered harshly as half
the homeless people in the station started closing in on
them.

In a panic, Ripley scanned the faces of the undercover
agents, only to realize that the homeless men were real
homeless men. Nelson's dearly beloved face was right
in the middle of them. He winked at her. It was all she
could do not to smile back.

"No problem," she said to Christine's request.

Ripley slammed the locker door open and right in
Christine's face, reaching for the purse at the same
time.

The homeless men, led by Nelson, swooped down
on them from all sides. Nelson reached to help Ripley.

The non-homeless agents had finally caught on and surrounded the others that surrounded them.

Only, unlike Nelson, they thought *she* was Christine.

"Wrong woman," Nelson shouted, grabbing an agent away from Ripley.

Ripley had a stranglehold on Christine's purse with one hand and reached up to pull off the wig with the other. The agents hesitated, obviously confused. Christine regained control of the gun and hit Ripley upside the head with it. Ripley smacked into the lockers, the din echoing through the station. In that one moment, she realized Christine might get away. Due to the agents' advance on them through the horde of homeless men, the path to the exit was left completely unblocked. Christine made a run for it. And with Ripley's sneakers, she just might make it.

A sound swirled up Ripley's throat, and she launched herself at the retreating figure, catching her around the knees and pulling her straight to the floor with a dull thud.

"Freeze!" someone finally yelled, and Ripley was half afraid it was she.

She turned to find it hadn't been her. Nelson, of all people, had shouted the command. The agents were all over her and Christine. They pulled Ripley to her feet, then confiscated Christine's purse and cuffed her on the spot.

Ripley gasped for air, trying not to notice the way her breasts threatened to spill out of the top of the dress or ponder the reason she was getting entirely too much of a breeze on her behind. Nelson gently moved her away from the ruckus.

She blinked at him. "How did you spot Christine?"

He grinned at her. "Simple. I know all the ho's that work the station, and she wasn't one of them."

Ripley laughed.

"Besides, she dressed more like the hundred-dollar variety, instead of the ten-dollar ones we usually get down here." He eyed her. "Red suits you."

"I'll remember that." Ripley turned to look for Joe, and her gaze fell instead on somebody else—a figure near the opposite door standing in partial shadow. The person stepped briefly into the light, her black vinyl rain slicker shimmering.

Nicole Bennett.

Ripley blinked as Nicole smiled.

Then she was gone.

CHAPTER FOURTEEN

JOE PATIENTLY APPLIED antiseptic to Ripley's skinned knees. She sat at the dining table that dwarfed the room it was in. The apartment was small but neat, unassuming but filled with quality items, much like the woman herself. He swapped knees, and Ripley flinched. It was all Joe could do not to take a peek under the hem of the cotton shorts she'd put on after her shower to see what color underwear she had on.

He dragged the back of his hand across his forehead, thinking the place could stand some air-conditioning.

He slowly tuned in on Ripley's nonstop litany of the evening's events. The only time she'd hesitated in her speech was when he first hit each of her surface scrapes with the antiseptic.

"I about died when she told me to strip out of my clothes," she was saying, her brown eyes animated, her slender, sexy body radiating energy. "But you'll never guess who I saw after Christine's apprehension, standing calm as you please at the other end of the station."

Joe put the cap on the bottle and wadded up the cotton balls. "Who?" he asked without enthusiasm.

"Nicole Bennett."

That did prick his interest, but only because during two hours of grilling by Miller and his men, in which he and Ripley had had to repeat and repeat again everything that went down, Ripley had neglected to share that little piece of information.

Her smile was anything but repentant.

He sank back on his heels and rested his forearms on his thighs. "Let me get this straight. In the middle of everything going down, Nicole stood watching from the corner?"

"Uh-huh." Ripley got up, went to the refrigerator and took out two bottles of what looked like chocolate milk. She held one out to Joe. He took it even though he could have used a beer or something stronger right about then.

"So I guess we don't have to wonder where the diamonds went, then, do we?"

Unfortunately, Miller didn't seem all that convinced that Joe and Ripley weren't behind the missing gems. After all, they'd had the key in their possession until an hour before the grand opening of the locker.

Ripley led the way into the living room and he followed, sitting on the arm of an easy chair while she sprawled across the sofa. She took a long swallow of milk. "It was nothing but a wild-goose chase," she said half to herself. She turned her head to look at him. "The trip to Memphis, the pawnshop owner. When Nicole Bennett took that job at Christine Bowman's, she knew exactly what she was looking for. And it's my guess she had the diamonds five minutes after she got the key."

"But why the wild-goose chase?"

"Simple. She had to make sure Bowman was out of the picture or else she'd have her on her tail for however long it took to find her." A thoughtful expression wrinkled her lovely face. "She must have known the

FBI had Christine under surveillance." She pulled at the label on the bottle. "I can't figure out how she got to the diamonds, though. Didn't Miller say they'd had the station staked out for the past two months?"

The more she talked, the more distant Joe became. He couldn't quite believe this was the same woman who'd had the muzzle of a gun pressed against her forehead, was forced to strip out of her clothes at gunpoint, then struggled with an armed woman all within the span of an hour.

She was looking at him. He sighed. "It's my guess that once Bowman picked up stakes here and they followed you to Memphis, they lightened manpower at the bus station. It wouldn't have taken much for her to have arranged for some sort of distraction, taken the diamonds, then returned to Memphis."

She sat up. "That's right. Nicole didn't sell the box to the pawnshop owner until a day later."

Joe stared at the bottle in his hand, started to take a drink, then grimaced. He put it on the coffee table, untouched.

Now that the mystery was solved, Ripley seemed to have run out of gas. Unfortunately, Joe had run out of gas somewhere between Memphis and St. Louis. And with the threat hanging over their heads gone…well, he felt more at odds than ever.

"Joe?" Ripley said quietly.

When he looked at her, the frown she wore told him it wasn't the first time she had said his name.

"Is everything all right?" she asked.

"Everything's fine," he said. But the moment the words were out of his mouth, he recognized the lie for what it was. He pushed from the chair arm and paced a short way away, running his hand over his hair. "Actually, no. Everything's not fine."

While she was in the shower, he'd used a towel to dry his hair then stripped out of the T-shirt she'd loaned him. He was in his trusty old white shirt, tie and slacks. Only, when he looked down, he barely recognized himself. What did it mean when a guy didn't feel comfortable in his own clothes?

He turned toward Ripley, his gaze settling on her unforgettable face. A need so intense, so overwhelming, gripped his stomach, making him want to stride across the room, sweep her up from the couch and carry her off to the bed that lay behind the door just a few feet away.

"I've got to go."

Joe heard the words. Saw Ripley wince from the impact. But for the life of him he didn't think he'd said them. But there they lay. Hovering between them like a bird neither of them wanted to catch.

Ripley was the first to glance away. She slowly put her bottle on the table next to his, the pain on her face ripping him in two.

"I see," she said quietly.

Joe strode to collect his suitcase from the dining room and placed it next to the door. "Do you? Because I sure as hell don't see much right now."

She got up from the couch. He nearly held his hand out and shouted, "don't," for fear that he would never get out of that door if she moved within touching range.

Instead he stood pole straight, his throat tight and raw as she stepped haltingly in front of him. She looked about to hug him, withdrew, then went ahead and threw her slender arms around his neck anyway, resting her cheek on his shoulder and facing away from him. Joe closed his eyes and swallowed hard. Her breasts pressed against his chest, making his heart kick up, while her hips nestled snugly against his, making other parts of his anatomy kick up. Parts he didn't want to acknowledge. Hadn't they already gotten him into enough trouble?

"Thank you," Ripley whispered in his ear, pressing her soft lips against his neck.

Joe groaned, unable to hold back. His arms curved around her, tugging her closer, every part of him reveling in the feeling of her nearness. He'd never experienced emotions so pure, so out of control, before. And, simply, they scared him more than the gun Christine had wielded.

Looking back, he realized he'd always had a certain vision of his life and how it would turn out. And everything that had happened over the past few days was so far outside that as to emerge surreal. He had the company he'd built up with his own two hands, his family in Minneapolis—everything that was familiar and safe and his.

"Where will you go?" she asked, her arms holding him even tighter.

"To Memphis, I guess. I'll get my car." And attempt to put his life back into some sort of order. Maybe contact the reps at Shoes Plus and try to make amends. Or maybe he'd drive straight to Minneapolis. Being home might help snap him out of his zombielike state.

He heard her breath catch. "You, um, could stay here."

Joe nearly groaned at her whispered words.

"You know, for tonight. You could leave in the morning."

Of course. What had he expected? That she was asking him to stay for good? And what if she had? Would he have stayed? Joe didn't know. And that scared him more than everything else combined.

He somehow found the courage to set her away from him. "I can't." He'd rent a car and drive to Memphis if he had to. He didn't care. He knew he had to get out of here...now, before he made an even bigger fool of himself.

Ripley's brown eyes were soft and watery.

He turned toward the door.

"Joe?"

He braced himself but refused to face her.

"Will I see you again?'

He silently cursed. "It depends."

"On what?"

"On whether business brings me through St. Louis or not."

He hated saying the words, but for the life of him he couldn't come up with anything else.

He opened the door and walked out.

RIPLEY STOOD STARING AT THE closed door for so long her eyes hurt. She couldn't quite bring herself to believe he'd just walked out like that. Every bit of adrenaline that had been roaring through her system from the night's events had stopped midstream. What had just happened? Was it something she said? Something she did?

Forcing her legs into action, she hurried toward the

window, peering out much as she had earlier. But instead of trying to spot the FBI surveillance vehicles, she sought Joe's familiar silhouette. There. There he was. He'd crossed the street and was walking, head down in the rain, toward downtown. She opened her mouth to call to him through the open window, but that's how her mouth stayed. Open. Silent.

What could she say to him? "Come back?" She'd already asked him to stay, and he'd turned her down cold.

He turned the corner and walked out of sight.

Ripley felt as if her heart had dropped to the floor at her feet and if she wasn't careful she'd step on it. Just as surely as Joe had stomped all over it just now.

Was she a little slow on the uptake or what? She'd been so consumed with the Bowman case she hadn't even stopped to examine what was happening between her and Joe. She absently ran a hand down her face, surprised to find tears clinging to her cheeks. She remembered him trying to talk to her earlier, when they had returned to her apartment. Recalled the somber expression he'd been wearing since before then. What had he been thinking? What had he wanted to say?

She didn't know what was worse. That she didn't know. Or that she would never know.

She sank to the floor, her back against the wall beneath the window, mindless of the spray of rain the wind blew in every now and again.

One thing she did know was that for the first time in her life, she'd fallen in love with a guy. Hard. Kissing asphalt hard. She'd said and done things to and with him she'd never done with another man. She waited to feel ashamed. Instead she felt a pain the size of Missouri spread slowly across her chest.

Had she really been that shortsighted not to notice until it was too late the signs that she loved Joe? Or had she simply been too afraid? Had she poured so much of her courage into her career that she didn't have any left over for him? For love?

Some private investigator she was. Oh, sure, she'd done a bang-up job on the Bowman case. But when it came to her personal life, she couldn't tell the difference between great sex and full-blown love. And she'd just let the best thing in her life walk right out that door.

She remembered what Polk had once told her. That he hadn't met a woman who lived up to his idea of one. She questioned that wisdom. In fact, the more she considered it, the more she thought it was just so much bull. It wasn't that the idea was better. It was that he'd probably spent so damn much time on his job, he hadn't paid attention to what was standing right in front of him.

And here she'd gone and made the same stinking mistake.

CHAPTER FIFTEEN

TWO MONTHS LATER, RIPLEY leaned back in her scratched and dented office chair and lifted her feet to prop them on the desktop. The spring in the chair threatened to dump her onto the floor. Grabbing the edge of the desk, she righted herself.

To add insult to injury, her mentor and coconspirator Nelson Polk was watching her from the other side of the rented office space, his bushy gray eyebrows hovering over his amusement-filled eyes. "Careful there. You don't have disability insurance yet. You just opened this place. Be a shame to have to close it so quickly."

Ripley settled for sitting back carefully and folding her hands over her stomach. So she was in jeans and a sweatshirt rather than a wrinkled old suit and overcoat, but what mattered was how she felt. And she felt like a private investigator through and through. From the green and gold lettering she'd splurged on for the front window announcing that Ripley Logan, Private Investigator, had arrived, to the newspaper clippings she had framed and hung on the wall to her left, her dreams had come true.

Her mood dampened considerably.

Well, almost. She hadn't known she wanted that other dream, so it didn't really count, did it? A grainy picture from the St. Louis *Times and Tribune* caught her eye. It was a shot of her and Joe coming out of the bus station, Joe holding a newspaper over her head as rain pounded down on them. It was her complete rapture as she looked at him that made her heart skip a beat.

Okay, so maybe things hadn't completely turned out the way she would have liked them to. She got the job but lost the man. But at least she'd had him for a little while, which was more than a woman like her should expect. Right?

She made a face. What a crock that one was. That's exactly what the old Ripley would have thought. The Ripley who whined about paper cuts and filing and the general miserable state of her life. A woman who hadn't gotten a lot out of her love life because she hadn't expected much from it. Now... Well, now she demanded more. In her professional life, she'd lived by two philosophies—put everything on the line and let the dice fall where they may. Thankfully, they'd given her a winning combination until now. Unfortunately, she wasn't so brave when it came to her personal life.

But she planned to change that, as well.

She cleared her throat, watching Nelson fix a filing cabinet on the other side of the large room. He slid the drawer in and out, then picked up the screwdriver again.

After Joe left, she leaned on Polk more than she ever had before. Thankfully she'd never again seen him in the state he'd been in the day she'd sobered him up and he'd told her where the locker was. In fact, she was beginning to suspect he'd put the drink away for good a few weeks ago.

She couldn't be completely sure what had caused

him to drink himself into a stupor that afternoon, but she guessed the young man she'd seen him with the other day had something to do with it. His son? She suspected so. He only had one, and she knew from what he'd told her during one of their many conversations that he hadn't seen the boy since he was three years old. His showing up after so many years would be enough to send anyone diving into a liquor bottle. It also appeared to be a catalyst for him to stop.

Of course, she didn't think the Bowman case had hurt any, either. At the bus station when he'd helped apprehend Christine, she didn't think she'd seen Polk so alive. So alert. And then changes began occurring little by little in his everyday life. Gone were the tattered, smelly clothes, replaced with clean new clothes she'd helped him shop for with the money he'd had stashed in a savings account but hadn't accessed for years. He'd gotten a haircut, shaved every day and had moved into a boardinghouse not far from the office. She'd thought she'd be doing him a favor when she hired him to work part-time at the office. The truth was, he was doing her a favor. She'd had no idea how to handle the avalanche of clients that had come knocking after the press coverage of her involvement in the Bowman case. She was turning people away.

"Nelson?"

"Hmm?" He looked up from the filing cabinet.

"Do you ever wonder if you let the business run you instead of you running the business?"

He squinted at her. It was hard to believe that a short time ago he'd been little more than a park drunk who could play a great game of chess and had tons of stories about his P.I. adventures. "What's that again?"

Ripley fingered a file in front of her. It was bursting at the seams. "I just wonder if you ever regret not giving as much attention to your personal life as you gave to being a P.I."

"Every day I open my eyes."

She didn't say anything. She nodded, then absently opened the file in front of her. A picture of Joe Pruitt virtually jumped out at her.

Okay, so maybe she hadn't completely let him go. While physically he was no longer a part of her life, she'd made him a part of it by scrounging every last bit of information she could on the college basketball player turned entrepreneur. She cringed as she remembered introducing him as a shoe salesman. From what she had gathered from news pieces on his success, that would be akin to his calling her a bike messenger.

She turned over the promotional photo she'd obtained by contacting his PR department and looked through the various news clippings she'd compiled. From posing with sports stars even she recognized to hosting charitable events, he was a man unfamiliar to her. Sure, he looked the same, but the Joe she knew couldn't have been more different from this man.

She turned over a press clipping and stopped to stare at another one. It was the last one she'd collected before calling a halt to her efforts a month ago. From the society pages of the Minneapolis *Star*, it showed Joe with a pretty brunette at some event or another. A formal one that spotlighted Joe in a tux and the woman in something sexy and shimmering. The columnist predicted future wedding bells for the couple, Joe a self-made man, the woman from a successful, wealthy Minneapolis family.

Ripley predicted the end of her mooning over a man she'd let slip right through her fingers. At least she hoped it would end.

"Go after him."

She blinked several times then stared at Polk. He'd finished with the filing cabinet and was putting a fern on top of it. "What?"

He grinned, and she knew he wouldn't repeat himself. They both knew very well that she'd heard him.

"Mail call." Nelson opened the door and collected the morning delivery from the mailman.

Ripley sat up and accepted the small pile of mail from him. She'd only been in the office a month, so she wasn't expecting much. Water bill, gas bill, telephone bill, a letter from the Grand Bahamas...

She turned the envelope over, then over again. Nothing to indicate who the envelope was from. Just a postmark. She checked the address. Sure enough, it was directed to Ripley Logan, Private Investigator.

"What is it?" Nelson asked.

She shrugged. "I don't know."

She opened the middle desk drawer, starting when the drawer nearly fell out of its track and into her lap. She freed her letter opener and slid a neat opening into the envelope. Blowing between the flaps, she turned the envelope upside down and watched as a yellow slip of paper the length and width of the envelope drifted down on the air, then landed smack dab in the middle of her desk.

She leaned closer for a better look. It was a cashier's check…made out for ten thousand dollars.

Ripley nearly swallowed her tongue.

"Well, if that isn't a nice chunk of change," Polk said, lifting a coffee cup she hoped was filled with only coffee or else she might be tempted to down the contents.

"Um, yeah."

The question was, where had it come from? She was almost afraid to touch the check. Merely looking at it, she felt like she was breaking the law. She slid the letter opener under the right-hand corner and gave a flick. The check flipped to lie face down. The initials NB were written right in the middle, along with a smiley face.

Nicole Bennett.

"Oh, boy. She did get the diamonds."

"What? Who?"

Ripley stared unseeingly at Nelson, then slowly brought him into focus. "Nicole Bennett."

Polk grinned and took one of the mismatched visitors' chairs in front of the desk. He didn't have one problem with his chair when he propped his feet on the corner of the desk. "Smart cookie, that one."

Ripley blinked at him. Smart cookie had to be the understatement of the year. The brunette had played them all like a fine-tuned guitar, making it appear that she had unwittingly stolen from another thief, leading them on a wild-goose chase to Memphis to get them out of St. Louis, then setting up the original thief with the skill of a professional. Unfortunately, the dead pawnshop owner probably didn't find the whole fiasco amusing. But from what Ripley had read about the initial robbery in New York, the Memphis man hadn't been Christine

Bowman's first or only victim. Two security guards had been shot and killed in the heist, a third paralyzed for life.

Ripley sat back and stared at Polk. "What should I do with it?"

"What do you mean what should you do with it? You should cash it, of course." He grinned at her, showing the result of recent dental work. "And give me a raise."

"But it's blood money."

"Blood you had no hand in spilling, and neither did Nicole Bennett." He sighed and glanced at the wall where an FBI artist had drawn three different composites of the mystery woman in question. "All thieves should be as savvy as her. Commit victimless crimes."

Ripley sat back and shook her head, still staring at the check. "There's no way I can cash this."

"Take the money, Ripley. You earned it."

Her breath caught in her throat, her gaze flying to the man who'd spoken from the doorway.

Neither she nor Nelson had heard him come in. Checks of this amount probably had a tendency to do that to people.

"How are you doing, Joe?" Nelson got up, walked over to the stud in athletic shoes and shook his hand.

Joe's gaze strayed from Ripley's face to consider the older man. He blinked several times. "Nelson Polk?"

"One and the same." They dropped hands then Polk glanced at her. "I think I'll just go...run that errand now."

"Errand...right," Ripley repeated dumbly.

The door closed behind him. Peripherally she saw him pause in front of the glass window, indicating she should proceed. Do something. Then he threw his hands in the air and continued down the sidewalk.

"Um, hi," Ripley said.

Forget chair springs. Joe's grin nearly knocked her chair legs right out from under her. He sauntered to the front of the desk. "You should take it, you know. The money."

She finally forced herself to blink.

"After all, you never did get paid the rest of your fee."

"Yes, but the total would never come to this much."

"Then consider it a bonus."

A thought occurred to her. "You...you wouldn't happen to be behind this, would you?"

"Me?" He seemed to understand what she was asking. "Oh, God, no. But I'm thinking that maybe I should have done something."

So Nicole really had sent her the check. And Joe Pruitt was really standing in front of her looking more delicious than ever.

Her gaze flicked over him. Gone were the white shirt, tie and slacks. In their place were a pair of gray sweatpants and a dark blue T-shirt that brought out the color of his eyes. In fact...

"You didn't run all the way from Minneapolis, did you?" she asked.

His chuckle did funny things to her stomach. "No." He looked around the office, then his gaze stopped on something on her desk. After a long moment, Ripley realized it was the file she'd compiled on him.

She smacked it closed and shoved it into a desk drawer.

"Just some…" She wasn't sure what to say. They both knew what the file was.

His grin widened. "Actually, I'm living in St. Louis now."

Forget the chair legs, Ripley nearly fell clean off the chair. "What? When? How long?"

He motioned toward her drawer. "Had you kept up on your information, you would have known it was a month ago." He cleared his throat. "About the same time you opened the doors here."

He knew she'd opened her own agency? He'd moved to St. Louis? And he hadn't contacted her?

"You're confused."

"Um, yes, I am. How—why haven't you tried to contact me before now?"

The grin disappeared, and that serious expression she'd learned to fear came back. "I could ask why you didn't pursue me to Minneapolis."

"If you'd asked, I'd have told you. Because I'm a coward."

His eyes practically devoured her, as if she'd said the one thing he'd needed to hear most.

He crossed his arms over his wide chest, drawing attention to the sweat stains. He looked as if he'd been jogging. The idea that he'd been running by her office for the past month without her knowing it made her feel suddenly dizzy.

"Actually, there's a specific reason I stopped by now."

She searched his eyes. "Oh?"

He nodded. "You see, I want to hire you to help me find someone."

"I see." She tried to hide her disappointment. She'd thought he'd stopped by to see her, and instead he was in need of her services. She shakily pulled her yellow legal pad in front of her and grabbed a pen. "Who?"

"Me."

She slowly looked up.

He shifted from one foot to the other. "You see, there's this guy I used to know." His voice dropped to a low murmur that skated over her skin. "This guy...we'll call him Joe. And Joe, well, he used to be pretty satisfied with his life. He'd accomplished more than either of his parents had ever expected of him, built a successful business from the ground up, and generally enjoyed what he had—which, from a material standpoint, was a lot." His gaze swept everywhere but over her as he spoke. "Then one day he met this woman." He finally looked at her. "We'll call her Ripley."

Her heart dipped to her feet then bounded up again.

"And she...well, she turned everything upside down. She made down look up. She made white look black. And she made Joe realize that he'd never really been happy with what he had. She showed him that he'd merely settled. Taken the road well traveled.

"This woman, Ripley, well, one day, after some of the most incredible sex Joe had ever had, she asked him what he would like to do if he could choose to do anything in the world. You see, he didn't answer her. Because to do so would be to open a door that could reveal something he didn't want to know.

"Then he left her, Joe did, even though it ripped his heart out to do so. He thought that if he just went home, got back into the same routine, everything would be fine. He wouldn't have to think about that question, the mind-blowing sex or the woman who had given him both.

"The only problem is, there was no going back. No matter how hard Joe tried, he couldn't forget the incredible woman who had swept into his life, this Ripley. It took him a month to figure out that he probably never would. He's got a hard head, this Joe."

Ripley stared at him, spellbound.

"So Joe named his secretary CEO of his company headquarters in Minneapolis and not only answered that question Ripley had once asked him, he pursued it. He's now in St. Louis and is first assistant basketball coach at Washington University in St. Louis."

Ripley didn't quite know what to say. So she said nothing.

"And now Joe would like to know how the woman, this Ripley, feels about everything he's just told her."

How did she feel? Ripley searched her heart and her mind. She felt like the most important woman on earth for having done something to deserve the man in front of her. Like she must not have totally screwed up for him to have come back to her.

She catapulted from the chair and practically dove into his arms, catching his head in her hands and planting a kiss on him that had them both panting for air. He tasted like fresh air, sweat and the man she loved.

"So?" he asked, running his thumb over her bottom lip. "What do you say? I can promise you you'll never want for another pair of shoes again in your life."

She scanned his handsome face from forehead to

chin, wondering if she'd ever missed anyone so much. "Joe, my feet are yours to do with what you will. But try putting a wedding ring on my toe instead of my finger and you're in big trouble."

"I have other things in mind for your toes," he said with a sexy grin. "And, just this once, let me get in the last word."

Just before he silenced her with one of his breath-stealing kisses, she murmured, "Never."

* * * * *

BREATHLESS

Kimberly Raye

For my oldest and dearest friend,
Liz Eden Kasper.
For great memories and a timeless friendship.
You're the best!

CHAPTER ONE

SHE KNEW HIM IMMEDIATELY.

A girl didn't forget the first man she'd ever made love to—the *only* man—even if it had been ten years ago.

He sat several feet away at a small table near the center of BJ's, the town's only honky-tonk. With his legs propped up, arms folded and eyes closed, it appeared that he'd stretched out and fallen asleep, despite the fast-paced George Strait song blaring from the speakers.

She moved forward and made her way through a maze of tables. It seemed as if the entire population of Inspiration, Texas, filled the small place. Then again, it was Friday night. Time to let down your hair and kick up your spurs. The tables were jam-packed, the dance floor to her left full of sliding boots and wiggling Wranglers.

She saw more than one familiar face as she scooted past this chair and squeezed by that one, not that anyone acknowledged her. The women either stared past her as if she didn't exist, or shot her a look of pure contempt. And the men... Open, hungry stares without an ounce of respect roved over her and picked her clean.

Annie Divine didn't shy away or wince or show any of the dozen emotions whirling through her. Shoulders back, head held high, she kept walking.

The country two-step ended just as she reached him.

The sudden pause magnified every sound around her. The spurts of laughter. The murmur of conversation. The *clink* of beer bottles. The *ding* of a pinball machine. Her heart echoed in her ears, pounding out a furious tempo that betrayed the composure she was trying so hard to maintain.

As if it even mattered.

Tack Brandon was drunk, maybe passed out, from the looks of him. Definitely passed out, she corrected when a nearby pool player hit an eight ball. A round of cheers erupted and the next song started with a loud guitar riff, but Tack didn't so much as flinch. He simply sat there, completely unaffected by his surroundings, by her.

The realization eased the panic beating at her senses, and she took a deep breath. The moment held a sudden surreal quality, as if she wasn't really living and breathing the here and now, but imagining it. She would open her eyes soon and find that this was all a dream. Cooper Brandon, Tack's father, would be alive and well and Tack would be anywhere but here. Anywhere but *home*. The thought filled her with an overwhelming sadness and she found herself holding her breath, holding the moment. He was here. Now. Right in front of her.

She almost didn't believe it. When he hadn't shown up for his father's funeral earlier that day, she'd started to wonder if he really did hate Cooper Brandon as much as he'd claimed. The question had weighed heavy on her, filling her with a mix of relief and despair. Both ridiculous, considering she shouldn't care if she ever saw Tack again.

She shouldn't, but she did.

The prodigal son was home.

Only he hadn't come home. He'd come here, she thought, her gaze going to a blazing neon Coors sign. A place to drown his troubles. To find trouble, if he had a mind. And from the stories Coop had told her over the past few years, Tack certainly had a hankering for that.

"How're you holding up, sugar?"

A warm hand closed over Annie's shoulder and she turned to see Bobby Jack, the club's owner, standing next to her.

She shrugged. "A little tired. Today was more difficult than I expected."

"Sorry I had to add to your troubles and drag you out of bed, but I didn't know who to call. I figured you was the closest thing to family Tack's got now. I been pouring coffee in him for the past hour, but he still ain't fit to drive."

"I couldn't sleep anyway." Or eat. Or breathe easily. She blinked. "I can't believe he's really here."

Bobby Jack gave her shoulder a reassuring squeeze. He stood a few inches shy of Annie's five-nine, but what he lacked in height, he made up in brawn. Built like a pit bull, he had a face only his mama and Norma Jean Mayberry, his fiancé, could love. His nose, a little too wide and flat, gave the impression he'd taken one too many punches. Then there was the bruise darkening the left side of his face…

He noticed the direction of her gaze and shrugged. "When the coffee didn't work, I tried a pitcher of ice water over his head. It always does the trick for Dell Carter. That old drunk comes up sputtering sober every time."

"But Tack came up punching?"

"Knocked me clear across the dance floor before he sank back into his chair and reached for another drink." Bobby rubbed his jaw. "Boy's got damn fine aim considering he guzzled close to a full bottle of tequila." He handed her a pair of keys. "I wrestled these off him a few minutes ago. Belong to that big bitch of a motorcycle parked out front..." His words died as someone motioned to him from a nearby table.

"Looks like I've got customers."

"You go on. I can manage."

"I'll be back to help you as soon as I can." Instead of rushing away, however, Bobby Jack paused. "I didn't get a chance to tell you at the funeral, but I'm real sorry about Coop. He was a good man." He shook his head. "Never thought I'd say that about him."

"It's all right, Bobby Jack. Coop knew he wasn't in the running for any popularity contests."

"Ain't that the God's honest. He was always a hard-assed SOB, but these past few years he seemed to soften up." He squeezed her shoulder again. "You did good, Annie. Your mama woulda been real proud." Then, as if he'd said too much, he pulled his hand away. "You need anything, anything at all, you let me know."

His concern touched her and she slid her arms around his wide shoulders for a quick hug. Bobby Jack had always been one of the few in town who treated Annie like a person, a friend, and not Wild Cherry Divine's daughter.

Not that her parentage bothered her. Annie had long ago come to terms with who she was. The moment Tack Brandon had roared out of town, and out of her life.

"Thanks, Bobby Jack." She gave him another quick hug before pulling away, Tack's keys clutched in her hand.

"*Anything,*" Bobby said again.

She nodded and watched him disappear into a cloud of cigarette smoke, then she turned back to the matter at hand.

To him.

If only she'd brought her camera, she thought as she stole the next few heartbeats just to look at and appreciate the changes ten years had wrought. Time had turned the gangly teenage boy into a hard and muscular man. His white T-shirt—soaking-wet from Bobby Jack's douse of ice water—clung to his sinewy torso like a second skin, revealing a solid chest, a ridged abdomen. Her gaze lingered at the shadow of a nipple beneath the transparent material, and a dozen erotic memories rushed through her.

Her lips closing over the flat button, tongue flicking the bud to life. His deep, throaty groan echoing in her ears, his hands buried in her hair, urging her on...

She took a deep breath and moved her attention to the damp jeans molded to his thighs, his calves. Scuffed black biker boots completed the outfit. His entire persona screamed *danger*. Tack Brandon was a womanizer, a use-'em-then-lose-'em type with a taste for sin and a body to back him up. He was the sort of man every mama warned her daughter about.

Every mama except Annie's. But how could Cherry have warned her daughter off the very type she herself had spent a lifetime trying to catch? The woman had been a lot of things, but never a hypocrite. She'd been loud and a bit gaudy, quick to rile and even quicker to forgive, naive in so many ways, yet experienced to the point of being the town Jezebel. Trustworthy and too easy to place her own trust, and loyal to a fault. Cherry Divine had given up her hopes and dreams and gone to her grave loving Cooper Brandon even though he'd never loved her back. Not the way he should have.

Like father, like son.

In appearance as well as deed, she thought, her gaze going to Tack's face. He had his father's features, the strong Brandon cheekbones inherited from a Comanche grandmother, as well as a straight, sculpted nose. Obscenely long sable eyelashes fanned his cheeks. A few days' growth of beard covered his jaw, crept down his neck. His brown hair, as damp as his shirt, curled down around his neck, the edges highlighted the same gold as the inch of tequila left in the bottle sitting in front of him.

Her palms burned as she remembered the softness of his hair—velvet strands stroking her breasts, trailing over her navel, brushing the insides of her thighs… Heat flamed her cheeks and she said a silent thank-you to the heavens and Cuervo Gold that his eyes were closed.

The fire cooled with several deep breaths and she continued her inspection. Tiny lines fanned out from the corners of his eyes. A scar zigzagged from his right temple and bisected one dark eyebrow. The subtle changes made him seem much older than the boy of eighteen who haunted her memories.

This was no boy. He was all man, and he had the hard look of someone who'd seen too much, spent the better part of his life sacrificing and doing without.

Ridiculous, she knew. Tack Brandon had never done without anything. He'd had everything he'd ever wanted, including her. Then again, he'd never *really* wanted her, not the way she'd wanted him.

Thankfully.

She focused on the thought and tried to restrain the emotions swirling inside her. To ignore the memory of his body covering hers, his hands stroking her bare skin, his tears wetting her palms... She didn't want to remember the way his touch had set her senses blazing. The way his gaze, usually so guarded and emotionless, had gleamed with raw feeling for those few moments when she'd been in his arms and he'd been inside of her.

The past was over and done with. She wasn't going to fall in love with him again, she told herself for the hundredth time that day. She *wasn't.*

The trouble was, Annie Divine didn't think she'd ever fallen out of love with Tack Brandon. And when his eyelids fluttered and he stared up at her with a gaze as blue and enticing as a clear midnight sky, she feared she hadn't.

Like mother, like daughter.

Tack Brandon hadn't taken just her innocence the night of their senior prom, the night his mother had died and he'd left Inspiration. He'd taken her heart, as well.

No. The past was over and done with and Annie had learned her lesson where he was concerned. Never again.

"Hey there, sweetheart."

He sounded more sober than drunk, but his gaze, red-rimmed and glazed, told a different story. Then there was his smile, a wicked tilt to his lips that stopped her heart for several long seconds. Definitely drunk, she thought. Because the last thing Tack would offer her would be a smile. His boot up her backside maybe, once he realized she'd befriended the one man he'd always hated. A man she'd hated herself up until the moment her mama had passed away. Things had changed then. Cooper Brandon had changed.

She made a point of keeping her fanny aimed away from Tack as she scooted around and worked her hand beneath one heavily muscled arm.

"Come on, cowboy. Let's get you home."

Her words seemed to trigger something and his smile died. "To hell with that. Motel," he mumbled, and she noticed the room key sitting on the table next to his wallet and the tequila bottle. He must have emptied his pockets digging for money to pay for his liquor, she thought, scooping up his possessions and aiming for her own pocket.

His hand clamped around her wrist and she found herself jerked onto his lap, his face inches from hers.

"Take it easy," she told him. "I'm just going to hold on to this stuff for you while I get you out of here."

"You pickin' me up, sugar?" He smiled again. "This must be my lucky night." His breath, a mingling of lime and tequila and a sweetness she remembered all too well, rushed softly against her mouth. Then his lips were there, nibbling at the corners of hers. "Best luck I've had in a hell of a long time."

Her mind replayed a dozen memories and it was all she could do to turn her head to the side and keep from meeting his kiss.

"I'm just helping you back to your room. You're drunk."

"And you're…" He leaned back and squinted, as if he couldn't quite see through the liquor fogging his senses. "Do I know you?"

"Maybe," she said, doing her best to ignore the pang of hurt that shot through her at the simple question.

Calm.

She pushed herself up off his lap, her hand plastered against the rock-hard wall of his chest. Her palm caught fire from the simple contact and she nearly cried. It wasn't fair that his effect on her should be so potent, so powerful after all this time.

Cool.

He grabbed for her again, but she sidestepped him. "Come on," she said, sliding a hand under one large bicep and urging him from the chair.

It took her several tugs, but finally she managed to get him on his feet. She slid an arm around his waist and six-feet-plus of warm male leaned into her.

"What's your name, sugar?" he drawled, his voice as lazy and thick as molasses.

"Sugar's, fine." She ignored the prick at her ego, her heart, and concentrated on holding him up and urging him forward.

Indifferent.

"I swear," he slurred, "I…know you…from some-where." He shook his head. "You an old girlfriend, sugar?" He didn't give her a chance to reply. "You are. I knew it!" He slapped his knee, the motion making them both stumble. She caught the edge of the table and he sagged against her. "A blast from the past," he mumbled.

"That's me. Now, hut-two, cowboy." She motioned for Bobby Jack who'd just served up a round to a nearby table. At five-nine, Annie towered over most of the women she knew, as well as a few men, but Tack was still a good head taller and she needed all the help she could get. "Let's see about drying you off and putting you to bed."

"Bed," he muttered, his head dropping onto her shoulder, his lips nibbling at the curve of her neck. "Now, there's a fine idea."

HE'D HAD THE DREAM MANY TIMES.

She leaned over him, her pale hair falling down around her face like a shimmering curtain of silvery silk that tickled across his belly as she worked at the button of his jeans.

"Just my luck Bobby had to pour ice water over him," a soft, sweet voice grumbled from someplace far, far away, "...my even worse luck it's colder than Iceland in here...should've let Bobby follow me...but no, I had to tell him I could handle it." He heard a few more mutters about motel air conditioners and pneumonia before her fingers slipped and grazed Tack's already growing erection. His heartbeat thundered through his head.

Again she tried to work the zipper, and instead, worked him into a frenzy. Every muscle in his body went tense, his breathing grew heavy, labored. He sucked for a deep breath.

Through the haze of tequila and smoke that hovered around him, he caught a whiff of her—the tantalizing smell of ripe peaches basking in the summer sunshine.

He drank in the scent, his nostrils flaring, his senses coming alive as her essence pushed aside the liquor-induced fog, to coax him back to life. Peaches had always been his favorite. He remembered so many warm days picking fruit down by Brandon Creek. There'd been nothing like biting into the sweet flesh, feeling the juice trickle down his chin...

Nothing as decadent, as satisfying.

Except her—the woman who haunted his past, his dreams, his *now*—and her soft-as-moonlight hair that whispered across his bare flesh and made his muscles quiver.

His zipper slid completely free. She sighed and he groaned, and then he reached for her, anxious for the part of the fantasy that came next.

He laced his fingers through the smooth strands of her hair and pulled her down on top of him.

A surprised "Oh!" bubbled from her lips before he claimed them in a kiss that was desperate, savage. He'd been far too long without a woman.

Without *this* woman.

Full, soft lips pressed against his. She drew back with a moment's hesitation that barely registered in his brain, then her mouth parted for him and her tongue flicked out to stroke his. He held her head in his hands, his fingers tangled in her hair, anchoring her to him as if he feared someone might pull her away.

Hell, he was afraid. He knew from experience he would wake up all too soon to find his bed empty and his body spent on another wet dream.

But at the moment, she felt like much more. *So real.*
The sound of her shallow breaths filled his ears. Her
hands trailed up his arms, over his shoulders, silky fingertips touching and stroking as if memorizing every
inch of him. Her heart pounded against his. Her nipples
swelled, pebbled against the thin cotton of her T-shirt.
Her hips rotated, echoing the same desperate urgency
clawing his belly.

Just a dream...

The best he'd had in a hell of a long time.

Clothes were peeled away, from her shirt and jeans
and wispy panties, to what was left of his. He urged her
up, sliding her sweat-dampened body along the aching
length of his until her nipple hovered a fraction from
his lips. He drew the quivering tip into his mouth and
suckled her long and hard, until she was gasping and
crying out his name.

He savored the sound of her response before he
moved on to the other breast. He suckled and nipped
until she bucked against him, so wild and untamed. The
way she'd been their first night together, once she'd shed
that damn potato sack of a dress. He'd peeled away the
fabric with gentle kisses and heated words, and along
with her clothing, he'd finally managed to strip her of
her inhibitions, as well. She'd matched his appetite, his
eagerness, just the way she did right now. The way she
always did when he had this particular dream.

He was near to bursting, his sex hot and heavy and
pulsing with a life all its own. Gliding his hands down
her back, he cupped her buttocks and lifted her. With
a shift of his hips, he touched her with the tip of his
erection, felt her warm and wet and waiting for him.

His fingers tightened on her firm bottom and in one smooth motion he slid her down his rigid length. Pleasure splintered his brain and sent an echoing shudder through his body. He gripped her hips and urged her to move, to ride him fast and furious.

"Wait." So soft and desperate, the word echoed through his head and pushed aside the desire drumming through his veins to jerk him back to reality.

But this wasn't reality. This was a dream. A very vivid, erotic fanta—

A splash of wetness hit his cheek and he knew in an instant that the woman in his arms was very real. His hands immediately stilled. He forced his eyes open, battling the damn fuzziness brought on by all the tequila.

He blinked and tried to focus, but the room was nearly pitch-black, so dark and blurry. He saw only the shadow of her face surrounded by a silver cloud of hair.

Her hair.

He forced the thought aside. It was a real woman, all right, but it couldn't be *her.* While the lights were out and lust clouded his brain, he saw what he wanted to see, felt what he wanted to feel, and man, she felt good!

Another splash hit his chin, slid down his jaw, and he raised a hand to wipe the wetness from her cheeks. He clamped down on his control, determined not to move, not to twitch inside her until he'd heard her answer. "I'm not hurting you, am I?"

"Yes. No." She sniffled. "I'm sorry. It's just been a long time." She drew a deep breath that ended on a ragged gasp when he reached up to thumb her nipple. "Too long," she added, leaning into his palm. "Much too long."

"Relax, darlin'." He stroked her back, felt her body bow toward him. "Just sit back and enjoy the ride."

At the coaxing of his hands, the slow, mesmerizing thrusts of his hips, she seemed to do just that. But not half as much as Tack, himself. When he came, it was like someone zapped his brain with a cattle prod. Heat sizzled across every nerve ending, consumed all rhyme and reason and thought, until he crashed and burned and his entire body went up in flames. And Tack Brandon had the second best orgasm of his entire life.

The first, of course, had been courtesy of the silver-haired beauty from his dreams. A memory.

A blast from the past.

The words echoed in his head, playing at his conscience, trying to remind him of something. But he was too tired, too spent, too pleased to think of anything except slipping an arm around this woman, *his* woman, nuzzling her neck and getting some much-needed sleep.

He'd have plenty of time to think tomorrow.

CHAPTER TWO

SHE WAS GONE.

Tack leaned up on one elbow and scanned the sparsely furnished motel room. With its orange shag carpeting and quarter-fed vibrating bed, the room, like all the others at the Inspiration Inn, served as home-away-from-home to truckers and eager lovers. Tack had considered himself neither when he'd signed the register yesterday. But now...

Visions of silky arms and long, long legs wrapped around him flashed in his mind. Heat skimmed over his bare flesh despite the air conditioner blasting ice-cold comfort from the wall unit not two feet away. *Eager.* That certainly described him last night. This morning, too, he thought ruefully, staring down at the portion of sheet raised in tentlike fashion over his prominent erection.

But his equally eager partner was nowhere in sight.

He took a deep breath and continued his visual search of the room. His wallet and keys sat atop a scarred dresser. His discarded clothes lay draped over the room's only chair, an orange vinyl number that made him want to reach for his sunglasses.

The rising sun didn't help matters any. A pale gold glow crept around the edges of the blinds to chase the shadows into the farthest corners. He clamped his eyes shut against the light as the first twinges of a major hangover needled his head. He was still sufficiently drunk that he didn't feel the full effect of the morning after, yet sober enough to recognize the hollowness in his gut.

She was really gone.

The dream was over.

But this hadn't been a dream. This had been a real woman, someone he'd picked up at BJ's. Maybe someone who'd picked him up. He searched his mind for a memory, but he couldn't grasp anything past Bobby Jack dumping that damn ice water on him. That and the crack of knuckles against his old friend's face. Tack had collapsed back into the chair, picked up the bottle again, and the world had faded away. The next thing he knew, he'd awakened to see all that angel hair trailing over his bare stomach.

His muscles shivered in response and he closed his eyes, feeling her over him, surrounding him, her body grasping him so perfectly. So warm and wet and—

What the hell had he done?

He wiped a hand over his face. He'd drunk himself into a stupor, that's what he'd done. Downed a full bottle of tequila when he never touched anything stronger than an occasional beer during off-season. While he raced the circuit, he stuck to sports drinks and bottled water. He *never* drank the hard stuff, any more than he slept with nameless, faceless women. Granted, he'd gone through his share of trophy girls when he'd started out, a rookie hotshot burning up the motocross tracks. Once he'd grown up, smartened up, he'd realized the women were just as bad for him as the booze. Distracting. Dangerous. He wasn't into one-night stands.

Then again, he hadn't really considered this woman a one-night stand. Just a dream. Another crazy fantasy. *The* fantasy that haunted him night after night.

But this had been real, with all too real repercussions. A dozen scenarios flashed in his head, all the result of unprotected sex. *If* it had been unprotected sex. Maybe she'd been on the Pill, or used a diaphragm or carried her own condoms. He clung to the hope and forced the doom and gloom aside. What was done was done, and Tack had never been one to linger over his mistakes. *Move on. Focus.*

Pushing himself up, he swung his legs over the side of the bed and spared a glance at the alarm clock. Half past seven and counting. Hangover be damned, he had to get dressed and get on with his business. Tucker was waiting for him—

The thought jerked to a halt as he remembered the sticky vinyl seat of a pickup truck, a woman's soft voice humming to a country tune playing on the radio. He went to the window, moved aside the blind and glanced out the window, squinting his eyes against the sun. Sure enough, there was no sign of his Harley.

Tack let the shade fall back into place. BJ's was on the other side of town, past the railroad tracks—at least a half hour on foot—while the ranch was only about a twenty-minute walk, fifteen if he took the shortcut he'd used after school as a kid.

He grinned, remembering the pathway that led directly past the creek and his favorite peach tree. Unwillingly, his gaze went to the soft indentation on the pillow next to him. The urge to turn and bury himself in the scent of her hit him hard and fast. He picked up the pillow and held it to his nose. Closing his eyes, he drank in the scent. *Peaches.* So sweet and warm and undeniably *her.*

He shook away the nostalgia and put the pillow down. It wasn't her. It never was when he opened his eyes. Never.

If only he knew the real woman's identity. Despite the regret swimming inside him, he also felt...different. More alive. Invigorated. She'd done that to him, with her body, her tears, her words.

Wait...it's been a long time. So long...

He searched for some memory, something distinctive, separate from his dream lover.

Nothing.

Cursing himself and that damn bottle of Cuervo, he headed for the bathroom. If he hurried, he could shower and change and make it to the ranch in time for his meeting with Gary Tucker, his father's attorney. Forever punctual, Gary was probably already at the ranch waiting, thrilled that Tack had agreed to come home for the reading of the will. No doubt he thought Tack was eager to get his hands on all that Brandon land and money.

But Tack hadn't wanted his father's legacy ten years ago, and he sure as hell didn't want it now. He'd spent his entire youth indebted to a man who'd seen his only son as an extension of himself rather than an individual with his own likes and dislikes. As the only son and heir, Tack had been bound to the Brandon land, chained to a lifetime of tradition. He'd been this close to fulfilling his father's expectations, but only because of his mother.

She'd loved the land as much as his father, but for different reasons. She'd never seen the ranch as a sign of wealth or power, but as her home.

She'd grown up on a neighboring spread, what was now the western portion of the Big B. An only child with a keen knowledge of cattle, she'd had dreams of taking over when her father passed on. The man, old and stubborn, refused to leave his single daughter—no matter how capable—in charge of thousands of acres of land. So she'd gone looking for a husband, and she'd found Cooper Brandon.

In his mother's eyes, Coop had been the perfect match. He'd been a rancher whose land bordered hers, one of the most eligible bachelors in the county, and most of all, her father had approved of him. Tack's mother had made a business proposition, and Cooper, greedy and eager to expand his cattle empire, had accepted.

Some say she'd been as cold as his father, but Tack didn't remember things that way. She'd always been kind and sweet, maybe a bit reserved, but some people didn't show their emotions as easily as others. Tack had forgiven her for that because whatever her shortcomings, at least she'd *tried* to be a good mother. But his father... There'd been no trying involved. Cooper Brandon had been a cattleman first, second and third, and his role as father had never figured in.

Tack's mother had died in a car accident the night of his senior prom and he'd left, determined to find his own way without the Brandon money and influence, without any help from his father, not that the man would have given any. Cooper Brandon would have sold his soul to keep his son on the Big B, but he wouldn't give the time of day to see him happy and content anywhere else.

Leaving had been hard. Making it even harder. But after years of blood, sweat and sacrifice, Tack had finally established a name for himself on the motocross and Supercross racing circuit. He'd raced for Team Suzuki, Yamaha, Honda and had just been approached to lead the Kawasaki team next year.

His gaze went to his duffel bag where he'd stuffed the new contracts that awaited his review and signature. He'd already received the go-ahead from his lawyer. A sweet deal, that's what Kenny had said. The best deal in the sport's history, and all because of Tack's reputation. One he'd built on his own.

No ties. No debts. *No roots.*

"Ain't nothing more important than this spread. The cattle, the land, it all comes first. Everything else is second."

The words echoed through Tack's mind, so crystal clear, as if his father had spoken them only yesterday.

Tack shook his head. He still couldn't believe his father was dead. The man had thrived on life and all it had to offer—money, whiskey, and especially women—sometimes indulging too much, always demanding more than anyone had a right. So domineering and manipulative and...*alive.*

Even standing at the grave yesterday after everyone had left, Tack had felt somehow, someway there'd been a mistake. He'd half expected his father to walk up, slap him on the back and launch into one of his speeches about responsibility.

Dead.

There'd been no mistake, no escaping the present or the past, though Tack had tried. He'd headed for the nearest bar to get wrecked, to forget the last time he'd seen his father, the words they'd exchanged, the guilt that still ate at him. The hatred.

As if he could.

He would, he told himself as he pulled on a clean T-shirt and jeans, and dropped into the nearest chair to pull on his boots. Cooper Brandon was dead. Tack was sorry for that, but he couldn't bring the man back to life any more than he could go back and change their bitter parting over his mother's deathbed.

Tack could only face today, the future, and his involved a very important race in six weeks, the Northwestern 250cc championship, a title he had to win if he intended to lead the Kawasaki team.

If.

A loud knock seemed to rattle the walls and he winced. He yanked open the door just as a ring-adorned fist reared back, ready to pound some more and torture his temples.

"Well, I'll be," exclaimed the old woman standing on his doorstep. "It *is* you. Why, I saw you yesterday morning, smiling for them ESPN cameras and racing some fancy-schmancy bike of yours up near Palm Springs."

"That was a rerun, Effie. Palm Springs was six months ago."

"Six months?" Effie Coletrain, owner of the Inspiration Inn, frowned. "That damn TV's getting to be as bad as that tabloid trash everybody reads. You never know what's what."

Effie was in her late sixties, by Tack's estimation, but

she made one hell of an attempt to hide it. Effie, alone, was responsible for the local Mary Kay rep's promotion from a pink Escort to the ultradeluxe pink Cadillac now zooming around town.

Today was no exception. Green eye shadow, hot-pink blush and matching lipstick worked to cover lines and wrinkles, but nothing could ease the rusty hint of her voice.

"Looks like somebody," she went on, "had himself a late night his first day back in town. Pastor Marley won't be too pleased about that. What other wicked things did you get yourself into last night?" Her gaze pushed past him.

He wedged his body between the open doorway and blocked her view. "Effie, I'm really in a hurry—"

"House rule number one—no carrying on in my establishment."

"Me?" He did his best to look innocent, the way he had so many times in the past when he'd been as guilty as sin and Effie had demanded the truth.

She studied him with a narrowed gaze. "House rule number two—no lying to an old woman who's heard more than her share. I can see right into them lady-killer eyes of yours, Tack Brandon. And I definitely see a man who did some hunting last night." She peered past him. "What I don't see is anything left over from the kill."

"Rule number one for lady-killers," he said grinning. "Never leave evidence hanging around. You might incriminate yourself."

She stared him down a second more, then shook her head. "Same old smart mouth, I see." Her tone was stern, but her eyes were soft, indulgent, the way they'd been all those years ago when she'd shooed Tack and his two partners in crime, Jimmy and Jack Mission, into her office after they'd been caught pouring bubble bath into the motel's swimming pool.

She'd been mad as a bull, yet when the sheriff had shown up, she'd declined to file any charges. Instead, she'd handed all three boys brooms and put them to work sweeping the parking lot. Afterward, she'd given out homemade cookies and lemonade, and he'd liked her from then on.

He eyed the tray she carried. "That wouldn't be—"

"For breakfast?" She flashed him a what-kind-of-woman-do-you-think-I-am? look. "Don't you know all that sugar stunts your growth?"

"I'm all grown-up now."

"That's a matter of opinion," she snorted. "You were too big for your britches when you were waist-high, and you're still too big. I ought to put you over my knee."

"You ought to, but you won't."

"Don't be so sure." She glared at him. "I'm not as sweet as I used to be."

"You're still as sweet as ever," he said, trying to coax a smile out of her. "Same old sweet-as-molasses Effie."

She sighed and her expression softened. "You got the old part right. Too old to be coming out here waiting on the likes of you." She held up the tray. "I don't usually offer room service—it's breakfast bright and early at 7:00 a.m. sharp in my dining room, or guests can fend for themselves, but I made an exception, seeing as how you just got back into town and all." She glanced at the tray. "Home cookin' guaranteed to put a spring in your step. And darlin', you sure as shootin' look like you need it."

"I'll savor every bite," he promised.

"Good." Her brown eyes filled with sympathy. "Your daddy was a bastard, but I always respected him. He was a straight-shooter. If he liked you, he liked you. If he didn't, he didn't. You always knew where you stood with Coop. I'm real sorry for you."

"Thanks, Effie." He took the tray from her hands and slid it onto the nightstand.

"Eat up, son."

He was actually tempted as he shut the door behind her and surveyed the meal she'd brought. Other than the headache, he felt none of the usual effects of a hangover. No churning stomach, aching muscles. Maybe he hadn't drunk as much as he'd thought.

Then why couldn't he remember more of last night? More of *her?*

The question niggled at him as he snatched his wallet off the dresser, grabbed a piece of sausage from the tray and headed out the door. Unfortunately, he didn't have time for a sit-down meal, not if he intended to make his meeting on time.

A soft whine stopped him just outside the motel room and he turned to see a pitiful-looking brown-and-white mutt—a cross between a German shepherd and a hound dog—eyeballing the sausage in his hands.

"Hey, buddy," he said, leaning down to stroke the animal's head. "You get lost on your way home?" Despite the question, Tack knew right away this was no one's pet.

The animal was painfully thin, his coat sticking to

his ribs as if he hadn't eaten in weeks. The way the dog trembled beneath Tack's soothing hand made it obvious no one had petted him for a very, very long time.

"You hungry, Bones?"

Bones replied by gobbling up the sausage link and licking frantically at Tack's empty hand.

"There's more where that came from," he said as he unlocked the motel room and led the dog inside. He wondered briefly which one of Effie's rules sanctioned no stray dogs, not that he cared. He would pay Effie any fine she required. Tack had always had a soft spot for strays.

Leaving Bones near the doorway, he placed a blanket on the floor in the far corner. Next he filled the motel's ice bucket with water and placed it, along with the breakfast tray, near the blanket.

"It's all yours, Bones."

The dog hesitated only a few seconds before ambling forward to sniff the food. He licked his chops once, twice, then started gulping down the breakfast.

Tack stroked the dog's matted coat. "We'll clean you up later, then see about finding you a home. Right now, I'm afraid you're on your own, buddy. I've got business." The dog spared him a glance before turning back to his breakfast, and Tack knew he'd already been forgiven for leaving.

Just as Tack turned toward the doorway, his gaze snagged on a piece of white silk nestled between the tangled sheets. A pair of panties, he realized with a grin as he pulled the scrap of silk and lace free. He stared at the tiny pattern dotting the fabric, and the air caught in his chest. *Peaches.*

His fingers tightened as a detailed memory of last night washed over him. Her body pressed to his, her hands touching him just so, her voice whispering through his head, each syllable softened with a honey-sweet drawl... *Familiar.*

He shook his head and stuffed the undies into his pocket. It couldn't be. The last he knew of Annie Divine, she'd been dead set on leaving town, heading for college and a career, and a life *away* from her mother. Annie had hated her legacy even more than Tack had hated his.

It couldn't have been her.

IT WAS HER.

Tack stopped dead in his tracks and stared across the sea of wildflowers. He blinked once, twice, but she was still there. Dressed in a sheer white cotton sundress, angel hair spilling down around her shoulders like a silvery cloud, she could have been a vision, for all he knew. Or wishful thinking. She'd been on his mind since he'd started out from the motel.

But this was different. *She* was different. He'd pictured her the way she'd been ten years ago, a girl on the verge of womanhood, her figure just starting to blossom. No way had he anticipated the woman who stood before him. She was all grown-up now, her body fully developed, ripe with lush curves that inspired wicked thoughts.

Like mother, like daughter.

Wild Cherry Divine had been quite a looker in her day. It was no wonder his father had been hooked the moment she'd stepped into town, and out onto the stage at the Watering Trough, a strip joint out on Route 62. Cooper Brandon, married man, loving father and pillar of the community, had staked his claim early on, and Tack had despised him for it ever since.

Not that any of that had to do with Annie. She'd hated the connection between her mother and his father as much as he had, but they'd been kids, maybe eight or nine when the affair had started, and they'd had little say-so.

That was a long time ago.

For a full second, it struck him how much she'd changed, how much she resembled her mother. Then she lifted an expensive-looking camera hanging from a strap around her neck and started snapping pictures of a particular cluster of flowers.

He smiled. Annie and her camera. It was a sight he remembered well. Annie standing on the sidelines at a high school football game, snapping pictures of players, the crowd, the cheerleaders. Annie tagging along on a group picnic, lingering on the fringes of the crowd, taking shots of the picnic goers, the countryside, the local wildlife.

She'd been a photographer on the yearbook staff, attending every event, always trying to mesh with the "in" crowd. She never had. She'd always been Cherry Divine's daughter and that had set her apart, made her different, even though she'd done her best to fit in.

She fit perfectly here, he thought. She stood amid an ocean of daisies and bluebonnets. Her dress—sleeveless and short and sheer enough to make him swallow—revealed smooth, tanned arms and an endless pair of legs. The material molded to her full breasts and nipped at her small waist. A soft breeze ruffled her hair and teased her skirt even higher. She wasn't dressed to kill or painted with the latest cosmetics, yet she looked every bit as desirable as any model. She was real. Daughter of the earth. Mother Nature's finest work. If Eve had looked half as good, it was no wonder Adam had eaten that apple.

Tack bit into the peach he'd picked a few yards back near the creek, but he didn't taste the succulent fruit. He tasted her the way she'd been last night. Warm and sweet and so damn addicting...

A blast from the past.

A herd of horses couldn't have stopped him from crossing the distance to her, from getting an up-close-and-personal view of Miss Annie Divine. Maybe being back in Inspiration wouldn't be as awful as he'd predicted. There was one bright spot to this town. There always had been. Annie.

CHAPTER THREE

"I NEVER KNEW YOU WERE a love-'em-and-leave-'em kind of girl." The deep voice startled Annie out of her inspection of a patch of bluebonnets. She whirled, fist flying through the air in a self-defense move her mother had taught her. Her hand connected with a rock-hard chest.

"Ouch!" A large, tanned hand rubbed the spot where she'd made contact. "Was I that bad last night?"

"Tack?" Her gaze swiveled up to see the man who'd crept up on her.

"In the flesh—ow!" He flinched as she punched him again. "I must've really stunk."

"That wasn't for last night. It was for sneaking up on me." She cradled her aching hand while her heart pounded at breakneck speed. "What are you doing out here?"

"The question, honey, is what are *you* doing out here?" he asked, biting into a half-eaten peach.

As his mouth worked at the sweet pulp, a trail of juice ran down his chin and she had the incredible urge to reach out, catch the drop and touch it to her own lips. Crazy. Touching him would be a mistake. Loving him last night had been an even worse mistake, but it was a sad truth she couldn't change. Better to forget and concentrate on today. Now. This moment.

Him.

Dark blue eyes caught and held hers, and she barely resisted the urge to turn and run. To avoid him and to avoid dealing with what had happened between them.

But Annie Divine didn't run. No matter how much she wanted to. She steeled her resolve and busied herself snapping a few pictures of a nearby cluster of daisies.

"You're a long way from Rose Street," he added.

"There isn't much to look at over there." Nothing but a big, run-down house and a neglected garden, neither of which she'd ever had the time to fix up. But that had changed. Cooper Brandon was dead now, Annie's debt was paid, her promise kept. Now she could get on with living.

She turned away from Tack and glanced at the surrounding landscape. "I come out here every once in a while. It's better when it's misty or foggy. Wildflowers photograph best in a subdued light, but early morning can lend itself to some good shots."

He motioned to her camera. "I figured you would have turned that into a career by now."

"I have. I'm a reporter for the *Inspiration In Touch*. I cover stories and do my own pictures."

"I wasn't talking about here. I thought maybe you'd gone big time. Houston, Dallas, maybe even out of state."

"Plans change. My mama got sick right after you left and so I stayed to take care of her."

"I heard she died. I'm sorry."

She met his gaze. "You never liked her."

"True enough, but I'm still sorry. Sorry for you."

"And I'm sorry for you. You missed a beautiful funeral yesterday."

He shrugged, his expression closing, and she knew she'd touched a subject better left alone. "So you like this place, huh?" he went on, as if eager to move to a safer topic.

She cast a sweeping glance around her and a sad smile curved her lips. "It holds a certain charm."

Blue eyes twinkled in the sunlight. "Last time I looked, you weren't too fond of Brandon land."

"It's been a long time since you looked."

He stared at her for a drawn-out moment. Insects buzzed, birds chirped and her heart double-thumped. A gleam lit his eyes. "I'd say too long, judging by last night." He pitched what was left of the fruit and rubbed his hands together. "You hightailed it out pretty early this morning. I didn't even have a chance to say hello."

"I'm not much for conversation." She did her best to ignore the whirlwind rushing through her. The regret. The elation. The despair. The joy. It was a volatile mix, one that threatened to send tears streaming down her face.

But not in front of Tack. That's where her mother had made her mistake. She'd let Cooper Brandon see what she felt for him. By pouring out her love, she'd fortified the hold he already had over her. Annie refused to do the same, to wear her emotions on her sleeve. It was better to keep them buried, to stay in control.

Not that she *loved* him. Not now. Not ever again.

"We could have skipped the pillow talk then," he went on. "And said hello another way." He reached out, his fingertip skimming her cheek. Electricity sizzled along her nerve endings.

Eager for a distraction, she turned away and studied the landscape as if she were searching for just the right amount of light and shadow to add texture to her next photograph. "I had to get home and I didn't see any point in waking you. You really tied one on last night. I'm..." She swallowed. "I'm surprised you even remembered what we...what happened."

"I remember, all right." His voice, so deep and smooth, slid into her ears and made her insides quiver. "You and me, together. What I don't remember is how we ended up—" his hand closed over her shoulder and forced her to face him "—*together.*"

"You were drunk and Bobby Jack thought it was better if you didn't drive home. He asked me to give you a ride."

A slow, wicked smile spread across his face.

"Not that kind of a ride. A lift back to your motel."

His smile widened. "Then the ride."

She frowned. "Haven't your hormones calmed down since the twelfth grade?"

"I thought so," he said seriously, "until last night." He grinned and gave her a wink. "But then, you always did get me hot and bothered, honey."

His words stirred so many old memories. Quick kisses beneath the bleachers after a Friday-night football game. Endless necking sessions in the bed of his daddy's pickup. Midnight swims down by the lake.

Despite her determination to stay cool and aloof and unaffected, a smile tugged at her lips. "You were forever trying to get into my pants."

"And last night you seduced me right out of mine."

"*I* seduced *you?*"

"You undressed me. I don't remember much, but I distinctly remember looking down and seeing you unzip my pants. *Feeling* you unzip them."

"The material was soaking-wet and the air conditioner was stuck. If I'd have left you in those damp things, you would have come down with pneumonia." She reached into the camera bag at her feet and pulled out a zoom-lens attachment. *Stay busy,* she told herself. *Then you won't have to look at him.* "And don't call me honey."

"A convenient excuse, and I like calling you honey." Before she could stop him, he slipped one strong arm around her waist and pulled her close. The lens attachment sailed to the soft grass and the camera sagged against its strap. Tack leaned down, his lips skimming the side of her neck as he took a whiff. "Because you smell so sweet."

She managed to get one hand between them and push him away, a halfhearted gesture that did little to ease the thunder of her heart. "I'd appreciate it if you didn't ruin my camera equipment."

He glanced at the piece lying in the grass. "If it's broken, I'll buy you a new one."

"That's not the point."

"Then what is the point?"

"That you've got your arm around me when I don't want it around me."

He pulled her closer and the camera jabbed into her stomach, just an inch above the spot where a very prominent part of his anatomy was doing some jabbing of its own.

"I didn't see you putting up a fuss last night."

"That was then." She tried to keep her voice from sounding as breathless as she suddenly felt. "This is now."

His eyes glittered. "Not up to ripping my clothes off and taking advantage of me again?"

"You can think what you want about last night, but I did have noble intentions. At first, anyway." She shook her head and stared at a point just over his shoulder, anywhere to keep from looking into his eyes, from losing herself in them the way she'd lost herself less than ten hours ago. After all these years, he still set the butterflies loose in her stomach. She stiffened and fought back the feeling. "Could you please let me go?"

Catching her chin, he urged her to meet his gaze. He stared at her long and hard, as if trying to see inside. "You know, I could always tell what you were thinking, Annie. Always. Everything was always right there in your eyes, on your face."

"And now?"

"It's different." He released her with a puzzled shake of his head. "You're different."

"Ten years is a long time." She turned away from him. "People change." She snatched up the zoom attachment, walked a few feet away and tried to concentrate on attaching the new lens to her camera. "If you don't mind, I came out here for some quiet time." *Go away, go away, go away,* she silently begged.

"We need to talk." He came up behind her.

She inched forward. "About what?"

"About last night."

"What about it?"

"We slept together."

"And?"

"And—" he sounded exasperated "—we *slept* together."

She aimed her camera and zoomed in on a vibrant-looking daisy. "And?"

"Dammit, Annie." His hand closed over her upper arm and pulled her back around to face him. "There are things we need to talk about."

"Like what?"

"Like what's bothering you."

She had to hand it to him. He looked genuinely concerned. For the space of a heartbeat, she wanted to throw her arms around him and tell him how mixed-up she felt. That she was glad he was home, and sad at the same time. That last night had been wonderful, yet heartbreaking. That she wanted him to stay almost as much as she wanted him to leave.

"Nothing's bothering me," she managed to say in her most nonchalant voice.

"Then how do you feel?"

"Fine. I was sneezing a few days ago, but the reason for it turned out to be a high pollen count in the air."

"That's not what I'm talking about." He ran a frustrated hand through his hair. "How do you feel about what we...*did* last night?"

"We had sex."

"Jesus, Annie." He threw up his hands. "I think it was a little more than that. This is you and me we're talking about. We have a history. We were friends. I was your first."

"Okay, it was great sex. Nostalgic sex. Making-up-for-lost-time sex. It was still just sex."

"Sex?" He gave her an incredulous look.

"As in two people satisfying mutual urges. I was needy, you were needy, we happened to be needy at the same time."

"That's really all it was to you?"

"Why are you making a big deal out of this?"

"Because it *is* a big deal."

"Why?"

"Because…" He seemed to grapple for words. "Because there…there are consequences."

"Like what?"

"Like…" He gave her a stern look. "Like you could be pregnant for one."

"I'm on the Pill." Instead of looking relieved, he simply stared at her as if she'd just grown an eye in the middle of her forehead. "Geez, Tack, don't look so shocked. A lot of women take birth control pills."

"We're not talking about a lot of women, we're talking about you. *You,* the girl who nearly had a fit when I suggested it that time before we…got together. No way, you said. You were convinced everybody would think you were loose like—"

"My mother," she finished for him. "That was then," she repeated, "and this is now. I'm not an ignorant teenager anymore. I'm twenty-eight years old." And irregular, she added silently. And that was the only reason she'd gone on the Pill even though her best friend and editor, Deb, had hooted and hollered that now was the time for Annie to start having some fun. "And I take responsibility for myself. There's no need for you to worry about any little surprises popping out in nine months." She pulled the camera from around her neck and packed it away in her bag. "I really need to get going."

"We're not finished." His fingers closed around her wrist.

She pulled her hand free, zipped up her camera bag and glared at him. "You're making an awful big deal about this. There's no chance I'm pregnant, so what's the problem?" Understanding dawned a heartbeat later and her mouth dropped open. "You're not trying to tell me... Oh, no! I can't believe I'm so stupid. Stupid, stupid, *stupid*."

"What are you talking about?"

She turned an accusing stare on him. "You have some sort of communicable disease, don't you? That's what this interrogation is all about. You're trying to find a way to tell me you contracted some deadly disease and now my insides are going to shrivel up and fall out and—"

"Hold on a second. For the record, I just had my yearly physical last week, including a blood test, and I'm as healthy as a racehorse." At her obvious skepticism, he added, "Despite my enthusiasm last night, I'm not in the habit of picking up women. And whenever I am with a woman, I use a condom. And I have a clean bill of health from the best damn team doctor in L.A. to prove it."

"Well—" she took a deep breath and tried to calm her panicked nerves "—that's a relief."

"Not completely." He folded his arms. "Since we're cleaning out closets, is there anything I should know about? I don't want anything shriveling up and falling off either."

"Because of me?" She bristled. "I certainly don't have any sort of disease."

"And what about your past partners?"

Past partners? As if she had any. She shook her head. "Nothing to worry about there."

He didn't seem convinced. "How many have you had?"

"Why does it matter?"

"Because I don't like playing Russian roulette."

"You weren't very concerned last night."

"I was barely conscious last night—" His words died as his gaze dropped to her hand. Relief smoothed his suddenly tense expression. "At least you're not married."

She erupted then. "Of course I'm not married! Geez, do you think I would have slept with you if I were?" She poked a finger at his chest. "What kind of person do you think I am?"

Like your mother. He didn't have to say the words. She knew what he was thinking, what everyone was always thinking. The trouble was, it didn't hurt with everyone else. She'd stopped caring about what the people of Inspiration thought a long time ago, with the exception of the few she called friends. But Tack...

"Look, Annie, I didn't mean—" The honk of a horn drowned out the rest of his words. Both Annie and Tack turned just as a Jeep topped the horizon and plowed across the pasture headed straight for them.

"I'd just about given up on you, boy." Gary Tucker shouted to Tack as he brought the vehicle to a jarring

halt and killed the engine. Clad in jeans, a chambray
work shirt and faded cowboy boots, the man looked
more like a ranch hand than an attorney. "Would have,
but then one of the boys said he passed by the road over
yonder and saw you out here talking to Annie. Come
on." He lifted his cowboy hat to brush back his gray
hair. "I'll give you two a lift."

"What do you say, honey? Can we drop you
someplace?"

"Actually—" she met his stare "—I was headed your
way."

Tack's forehead wrinkled in a frown. "The house?
Why?"

"For the reading of the will," Gary interjected. "Coop
left specific instructions that he wanted Annie there."

Tack's attention shifted from Gary to Annie, and his
blue eyes narrowed. "Why would my father want you
at the reading of his will? Last I knew, you didn't like
him, he didn't like you."

She shrugged, despite the sudden pounding of her
heart. "We got to know each other these past few
years."

"You and my father?"

"Turned out to be pretty good friends," Gary said,
climbing from the seat of the Jeep.

"You and my father?" Tack repeated, as if the words
wouldn't register in his brain. "But you always hated
him."

"Half the county did." Gary slid a protective arm
around Annie's shoulder. "But Annie changed that,
didn't you, gal? Softened that old hellion right up."

"*You* and my *father?*" he said, the words more

accusation than question as anger chased shock across his handsome features.

She summoned her courage and met his murderous glare. "I never actually hated him, Tack. I never really knew him. Once I took the time, I realized he was a good man."

"I'll just bet he was good." Blue eyes drilled into hers and she came this close to taking a step back. "What I want to know, honey, is just how good he was. And more importantly, was he better than last night?"

CHAPTER FOUR

ANNIE FIXED HER GAZE ON the sprawling ranch house just up ahead and tried to ignore the man seated directly behind her.

Was he better than last night? Her face still burned from the question. Not because he'd asked right in front of Gary. The attorney was too much of a gentleman to even acknowledge the question. He'd simply started toward the Jeep as if Tack hadn't said anything out of the ordinary. She wasn't embarrassed. No, she was mad at herself for not telling Tack right away that she was doing more out this way than simply taking pictures.

She chanced a peek in the side mirror and saw him staring back at her. *Traitor,* his gaze seemed to say, and she couldn't blame him. He was right. While she'd never slept with Cooper Brandon, she had befriended him. She'd given up her anger and her principles to embrace a man she'd never held anything but contempt for, and she'd done it willingly.

Look out for him, Annie. Don't let him hurt alone. It had been her mother's dying plea, and Annie's last promise.

She'd approached Cooper after her mother's funeral, to set aside her resentment and offer thanks that he'd come, that he'd sent vanload after vanload of fresh daisies—her mother's favorite. It had been little more than an automatic response, a proper display of politeness. But it had turned on her. She'd touched his arm and he'd faced her, his usually hard eyes shining with remorse, guilt, affection. At that moment, Annie had actually softened toward Cooper. Over the next few years, she'd even started to understand him.

She felt Tack's gaze in the mirror, but she refused to look. It didn't matter what he thought of her. She didn't owe him the time of day, much less an ounce of loyalty, an explanation or an apology. She'd befriended his father and too bad if he didn't approve. She didn't have to justify herself to him.

Despite what they'd shared ten years ago.

And last night.

It shouldn't have happened. No matter how right it had felt, how wonderful. They were too different. Just as his father and her mother had been worlds apart, wrong for each other because of where they came from and where they were going, so were Annie and Tack.

Annie was Wild Cherry Divine's daughter. Tack would never forgive her for that. Or more importantly, for the fact that she no longer wanted his forgiveness. She was who she was. No longer ashamed. Or regretful. And she wasn't falling in love with him again.

Unfortunately, she was all too aware of his proximity. With each passing moment, her breaths grew shallow. Her heartbeat stampeded like a team of frightened horses, particularly when the Jeep hit a nasty rut in the road. The truck lurched and Tack's hand closed over the edge of the seat just a fraction shy of touching Annie's shoulder.

"...the house hasn't changed much."

Gary's voice pushed past the pounding in her ears and she focused on the words, intent on gathering her control and ignoring Tack. Mind over matter, she told herself. *Your mind over his matter.*

"Coop did have the foreman's house remodeled for Eli and his wife," Gary went on.

"Eli's *married?*" Tack shook his head in disbelief. "The same Eli who's been cowboying for my father since he was fifteen? The same Eli who used to brand those little x's into the side of the bunkhouse for every woman he talked into bed?"

Gary chuckled. "Kept track for more than twenty years. A few more brands and the wall would have dissolved in a heap of ashes."

"I never figured him for the marrying kind."

"Got himself a couple of kids, too. Twin boys, 'round seven or eight, and a baby on the way. Wife's name is Vera."

"Vera Marley? The preacher's daughter? But she hated Eli."

"That's what everybody thought," Annie said, praying she didn't sound as breathless as she felt. But she needed to talk, to do something besides feel the way Tack's deep voice, his presence, affected her. "I think Vera and Eli were more shocked than anybody. One minute they were fighting. The next thing you know, Eli kisses Vera, she kisses him, and the war was over."

"That was on Friday," Gary added. "Went on their first date Saturday night, got engaged Sunday, much to her daddy's upset, married at the judge's office on Monday and been together nine years now."

"Nine years. Talk about luck." Tack's voice sent a

waterfall of heat cascading down Annie's spine. Her nipples tingled, her thighs burned, and she remembered his words the night before. *Best luck I've had in a hell of a long time.*

"Not luck," Annie replied before she could stop herself. "Love. There's a big difference."

"HE DID *WHAT*?" The question echoed off the walls of Cooper Brandon's study. Tack bolted from a brown leather chair to tower over his father's desk, where Gary sat reading the man's last will and testament.

The attorney slipped off his glasses and met Tack's stare. "He left that stretch of wildflowers that borders the south road to Annie. An acre and a half, to be exact. The rest, as you've been told, goes to you."

"I don't believe it." Tack tried to digest the news while Annie barely resisted the urge to jump from her seat and shout for joy. Coop had given her more than an acre of land, or more importantly, *the* acre and a half of land.

"He gave away Brandon land? My father handed over some of his precious ranch? That's crazy. He would never let any of it fall into outside hands. When Clem and his wife moved into that old deserted cabin down by the river after their place burned, he called the sheriff and had them thrown off. *Thrown off,* for Christ's sake. They didn't have anyplace to go, not a penny to their name, but he didn't care. They weren't Brandons, and this is Brandon land, he said. He wouldn't give one square inch away." His gaze strayed to the portrait of Cooper Brandon, looking so serious and stiff, on the far wall. Tack just stared, long and hard, the muscles in one jaw working as if he wanted to rip the thing from its mount. "He couldn't have been in his right mind."

Annie didn't miss the strange light in his eyes, the turmoil, and she barely resisted the urge to reach out. Instead, she curled her fingers into the rich leather of the armchair where she sat.

"He was lucid, all right," the attorney went on. "Sane right up until he shut his eyes for good, and this was one thing he insisted on. He wanted to make things right."

"My point exactly," Tack said angrily. "Cooper Brandon didn't go around doing the right thing. He did what was most lucrative for this ranch, and giving away land isn't very lucrative." He turned to Annie. "Why?"

Her gaze met his. "Because that land means something to me."

"Why?" he persisted. He smiled, but there was nothing friendly about his eyes. Something dangerous, maybe. Very dangerous. "You and my old man have fond memories of the place?"

"Something like that."

Tack's expression drew tight as images filled his mind. Annie talking with his father, laughing and smiling and...

Anger rushed through him like flame eating up a fuse.

"The two of you have romantic picnics out there?" he pressed. "Go stargazing? Have a little roll in the wildflowers?" He saw a glimmer of pain in her eyes, then it vanished and there was no indication his words had affected her.

She didn't show a damn thing, but he knew she hurt,

because he hurt. Saying it, thinking it, feeling it. Christ! Annie and his *fath*—

A pounding on the front door echoed through the house and shattered the dangerous thought.

"Tack Brandon!" came Effie Coletrain's muffled shout from outside, followed by several frantic barks. "You get on out here and get this mangy mutt that ripped apart my motel room!"

"I really need to get going." Annie stuffed the deed Gary handed her into her camera bag. "Thanks for everything, Gary."

"Tell me, Annie." Tack's voice followed her to the door. He needed to hear the truth from her, to wipe away the niggling doubts, the confusion. "What could mean so much that Coop Brandon would give up a piece of his precious land? *What?*"

"My mother," came her calm, cool voice as she paused in the doorway. "She's buried there."

"IT'S SATURDAY." Deb Strickland, the editor of the town's only newspaper, stood across the room, coffeepot in one hand, ceramic mug in the other, and gave Annie an accusing stare. "What are you doing here?"

"I usually work Saturdays." Annie set her camera bag on her desk and turned on her computer.

"I know, but the funeral was yesterday." Deb finished pouring and headed for Annie.

Dressed in a red silk blouse, matching skirt and three-inch stiletto heels, the brunette looked as if she should be walking a runway rather than cracked linoleum. She sipped steaming black coffee from a mug that read 100ASCII 228 Bitch and eyed Annie. "I thought you might want the day off."

"I haven't taken a day off in over three years."

"My point exactly. You're due."

"I'm all right, Deb." Or she would be once she settled down at her desk and put the morning behind her. *Distance.*

"I know I probably seemed like a real witch because I didn't go to the funeral, but ever since my granny died, anything involving cemeteries really creeps me out. Just because I wasn't there for you yesterday, though, doesn't mean I'm not here for you now. Take the day off or cry on my shoulder, or whatever you feel like doing."

"Coop and I were friends and I'll miss him, but he's gone. I just want to have a normal day. Business as usual, okay?"

"Are you sure?" Deb gave her a searching glance. At Annie's nod, she finally shrugged. "If that's what you want." The expression of sympathy on her face faded into her typical I'm-the-boss look as she glanced at her watch. "You're an hour late." She took another sip of coffee and headed for her desk.

Deb slid into the role of slave driver so easily, but it was more for show than anything else. The *Inspiration In Touch* was a typical small-town newspaper with only Deb, Annie and Wally Wilkins, a nineteen-year-old journalism major, on the payroll. The three of them were like family. They put out a weekly edition with a Friday deadline and a Sunday distribution. Deb took care of the advertising, edited and did a few columns, while Annie covered the news and took all the pictures, and Wally did his best to convince both women that he should be doing more than running copy or fixing the ancient printing press that was forever breaking down. They bickered, laughed and supported one another.

Deb and Wally were the only two things about Inspiration Annie knew she'd miss.

She opened her planner, as she did every Saturday morning, to go over her weekly schedule and get ready for a new edition. *Business as usual.*

She told herself that, but the tremble in her thighs, the ache between her legs, refused to be ignored.

Had she really slept with Tack?

Yes, and the trouble was, she wanted to do it again.

Not that she would. She might have been weak last night, seeing him in the flesh after all these years. She'd been in love with him, after all. Precisely the reason she wouldn't sleep with him again.

Annie wasn't going to risk falling in love all over again. Not the I'll-love-you-'til-my-dying-breath kind of love her mother had had for Cooper Brandon. Annie had watched the woman throw away so many hopes and dreams for a man, and she wasn't going to make the same mistake.

With Tack Brandon it would be all too easy. Ten years hadn't dulled his looks or his charm or the way he made her feel when he smiled. Warm and hungry and oblivious to everything except him.

That was the *real* trouble.

"Annie?" Deb's voice penetrated her thoughts. "You're not all right, are you? I'm sorry. I shouldn't have said anything about you being late, but I was just going through the motions—"

"It's not you."

"—because you know I completely understand your being late, I just thought you wanted me to act like my bitchy self—"

"It's not you. It's me."

"I knew it. You're upset about Coop."

"No. I'm just tired, that's all." Tired? Since when did she make excuses to Deb? Not only her editor, but her best friend? She didn't. Not anymore. Not since she'd promised herself never to let other people's opinions of her dictate who she was. Annie Divine had taken control of her own life, and she intended to keep it. "I had a late night because—" Her words faded into the shrill ring of the newspaper's hotline, a bright red phone that occupied the corner of Deb's desk.

"Hold that thought." Deb snatched up the line. "*Inspiration In Touch,* you're in touch with Deb." Seconds later, Deb slid the receiver into place, a knowing grin on her face. "You're tired because you picked up a cowboy."

"Says who?"

"Effie Coletrain just informed me that Tack Brandon, *the* Tack Brandon, Supercross superstar and the long lost son of Cooper Brandon, rolled back into town yesterday. Good sources have it that he rolled straight to BJ's, got rip-roaring drunk and you gave him a lift back to his motel *and* went inside. And didn't leave until much, much later." At Annie's incredulous stare, Deb shrugged. "Hazards of living in a small town. Gossip spreads like wildfire." A gleam lit her eyes and she clapped her hands. "I don't believe it. Goody-goody Annie finally got down and dirty with a lean, mean, cow-punching machine!"

She fought back the sudden pounding of her heart and gathered her composure. "I am not a goody-goody."

"Trust me, you're about as goody-goody as they get—I don't care what folks used to say about your mama." Deb perched on the edge of Annie's desk, took a sip of coffee and beamed. "I thought you looked different this morning. Your cheeks are flushed."

"That's because my air conditioner went out last night and I spent the morning in hell." Then, of course, she'd met up with the devil when she'd been taking a few early-morning pictures.

"Effie said you two were an item once."

"Effie talks too much."

"So she lied?"

Annie shrugged. "We went out a few times."

"As in, let's do homework together or let's get naked in the back seat?"

"As in, I had a crush on him throughout high school and he rarely glanced my way. One night, after our senior homecoming game, he offered to give me a lift home. He was always doing things like that, always helping people. He used to carry Pattie Mitchell's tuba every day. Fatty Pattie—that's what the boys called her—was so shy. She never smiled, but Tack always took the time to coax one out of her and tote that tuba to the Band Hall. He used to help old Mrs. Witherspoon down the aisle at church, too. She had a walker and a hip replacement. The other kids would make fun of her, but not Tack. He'd been so determined to accept people for who they were, to see beyond looks, wealth, power, the way his father never had. To be different from the bastard Coop had been back then."

"Sounds like a saint."

"Sometimes." And at other times, he'd been every bit the sinner, with his wicked grins and his sweet, intoxicating kisses.

"Annie?"

"Um, yeah?"

"You were saying?"

Annie forced the image of Tack away and cleared her throat. "I, um, thought he was just being nice."

"But he secretly lusted after you?"

"Not at first. But once we talked and got to know each other—"

"Then he lusted after you."

"Sort of." At Deb's get-real look, Annie added, "Okay, so he lusted after me."

"And you lusted after him."

"Yes," Annie admitted. "We went out several times and became a couple until our senior prom. His mother had a car accident late that night. We spent half the night pacing the emergency room, waiting for the doctors to do what they could, and waiting for Tack's father to show up."

"Where was he?"

"With my mother. He didn't get word and make it to the hospital until ten minutes after they'd pronounced Tack's mother dead. He and Coop got into a fight and he left." Annie shook her head. She could still smell the disinfectant, feel the cold floor seeping up through the soles of her shoes as she'd sat there and watched him storm away without so much as a backward glance. Her heart had hurt so bad. Not for herself, for her own loss, but for his.

That's the way it had always been with Tack. She found herself so caught up in the sight and sound and feel of him that her own needs fell by the wayside.

"He left you? Just like that?"

"We weren't exactly married." While Annie knew he'd cared for her, she'd never had any illusions about Tack Brandon loving her the way she'd loved him. When he left, she'd hurt, but she'd also understood, and later, she'd been grateful for the hard lesson learned. "We were kids. He did what he had to do under the circumstances. End of story."

Deb gave her a searching glance. "Sounds like you guys started working on a sequel last night."

Annie averted her gaze and searched through her drawer for a computer disk. "Last night was just overactive hormones. It was bound to happen. You said so yourself, if I kept going home alone, my hormones were going to erupt one day and I'd find myself grabbing a little gusto with the first cowboy I could find. Well, I went into hormone overload and Tack just happened to be there."

"You're not still carrying a torch for this guy, are you?"

"Of course not." She retrieved the disk and turned to rearranging some of her notes. "Why is everybody making such a big deal out of this? It was only sex. It's the nineties. I'm a healthy woman. I'm entitled to a little fun."

"*Fun* being the operative word. You should be smiling right now, honey—" Her words faded into another shrill ring of the hotline.

A few seconds later, Deb turned to Annie.

"Don't tell me. Another update on my sex life."

"No, though I'd be glad to hear it because I think you're holding back. It was Tess Johnson. Shotzi just had her litter."

"Shotzi?"

"Tess's prizewinning pig, the one that took first place at the FFA championships in Dallas last spring. She just had the largest recorded litter in Texas in fifty years. I'd do this one myself, but I've got an interview for the This Is Your Neighbor column, then a manicure at the beauty salon."

A pig? "Remind me again why you left the *Dallas Star?*"

"Because my father owns the *Star,* and everybody who works for him." Deb grabbed her briefcase and purse. "That's why I took the money my granny left me when she passed on and reinvested it in this place. It's small, but it's mine, and it does have its advantages. You don't have to go neck and neck with some ruthless colleagues to get the best stories."

"You're right. I'd hate to have to worry about someone stealing the Johnson-pig exclusive right out from under me. Why don't you send Wally?"

"He's not ready."

"Who's not ready?" Wally, his shoulder-length blond hair pulled back in a ponytail, spectacles perched low on his nose, crested the back staircase and walked into the office. Black newsprint covered his hands and forearms. "I've got two years at the local community college and I'm ready for anything."

"In time, grasshopper." Deb did her best *Kung Fu* imitation, and Wally frowned.

"Discrimination." He leaned down and started rummaging in a cabinet. "That's what this is. Give the guy all the manual labor, make him fight with a dadblastit press that keeps spraying ink everywhere." He paused to pull out a bottle of cleaning solution. "And save the good stuff for yourselves."

"Good stuff?" Annie shook her head. "As in pigs? Yeah, right, Wally."

"Come on, Annie," Deb said. "I bet they're cute."

"I'm sure they are, but after covering that baby raccoon stuck up in Mr. Miller's tree last year, I promised myself no more animal exclusives."

"That was a great story."

"The raccoon attacked me."

"He was just a little scared of the flash."

"He went berserk. I had to have a rabies shot at the hospital over in Georgetown."

"She gets to have all the fun," Wally grumbled as he yanked open another cabinet and launched into a search for extra rags.

"How long do those rabies things last?" Deb asked.

"A few years."

"So you're all set in case the pigs decide to gang up on you." Deb gulped the last of her coffee. "Gotta go or I'll be late for my interview." She paused in the doorway. "So is Tack Brandon really as cute as Effie Coletrain said?"

Annie stuffed a notebook into her purse. "How many pigs did you say Shotzi had?"

"Come on, Annie. I'm not from around here, remember? Give me a hint. Blond or brunette?"

"And it's the biggest recorded litter, you say?"

"The biggest?" Wally slammed the cabinet shut. "Aw, man, she gets all the breaks." He stomped back down the stairs.

"Bulky or lean in the muscle department?" Deb smiled and resumed her line of questioning.

Annie grabbed two extra rolls of film from her top desk drawer and stuffed them in her case. "I'll check with the *Farmer's Almanac* and the state FFA group just to get my facts straight. They keep track of all those things."

"You know, Annie, it's all right to let your hair down once in a while, despite what all those old biddies down at the bingo hall might say. You should call up your cowboy and go for round two. Use it before you lose it, honey," Deb said before she closed the door behind her.

If only it were that simple.

But Tack Brandon wasn't just some cowboy Annie had picked up to satisfy her needs as she'd said. He was *the* cowboy. With bedroom eyes and a heart-thumping smile that made her think beyond long nights filled with mind-blowing sex. To weddings and babies and happily-ever-afters.

A man she could fall in love with all over again if she gave herself the chance.

Which she wasn't about to do.

She had a future that didn't include him. She longed for front-page stories and bigger bylines, and now that her promise to her mother had been fulfilled, she could make her dreams come true. She would. Yesterday, after she'd said goodbye to Coop, she'd stopped at the post office and mailed off résumés and tear sheets—page samples of her work—to the editors of the top five newspapers on her Top Twenty list, with Deb's full support. Meanwhile, Annie would seize every opportunity to beef up her portfolio.

Or in this case, pork it up.

Grabbing her camera equipment and purse, she headed downstairs. Today was the first day of the rest of Annie Divine's life, and she intended to make the most of it.

CHAPTER FIVE

"My life stinks." Annie stared down at her soiled dress later that afternoon and grimaced.

"I've got news for you, girlfriend. It isn't your life. It's you." Annie glared and Deb smiled. "Fieldwork is tough. Think of this as training."

That's exactly what she'd been thinking as she'd fled *sixteen* squealing piglets, only half the litter, and run straight into a mud puddle. She sniffed. At least she'd thought it was mud.

"You should have sent me." Wally sat at a nearby desk compiling ads for next week's edition. "I raised two pigs in high school and I know what makes them oink. But does anybody listen? Heck, no."

Deb ignored Wally and turned back to Annie. "I guess you're not up for drinks at BJ's."

Annie leaned down to tug off her mud-covered sandals. "The only thing I'm up for is a nice, long soak in a hot bath."

"Now that sounds like the best idea I've heard all day." The deep voice rumbled up and down Annie's spine and she froze in place.

Then her head snapped up and she found herself staring at jean-covered hips. She straightened, and her attention shifted slowly upward to drink in the man who stood in the doorway. Her gaze roamed over a trim waist, a crisp white T-shirt stretched over a broad chest, to a stubbled jaw, before colliding with twinkling blue eyes, as blue as a rain-washed sky. The air snagged in her chest.

"You must be Tack Brandon," Deb said.

"Tack?" Wally pushed his glasses up to take a good look. "Well, bust my behind, you *are* him! *The* Tack Brandon. The motocross racer."

Tack winked and stopped in front of Annie's desk. "The last time I looked."

"What are you doing here?" Annie blurted, all too aware of Deb's smile and Wally's curious expression.

"You forgot something." He pulled a white pair of panties dotted with tiny peaches from his pocket.

Annie's heart stopped beating, Wally chuckled and Deb barely caught a giggle as Tack dangled the skimpy silk from one tanned finger.

"I, um, we really have to get going." Deb motioned for Wally. "I'm dead tired and it's way past Wally's bed-time." Before Annie could blink, Deb hauled Wally from his desk and they both disappeared into the darkened stairwell.

"I thought you might need these." Tack rubbed the silky material between his two fingers in a sensuous caress she felt from her head, clear to the tips of her toes, even though he wasn't touching her.

Ah, but he had. That was the trouble. That had always been the trouble. One touch made her want another. And another.

Heat uncoiled in her stomach, along with a slow burning anger that spread through her. She came so close to snatching the panties from his hand, but she wasn't about to give him the satisfaction of knowing she was the least bit affected by him.

Calm, cool, indifferent. The silent mantra echoed in her head and she shrugged. "Thanks for the gesture, but I'm wearing new ones."

"Then I'll just keep these." He stuffed them into his shirt pocket and perched on the corner of her desk. "So this is where you work?"

"It isn't the *Times,* but a girl has to start somewhere." Her gaze narrowed. "Is that why you came? To see where I work?"

"Actually—" his voice took on a softer note and she read the regret in his eyes "—I wanted to say I'm sorry about today, about the things I said. Gary told me you and Coop were just friends, and I had no call to act like such a jerk—"

"A slime bucket," she cut in.

"A creep," he conceded.

"A bast—"

"Ouch, Annie," he interjected. "You sure know how to hurt a guy." His grin dissolved into a serious expression. "But I know I deserve it. I was way out of line. It's just the thought of you and him and… It made me a little crazy."

"I didn't sleep with him, but I was still his friend. No more, but no less."

"Because your mother asked you to," he pointed out.

"And that makes a difference?"

"It shouldn't, should it?" He raked tense fingers through his dark hair. "But it does. I'm not thrilled with the idea of you and him being friends—I can't quite understand it—but I'm not mad. I'm just sorry for drilling you about the land the way I did." His sensuous lips curved in a teasing grin. "Sorry for being a jerk/slime bucket/creep/bastard."

"Apology accepted." A smile tugged at her lips despite her best efforts to remain aloof.

Indifferent.

"So you forgive me?"

She eyed him a long moment and saw the sincerity in the blue depths of his gaze. "Maybe."

"I was hoping for a yes."

"It's the closest you're going to get."

"I'll take it." He winked. "And since you're being so charitable, how about doing a job for me? I need somebody to take pictures of the ranch so prospective buyers can see what they're getting."

Buyers. As in…

"You're *selling?*" He nodded and Annie's stomach went hollow. "But that ranch has been in your family for years," she pointed out. "Your father lived and breathed that place. Your mother, too. It's part of them. They're a part of it."

"But I'm not." He shook his head. "Hell, Annie, I never was. I pretended for a long time, but it's just not in my blood. I know my mother would want it to stay in the hands of a rancher who would love it the way she did. I can't. I never could."

"When?" she asked, tamping down the strange ache the notion stirred. Selling was good. *Great.* No Tack, no temptation, no falling in love.

"A month or so to circulate a sales package and find a prospective buyer, a cattleman—the Big B is a ranch and it'll stay that way. Every hand stays on as part of the sale, for the next year anyway. I want the cowboys to have a chance to prove themselves to a new boss."

A strange sense of admiration crept through her. For all his bitterness, Tack had grown into a fair and decent man. Just like the fair and decent boy who'd helped old Mrs. Witherspoon down the aisle in church every Sunday.

She forced the feeling aside and asked, "In the meantime?"

"I'll be staying at the ranch until it's sold. Eli isn't used to running things on his own."

"What about your racing?"

"I'm not due in L.A. for another six weeks. I'll bring in some bikes, do laps out in one of the unused pastures in the morning and oversee the ranch during the day."

"Sounds like you have everything figured out."

"Almost everything." His blue gaze pinned her to her chair. "So much has changed." *You*, his eyes seemed to say.

She shrugged. "You can't expect time to stand still, even in Inspiration. We've got cable television, and Mabel at the beauty shop had a tanning bed installed, and Mitch Freeman's running a computer-repair shop out of the back of his feed store."

"That's not what I was talking about."

"Effie Coletrain even put in a whirlpool spa over at the motel," she went on as if she hadn't heard him. "And Bobby Jack computerized the club's sound system. Then there's Jimmy Mission. He's been advertising his stud bull on-line." The last bit of information snagged his attention. Thankfully.

"Jimmy's here?"

"Been running the Mission Ranch for the past year."

"A rancher? *Jimmy?* The last I heard of him, he'd joined the air force and run off to play soldier boy."

"He did that." Her gaze collided with his. "And then he came home."

As if her words hit their mark, he averted her eyes. "So, are you interested in the job?"

She pushed a strand of muddy hair from her eyes. "I already have a job."

He slipped into the old bad-boy Tack with his heart-breaker smile. Devilish delight flashed in his eyes as he leaned over the desk to finger one soiled strap of her ruined dress. "Wrestling pigs? Honey," he drawled, his voice like warm syrup dripping over her favorite blueberry pancakes, "I always had higher aspirations for you."

She leaned back in her chair, away from the warm fingertips playing havoc with her sanity. "For your information," she managed to say, focusing on her irritation rather than the strange sensations stirring in her belly, "I've just covered a historic event. Largest recorded litter in Texas in fifty years."

"The pay's pretty good."

He placed an envelope on her desk, and Annie couldn't help herself. If, *when* a journalism job came through with one of her Top Twenty, she was sure to need extra cash to finance a move. "I can take the pictures at my leisure?"

"As long as I have the prints by close of business on Friday."

"I guess you've got yourself a deal then." He didn't budge, just stared around him and she asked, "Is there anything else?"

"Just looking." He got to his feet and studied the framed articles lining the wall. "Are these yours?"

She nodded, leaning her elbows on the desk, relaxed now that he wasn't stripping her bare with those bluer than blue eyes of his. "Our football team won the state championship last year. Deb's not into sports, so it falls to yours truly."

"These are good—better than good." He indicated a collection of pictures. His attention lingered on one in particular of a young boy walking off the field, the game ball in his hands, victory gleaming in his eyes.

"That was last year's quarterback. He was great. The best we've seen since you took us to a state championship."

His expression eased into a grin. "We had a good team our senior year."

"You pushed the other guys, made them think that a small-town team could really go up against the big-city boys." A smile played at her lips as she remembered the games. She'd stood on the sidelines so many times and watched him, the way he moved, smiled, frowned, yelled, *everything*. "You had a competitive streak even then."

Tack studied a few more pictures. "You're really talented, Annie." The way his gaze shifted to hers, touched her lips, her neck, and lower, she knew he wasn't just talking about her work.

She tried to ignore the sudden change in temperature. "I hope you're right. I'm a jack-of-all-trades here, but the bigger papers employ straight photographers, and that's what I'm after."

"A picture tells a thousand words, huh?" He held her gaze a few seconds more, blue eyes pushing deep, searching, before he turned his attention back to the photographs and gave Annie a chance to study him.

His dark hair and shadowed jaw lent him an air of danger. At the same time, the dimple that cut into one cheek when he smiled softened the edge and gave him a certain charm.

Charm?

She shook away the notion. Focus on his bad habits: his double dose of cockiness, his enormous ego, his rattle-her-nerves smile.

"If all your stuff is this good, you'll land a job soon." He leaned on the corner of her desk, hands resting easily on his thighs. He rubbed his open palms up and down the faded material. An innocent gesture, little more than a habit, but it caught Annie's attention.

She'd always loved his hands. Large and strong, yet oddly gentle. He'd been able to throw a football fifty yards, and pick wildflowers without losing a petal.

His palms continued to stroke up and down the material, the movement a sensual reminder of last night, of those same movements on her back, her buttocks, her belly...

So much for bad habits.

"Annie?"

She licked her lips and tore her gaze away. "Um, yes?"

"I asked how long you've been with the paper."

"Uh, all day." She glanced at her watch. "Speaking of which, I really need to get home."

"I meant, how many years."

"The six since my mother died. Before that, I took care of her and worked odd jobs while I went to school." She grabbed her purse and camera bag.

"We still have something else to talk about." He caught her wrist. The pads of his fingertips pressed against her thudding pulse and heat skittered along her nerve endings.

"Sex," she growled, her senses going into temporary overload. "S-E-X, Tack. Can't you get that through your head?"

"I was thinking more along the lines of a kiss." His hand went to the button of his jeans. A wicked, teasing light flashed in his eyes. "But if you'd rather give up the preliminary round and go straight to the main event—"

"No! Stop!" Her fingers closed over his before she could think better of it. Her thumb brushed the hard ridge straining beneath his jeans and she snatched her hand away as if she'd touched a live wire. "I—I thought you meant we should talk about last night."

"Last night was last night. I'm more interested in tonight. Right now." His gaze held her captive. "I was going to ask you for a kiss."

Her heart launched into overdrive. "No."

"I didn't ask yet."

"Well, I'm saving you the trouble." She took a deep breath. "No." Hell no. Please no. Oh no.

"Why?"

"Because." *Because one kiss might lead to two and two to three and...*

Calm, cool, indifferent.

She forced her gaze from his to glance at her watch, determined to ignore the sudden anticipation that rushed through her veins. "Because I'm late. I have to stop at the hardware store before they close and pick up the new paint for my house."

He eyed her. "Is that the only reason?"

She gave him an innocent look. "Why else?"

"Then this won't take long." His hands came up to cup her face and his lips closed over hers, firm and purposeful, before she had a chance to breathe, much less summon her defenses.

"Open up, honey, and let me in," he murmured against her mouth.

Her lips parted. He was just so close and so warm and he was touching her. Ah, he was touching her.

With firm, hungry lips that slanted so perfectly across her own. With a gently thrusting tongue that probed and stroked and tangled with hers. With strong fingers cradling her cheeks, tilting her face so he could deepen the kiss.

There was none of the old Tack in this kiss. None of the teasing, butterfly pecks a young boy had used to coax an uptight virgin out of her shell so long ago.

This was a man's kiss. Hot, wet and mind-blowing. Intimate. Powerful. *Possessive.*

Realization zapped her, a lightning bolt through the thick fog of desire that blinded her.

What the hell was she doing?

Letting him kiss her. Wanting him to kiss her. Kissing him back— *Oh no!*

She forced herself away and stumbled backward a few steps, gaining some blessed distance.

"That didn't take too long, now, did it?" The words were light, teasing, but there was none of it reflected in his gaze. Bright blue eyes lingered on her lips as if he fought the urge to kiss her again. And again.

"Long enough," she said shakily. *Too long.*

"You look a little unsteady, honey. You all right?"

"Fine," she choked out. Confused. Happy and sad and angry and joyful and—

Calm, cool, indifferent.

Annie gathered her composure, unwilling to let Tack know how deeply he affected her. "I'm *really* late." Her lips tingling, she snatched up her equipment and headed for the door, her steps practiced and sure, despite the pounding of her heart as she walked away.

What she should have done last night.

Breathless moments later, Annie climbed into her battered white Chevy pickup and shoved the keys in the ignition. Her gaze hooked on the sleek, black Harley parked across the street. The urge to climb on, feel the powerful machine vibrate beneath her, hit her hard and fast, and heat speared her body.

But it was nothing compared to the fire that flared, raged deep inside when she saw Tack exit the building, strut toward the motorcycle and straddle the seat. His eyes locked with hers and suddenly it wasn't the machine she wanted to feel beneath her, but him.

"No," she said, gunning the engine. It was one night, and now, one kiss. Annie would be damned if she'd let it turn into something more, if she'd find herself caught in the same trap that had kept her mother chained to a town she hated almost as much as it hated her.

One month, she told herself. Then he would be moving on, out of Annie's life forever.

Until then, she would simply concentrate on finding a new job and fixing up her house, and forget all about Tack Brandon and the fact that he still had her underpants tucked away in his pocket.

TACK SAT ON THE SIDE of the small twin bed and fingered the silky material. The scent of her filled his nostrils and he got all hot and bothered again. Not that he'd calmed down. Three hours kicking up dust and peeling down a maze of country back roads, and he'd still had a hard-on when he finally climbed off his bike and walked inside the ranch house.

Hell, he didn't even have to see her. Thinking about her was just as powerful, and as frustrating as hell. Because as badly as Tack wanted a repeat of last night, he wanted to know why she'd slept with him in the first place.

He didn't buy her initial story. Annie wasn't a *just sex* sort of girl, at least not the Annie he remembered. The Annie who'd blushed and trembled and hidden herself behind ugly sweatshirts and baggy pants.

But this Annie was different. She wore flattering sundresses, looked him straight in the eye and called him out when he damn well deserved it. Her skin was tanned a soft golden hue, and he hadn't once seen her tremble.

But he'd felt her tremble. Last night when she'd been in his arms and he'd been inside her.

Just sex didn't explain her tears, the whisper-soft, "It's been a long time." Nor did it explain the flash of fear in her eyes when he'd kissed her tonight, an expression so quick he would have missed it if he hadn't been paying attention.

But he'd always paid attention where Annie was concerned.

He remembered she'd fancied herself in love with him way back then, though she'd never said the words out loud. He also remembered that the prospect had scared the daylights out of him, and thrilled him at the same time.

Because he'd loved her?

No, but he had felt more for her than he'd ever felt for anyone before. Anyone since.

He'd gone through enough women over the years, prime, experienced, grade-A females, and not one of them had lingered on his mind, or on any other part of his anatomy. Not one.

Only this one.

"Thought you might need an extra blanket." The familiar voice drifted through the crack in the bedroom door, cutting short Tack's thoughts.

He glanced up just as a man entered, a blanket in one arm and a box under the other.

With a crew cut and a baby-smooth face, Eli Sutton looked a hell of a lot different from the long-haired, mustache-wearing wrangler Tack remembered. Eli had been so wild, reckless and carefree back then that Tack had barely noticed the man had fifteen years on him.

He noticed now.

While Eli didn't look a day over his forty-two years, he seemed...tamer. Settled.

Married.

Content.

Eli handed Tack the blanket. "Vera would have come herself—she's been wanting to get up here and say hello—but she don't get around so good with the baby so close to coming. She didn't know if you'd remember where the linens were kept."

"Second shelf, hall closet. A few things haven't changed." His gaze darted to the large shelf filled with sports trophies, from Little League to high school. A half-finished model airplane sat on the corner of a crowded dresser. In the eighth grade he'd started the model as a class project, but he'd never been able to sit still long enough to finish the wings, never been good at anything that kept him chained to a desk or chair. He'd done well in school, but it hadn't come from studying. He had a good memory and he caught on quick, and so he'd pulled in mostly A's and kept a GPA high enough to get him into his father's alma mater, Texas A & M.

The acceptance letter still sat framed on his desk.

"When Vera and I got married and she started cleaning up here, she had me talk to your daddy about packing some of this stuff up into boxes—it's hell to dust all of it—but he said no. Said he wanted a reminder of all you'd given up, all you'd left behind so he could keep on hating you."

Leave it to Eli to speak his mind. "And did he?" Tack asked.

"He tried. He'd come in here every night, but I finally

realized it wasn't 'cause he wanted a reminder of why he should hate you, he just wanted a reminder of you. That's why he collected all them videotapes."

He cast a sharp glance at the ranch foreman. "What videotapes?"

"Third shelf in the library. Recorded every one of your races ever televised. He missed you, Tack."

His heart pounded and his chest tightened before he could fight back the feeling, the hope. "He never picked up the phone."

"And neither did you."

But I came close. So close.

The clock ticked away a full minute as both men stood there. Finally, Eli seemed to remember something. He pulled the box from under his arm and handed it to Tack. "Me and the boys got you a little welcome-home present. Thought you could use it."

Tack opened the box and saw a straw Resistol sitting inside.

"It ain't the same one you used to wear, mind you—that thing died a long time ago. But it looks like it."

He couldn't help the grin that spread across his face. "I wore that hat every summer from the time I turned thirteen to the night I..." *Left.* The word caught in the sudden tightness in his throat and his mouth drew into a thin line. "Thanks, Eli, but I won't be needing it."

"I figured that. Rumor has it you're selling."

Tack put the hat back into the box. "Good news travels fast."

"It ain't such good news, but it don't come as much of a surprise. Bets had it that you wouldn't even make it home, much less stick around. Some boys lost a hell of a lot of money when you showed up."

"What about you?"

Eli grinned. "I made enough to buy Vera that cradle she's been wanting." When Tack tried to hand him back the hatbox, he shook his head. "You hold on to that. You never know when it might come in handy."

TACK REPLAYED THE conversation with Eli as he stripped off his shirt and stretched out on the bed.

No, he'd never called his father, but he'd thought about it. Thought about picking up the phone and calling to hear Coop's voice. Then he'd think about what his old man would say.

Ain't nothing more important than this land.
If you walk away, don't bother coming back.
You ain't welcome—
Stop it! The past was over and done with.
Forget. *Focus.*

He clamped his eyes shut, but try as he might, he couldn't seem to clear his head, to think about the next training session, the next race.

His eyes opened, drinking in the display of trophies, the knickknacks, the hatbox—all reminders of the life he'd left behind.

Climbing from the bed, he pulled on his jeans, snatched up a blanket and headed outside. For some cool air. Some freedom. Some blessed distance.

From the past.

From the present.

He ended up down by the creek, watching the play of moonlight on the mirrorlike surface, listening to the trickle of water and the buzz of insects. The sounds pushed inside his head and shoved aside Eli's voice, his father's, everything except the soft, sweet whisper of water.

He stretched out on his back and stared up at the sky, but he didn't see the stars or the moon. He saw her. A halo of silver hair framing the sweetest, warmest woman he'd ever had the pleasure of sinking into.

She'd fueled his dreams for so long, made him toss and turn and swell until he was rock-hard and desperate for release. Even when he'd slept with other women, Annie had always been there, living in his memories, a shining ray in his stormy past.

However persistent, she'd always been a dream. A nighttime reprieve from life on the road, the stress of going from race to race and keeping himself primed and pumped and focused.

Not anymore.

He was wide-awake now, and she was right in front of him. Not the same soft, sweet girl who'd lingered in his head all this time, but a woman, her features sharp and defined rather than fogged by time and a young boy's memory. *Real.*

He felt her quivering and needy in his arms. Heard her tiny, high-pitched whimpers. Saw the fine sheen of sweat covering her shoulders and breasts. Smelled the steamy heat and the faint scent of peaches that clung to her naked body.

The blood rushed through his veins, surging straight to his groin...

He couldn't stop thinking about her, but not just about the way she'd felt surrounding him, riding him, but about the tremble of her voice when she'd whispered in his ear, the warmth of her tears on his skin, the way she'd touched her lips to the pounding of his pulse, as if she could feel, taste the life pumping through his veins. As if she wanted to.

Those lips at his throat. That's what he couldn't forget.

What he wanted to feel again.

He would. As many times as necessary to slake the lust eating at his common sense. As intent as Tack was on selling the Big B, he was suddenly just as determined to purge himself of the beautiful Miss Annie.

This time when he left Inspiration—for the last time—he would be rid of the dream that had haunted him all these years. He could make a clean break, no lingering memories. No regrets.

He had to work Annie Divine out of his system.

And that meant he had to get her back into his bed.

CHAPTER SIX

"TELL ME EVERYTHING," DEB DEMANDED the minute Annie picked up the phone early Sunday morning.

"Good morning to you, too."

"The man has your panties, for Pete's sake, and you didn't tell dear old Deb."

"No, no, you didn't wake me. I've been up for hours. What's new with me? Well, my roof sprung a new leak after last night's rain and my air conditioner's still out."

"Okay, it's five in the morning, I shouldn't have called so early— Bless my Gucci-loving soul, he isn't there, is he? Because I may be insensitive, but if I interrrupted the two of you while you were—"

"It's just me and the twins." A loud clatter drifted from outside and she added, "And Mrs. Pope."

"You have to get a life, Annie. Sleeping with two collie puppies isn't my idea of a hot Saturday night— *Mrs. Pope?* The old lady's in bed with you?"

"She's in her side garden, about thirty feet from my bedroom window, making enough racket with her gardening tools that she might as well be in bed with me."

"Gardening at five in the morning?"

"More like revenge." Tools clattered and Mrs. Pope launched into her fourth chorus of "Amazing Grace."

"She's mad at me because I was up late stripping my kitchen floor a few nights ago and had all the lights in the house blazing. She said the glare kept the entire neighborhood awake."

"She's the only neighbor you've got for two miles."

"She also wants me to reimburse her seven dollars or she's going to report me for disturbing the peace."

"Why seven dollars?"

"She went to bingo early the next morning and lost seven dollars because she was tired."

"Bingo isn't about skill. It's about luck."

"That's why I gave her a copy of *Bingo for Bucks*."

"Was she appreciative?"

"I don't think so. I can hear her hooking up the sprinklers." Annie crawled out of bed and reached the window just as a shower of spray splattered her. "Ugh," she sputtered and shoved the window down.

"What's wrong?"

"I'm all wet."

"Speaking of wet, tell me *everything* that happened after I left last night."

"You're shameless, and nothing happened." Her lips tingled at the memory and she stiffened. *Calm, cool, indifferent.* "We spent one night together, and it's over. I don't see what the big deal is. It wasn't even an entire night. Just a few hours."

"Hours?" Excitement bubbled in Deb's voice. "I heard athletes had stamina, but *hours?* Where can I get one?" Annie tried to ignore the niggling anger when she thought of Deb "getting one." Or more importantly, when she thought of Deb getting Tack.

Jealousy?

She shook away the notion. Before Deb could ask another question, she added, "I've got a leaky roof to fix. See you at work tomorrow," and punched the disconnect button on her cordless.

She showered, donned a pair of shorts and a tank top and pulled her hair back into a ponytail. Then she ushered the twins out the front door to do their business. Grabbing a red ball, she walked to the edge of the front porch, pitched the toy into a batch of bluebonnets in Mrs. Pope's front garden. The twins scurried after the ball and Annie headed back inside.

She managed two steps before she heard Mrs. Pope shriek at the top of her lungs.

"Annie Divine! Those mongrels pooped in my flower bed!"

Annie leaned out the front door and smiled. "Then I guess we're even."

"Even? How do you figure that?"

"Do you know how much fertilizer costs at the feed store? At least double what you lost at bingo. But seeing as how we're neighbors, I'll call it even. By the way, how did you like the book?"

Annie ducked back inside seconds before a spray of water splattered the screen door where she'd been standing. She chuckled. Never a dull moment.

Taking a deep breath, she turned to her next order of business—fixing the oval-shaped spot marring the already cracked living-room ceiling. Her gaze dropped to survey the room, from an old worn sofa and chair, a scarred coffee table, to the far corner where she stored tripods and several camera cases. The entire place needed an overhaul—from the chipped and peeling outside, to the inside—if she ever intended to get a decent offer when she put it up for sale.

But first things first...

She took a deep breath and moved the sofa out of the way, then the coffee table. Her elbow bumped an old pink embroidered photo album that sat on top and sent it sailing to the ground. She spent the next few minutes gathering pictures and placing them back inside. Her gaze traveled over photos of herself as a child, the house, Coop—everything Cherry Divine had loved in her life.

Annie's gaze lingered on a prom photo she'd taken with Tack. He smiled back at the camera and her chest tightened.

She steeled herself against the feeling and shut the album. One month, she told herself as she placed the book back in its spot. Then Tack Brandon would be leaving.

If only that thought didn't bother her almost as much as the idea of him staying.

"SHE'S A WILD ONE. Fern won't let not a one of the men around here touch her, much less take a ride."

Tack stood next to Eli just after sunup and stared across the corral at a dark brown horse. "She looks tame enough."

"Looks can be deceiving. I broke many a horse in my day. Been in charge of the breeding stock here for your daddy going on twenty years now, but this one's got me by the balls. Coop actually got close enough to stroke her once, but I ain't had the same luck." Eli shrugged. "I suggested using her as a broodmare, but you know old

Coop. He always loved a good challenge. Wasn't about to give up on this one without a fight."

Bones chose that moment to bark, effectively killing the subject before Tack did it himself. "Come on, boy." Tack slapped his thigh and Bones came running up.

"That the mutt Effie was hollering about yesterday?"

Tack stroked the dog's shiny coat. "One and the same. He spent the night at the vet and had a thorough checkup. He's a little lean, but healthy." Tack eyed Eli. "Those boys of yours like dogs?"

"Too much for their own good." Eli grinned. "I'll tell you what, I'd be willing to take this dog off your hands if you'll ride fence with Bart for me this morning. That'll give me a chance to take Bones here home and get him settled in."

"And?"

Eli looked sheepish. "Drive Vera to church. She's too big to fit behind the wheel of that little car of hers, and she ain't very good at driving my truck. I used to drive her and the boys while Coop did fence duty, but with him passing on this past week, we're a man short—"

"Go," Tack cut in, giving Bones one last rub.

"You sure?"

"I haven't set a saddle in a long time. But I'll do my best." Tack turned and headed for the barn.

"Just remember," Eli called after him, a chuckle warming his voice, "it's like making love. Once you take a good ride, you never forget how."

IT WAS THE BEST RIDE he'd had in a hell of a long time.

Tack kneed the quarter horse and raced over the open

pasture, leaving Bart working on a stretch of barbed wire while he headed down the fence to mend a break he'd spotted earlier. The sun blazed, sending drops of sweat trickling between his shoulder blades. The wind whipped at his face. The motion of the horse worked his thigh muscles, drawing a steady, throbbing ache.

Tack loved every second.

He didn't even mind the work itself. With a boot top of staples and a hammer, he threw himself into the tedious chore of stretching loose fence and hammering it back into place, grateful for something to do besides think about his father or the ranch. Or Annie and her starring role in last night's fantasy.

He could still see her as she'd been in his thoughts, his memories. Waist deep in the river, her breasts wet and glorious in the moonlight, her nipples dark, puckered tips begging for his mouth... *Man, oh, man, you got it bad—*

Focus!

He concentrated on the hammer in his hand and spent the rest of the day working himself into exhaustion. The sun inched below the horizon by the time he rode back to the house, sore and tired. At the same time, his muscles tingled and his nerves twitched with awareness. He felt invigorated. Alive. The way he felt after a good race or a rigorous training session.

Or a hard day cowboying.

Not that the feeling would last. It was his first day back in the saddle. Once the newness wore off, so would the pleasure. Then he would start to feel stifled, trapped. Just like before.

A loud bark drew Tack's attention and he turned to

see Bones jump off the back porch of the house and run toward him.

"What happened?" he asked Eli, who followed the dog. "The kids didn't like Bones?"

"They were crazy about him. It was Vera. And it wasn't Bones, specifically. More like his eating habits. He ate an entire apple pie meant for the church bake sale and half a Bundt cake. Vera was mad as a hornet and told me to bring him back to you." He shrugged. "Sorry, man. Hey—" his face brightened "— Bart's got a little girl and his wife likes dogs—got one of her own. I could ask him to help you out."

"I'd appreciate it."

Eli took Bones and headed to the bunkhouse to catch Bart before he went home, and Tack started for the house. His gaze snagged on Fern and he found himself backtracking to the corral.

Wild or not, she was still beautiful. One of the finest horses he'd ever seen. Glossy brown coat. Strong hind legs. Intelligent eyes.

He wasn't sure what drew him, but he found himself unhooking the latch and slipping inside the corral before he could think better of it. He wasn't a cowboy, but a dirt-bike racer, and he was as far out of his element as a man could get.

The animal glanced at him and he saw a flicker of apprehension before it disappeared in the black depths of her eyes. Muscles rippled and tensed beneath her sleek coat. Tack took a step closer. The walk, the approach, came back to him in a rush and he remembered sitting on the fence, watching his father soothe a new gelding.

The animal snorted a warning, but Tack was careful, sure, as he reached out. Soft, silky horsehair met his callused palm. Surprisingly, the animal didn't bolt. Ten years faded away and he was eighteen again, soothing his own horse, a prized Arabian his father had purchased as a graduation present.

Cooper Brandon had always had an eye for beauty, and a hankering for a good challenge—

Over and done with, he told himself again. *Forget and focus.*

He shifted his attention back to the horse, to the soft feel of hair beneath his palm. Another stroke and the animal trembled. "Don't worry, girl. You're safe with me. I'd rather bust my balls on metal than horseflesh." He said the words, but his hand lingered a few seconds on the animal's mane.

Tack forced himself away, toward the house for a shower and some supper before he headed back outside for another night of freedom beneath the stars. Like the horse, Tack Brandon had a wild streak of his own. He'd lived too many years under his father's stifling rule. Now he craved air and space and distance from any and everything, especially the house filled with so many reminders.

The fantasies were another matter altogether. Those he welcomed the moment he closed his eyes.

ANNIE WAS NOT GOING TO LOOK.

No matter how perfectly the first light of day spilled through the trees and sculpted the man standing between two big cedars not more than ten yards away.

No matter how the surrounding foliage cast just the

right amount of shadow to accent the corded muscles of his shoulders and arms.

No matter how bronze and beautiful and *naked* he was... Well, almost.

His back to her as he stared out over the crystal creek bed, he wore a pair of snug, faded jeans, but instead of camouflaging what lay beneath, they molded the shape of his buttocks, his lean hips and strong thighs. A rip in the denim bisected his right thigh, giving her a peek at silky dark hair and tanned skin.

She sighted through the lens, moved a half inch this way, a fraction that way. Closer to find just the right angle... *No!*

Her finger stalled just shy of the shutter, her hand tightened on the camera. What was she doing? She was supposed to be taking pictures of the ranch. She'd purposely dragged herself out of bed before daybreak, knowing the light would be just right to shoot without a flash and portray the quiet serenity of a Texas sunrise at the Big B. The less she had to use flashes or strobes, the more *real* her pictures. Tack might want a few photos, but she always sought to tell a story with her work, even if the pictures were only meant as a sales tool.

She intended to show the natural charm of a winding creek lined with cypress and cedar trees, the breathtaking quality of the hills, the strength of the land. Not to snap pictures of the bare-chested owner with a tantalizing rip in his too-tight jeans—

The thought stalled as Tack reached overhead to stretch. Muscles rippled. Shadows chased sunlight across his bare torso and the air lodged in her throat.

If a picture told a story, Tack's was certain to be

a triple-X feature. It was just a casual stretch, yet everything about the movement screamed *sex*. From the sensual arch of his back, his hips thrust out just enough to emphasize the bulge beneath his zippered fly, to the stroke of long, lean fingers through his dark, sun-kissed hair.

She stared at the image in the viewfinder, unable to tear her gaze away, to get while the getting was good. She should go back to her truck, get her tripod and large-format camera and do some panoramic shots from the top of Brandon Bluff. At least the morning wouldn't be a total waste. The creek shots she could get later. Much later, after Tack Brandon was gone and Annie Divine wasn't so fresh from a night of tossing and turning and thinking about him.

Wanting him.

He turned, giving her his profile as he reached up and picked a peach from a nearby tree. She watched as he dusted the fruit off on his jeans and bit into the pale flesh. Juice spurted, trailing over his tanned fingers, dripping down his muscled forearm.

Annie couldn't help herself. Her trigger finger itched. The shutter clicked.

Tack stopped chewing for a fraction of a second and she froze. He'd heard. She knew it. She was too close, the sound too pronounced in the hushed morning. She lowered the camera, bracing herself for a confrontation.

He didn't turn toward her. He simply stood there for a long, drawn-out moment. Then his mouth moved, his stubble-covered jaw worked at the fruit again, as if he was unaware of her presence.

That, or he was ignoring her.

No. Tack wasn't a man to look the other way, not when he wanted something, and he wanted her. He'd made no secret that he'd like a repeat performance of their night together.

He had no clue she was there.

What harm could it do to take a few pictures? It was the touching she had trouble with. Letting her guard slip and pushing her fears to the back burner, Annie indulged herself. Just this once.

Raising the camera, she sighted him again, following his every movement through the viewfinder. His teeth sinking into the soft pulp, the decadent spurt of juice over his tanned skin.

He abandoned the peach to catch a trickle of sweetness along the inside of his forearm. The tip of his tongue caught a golden drop before gliding up along his smooth skin, and Annie's heart stalled.

Heat flooded between her legs as she remembered his touch. The wet flick of his tongue on the inside of her thigh.

A last, lingering lick at the tender side of his wrist and Annie's knees trembled.

He took another bite, lips working at the flesh, teeth nibbling, and Annie's body responded once more. To the sight, the sound, the memory of his hungry mouth feasting on her the way he feasted on the peach.

There was something about Tack that stoked the passionate fire deep inside her, fed the flames until they blazed hot and bright. Consuming. He drew a physical response from her that was unlike anything she'd ever experienced.

Physical. She focused on the thought, intent on keeping her emotions separate. Protected. Buried.

He sank his teeth deeper into the succulent fruit. Her breathing grew harsh, her heart drummed a frantic tempo. The camera slipped from her grasp and stopped at her waist, anchored by the strap around her neck. The firm edge of the canvas grazed one throbbing nipple and she gasped. The sound echoed in her ears, thundering through the silence separating them.

Tack didn't so much as flinch, much less turn accusing eyes on her. He took his last bite of peach, pitched the core and licked his fingers, and Annie felt her first spasm. A soft clenching that made her entire body vibrate as it worked its way from between her legs, spreading through her the way the peach juice had drenched Tack's lean fingers.

By the time he'd licked the last one clean, she'd managed to catch her breath. But she couldn't move. She leaned against the tree, quivering and spent and still needy. While she'd had an orgasm, it wasn't enough to quiet the hunger inside her. She'd had a taste, or rather, he'd had the taste and she'd felt it, and now she wanted to feel more.

To feel him.

Closing her eyes, she fought to summon her defenses and pull herself together. She had a few yards on him. If she bolted, she could get away before he walked toward her, touched her, and she lost what little resistance she had.

Resistance? She was this close to falling at his feet and begging him to make love to her. But it wasn't the sex act itself that posed the threat. It was the begging.

The *need*. The last thing Annie wanted was to need Tack Brandon, to crave more than a few moments of carnal bliss to the point that she stopped thinking of herself and wanted only him.

She stiffened and her eyes snapped open. She would not fall for Tack all over again, not without a fight. No matter how fierce the attraction—

He was gone.

She stared at the empty patch of grass and disappointment crept through her, followed by a rush of relief. He really hadn't seen her.

Snatching up her camera bag, she forced her legs to move back down the path to her truck. He might have reduced her to a quivering mass of hormones, but at least he wasn't aware of it, and that meant he had no idea how he affected her. Annie intended to keep it that way, to keep her precious control. Over her life, her destiny. Her dreams.

Now if she could just add her traitorous body to the list.

TACK WAS THIS CLOSE TO going up in flames by the time he made it back to the ranch house and his old bedroom. He could still see Annie, leaning back against the tree, her breasts heaving, erect nipples outlined by the thin fabric of her pale pink blouse.

God, he wanted to be inside her, and she wanted him there. He knew it. She'd been so absorbed in what she was feeling, she hadn't even realized he'd been looking at her. He'd seen the desire on her face when he'd licked away the last of the peach.

The sweetness lingered on his tongue and a bolt of

heat shot straight to his already throbbing erection. He slid the button of his jeans free and eased the zipper down enough to give himself some much-needed room. Man, he was hard. *Hungry.*

For more than a piece of fruit. He wanted the real thing. *Her.* Five long strides and he could have had it.

Annie. Beneath him. Surrounding him. Sending him to heaven.

Not yet.

Not until he figured out what she was all about. He wasn't pushing inside her sweet body until he'd managed to push inside her pretty little head and get some real answers.

In the meantime...

Tack walked into the bathroom, twisted the cold-water knob and started to push his jeans and underwear down. A door slammed somewhere in the house and an angry shout carried down the hallway.

"Tack Brandon! I've got a bone to pick with you."

Yanking up his jeans, he grimaced as the fabric fit tightly over his throbbing length. Man, oh, man, he had it real bad.

"Tack Brandon!" The voice echoed louder. Closer.

He reached the bedroom doorway just as a large woman, salt-and-pepper hair pulled back in a bun, rounded the corner, carrying Bones.

"Don't tell me. You must be Bart's wife."

She frowned, her round, pudgy face pinched into a frown. "And you're the sorry SOB who sent this mongrel home with my husband." She plopped Bones on the ground and dusted dog hair off her neon-blue housedress.

"What did he do?"

"Ate three loaves of my pumpkin bread, but that's beside the point. This poor excuse for a stud was putting major moves on my Camille."

"Camille?"

"My prizewinning poodle. She was enjoying her favorite biscuit when this mutt corners her in my kitchen. She's whimpering and crying when I come in and see you-know-who about to...to..." The woman colored and waved a hand in Bones's direction. "Well, you get the idea."

Tack shifted his stance to give his crotch a little more room. Unfortunately, he got the idea all too well.

"Anyhow," the woman went on, "it took a rolled newspaper over his head and a lot of tugging and pulling to get him away from her."

"Maybe she's in heat."

"Not my sweet little Camille!"

"Sounds like a possibility, if you ask me. Poor Bones here is a healthy male. He's got needs. This Camille's obviously got needs."

"I will not have Camille breeding with every two-bit Casanova that sniffs in her direction, nor will I have this sack of bones raiding my pumpkin bread." She turned on her heel and stormed down the hallway. The front door slammed shut and Tack's accusing gaze dropped to Bones.

"Looks like you just got yourself kicked out of home number two." Bones's tail thumped enthusiastically and Tack shook his head. "I know it's not all your fault, but you have to behave yourself, Bones, or we'll never find a place for you. That means staying out of the kitchen."

Bones barked, and Tack added, "I know, I know. It wasn't just the food you were after this time, but you still need to learn some self-control."

He walked back into the bathroom, pulled off his jeans and briefs, wincing as the material grazed the hard evidence of his own lack of self-control. Thankfully, Bart's wife had been too mad to notice, otherwise, she'd have taken a newspaper to Tack for sure. A Sunday edition, by the size of things.

The dog whimpered, and Tack turned to see Bones had followed him into the bathroom. The dog's mouth hung open, tongue lolling to the side as he panted from the morning heat. That, or he was still worked up over Camille.

"I know the feeling, buddy." Tack turned on the spray, stepped into the shower and let the cold tame his eager body. "I know the feeling all too well."

"WHAT'S WRONG WITH YOU?" Deb asked Wednesday morning when Annie walked into the newspaper office.

"What do you mean?" She flipped on her computer and stowed her camera bag and purse beneath her desk.

"You look flushed. Are you coming down with something?"

"No." Just a bad case of stupidity, Annie thought as she pulled out her notes on the luncheon she'd covered yesterday and tried to still her pounding heart.

Pounding, even after twenty minutes, an ice-cold diet soda and a drive into town with the truck's air conditioner blasting. But nothing short of a dip into a river of ice cubes could have lowered her body temperature after another early-morning down by Brandon Creek.

Her third to be exact.

She should have known he'd be there. She *had* known. After spotting him again on the second morning, she'd known as soon as she walked down the path that she'd find him at the same place. Looking as sexy as ever in worn jeans and nothing else. Nothing but a peach in his hand.

The second two days had been a repeat of the first morning. Tack devouring the fruit, licking his hunger away while Annie watched him. *Felt* him.

She flipped open her notebook and noted the tremble of her fingers, the strange tingling of her skin. For all her disapointment that she'd given in to her baser desires again, she felt oddly exhilarated. Reckless. Daring. The way she'd felt when she'd walked around wearing her first pair of skimpy lace panties.

After a lifetime of nice, conservative granny panties, as her mom had called them, Annie had bought a pair of French-cut bikinis the day she'd enrolled in college. She'd been celebrating the start of her new life away from Inspiration.

Things had changed a few days later. Her mother had been diagnosed with cancer and Annie had made the decision to commute to the University of Texas and live at home to tend Cherry.

As disapointed as Annie had been, she always re-membered that first day walking around Austin wearing her new, sexy lingerie. No one had known, but she had, and it had made her feel good about herself.

The way she'd felt this morning, taking her pleasure

and not fearing for her peace of mind at the same time. Tack had been oblivious, far away from touching her and stirring the emotions simmering deep down inside, and Annie had been...on fire.

If only it was enough.

She ignored the thought and fanned herself with the edge of the notebook.

"You're definitely coming down with something." Deb took a sip from her newest mug, Ballbuster And Proud Of It. "Maybe you've got a fever."

"I'm fine, Mom."

"I am not acting like a mother."

"Oops, I said the three-letter word."

"It's not that I have anything against mothers," Deb said, "except my own, which is why I have no desire to squeeze out a little bundle of joy anytime soon."

"Bad parenting isn't genetic, you know."

"And poor choices aren't either," Deb said.

"What's that supposed to mean?"

"Just because your mother had a miserable love life, doesn't mean you're doomed to the same. Live a little, Annie, and stop worrying about making the same mistakes Cherry made. Tack Brandon's the best-looking cowboy I've seen in a long time."

"He's not a cowboy." Annie braced herself for a barrage of questions, but Deb simply sipped her coffee and walked back over to her own desk.

"By the way, I've got to drive to Austin, so I need you to cover the This Is Your Neighbor for this edition."

"I can get to it after I finish this piece on the weekly seniors luncheon. So who is it this week? I hope it's Granny Baines. She kept hinting about it through lunch yesterday." Granny Baines was one of the few older citizens of Inspiration who didn't look down her nose at Annie. While she hadn't approved of Cherry, she'd always treated Annie decently.

Of course, she also wanted to get her picture in the paper.

"It's not Granny Baines," Deb said. "It's a he."

Annie arched an eyebrow at her editor. "And you're not covering it? He must be too old to qualify as hunk material. That or married."

"Neither."

"Young and single? Are you sure you're not the one who's coming down with something?"

"The fact of the matter is, Mr. Young and Single requested you."

"Me?" Her eyes narrowed. "Who is it?"

"Your gusto-grabbing cowboy."

"Oh no." Dread churned fast and furious in Annie's stomach and she groaned. "On second thought, I think I am feeling sick."

"A touch of flu?"

Annie shook her head. "Too many peaches."

CHAPTER SEVEN

ANNIE GRIPPED HER NOTEBOOK and camera bag, rang the doorbell and ignored the urge to bolt.

"It's just an interview," she told herself for the hundredth time since Deb had dropped the bomb. It *was* just an interview, despite what had happened between them.

"Just stay calm," she muttered. "Calm and cool and indifferent—"

"Indifferent to what, honey?"

The deep voice brought her whirling around to see Tack clad in nothing but a pair of jeans, a white towel hooked around the strong column of his neck. Drops of water slid down his deeply bronzed shoulders and arms to bead in the black mat of chest hair that stretched from nipple to nipple. The forest of ebony thinned and narrowed to a silky funnel that bisected his washboard stomach and disappeared between the gaping waistband of his unbuttoned jeans. Annie's gaze lingered on the hard ridge beneath the zipper.

"Cold showers aren't what they used to be."

Her gaze snapped up at the sound of his voice. "W-what?"

He grinned, a sexy slant to his lips that made Annie's heart stop for a long moment. "I said, a cold shower isn't enough to beat this heat."

Annie wiped a trail of perspiration from her forehead. "The weatherman said we're headed for a record-breaking day. Ninety-eight degrees."

He winked. "I wasn't talking about the temperature outside, honey." He scrubbed at his damp hair with the towel. "And you didn't answer my question. Indifferent to what?"

You. The word rushed through her thoughts and straight to her lips where she bit it back. Annie couldn't help the strange emotions stirring deep inside, but she could keep them contained. Controlled.

She took a deep breath. "To the heat," she said matter-of-factly. "Calm, cool and indifferent. The only way to cope with a Texas summer." She wiped another trail of sweat from her temple. "So where do you want to do it?" She indicated her notebook. "I've got a tight schedule today—a luncheon at city hall and a follow-up on Tess Johnson's litter—so if we could hurry this up, I would really appreciate it."

He stepped back. "How about the kitchen?"

"Fine," she said as she slipped past him. Her shoulder brushed against one muscular arm and heat zigzagged down her arm to make her fingers tingle. She managed a calm voice. "I can find my own way while you finish dressing."

"Sure thing." Two strong fingers slid the button of his jeans into place and he grinned. "All done."

"What about a shirt?"

"I'm pretty comfortable the way I am, but if it bothers you…" Blue eyes drilled into her. "Does it bother you?"

Yes! She shrugged. "Suit yourself."

"I intend to, honey," he murmured as she turned to precede him into the house. "I surely do."

Minutes later, Annie sat at the kitchen table sipping a diet soda while Tack stood at the counter and poured a glass of iced tea.

"Let's see…" She studied several pages of the notebook and tried to calm her pounding heart. "You'll have to give me a second to find the questions. Deb's got the handwriting of a serial killer and she does all the interviews for this column, except the one with Jimmy Mission." At his questioning glance, she added, "They don't get along too well."

"A woman exists that Jimmy doesn't get along with?" Tack dropped two spoonfuls of sugar into his tea and stirred.

"Deb's not your normal woman. She's got…attitude."

"You mean balls."

"That's what Jimmy told her."

He sipped the tea and added two more heaping spoonfuls. "It's no wonder they dislike each other."

"I think *hate* would be a better word. Jimmy volunteered for the dunking booth last year at the annual spring carnival—"

"Are we talking about the same Jimmy who won't go within a stone's throw of the river?"

"The one and only. The mayor persuaded him by saying that it was a shallow tank and Jimmy probably wouldn't even get wet since the girls' baseball team was on a seven-year losing streak and all the boys would be at the kissing booth with Mary Jo Madden—she was the Southwest Rodeo Queen. Mostly, Jimmy was supposed to sit up there, bare-chested, while the girls oohed and aahed and forked over a buck to make themselves look charitable. He didn't count on Deb seeking revenge for the balls statement, or the fact that she grew up with three jock brothers."

He chuckled. "She dunked him?"

"Seventy-two times. It was the highlight of the carnival. That and the yelling match that used so many four-letter words the church ladies called an emergency prayer meeting right there on the spot. Deb and Jimmy haven't spoken since…" Her words faded as she watched him dunk two more spoonfuls of sugar. "Why don't you just add a few ice cubes to the sugar bowl?"

He grinned. "What can I say? I've got a sweet tooth."

It wasn't his words so much as the gleam in his blue eyes that made her think of long dark nights and tangled sheets and lots of sweet, sweet heat.

"What about you, honey? You like sweets?"

Yes. She fixed her gaze on the notebook. "On occasion. Question number one. Occupation?"

Tack turned a kitchen chair, straddled it and rested his forearms on the back, the ice-cold glass cradled in his palms. "Professional motocross racer. Eight years riding pro. I started out working as a mechanic in a motorcycle shop after I left here. The owner raced as a hobby and he showed me the ropes. I started my first pro season a year later. So you've been with the *In Touch* how long now?"

She penciled his answer down. "Six years."

"And before that?"

"I worked my way through college. I've got a bachelor's in journalism and a minor in communications. Now, on to the next—"

"A bachelor's?" he cut in. "You couldn't do that at Grant County Community College."

"I didn't. I went to the University of Texas."

"I thought you stayed home and took care of your mother?"

"I did," she said tightly. "I commuted. Now, about the second question—"

"But that's a two-hour drive each way."

"I scheduled all of my classes on Tuesdays and Thursdays and took six years to get a four-year degree."

Tack thought of sweet, shy Annie driving hours on end, burying her head in schoolbooks, hanging in there and staying focused while her classmates lived on campus, went to parties and football games. Warmth swelled in his chest. "You wanted a degree that bad?"

"Yes," she said through clenched teeth before giving him a pointed stare. "This is your interview."

"Annie, Annie," he clucked. "You need to relax. Don't be so uptight. I'm just curious to know what you've been up to all these years."

"I am not uptight."

"Then you must be nervous." He took a long gulp of iced tea and watched the way her gaze riveted on his mouth. "Do I make you nervous, honey?"

"Of course not." Her words were so cool, so matter-of-fact, he almost bought her indifference, except for the white-knuckled grip she had on the pencil.

As if she noticed the direction of his gaze, she relaxed her hand. "I'm just pressed for time, that's all. So what about you? Did you make it to college?"

He shook his head, his grin fading as he thought of those early years. "I was busy surviving. When I left home, things were tight. I could barely feed myself, much less pay for school."

"What about that football scholarship to Texas A & M? You could have played college ball, all expenses paid and gotten an education in the process."

"I thought about it. Hell, I even came close to driving up to College Station. I really liked playing football. But not enough to go head-to-head with guys who loved the game. I only played high school ball to get away from the ranch. Once I was on my own, I didn't need a way out anymore. I lost my drive."

Her green eyes caught flecks of sunlight as her gaze rose to meet his. "But you found it again with motorcycle racing."

"I was the hungriest rookie to ever hit the track."

"And now?"

He thought of the contracts tucked away in his duffle bag, still unsigned, and shrugged. "I'm still hungry, but I'm getting older. Most of the guys coming into the circuit are young, eighteen and nineteen. Talented kids like Jeff Emig, Jeremy McGrath, Ezra Lusk. I've got nearly ten years on all of them." He took a long drink of iced tea and grinned. "The competition is tough, but it makes winning all the sweeter, and you know I like sweets."

A smile played at her lips. "Still a sucker for a challenge?"

"Yeah, I am," he said, his thoughts shifting from racing to Annie. A grown-up, voluptuous Annie standing near the creek bed, her lashes at half-mast, her lips parted, a soft sigh quivering from her throat. Heat fired his blood and his gaze captured hers. "When it comes to something I really want."

The tension coiled thick between them for several long moments as Tack let the meaning of his words sink in.

"What is it you really—" Her question faded into a series of loud barks as Bones bounced through the doorway to beg at Tack's feet. "I—I think the dog must be hungry," she blurted, as if she'd just realized what she'd been about to ask.

"He's always hungry." Tack glared at Bones, got to his feet and retrieved a can of dog food from a nearby cabinet.

"This is your dog?"

He shook his head as he opened the can and poured it into a bowl. "A stray I picked up at Effie's. I call him Bones."

"For such a skinny dog, he sure likes to eat," she pointed out as Bones started lapping up the dog food.

"There's no like about it. He loves to eat." Tack returned to his seat. "Come to think of it, so do I." He reached into the fruit bowl at the center of the table and grabbed a peach. "How about you, honey? You hungry?"

Annie stiffened and shook her head, her gaze riveted on the piece of fruit.

He cast her a sly grin. "And here I thought you liked peaches."

Worry lit her eyes, and by her erect posture he knew she was bracing herself, fully expecting him to call her out about her harmless voyeurism. To tease her. Hell, he was half tempted just to see if she would turn that enticing shade of pink he remembered so well.

As much as he liked to see her blush, he wouldn't break the connection her simple act had forged between them. The small thread of trust. For the first time, Annie had taken the initiative. She'd taken her pleasure as bold and brave as you please, revealing how much she had changed.

And he liked it.

He'd always had to coax the smallest kisses from her, charm her out of those big baggy clothes. She'd never been comfortable with her luscious body, afraid people would think she resembled Cherry in more ways than appearance. She'd never initiated a kiss, never been daring or flirty like the other girls who'd pursued him back in high school.

At the time, Annie had been a breath of fresh air. Pretty and sweet. As appealing and challenging as that innocence had been, Tack wasn't interested in picking up where they'd left off. The hunter and his prey.

He wanted an equal partner this time. A *woman*. One just as bold as she was shy, as greedy as she was giving. One who burned as fiercely as he did and didn't try to hide her desire.

He wanted the sexy woman his sweet little Annie had become.

The sun filtered through the kitchen windows, bathing them in a warm glow that drew a line of perspiration from her temple, despite the cold air blowing from the air-conditioning vents.

"You hot, honey?"

"It's a little warm in here, but bearable," she replied

in a cool, calm voice. So damn calm. "My notes say that you've won eight national motocross championships, and have raced for Suzuki, Honda and Yamaha. So where's home base? Coop said something about California."

As always, the mention of his father sliced through him like a dull razor, dicing his thoughts. He cast her a sharp glance. "He knew where I was living?"

"He kept up."

A strange sense of hope surged deep inside, but he forced the feeling back down and shrugged. "Yeah, I guess he did. It wasn't as if he had to go to any trouble. Just tune in to the latest sports channel and watch a postrace interview."

"Or maybe he kept tabs on you—"

"Can we get back to the interview?" he cut in, determined to change the subject, to ignore the hurt, stay one step ahead of it for as long as possible.

Forever.

She stared at him, her green gaze searching, comforting. Understanding lit her eyes and Tack glimpsed the old Annie. The one who'd listened and comforted whenever he'd been mad at Coop. As much as he wanted the woman she'd become, it gave him an odd sense of peace to know a little of the old Annie remained. The friend she'd been before she'd been his lover.

At that moment, he wanted to sit with her, gaze at her, talk to her even more than he wanted to take her to bed.

As if she sensed his thoughts, her eyes dropped, breaking the spell as she glanced at the pad. "Where in California?"

"Encino. I've got a little place near the track where

I do laps. So, honey—" he took a bite out of his peach and winked at her, comfortable now to be back on track, focused on the present, rather than on his damnable past "—you work all day and go home to an empty house?"

"Yes and no." She plowed into the next question as if to stay focused herself. "Now, about hobbies…"

"I lift weights, jog, work on my dirt bikes."

"All that's work-related. Our readers want to know what you like to do for enjoyment."

"Let's see… *Enjoyment*." The word dripped from his tongue with just enough intimacy to lure her gaze to his. "I think you, of all people, should know the answer to that one."

"How would I know…?" The question faded as a knowing light lit her expression. "You sleep around for enjoyment. That's what you're getting at, isn't it?"

He grinned. "I can promise you, honey, there's no sleeping involved." His grin widened.

Several seconds ticked by before the tension in her muscles eased and her mouth hinted at a smile. "You're pulling my leg, aren't you?"

"I'm doing no such thing." His eyes widened in mock innocence. "I'm not even touching you." *Yet.* The unspoken promise hovered in the air between them and the temperature in the room rose another degree.

"You said yesterday that you didn't sleep around."

"I don't. You asked what I *liked* to do for enjoyment, not what I actually do."

"Which is?"

"Lift weights, jog and work on whichever bike needs it the most."

Her lips parted and her mouth curved into another smile. "You always did like to shock me."

"You were easy to shock back then. All I had to do was say a few naughty words, wink at you or look a few seconds too long, and you turned a bright shade of pink." He reached across the table before she could pull away and touched her. Not a real, hand-gripping touch. Just the slow glide of his fingertip down her forearm, to her wrist. "I've looked and winked and talked as naughty as I can with an audience around—" he motioned to Bones "—and you're still snow-white."

She met his stare. "I'm immune to your charm now that I'm all grown-up."

Another seductive slide of his finger and goose bumps rose along her arm. He smiled. "Looks like you're not so immune, after all."

"I…" She grimaced. "It's cold in here."

"You're sweating."

"I'm coming down with a cold." She pulled her arm away from him. "You shouldn't get too close." She made a pretense of coughing. "Back to the questions."

"My thoughts exactly. Now, what about the going home alone to an empty house? You said yes and no. What did you mean?"

"Yes, I go home alone, but not to an empty house."

"Meaning?"

"I share it with twins."

"As in roommates?"

"Babies. My babies."

"You've got *kids?*"

"Barely six weeks." She grinned. "Two healthy,

bouncing baby boys who just learned how to tinkle on a newspaper."

Kids. Annie had kids. Bouncing boys who tinkled on a— "Come again?"

The warmest laugh he'd ever heard vibrated from her full lips. "They're collie pups from the same litter."

Relief crept through him. "You really had me going."

"You played right into my hands."

He winked. "Right where I want to be, honey."

Her smile dissolved and she cleared her throat. "On to the last question. Your, um, fondest memory of Inspiration."

"That's easy. The homecoming game. Or rather, afterward." Tack shifted his attention to her mouth. Her full bottom lip trembled just enough to send a lightning bolt of need straight to his groin. "I was still pumped, throwing the football around on an empty field, and there you were sitting on the bleachers with no particular place to go because you were the only girl in school without a date for the homecoming dance."

A soft smile played at her lips, and he knew she was remembering, too. The darkness. The moonlight. The two of them. "I didn't know how to dance."

"If I recall, you learned pretty quick."

"I hardly moved."

"Trust me. You moved just enough, sweetheart."

"How do you know? It was so dark down by the river. There wasn't even a moon out. I couldn't see a thing."

"I didn't have to see you, Annie." His voice grew husky, raw with the sudden need clawing inside him. "I felt you. Every move. Every sigh. Every beat of your heart. You know, leaving you was the one thing I regretted more than anything."

"You didn't love me."

"I came the closest to loving you as I'd ever come to loving anybody."

He watched the play of emotions on her face, the flash of longing in her eyes, the same look he'd seen down by the creek that morning, then it disappeared, snatched away by the beautiful, controlled woman sitting across from him.

"I'm not that same naive, young girl you danced with in the flatbed of your daddy's pickup." She gathered up her camera bag and notebook and started toward the back door. "And I'm not falling into bed with you again."

"Actually," he said as her gaze collided with his one last time and the fantasy that had been haunting him night after night flashed in his mind. "It wasn't a bed I had in mind."

CHAPTER EIGHT

TACK CLIMBED ON HIS BIKE early the next morning, flipped the key and gunned the engine. A roar split open the morning silence, drowning the quiet that had haunted him all the way from the creek.

No soft footsteps or the faint *click, click* of a camera. No hushed sighs or barely contained moans. No Annie.

Starts, he told himself, determined to shift his thoughts. To focus.

He had to work on his starts.

He took a last visual survey of the makeshift track, an empty pasture covered with fresh, hard-packed dry dirt delivered just yesterday. Ruts cornered the pasture, along with several whoop sections—long rolls of dirt gutted with sharp grooves—and a few jumps. It wasn't even close to the track he trained at back in California, but it would do.

Moving his body up toward the fuel tank, he leaned over the bar and pushed his head over the front of the bike. Two fingers on the clutch, he squeezed the bike with his thighs and applied steady throttle. The motorcycle bolted forward, straight and smooth, eating up ground at a frenzied pace. Bones kept up with him for a few seconds, until Tack opened up the Kawasaki all the way.

He squared off a sharp corner the way he always did, using the rut as a traction device. *Extend your inside leg. Feed out the clutch and roll on the throttle. Easy now...* He hit the pivot point, pulled in the clutch and locked up the rear brake to get a little skid going.

Dirt flew, his body twisted and the bike gobbled up the next stretch, headed for the first whoop section up ahead.

No Annie.

It shouldn't surprise him. Hell, it didn't, not after she'd made it very clear that she wasn't sleeping with him.

But for a few days she'd come to watch him. And though he much preferred a little one-on-one, watching Annie, seeing her take her pleasure, had been as fulfilling as taking his own. Her lashes at half-mast, her lips parted, pure rapture on her sweet face. It was a sight he wasn't likely to forget for a long, long time—

The thought shattered as his front tire hit the whoop. *Wheelie in, man. Wheelie in!* But it was too late. He pulled back, the front wheel snapped up, then slapped back down and the bike jumped. Tack gripped the handlebars and fought for balance. Brakes screeched as he brought the motorcycle to a bone-jolting halt.

"Shit!" He cursed at his loss of control, his wandering thoughts. But most of all, he swore because he wanted Annie and he couldn't have her, and that realization bothered him a hell of a lot more than the fact that, for the first time in years, Tack Brandon had lost his precious focus and nearly busted his ass.

A low whistle split the air. "I heard tell that Mr. All-Star Motocross Racer had taken up residence out here, but after witnessing that pitiful ride, I'd say I must've heard wrong."

Tack yanked off his helmet and glanced at the cowboy who stood on the other side of the fence, hat tipped back, a grin curving his familiar features.

At well over six feet, James Mission towered over most of the men in Inspiration. Except Tack.

They'd been the same height in school, always next to each other on the top row in a class picture, and side by side when it came to getting into trouble. Double Trouble, that's what everybody had called them, particularly the women. Jimmy, with his blond hair and green eyes, had been every girl's dream, and Tack, with his dark good looks and wicked charm, had been every mama's nightmare.

Tack grinned, climbed off the bike and strode toward the fence. "It's been a long time." He clasped Jimmy's hand while Bones barked his own greeting from the other side of the pasture where he'd spotted a rabbit.

"Eli said I'd find you out here. He said you were doing laps, but it looked more like that lap was doing you, buddy."

Tack shrugged at the observation. "I was just warming up."

"You'd better get a hell of a lot warmer if you intend to lead the Kawasaki team."

Tack eyed his old friend. "You follow motorcycle racing?"

"I catch it every now and then on cable. So what's the scoop? I swear, every sportscaster from here to New York is speculating on what the hell's taking you so long to make up your mind. You racing for Kawasaki or not?"

"Hell, yes. They made a damn good offer." One he'd be a fool to pass up. So why hadn't he signed the contract? He forced the question aside and smiled. "How have you been, Jimmy?"

"Busy." The man pulled off worn brown work gloves. "Otherwise I would have come here sooner. I'm running three thousand head over at my place and there's always something to do."

"What about that little brother of yours?"

"You know Jack. Can't sit still long enough to tie his shoelaces much less look after a ranch. Last I heard, he was in New Mexico training horses for some rancher, but that won't last long. It never does with Jack. Once the newness wears off and he's met the latest challenge, he's on to something else. Someone else."

Tack chuckled. "I won't ask if he's settled down with a wife and kids."

"No kids, thankfully, but he's been married twice, and divorced three times."

Tack wiped the perspiration from his forehead. "Hell, Jimmy, I never paid much attention in Mrs. Spades's math class, but isn't the second one supposed to be less than or equal to?"

"That's what I said, but Jack never did explain that one."

"What about you?" Tack asked. "Anybody waiting at home?"

The man shook his head. "Not yet, but I've been shopping around." He winked. "Sampling the merchandise, too. How about you?"

"I'm not in the market."

"That's not what I hear." At Tack's sharp glance, Jimmy grinned. "It's a small town, Brandon."

"I thought Annie and I might get reacquainted while I'm back in town, but she's putting up one heck of a fight."

"Sounds like Annie."

"Not the one I used to know."

"You haven't been around for a long time. Annie isn't so worried about everybody liking her like when we were kids. She's got a little vinegar in her now. Like that in a woman, myself."

So did Tack. Annie had turned out to be strong and sassy and sexy as anything and he *really* liked it.

Tack's fingers clenched for a long moment, until Bones bounded up, jumping and barking, demanding a snack. He reached into his duffel bag hooked over the fence post, retrieved an orange and tossed it. The dog raced off in hot pursuit. "You seem to know an awful lot about her."

"A buyer's market. A guy's got to know the local product." At Tack's cutting look, Jimmy grinned. "Don't get yourself all worked up. She's a pretty thing, but she's not my type."

Tack raised an eyebrow. "Not enough balls?"

Jimmy frowned. "Deb Strickland gives the entire female population a bad name."

"She seemed nice enough to me."

"She's nice to everything in pants. That's half the trouble."

"And the other half is she doesn't drop her panties when you walk into the room?" At Jimmy's sharp glance, Tack chuckled. "That's it. They finally made a woman immune to Jimmy Mission's charm and it doesn't sit too well."

"Did I say it was good to see you?"

"No."

"That's because it isn't."

Tack chuckled. "You're just as glad to see me as I am you. It's been too damn long."

"And it's going to be a brief reunion if the rumor I heard is true. You really selling?"

Tack nodded and wondered why the one action bothered him so much. "I'm not cut out to cowboy."

"You made a pretty decent cowboy way back when. Remember when we used to go out chasing calves?"

Tack grinned. "I recall a few calves chasing us."

"Before we figured out how to do it right. Once we did, we put on a hell of a show. Eli said you took to the saddle again like a hog to a mud puddle."

He shrugged. "I ride bikes for a living. Same concept."

"Or maybe you're good at it, and that doesn't sit too well with you." He scratched his temple and stared off at the open pasture. "I suspect that's probably why you're selling. Afraid you might turn out to have something in common with the old man, after all."

We have nothing in common. He was a cold, manipulative bastard. A killer. The denial jumped to his tongue, and stalled there. He shook his head. "I've got a life someplace else now that has nothing to do with horses or cattle or land, and I like it that way." It was *his* life, a life he'd carved out for himself, on his own. *No ties. No debts.*

"If you're determined to let the place go, then I'd like to make a bid. Your place borders mine and the land is too good to pass up." At Tack's nod, Jimmy added, his voice somber, "I'm real sorry about Coop. If there's anything I can do, just say the word."

Tail wagging, Bones found his way back to Tack, went up on his hind legs and begged for more food.

A smile tugged at Tack's mouth as he turned to Jimmy. "You know, there is one thing..."

ANNIE EASED BACK INTO THE TREES, careful that the two men standing near the fence didn't see her.

She leaned back against a tree trunk and closed her eyes, her heart pounding frantically. So much for trying to avoid Tack. She'd purposely decided to work on land shots—some views of the pasture, the herd—all far away from the creek and, most of all, him. After their interview yesterday, the heat his hungry gaze and his charming smiles had generated, Annie wasn't about to risk seeing him again.

Not with a peach in his hand and sin on his mind.

She wanted only to finish her job. The sooner she finished the pictures, the sooner the sales package could be put together and a buyer found. The sooner Tack Brandon would leave Inspiration.

She peered around the tree, her heart jumping into her throat as she drank in the sight of him. He wore only a sleeveless black racing vest with Take the Dare emblazoned in liquid blue. Matching black pants hugged his thighs and calves. Biker boots completed the outfit. His hair was damp. Perspiration dripped off his chin.

Bare muscular arms gleamed with sweat. He looked tired and hot and…incredibly sexy.

Her pulse quickened and heat uncurled low in her belly, spiraling to the sensitive tips of her breasts. She became acutely aware of the way her lacy bra rasped against her nipples with every deep breath.

Distance, she told herself. *Turn around and don't look back.*

Surprisingly, her body obeyed. Fifteen minutes later, she climbed into her truck parked on the side of the dirt road that bordered the wildflower field, *her* field, and tried the key. The engine refused to catch.

"Please don't do this to me now." She tried again.

Click, click, click…

She slammed her palm against the steering wheel and let loose Deb's favorite four-letter expletive. "First the stupid air conditioner at home, and now this. Why me?"

She wallowed in self-pity all of five seconds before she climbed out, popped the hood and tried to figure out what she was looking for. She checked the oil, the water in the radiator and tapped and knocked a few places. Another turn of the key and still nothing.

So much for speeding up Tack's departure. If she didn't get the film to the lab before noon, she would never have the pictures by five. That meant waiting until Monday. Three extra days.

Annie grabbed her camera equipment and started walking.

A few minutes down the road, the roar of a motor-cycle filled her ears and she moved to the shoulder just as a familiar black Harley grumbled to a stop beside her. Tack sat there, hands on his hips, blue eyes roaming from her head to her dust-covered sandals.

"My truck quit," she explained.

"I saw it a ways back. Could be the transmission. It was leaking fluid."

She shook her head. "Just my luck."

He grinned. "You could get lucky in a second, honey, if you wanted to." There was no missing the double meaning.

"I'm not interested in getting lucky."

His unreadable blue eyes assessed her. "Or maybe you're just afraid."

"Of you?" Her laugh sounded rusty.

"Of finding out that you're a hell of a lot more affected by me than you care to admit."

He couldn't have been more wrong. Annie already knew the truth, felt it in the bone-melting heat that gripped her body, the electricity that skimmed her nerve endings when he was near.

She tried for a laugh. "That'll be the day."

"Then get on." His eyes gleamed with challenge and Annie knew she had no choice. She either climbed on or walked, and walking would be as good as admitting that Tack Brandon did, indeed, get to her.

"I only need to go as far as Moby's Service Station. He's got a wrecker." She straddled the spot behind him and gripped the sides of the seat, careful to avoid touching him.

As if he sensed her reluctance, he said, "You'd better hold on to me unless you want to find yourself lying by the side of the road." He chuckled, a soft, warm, sexy sound that vibrated the air around them. "I won't bite, honey. Unless you want me to, that is."

"No, thanks." She took a deep breath, braced herself and slid her arms around his waist. "Okay, I'm ready."

And so was he, she realized when he shifted the bike into gear and zoomed forward. They jumped and Annie's hands grazed the bulge in his jeans.

She stiffened and he chuckled again. "The service station?" he asked. "You sure that's as far as you want to go, honey? Because I could take you for a long ride." The deep huskiness of his voice told her the ride he referred to had nothing to do with motorcycles and everything to do with a man and woman and lots of sweet, breath-stealing bumps and curves. "Long and slow. Short and fast. Any way you want it."

She wasn't going to let him bait her. "Moby's is plenty far enough."

But Tack had other ideas. He took her to Moby's and helped make the necessary arrangements to have her truck picked up. Then he steered her back onto the Harley, determined to see her safely to work.

By the time Annie climbed off the back of Tack's motorcycle, she was this close to throwing herself across the front of his bike and begging him to touch her, kiss her, love her.

Close, but not quite there. *Yet.*

"Don't I get a thank-you?"

"Thank you," she said, grabbing her camera bag.

"I was thinking of something a little more... *active.*" He grinned, oblivious to Mr. Hopkins and several others who stood out in front of a nearby grocery store, their gazes hooked on Tack and Annie. "Like a kiss."

"Didn't you hear anything I said?"

"That you're not falling into bed with me again. I don't see a bed around, honey. It's just a kiss."

"Forget it." She glanced pointedly at Mr. Hopkins.

"Afraid people might get the wrong idea about us?"

Or the right idea. "I'm not kissing you, and I don't give a fig what anyone thinks."

"Well, then." He climbed off the motorcycle to tower in front of her. "I guess I'll have to kiss you."

Before she could blink, he hauled her up against his chest and covered her lips with his. His tongue slid into her mouth to stroke and tease. Strong hands pressed the small of her back, holding her close as he kissed her long and slow and deep the way he had in the newspaper office Saturday night. But this time she could feel every inch of his body, from chest to hips to thighs, his desire pressing hard and eager into her belly.

He smelled of leather and fresh air and a touch of wildness that teased her nostrils and made her breathe heavier, desperate to draw more of his essence into her lungs.

She was a heartbeat away from sliding her arms around his neck and clinging to him, when she heard the high-pitched whistle followed by a few shouts of encouragement from their audience.

Annie did what any woman would have done in her situation. She grabbed an inch of Tack's upper arm and pinched for all she was worth.

"Ouch!" He released her with a suddenness that sent her stumbling backward a few steps. "What the hell was that for?"

"For kissing me when I didn't want a kiss."

He rubbed his arm. "You could have tried telling me to stop before you decided to take off an inch of flesh."

"You weren't giving me much room to get a word in edgewise."

He examined his arm. "Hell, it's bruising."

"It was only a little pinch."

"I think you broke the skin," he said accusingly.

"I did not." She leaned in and rubbed a fingertip over the spot of angry red skin. "Don't be such a baby." She summoned her courage and ignored a pang of guilt. "And don't kiss me again. Otherwise, I just might break the skin."

Despite his bruised arm, he chuckled. "You know, honey," he said, his eyes darkening to a deep sapphire blue, "I might be inclined to think you don't like me, except that you were really into that kiss."

She bristled. "In your dreams, buddy. I pinched you, remember?"

"*Before* you pinched me. You kissed me back, Annie. Both lips, tongue, the works, baby. *You* kissed *me*." With a satisfied smile, he turned, climbed on the motorcycle and left her staring after him.

She wasn't sure how she made it across the sidewalk and up the stairs to the newspaper office. Divine intervention. Or maybe the fact that she could feel the eyes on her, boring into her back after Tack's blatant disregard for their rapt audience.

He'd kissed her on Main Street in front of God and everyone.

It doesn't matter what people think.

Ordinarily, but this wasn't some misconception based on ignorance. Anyone who saw the kiss would know that Tack Brandon wanted Annie Divine.

At least they didn't know that she wanted him back. She'd pinched him and put him in his place. If only she'd done it a moment sooner. Before she'd kissed him back with both lips, tongue, the works.

Her stomach jumped as she walked into the office and sat down to find a stack of mail on her desk. A quick thumb through the pile and her day went from bad to worse. Five rejection letters from the five résumés she'd sent out, and all in one week.

"It's a tough business." Deb walked by, her Bad To The Bitchiest Bone mug in her hand, sympathy gleaming in her eyes. "Don't let it get to you. Send out more tear sheets."

Annie nodded, filed the letters away in her drawer and pulled out her Top Twenty list. She crossed off the rejections and moved on to the next batch of five.

They were just a few rejections, a few stop signs on the road to her future, and it was just one kiss.

Okay, so technically it was two, but that didn't matter as long as the buck stopped here.

No more kissing. Nada. Zilch.

If only she didn't want to go for number three.

Annie wasn't taking any chances on another encounter with Tack. She dropped the ranch pictures by Gary Tucker's office at exactly 5:00 p.m., stopped off at the garage to check on her truck, then headed back to the office to finish some work.

She sat down at her desk and pulled out another manila envelope. The pictures she hadn't turned over to Gary.

She stared down at a particularly suggestive shot of Tack eating a peach down by the creek.

Now was her chance. Deb was still at the courthouse interviewing the mayor's secretary for a political piece. Wally was downstairs with the printing press that kept eating this week's issue.

Out of sight, out of mind.

She gripped the edge of one and started to tear. Her fingers faltered a fraction from his face. He wore such an intense expression, as if he put all his heart and soul into the simple task of devouring the fruit, sating his hunger, stirring hers. A smile tugged at her lips, and she tucked the photos into her camera bag.

What harm could a few mementos do?

"DID YOU GET PICTURES?" Deb stood in front of Annie's desk less than an hour later, a copy of Tack's interview in one hand and her Born To Bitch mug in the other.

"Pictures?" Annie's squeaked out, shifting a guilty gaze to her camera bag. "What pictures?"

"Of Tack. A head and neck shot for the This Is Your Neighbor column. We usually run the article with at least one picture."

"Oh, *that* picture."

"What else?"

"Nothing." Annie tried to still her pounding heart as she rummaged in her desk and pulled out the yearbook she'd used to fill in background information on Tack. "How about this?"

"An old yearbook photograph?"

"That's how the entire town remembers him. We can use a few football shots, the standard head and shoulders. It'll be like a tribute to the past." And the only thing Annie could come up with since she'd been so worked up during the interview, she'd forgotten to take a current picture.

"How about this prom photo?" Deb wiggled her eyebrows. "Geez, honey, you were a pretty girl, but that is the ugliest dress I've ever seen. All I see is a little blond head sitting on top of this navy blue...*thing.*"

"I wasn't a flashy dresser back then."

"And you landed the captain of the football team?"

"I think that was one of the reasons Tack liked me. I wasn't flashing my cleavage in his face every five minutes. He liked the challenge."

"This was definitely a challenge. I'd say the guy deserves a date just for the effort."

"I do not have any desire to date Tack Brandon. He's only back for a little while." Thankfully. "And I'm busy."

"Doing what? Your weekly stories are finished. We go to press in the morning. It's Friday night and you're free."

"Not completely. I already have a date."

"With who?"

"My living room. I'm wallpapering tonight. Ivory with mauve flowers," Annie said. "And it's gorgeous."

"Not half as gorgeous as this." Deb pointed to the photo of Tack.

But much safer, she thought as she headed across the

street to Heavenly Hardware to pick up the wallpaper supplies and the paste before she hitched a ride home with Deb.

And safe was all Annie could handle right now.

CHAPTER NINE

LATER THAT EVENING, ANNIE stood on a stepladder, struggled with a strip of wallpaper and tried not to think about Tack.

Or his kiss.

Or that she wanted, *really* wanted another.

Work. She steeled herself and tried to concentrate on the paste-laden strip of wallpaper rather than the restless hunger gnawing at her, the need to feel his lips on hers, his hands skimming her body, his heart beating strong and sure and frantic against hers—

The screen door shook with the force of a knock, shattering her thoughts. Thankfully.

"Come on in," she called out over the radio blasting an old Rolling Stones song. The wallpaper sagged with the weight of the paste and she struggled to hold the sheet upright. "They ought to give a warning with this stuff. Extra hands needed." She groaned as the edges started to fold over. The screen door squeaked and she added, "That was quick. Just put the pizza on the table."

"What pizza?"

The deep voice froze her hand in midair. The paper collapsed, slapping her cheek as she realized that Tack Brandon stood in her living room.

Worse, he was standing right behind her. He leaned

in, strong, muscular arms coming up on either side to help her hold up the paper.

His large, dark hands were a stark contrast against the dainty cream wallpaper as he anchored the edges in place. Annie managed to tear her attention away from the tanned perfection of his fingers long enough to retrieve the wallpaper blade from her pocket and smooth the strip into place. Her fingers trembled. Her heart drummed. Or maybe that was his. He was so close. Too close.

"I—I thought you were the pizza boy."

"Not the last time I looked."

His voice rumbled over her bare shoulder. Warm breath brushed her skin, sending a wave of goose bumps chasing down the length of her arm. She managed a few more swipes of the blade then slipped it back into her pocket.

"All done," she said, but he didn't move. Annie turned in his arms. The stepladder put her at eye level with him and their gazes collided. Locked.

"It looks good," he said, but his eyes remained on her.

"I—I always thought wallpaper would look nice in here."

"I wasn't talking about the wallpaper."

Suddenly, she couldn't get enough air. She drew in a deep breath, the motion pushing her breasts up and out. Her nipples kissed his chest. Heat spiraled from the points of contact to settle low in her belly.

"What are you doing here?" she managed to say in a breathy voice.

What would you like me to do? That's what his gaze

said, but his lips murmured, "You said you were fixing up the place." He spared the chaos around them a quick glance, from the sheet-covered furniture and scarred hardwood floor, to the torn screen door. Bones stood on the other side, wet nose pressed to the mesh, while the twins barked and jumped at him from the inside. Tack's gaze returned to hers and a slow grin spread across his face. "I thought I could help. I'm pretty good with my hands."

Too good. The thought blew through her mind a second before he touched her. A callused fingertip slid along her sweaty cheek, the damp skin of her neck.

Electricity skimmed her nerve endings, sending warmth pulsing to her nipples, her thighs.

"You're awful hot, honey."

She blew out a breath. "My air conditioner conked out. The hardware store special-ordered a part, but it's not in yet."

He didn't seem convinced. He stared at her as if searching for answers. Despite the radio blasting in the background and the twins yipping and yapping at Bones, she could hear the air drawing in and out of her lungs, the drumming of her own heart, the hum of blood as it zipped through her veins.

"That explains why you're so wet." His gaze dropped, roaming over her neck and shoulders covered with a fine sheen of sweat, down over the damp material of her tank top molded to her puckered nipples, the bare skin of her stomach glistening just above the waistband of her shorts. Blue eyes caught and held hers. "That *is* why you're so wet, isn't it?"

Before she could answer, the twins abandoned Bones

and rushed at Tack, effectively breaking the erotic spell holding Annie captive.

"I—I'm going to open another window." She didn't look at him as she ducked beneath one arm and stepped off the ladder, but she felt his grin.

"Hey, there, fellas." Tack hefted the twins into his arms. They licked at his face, tails wagging. "Gary said the pictures were really good."

"Thanks."

"He's handling the Echo Canyon sale in the next county and asked if you'd be interested in earning some extra cash. He said to give him a call." He nuzzled the puppies. "You cheated, you know," he finally said. "You were supposed to deliver the pictures to me."

She averted her gaze and fought to push the living-room windows as high as they would go. "Gary's in charge of the sale, so I thought I'd give them directly to him and save some time."

"Or maybe you weren't in any big hurry to see me again."

"Maybe I wasn't."

"Why not?"

She gave an indifferent shrug. "Why should I be?"

He stared at her as if searching for an answer, and she feared he wasn't going to let the subject go. Then a grin slid across his handsome face and relief crept through her.

"Because I'm cute," he offered.

"More like egotistical."

"Irresistible," he countered.

"Shameless."

"Helpful. You need an extra pair of hands, and here I am."

Speaking of hands...

Her gaze fixed on his, so big and strong and tanned and gentle against the small white puppies. *Gentle.* A warmth spread through her, soothing her jangled nerves. "I guess I could use the help." She wiped at the sweat beading her forehead. "I'll paste and you do the hanging."

"I'm way ahead of you on that, honey."

A quick glance down and she realized he wasn't speaking just figuratively. She blushed, he chuckled, and despite the sexual tension coiling around them, she actually relaxed.

She liked his laugh. The deep sound of his voice. The teasing. He could always make her feel at ease even though she knew he posed the greatest threat. Because Tack Brandon had been her friend, as well as her lover. Her best friend, and for some insane reason, that's all she remembered at the moment.

They spent the next half hour finishing one wall until the real pizza boy arrived. While Tack moved the sofa to the opposite side of the room so they could paper the next wall, Annie let the twins out to do their business. When she returned, she found him sitting on the floor with her pink photo album.

"It fell off the coffee table during the move," he explained as he turned page after page, his gaze drinking in everything from photos to a cocktail napkin from her mother's favorite restaurant, a dried daisy—her mother's favorite flower. "What is it?" he said, indicating the album.

"My mom."

He closed the book as his gaze locked with hers. "You mean it belonged to her?"

"I mean it *is* her. It's filled with everything she loved in her life. Whenever I get lonely, I look at it and it makes me feel closer to her." She held out her hand. "I'll put it away so it doesn't get messed up."

"That's nice," he finally said as he handed over the album, and Annie realized she'd been holding her breath. A strange sense of relief stole through her and she smiled.

She stored the album under her bed, retrieved two beers and some napkins from the kitchen, then joined Tack in the living room. She handed him a bottle dripping with condensation.

"I've never developed a taste for the stuff myself—this is Deb's leftover from our last gab session—but it's the only thing that's really cold in this entire house." She sank onto the floor and sat with her legs crossed, the pizza separating them.

He took a long swig of beer and glanced around.

Annie's gaze followed his, from the leak in the ceiling where water had puckered the sheetrock, to the scratched floor, to the broken screen door. "I was so busy making ends meet after my mom died that I let the place go. I mean, it never was much, but my mom kept up with everything. Minor repairs, fresh paint, waxed floors. Since I never had a dad, except biologically speaking, she learned how to fend for herself."

"Do you remember him at all?"

"Only what she told me. He was a truck driver. She'd just graduated high school and started waitressing at this honky-tonk out on the interstate. They were both young and in lust. She told him when she found out she was pregnant, and never saw him again after that. He left town. She had me and moved us here, as far away as her pocketbook and a Greyhound bus could carry us. She promised that Inspiration would only be temporary, just long enough for her to save some money and get us to Austin."

"What was in Austin?"

"The Silver Spurs, the biggest nightclub in Texas, or it was at the time. They had their own version of the Rockettes who wore these little cowgirl outfits and put on nightly shows."

"She wanted to be a dancer?"

"A respectable dancer. A showgirl. But she never made it."

"Because she met my father."

"And fell in love, and gave up her dreams, to stay here and be the town outcast." A mistake Annie had no intention of repeating. Her dreams had seen her through the pain of Tack's leaving and given her hope for something other than him riding back into town and sweeping her off her feet like the hero in some romantic fairy tale. "Not me."

"Which part?"

"All three. I've spent my entire life living for everyone else. Now I want something for myself. I want to take my career as far as it can go."

"I guess that means you haven't given much thought to settling down."

She shrugged. "Ted Riley asks me to dinner every once in a while. He's the youth minister over at the church. We've kissed a few times, but nothing more. We're mainly just friends." She watched a satisfied expression creep over Tack's face. "What about you? You ever think about tying the knot?"

He took another swig of beer and wiped his sweaty forehead. "No, and I intend to keep it that way. I'm not the marrying kind. I'm on the road a lot, living out of a suitcase. My racing takes one hundred and ten percent. That's no kind of life for a wife and kids." He paused, then said, "I'm not making the same mistake as my old man. He was too busy with his ranch to do right by my mother and me."

"Sounds awful cynical for the guy voted most likely to."

"To what?"

She grinned. "Just *to.* The Tack Brandon I knew would try anything at least once."

"And the Annie Divine I knew wanted a big white wedding and at least three kids."

Before Annie could think of a reply, Bones whimpered from the front porch. Annie got to her feet and let him in, grateful for the sudden distraction. He rushed over to Tack and begged for some pizza.

After the dog had devoured his fourth slice, Annie asked, "Does he always eat this much?"

"You wouldn't think so from looking at him. But he's a glutton, aren't you, boy?" He rubbed the dog's head and Bones wagged his tail. "I've been trying to find him a home, but so far he's been to three different places and has eaten himself right into a trip back to the Big B. He was with Jimmy until yesterday. Bones ate Jimmy's lunch, then left a little souvenir in Jimmy's boot."

"You don't mean—"

"Jimmy's still trying to get the smell out." Tack climbed to his feet, grabbed the empty pizza box and the napkins and stuffed them into a nearby trash bag Annie had erected for the wallpaper leftovers.

"He's kind of cute." Annie rubbed the dog's bulging tummy. "And he probably pooped in Jimmy's boot because he was lonesome for you. Dogs do that when they're homesick."

"The Big B isn't his home." Tack lowered himself to the floor, his back against the wall, his legs stretched out in front of him. "Damn, but it's hot in here." He pulled at his damp T-shirt and Annie caught a glimpse of a rock-hard abdomen dusted with dark hair.

She forced her attention back to Bones. "I meant, he probably missed you. Why don't you keep him?"

"I don't think he'd fit in my suitcase. I'm on the road two-thirds of the year, and I'm hardly home when I *am* home. I can't keep him."

Bones rolled over to waddle around Tack, and settle down beside him.

Annie laughed. "You might not be keeping him, but I think he wants to keep you."

"Actually, it's your floor he's getting real comfortable on. Help a guy out, Annie. Bones here would be in heaven. Animals like you."

"If memory serves me, they like you, too. I seem to recall a certain collie that followed you everywhere."

He grinned. "Mary Theresa."

"Who ever heard of calling a dog Mary Theresa?"

"Nostalgia, honey. Mary Theresa was the first female I ever had a crush on. My kindergarten teacher. Mary Theresa Berger. What about you? Name your first love."

"That's easy. Pastor Marley." At his incredulous expression, she shrugged. "What can I say? I liked the way he looked in that suit." She took a sip of beer. "I remember sitting in the last pew—I always sat in the last one because I had to ride the Sunday-school bus and, since I lived so far out, I was always getting there late. Anyhow, I would slide into my seat and sit there and think, if I could just marry Reverend Marley, my life would be perfect."

"Wasn't he bald?"

"And he wore glasses and had a potbelly, but it wasn't about looks."

"What was it about?"

Annie stiffened and shook her head. "I think we've strolled down memory lane enough for one night. This wallpaper won't hang itself." She started to climb to her feet. Large, strong fingers closed around hers.

"Come on, Annie. Tell me."

She wasn't sure why she did, except that he was touching her and she did crazy things when he touched her. "I thought that if I married Pastor Marley, I'd get to sit in the front row for once. People would shake my hand and smile at me instead of staring at me, or worse, pretending not to see me at all."

"I see you," he said, his thumb rubbing a tiny circle at the inside of her wrist. "I always did." He let go of her then, but it was too late. Her nipples tightened, tingled, and a low burning flame swept her nerve endings, and all because of that small, whisper-soft touch that had lasted all of two seconds.

She let out an unsteady breath. "It's really hot in here."

"I know the feeling." He drank the last of his beer and set the bottle down. Bones shifted and stepped over Tack. The bottle *clinked* to its side as the dog strolled toward the kitchen.

Tack eyed the fallen beer bottle, then a slow grin spread across his face. With a flick of his wrist, he started the bottle spinning. It shimmied to a standstill, the mouth pointing to Annie.

His eyes gleamed with challenge. "Truth or dare?"

Maybe it was the heat or the beer or his smile, maybe all three, that reminded her of so many hot nights sitting by the river, spinning a cola bottle in the back of his daddy's truck and playing kissing games. Regardless, she met his gaze, his smile, and whispered, "Truth."

"Did you miss me?"

She swallowed, thought about lying, then quickly discarded it. "You were one of my best friends. Of course I missed you."

"That's not the kind of miss I meant." He grinned. "But it'll do. For now. Your turn."

Annie's fingers trembled as she twirled the bottle, which came to point at her again. "I think this is rigged."

"Truth or dare?"

"Another spin?"

"That's against the rules." He eyed her. "But just to show you that I'm a nice guy, I'll give you another chance."

Annie smiled and twirled the bottle again. "Aha," she said, smiling triumphantly. "Truth or dare?"

"Truth."

"Did *you* miss *me?*"

"You were my best friend…" He started to mimic her answer and disappointment welled inside. "And my lover, and I missed both. You've been keeping me company at night, Annie." Fierce blue eyes caught and held hers. "In my dreams. But they've been even worse lately since I've been back in town." He paused, his voice dropping to a husky whisper, "And back inside of you—"

"Your turn," she blurted before he could say any more. "Your spin." She pushed the bottle at him. "Here. Spin."

He did. The bottle pointed to her. "Truth or dare?" he asked.

Annie wasn't up to any more questions. "Dare."

He didn't say anything for a long moment, just stared at her, his gaze dark, intense, stirring. "Kiss me like you missed me," he finally said. "Like you *really* missed me."

Pleasure tickled low in her belly at the prospect, and before she could call it quits, she got to her knees and scooted closer. It was just a kiss, one she wanted more than her next breath.

She focused on that thought, rather than the push-pull of emotion inside her, and placed her hands on his broad shoulders to steady herself.

"No pinching this time," he added, his warm breath feathering her lips.

She smiled. "And here I thought this was going to be fun."

"Oh, it'll be fun, all right. Just not life-threatening."

"Says you," she murmured as she touched her mouth to his.

One kiss, Tack told himself as she leaned in, one simple kiss. That's all she owed him, all he meant to collect.

Until her lips lingered, parted and a soft moan quivered into his mouth, and suddenly he wanted more than a kiss.

Suddenly he wanted more than teasing games. He wanted to make his dreams come true. To feel her pulse around him and shatter in his arms. To feel *her*, warm and quivering and real.

His hands came up, sliding around her waist and pulling her closer. One hand caught the back of her thigh, lifting her knee so that she straddled him. He grabbed her bottom and settled her more firmly against the bulge in his jeans.

The contact shocked them both. She gasped and rocked against him, and he worked frantically at the button of her shorts. The zipper hissed, the waistband fell open and his fingers dived inside. He cupped the soft flesh of her buttocks in his bare hands.

The heat burned fierce between them as they kissed and rubbed and worked each other into a frenzy. The air grew hotter, charged with the summer heat and the ripe smell of sweaty bodies and steamy sex and—

"Wait." His fingers tightened, stilling her movements. "Slow down, honey. I don't want this to go too fast, to be over too quick." He took a deep breath and rested his forehead against hers. "Damn, you make me crazy. I can't think."

"It's the beer," she murmured before claiming his lips in another kiss.

Another sweet, erotic shimmy of her body and the air lodged in his chest.

"I can't breathe either," he gasped.

"It's the heat."

Beer? Heat? He caught her face between his hands. Her gaze collided with his. "Like hell, Annie. It's you. Me. *Us*."

Denial raged in her eyes, warring with the passion that glittered hot and bright and needy.

He was so close to easing the fierce ache. A quick flick of a button, a swift jerk on his zipper and he could satisfy them both.

But for the first time in his life, Tack wanted more from a woman than physical satisfaction. He wanted to know why. Why the tears, the murmured, "It's been so long." *Why?*

"You do this to me," he said, arching so she felt every thick, throbbing inch of him through his jeans. "And I do this to you." He flicked her puckered nipple, making it quiver and tighten, before trailing his fingers down to dip into her shorts, her panties and stroke the moist heat between her legs. "I make you this hot, this wet."

"I haven't been with anyone in a while and—" she caught her bottom lip as his fingertip dipped inside her "—I...I'm only human. It's so hot in here and I have needs and..." The sentence faded into a whimper.

"Needs that could be satisfied by any man?"

"Y-yes."

He plunged deep and she shuddered. Her eyes closed, her full lips parted. He indulged her for two more deep, probing thrusts before stilling the movements, for his own sanity more than hers. She was so damn beautiful, so flushed and hot and ready, and he was only human. Only a man. *Her* man.

"You know, honey," he said when her eyes fluttered open. "I'm not nearly as convinced that what happened between us my first night back in town, that this—" another sweet probe of his finger and a ragged gasp broke from her full lips "—is just for convenience's sake, that you're hungry for a man and I happen to fit that description. There's more to it. More than the beer freeing your inhibitions or the heat making your body burn."

"There isn't," she said, despite the fact that she arched into him, her muscles contracting, drawing him a fraction deeper.

Ah…

He couldn't help himself. He kissed her, a deep, probing kiss that uncovered every secret and left no doubt in her mind that he wanted her.

"Just to prove my point," he murmured when the kiss ended and he finally found his voice, "I'm not going to press you, or touch you or kiss you again or—" he licked his lips in slow, sensuous promise "—do half the things running through my mind. Not until you say the word, until you ask me. That way, if you're not attracted to *me,* then you don't have a thing to worry about. I won't tempt you, and there'll be no fall from grace." He gathered his last shred of control, removed his hand from her shorts and felt her tremble at the slide of flesh along flesh.

She was hiding. Hiding her need for him behind convenient excuses that could explain her reaction in purely physical terms.

But this was more than physical. The chemistry between them was explosive because the feelings ran deeper than lust. Much deeper.

He fastened her shorts, set her aside and climbed to his feet. Then he walked away from her, because Tack Brandon wanted more than sex. For the first time in his life, he wanted a woman's heart, as well. He wanted Annie's.

ANNIE STOOD ON HER BACK PORCH, her body still hot and trembling, an undeniable reminder that Tack Brandon had roared back into her life, into her head and her heart.

Not for long, she told herself. He would be leaving again, and Annie would get on with her life, with her future, and she would forget all about the way his eyes darkened to a midnight blue when he looked at her. The way his hands trailed over her body, soft and tender, yet purposeful at the same time, the way he looked at her, into her, and saw all the things she tried to hide. Her desire. Her love.

Not love. Not completely. Not yet.

Out of sight, out of mind.

She opened the trash can, threw the photos inside and slammed the lid back on. Then she turned on her heel and marched inside.

She tossed and turned for the next few hours, trying to fall asleep. Just when she started to relax, she saw him standing down by the creek, eating the peach with enough zest to make her legs quiver. She felt him, too. His hands on her breasts, feathering over her skin, stroking between her legs until she was so close to coming apart—

She threw off the covers, hurried outside and retrieved the photos from the trash can.

"This doesn't prove a thing except that I hate to waste really good work." The pictures of Tack had been some of her best. They told their own story of passion and hunger, and while she wasn't about to add them to her portfolio, neither could she discard them.

She packed the pictures away in her picture box and stuffed it beneath the bed. *Safe.*

But Annie herself was far from safe. The night stretched ahead of her, the bed loomed big and empty, and Tack waited just the other side of sleep. To touch and tantalize and try to shake her precious control.

Tonight proved her point exactly. She had to keep her distance from him until he left. In the meantime, no touching, no kissing, *nothing.*

"MISS ANNIE?" ANNIE TURNED from painting the trim at the far corner of the house, to see Wayne Mitchell, the clerk from the hardware store.

"Did I forget something?" She glanced around at the gallons of paint, the brushes and rollers, the pan.

"No. You picked up everything yesterday. I've got a temporary air-conditioning unit that Mr. Heaven asked me to bring out here and hook up until the part comes in for yours."

"I didn't ask for a temporary unit."

Wayne shrugged. "All's I know is Mr. Heaven got a

call from Mr. Brandon, and here I am." He motioned to the truck. "I'll get the unit hooked up for you."

"Forget it. I'll wait for the part."

"But—"

"Take it back."

"Mr. Heaven will be mad 'cause Mr. Brandon's sure to be hot as a concrete pavement at noon if his orders ain't carried out."

"I'll take care of Mr. Brandon," she said through tight lips. "You can bet money on that."

Later, after she conned Wally into a ride, she found Tack in the barn at the Big B.

"I don't need you flaunting your money and renting air conditioners for me."

He finished saddling the horse and faced her. "I just wanted to make sure there wasn't anything clouding your opinion of what's going on between us."

"There's nothing going on between us."

"Did they get the unit hooked up?"

"I sent it back. If I want a temporary unit, I can rent one myself. I don't need anyone paying for me." *Buying* me. The way Coop had tried to buy her mother. He'd given her so many things to con her into staying, into needing him so much she'd given up her dreams of Austin so she could stay and be his mistress.

She slapped him in the chest with an envelope. "Here's the money you gave Mr. Heaven." She turned and stormed out. He caught her at the doorway, his hand closing around hers for a split second before he let her go.

"I wasn't paying for you, Annie, or trying to insult you. I was just trying to even up the playing field."

"There's no need, because we're not playing. Last night was a tie. End of season." Annie walked away, and Tack's voice followed her out.

"I've got news for you, honey. We're going into overtime."

CHAPTER TEN

IT WAS LATE SATURDAY AFTERNOON when Tack showed up on Annie's doorstep. Freshly showered and shaved, he looked heartbreakingly handsome in a white T-shirt and jeans. When he handed her a single daisy, her chest tightened.

"I thought you might want some company. My company."

She took the flower and summoned her indifference. "What would make you think something like that?"

"You don't have to be scared, Annie."

"Of you?"

"Of *us*."

"There is no us. I—I really have to go." It took everything she had to close the door in his face, but she managed.

She waited for the sound of footsteps, the roar of his motorcycle. She heard only the *bam, bam, bam* of her own heart.

He wasn't leaving. The knowledge hit her a few seconds later. She moved to the edge of the curtain in time to see him shrug out of his shirt, pick up a nearby can of paint and a brush and disappear around the side of the house. Annie rushed to the back bedroom and peered through the window, and saw Tack start on the trim she'd begun that morning.

As if he had nothing better to do than help her out. As if he enjoyed it.

Fat chance. It was a ploy to get into her house, her bed.

Annie promised herself to ignore him and concentrate on varnishing the newly stripped kitchen cabinets, but it wasn't easy. She heard every sound, from the swish-swish of paint near the kitchen window as he finished the side of the house, to the glug-glug of water when he finally rinsed up and called it quits just after sunset. His Harley growled and spewed gravel as he left her to a sleepless night filled with erotic dreams of a half-naked man who smiled and teased and ate peaches and made Annie feel both shy and wanton at the same time.

That was his plan, she told herself the next day. That and to make her feel guilty that he was outside working so hard on a Sunday afternoon while she sat inside with a cool glass of lemonade.

From the sofa where she sat, she could see him through the front window that overlooked the porch. He'd finally worked his way around and had just started to apply a fresh coat to the wooden railing that framed the porch.

He wore nothing but a pair of faded jeans and dusty black motorcycle boots. The denim hung low on his hips. His muscled torso gleamed with perspiration. She shook her head at the ache that twisted her middle. Longing. Anticipation.

She stomped to the window and yanked the blinds closed. There. That was better. She could enjoy her lemonade with no distractions—

Bones barked, shattering the thought. Annie peeked

through the slats to see the dog sitting under a nearby tree, panting. Her gaze shifted back to Tack.

Strong fingers clasped the paintbrush. Muscles rippled, bulged as he moved the brush back and forth. Annie forced her attention from the slow, smooth strokes, up, over a heavily muscled bicep, the curve of one broad shoulder, to his face. Sweat beaded his forehead. A drop slid from his temple, down to his strong jaw and dropped onto his chest.

Perspiration trickled from her own temple.

Maybe she should have forked over the money herself for a temporary air-conditioning unit. Then she wouldn't be so miserable. Not that it would have offered Tack any relief. He was outside, in the one hundred and ten-plus, record-breaking heat.

Seconds later, she opened the front door, thrust a glass of lemonade at him and placed a bowl of fresh water on the front steps for Bones. Then she picked up a brush.

"What are you doing?"

"Painting. If you think I'm letting you have all the fun while I bake in that oven of a house, you've got another think coming."

It *was* just painting. Harmless, innocent painting in full view of God and Mrs. Pope and anybody else who might wander by.

Tack grinned. "I knew you couldn't resist my charm."

But it wasn't his charm she was worried about resisting. It was all the rest of him.

"WALLY HAD A DENTAL appointment, so I told him I'd come by and give you a lift." Deb climbed out of her fire-engine-red Miata just as Annie stepped up onto the porch after giving her roses their Monday-morning watering.

"Thanks. My truck should be fixed later this afternoon."

Deb glanced around and let out a low whistle. "Wow. This place is really shaping up. I thought you'd planned to work on the inside this weekend."

"It wasn't her," came the gravelly voice next door. "It was that man, Coop Brandon's boy. He spent the whole danged weekend over there, traipsing around half-naked."

"Half-naked?" A smile split Deb's face. "Sounds interesting."

"Dreadful, that's what it was," the woman said. "If you youngsters want to play sex games, you should do it in the privacy of your own home."

"Good morning to you, too, Mrs. Pope," Annie greeted in her cheeriest voice. "Play bingo this weekend?" The woman frowned.

"Sex games." Deb's smile widened. "And here I thought I was the only one who kicked up her heels on the weekend."

"We did not play sex games," Annie told Deb. "We were just painting and drinking lemonade together."

"It was a shameful display," Mrs. Pope chimed in.

Deb motioned next door. "I thought she wore a hearing aid."

"I've never worn any such thing, missy," Mrs. Pope grumbled, stabbing the air in Deb's direction with her gardening tool. "My hearing's one hundred percent just like the rest of me. A rest home, my daughter Claire says. Why, she can shove her rest home where the sun don't shine..."

"I bet the rest home has weekly bingo," Annie called out as she grabbed Deb's arm and ushered her inside. "I swear, the woman's got bionic hearing, and the eyesight to go with it."

"At least you only have to worry about one neighbor since you live out here in the boonies." Deb poised on the edge of Annie's couch, an eager look on her face while Annie searched for her camera bag. "So tell me, are we talking so-so, it's-not-so-bad-but-I-live-in-red-neck-central shameful, or the ultra, even-try-anything-once-Deb-will-be-shocked shameful."

"Neither." Annie found her bag, then hustled the twins onto the fenced-in back porch and closed the door. "Nothing happened."

"He was here."

"Yes."

"And he did all that work outside."

"Yes."

"And you were both traipsing around naked."

"That's *half*-naked, and it was Tack who took off his shirt. I was fully clothed." With the exception of Friday night, she added silently.

"So he was here strictly in a home-repair sense." At Annie's nod, she added, "The guy's either stupid, or he wants you bad. I vote for the second. Either way, you should thank him."

"I did. I said thanks, kept him supplied with lemonade and even painted a little myself. Now, can we just go?"

Deb nodded and five minutes later they were zooming down the main strip through town.

"I don't understand why you're trying so hard to push this guy away," her friend said as she struggled to parallel park in a spot no sane person would try for, except Deb, who prided herself on her skill behind the wheel.

"You're cutting it awful close to that black Bronco behind us."

"Black?" Deb's head swiveled and she grinned evilly. "Say, isn't that Jimmy Mission's Bronco?"

"I think so."

"Oh boy. I should have known. With an ego the size of his, I'm not surprised he needs two parking spaces—oops." They rocked as her car backed into the Bronco's bumper. "I hope I didn't scratch anything."

"The Bronco looks pretty tough."

"I was talking about *my* car." She manuevered forward a few inches. "Now, about you and Tack..."

"I thought we closed this subject."

"*You* did. I was just getting started. Look, Annie. He's good-looking, famous...sort of, in a sports sense, and he obviously wants you. Not to mention, most men wouldn't spend two seconds doing a job if they thought it wasn't going to pay off. If you made it clear to Tack that there was no hope for the two of you and he still went out of his way, that makes him one hell of a nice guy on top of everything. This cowboy's a prize find."

"A temporary find." Thankfully.

"And temporary is exactly up your alley, or so you've said a thousand times. 'I can't take that cowboy home, Deb. This town is too small, I don't want to get serious with anybody, and sleeping with them might give the wrong impression, and what will I say when I have to face Tack and everyone else day after day?' Okay, you had a point, but you won't have to face Tack day after day. Just until he sells or you leave, or both. And nobody will get the wrong impression if the understanding is there right up front. He's leaving. You're leaving. Temporary. Perfect."

Deb was right, Annie thought as she headed up the stairs to the second floor and left her editor examining the rear bumper of her car. Or she would have been if Annie had been telling the truth.

But sex wasn't just sex, not with Tack. She didn't just like the way he made her feel; the way his kisses made her lips tingle or the way his hands drove her mindless with pleasure. She liked *him*. Everything from the deep timbre of his voice, his teasing smiles, the gentle way he cuddled Bones and played with the twins, to the strange light in his eyes when he stared at a Texas sunset as if he'd never really seen one before.

There could never be a temporary for them because Annie felt more for Tack than simply lust. She was falling in love with him again. It was only a matter of time before the emotion consumed her and she forgot all about her future beyond Inspiration. Beyond Tack.

She couldn't, wouldn't do that. No matter how gently he cradled the twins, or kept Annie company, or warmed her from the inside out with his smiles. *Never again.*

TACK CLIMBED ONTO the dirt bike, flipped the key and gunned the engine. A roar split open the morning silence, deafening even to his own ears that had long ago grown accustomed to the thunderous sound. He killed the engine. Quiet settled in, disrupted only by the distant trickle of creek water, the chirp of birds, the buzz of insects.

He stared at the empty stretch of pasture, drawn by the serene quality. The peace he'd traded for screaming engines and squealing tires and the constant roar of the track. Bitterness swirled inside him and clawed its way up his throat. Years of hard work, of pushing himself to the edge, training until his muscles screamed, and what did he have to show for it?

Trophies. A whole wall of them. So many there were still dozens stuffed away in boxes he hadn't the time or desire to unpack when he'd moved into his house in Encino.

Money. A nice, fat bank account that he rarely touched for anything other than living expenses.

A reputation. He was the best. The top of the game, in his best shape ever. King of the mountain. But for how long? Another race? Another season?

The trophies would tarnish, the money would dwindle. And the reputation would fade when he took a wrong turn, missed a jump or just got slow on his starts.

But this…

Green grass stretched endlessly, giving way to brown hills that jutted upward and kissed a crystal-blue sky.

This went on forever. Tomorrow. Next week. Next year.

The land would still be here, still green and fertile and *home*.

He shook away the thought and gunned the engine again. Kicking the bike into gear, he bolted forward, focusing on the next turn, the next jump, running from the peace and quiet, the memories, the damn present, because Tack had been doing it so long, he didn't know if he could stop. No matter how much he suddenly wanted to.

ANNIE SPENT THE REST of the week breaking in the new transmission on her truck, sending out résumés to more newspapers, taking pictures of Echo Canyon and another piece of property Gary commissioned her to shoot, and trying to resist Tack.

Not that he actually did anything to make himself irresistible. True to his word, he didn't touch her again. He simply showed up at her house each evening, freshly showered and ready to help. They talked a little, about people they used to know, Tack's racing and Annie's newspaper aspirations—always keeping the truce and steering clear of the taboo subject of his father. Mostly, however, they worked in companionable silence.

She found herself craving the deep, even sound of his breathing, his footsteps, the feel of his body not far away. It wasn't a sexual feeling but one of security that his presence stirred. She couldn't help remembering the two of them down by the lake, staring at the stars, or in the library, sitting side by side and doing homework. Not talking, just being together. Being friends.

Not friends, she told herself Friday evening as she finished installing the new screen door she'd ordered from Heavenly Hardware. The denial was a vain, last-minute attempt to bolster her defenses, to bury the truth that she'd admitted to herself days ago. That Tack meant more. She felt more. Wanted more—

"Home-repair buddies," she growled. "And that's it."

"Did you say something?" He stood on a stepladder, fixing the sagging porch eave.

Annie's head jerked up and she realized she'd spoken out loud. "I—I asked how the home repair was going, um, buddy?"

"I'm nearly done. How about you?"

"A few more screws and I'm home free." Annie focused her attention on the task at hand.

Tack shifted his stance, fabric brushed fabric as his weight transferred from one leg to another, and a strange sense of peace rolled through her. He was close. *Here.*

She fought back the feeling, tossed her screwdriver into the toolbox with a loud *clang* and blurted out the first thing that came to mind, anything so she didn't have to think about the silence between them, the comfort, and the fact that she'd missed it so much.

"You never did say if you liked my pictures of the ranch?" Annie finished the last adjustment.

"Other than the fact that you didn't deliver them to me personally, they were great." Tack climbed down off the ladder to wipe his hands and sit on the porch steps. "You've got a real eye for landscape."

"Nature offers a lot to the camera." She shrugged. "But the real test is whether or not they'll entice a buyer."

"They don't have to. Jimmy put in a bid a few days ago."

"Already." She busied herself packing up her toolbox. "Looks like things are moving pretty quick." Which meant he would be leaving soon. She forced aside the sudden ache in her chest and smiled. "That's great."

"So you think I should go through with it?"

"If you don't like ranching, selling makes the most sense, and Jimmy is right next door."

"And if I like it?" The question paused her hand in midair. She shot him a sideways glance, but his expression revealed nothing. He simply stared straight ahead at the fast-disappearing sun.

Her breath caught and held. "Do you?"

"Maybe." He shook his head. "Hell, I don't know. It's not as bad as I remember, but it's a lot of hard work."

"That's what Coop always said, but he loved it anyway. He was a cowboy through and through."

"And I'm not." Anger lit his eyes, drew his mouth into a frown.

"Or maybe you're just trying really hard not to be." What the hell was she doing? *Just leave things alone. Let him sell,* cried a small voice inside her. *Tell him what he wants to hear and save yourself.* But at that moment, Annie sensed Tack's fear even more than her own, and she had to say something.

"I know you don't like to talk about Coop." She pushed the toolbox aside, sat down on the steps and motioned to Bones, who flopped down in the space separating them. "But you've got a chip on your shoulder the size of Texas, and avoiding the subject of your father isn't helping anything. Face the past, Tack. Admit that you're still mad at Coop, and giving up the ranch is a way to get back at him. To have the last laugh, so to speak."

"I don't give a damn about revenge."

"You want it so bad, you can taste it." His only reply was a sharp glance. "But there's another part of you that's still holding on," she went on, "the way you were after that homecoming game, mad as anything because Coop had missed it, but still waiting. Still hoping, even though it was over and the stands had cleared, that maybe he might show up. That's why we got together, Tack. Why you were still hanging around when you should have been celebrating the victory with everybody else."

"Leave it alone, Annie."

At the warning note in his voice, it dawned on her that she wouldn't be saying such things to a mere acquaintance, a *buddy.* She wouldn't care enough to ease the hurt.

She did.

The admission fueled her determination. "You told me the other day that your father was too busy for you and your mom. He wasn't, Tack. He was just scared."

"I don't want to talk about this."

"Maybe you don't want to, but you need to, because you don't have a clue what to do with the ranch. You know what your head says, but it's not the same thing you're hearing in here." She tapped her chest. "You're torn. Admit it. Just admit it."

He shrugged. "Christ, Annie, everything's just so damn different. *Everything,* especially you." He spared her a long glance, anger and hurt warring in his blue eyes. "There was a time when you used to be on my side."

The words tugged at the whirlwind of feeling she fought to keep contained. Her throat tightened and her eyes burned. "There are no sides, Tack. Things aren't so different, it's just that we didn't understand them then. I didn't understand my mother and you didn't understand your father. But I stayed and let myself get to know her, and you left. I didn't agree with everything she did, but I finally figured out that it didn't matter. She raised me and loved me even when I was ashamed of who she was. Who I was." While Annie had made peace with her mother, she'd never actually said the words out loud to anyone but Cherry. Until now. "I loved her for that. I *loved* her, and I always will."

He stared at her while she held her breath and waited to see what he would do. Call her a traitor, tell her to shut up, to keep her nose out of his business, his pain.

His gaze finally dropped as he eyed the worn tips of his boots. "What do you think my father was afraid of?"

"Doing the wrong thing. He knew ranching, but he didn't know anything about raising kids, or being a husband. He never had a family, no mother or father, no brothers or sisters. Just the cattle. He knew how to ride shotgun on a herd, to breed the best stock, but that's all he knew."

"So I'm supposed to feel sorry for him? To sympathize?" Tack shook his head as the bitterness welled inside him, making his chest ache, his throat constrict. "How can I when it's his fault my mother died? She was driving *because* of him. She hated to drive. She barely knew how. The only reason she got behind the wheel that night was because she'd promised me. They both had. She and my father were supposed to chaperone the prom, but my father didn't come home as expected. He broke his promise—like he always did—so my mother drove herself." He pushed up from the steps and walked out into the yard, putting his back to Annie as he let the memory take full control. "I thought Coop was there with her that night. I was so busy staring at you, so awed by how you looked in that awful blue dress, I didn't even notice she was alone."

He closed his eyes, remembering the swirls of colored lights, the music, Annie in his arms and the brief glimpse of his mother, lingering near the refreshment table, a smile pasted on her face as if all were right with the world. She'd never shown her emotions, but he'd glimpsed her feelings that night. Not heartache. Love had never figured in with his parents. She'd been angry, embarrassed because her husband was with his mistress. Again. "He should have been there. He should have driven her." His voice broke then and the guilt that had haunted him for too many years poured out. "*I* should have driven her."

"It wasn't your fault, Tack."

Her hand touched his shoulder and every nerve in his body snapped to attention. She was so close, so warm. All he had to do was turn to her, take her the way he'd been wanting to the past few days, but he'd promised himself. And her—especially her.

"Don't do this to yourself," Annie said. "You didn't know. As far as your father goes, you're right. He should have been there, but he wasn't. He made a mistake," she went on. "He made a lot of mistakes, some on purpose, some not, but he still loved you."

Some small part of him wanted to believe, but he tamped the urge down. *No expectations, no hurt.* "You didn't know him."

"I think you're the one who didn't know him," she said. "You're a lot like him. He never liked to talk about the past, either. But there was one night, right after my mother died, when he told me how sorry he was that he'd failed so many people. He did a lot of selfish things, but there was one he regretted more than anything. One he'd do over in a second if he had the chance."

"What?" The word was out before he could stop himself.

"He'd see you play that homecoming game."

The words echoed through his head and something tightened in his chest. But Tack had hated much too long to let go of the feeling now, even if it was eating him alive. "Regret doesn't mean a damn thing. Life doesn't give second chances."

"Doesn't it? You're here. Home. Looks like a second chance to me."

"My father's dead."

"But you're not, Tack. You're the one with the second chance. A chance to make peace with the past, with your father's memory."

"Why don't you leave it alone, Annie? You hated him the same as me back then, and you certainly wouldn't have been caught dead singing his praises. Hell, you barely talked at all."

"I was also a naive teenager. Now I don't bite my tongue for anybody. If there's something that needs to be said, I say it."

"To hell with the consequences?"

"If the stakes are worth it, yes."

"And what are the stakes here?"

"You," Annie finally whispered. "Your peace of mind, your memories. You." Then she walked inside and left him standing alone in the fading sunset.

IT DIDN'T MATTER, Tack told himself as he stood in his father's library and fingered one of the many video-cassettes lining the shelves. The tape slid free easily enough, too easy, and Tack's fingers tightened around the black plastic.

So the man had tapes of him. So he'd kept up with races and kept tabs on where his son was living. So he'd actually regretted that one damn football game. So *what?*

It didn't matter. None of it. It was all in the past. Forgotten if not forgiven.

At least that's what he kept telling himself as he sat up the rest of the night and went through the shelves tape by tape, race by race, a bottle of his father's favorite whiskey in his hands. He sat in Coop's chair, the cowboy hat Eli had given him on the desk in front of him, next to the Kawasaki contracts.

Just a signature. That's all he had to give. But every time he picked up the pen, the videotape ended and he had to put another in the machine, or he had to take another drink or adjust the volume on the TV or run his fingers along the brim of that damn Resistol or… *something.* Always something.

He watched the images of himself, and did his best to drink away the ache in his chest. But it lingered until he'd run out of tapes, of Jack Daniel's, and there was nothing to fill the silence but the static from the television and the sound of his own breathing. And the voice.

Ain't nothing more important than this land. Nothing.
Not guilt. Or regret. Or hatred.
Not ten years or thousands of miles.

Not life, or death.

Tack turned toward the portrait of his father, met the intense blue gaze so much like the one he stared at in the mirror every morning.

"You're wrong," he growled, but he didn't feel the usual bitterness deep in his gut. Just a strange emptiness.

Grief.

"You were *wrong*." The words were softer, directed at his father, at that damn stubborn streak inside of himself that had kept him hating for so long. "But it's okay now."

And as he stretched out on the couch, straw Resistol tipped over his face, and fell into the first real sleep he'd had in days, it *was* okay.

Tack Brandon had finally made peace.

CHAPTER ELEVEN

"I'VE GOT GOOD NEWS AND I've got ridiculous news," Deb said when Annie walked in on Monday morning. "Which do you want first?"

"Give me the ridiculous news."

Deb took a sip from her Bitchiest Babe In Texas mug. "You're working for a wanted woman. Jimmy Mission, the slug, filed charges on me for failure to remain at the scene of an accident and damages to his precious Bronco. A phallic symbol if I ever saw one."

"Failure to remain... Didn't you at least leave him a note?"

"One that specifically told him not to be taking up two parking spaces—I know he did it on purpose—and that he should drive something a bit smaller, to go with the size of his brain and his—"

"You didn't!"

Deb chewed her bottom lip as a rare gleam of uncertainty flashed in her eyes. "You think I went overboard?"

"Don't you?"

"Okay, maybe a teensy bit, but you should have seen his face when he read the note. I was watching from the window. It was priceless."

"Worth a trip to jail?"

"I'm not actually going to jail. Not today. Just over to

the courthouse. The judge will set bail, I'll pay it, then we go to court on Monday. Now, the good news." Deb put down her mug and clasped Annie's hands. "Wally, a drumroll, please." Her excited gaze locked with Annie's. "A certain editor at the *Houston Chronicle* called me less than fifteen minutes ago. They wanted a reference. They're considering you, Annie. For a photographer's position." She smiled. "It's not in the bag, but it's pretty darned close."

Annie tried to grasp the wonderful news. "Me?" Reality sank in and she threw her arms around Deb for a fierce hug. "Oh my God, *me!*"

"That's right. I sent Wally next door to the grocery store earlier to pick this up." She handed Annie a bottle of champagne with a big pink ribbon tied around the neck. "We'll celebrate as soon as I get back."

But by late afternoon, Deb was still tied up in court, haggling with Judge Baines over the bail and the two fines she'd garnered by giving Jimmy Mission a piece of her mind over the entire episode, and Wally had left for an evening class at the college.

Annie grabbed the champagne, her purse and camera bag, and headed home. She pulled into the driveway, killed the engine and simply sat there, listening to the *knock-knock* as the engine sputtered then quieted. Her gaze hooked on the lifeless house and, for the first time, Annie dreaded going inside. Even the puppies weren't there. Deb had borrowed them to scare off the neighborhood cats that were trashing her garden.

Alone.

She was still sitting there, staring straight ahead when Tack pulled into the driveway and parked beside her.

He wore a faded denim work shirt, jeans and scuffed black boots. A day's growth of beard crept down his strong jaw. Fierce blue eyes caught and held hers as he climbed off the bike and walked the few feet to her.

"Did you just get here?"

"Actually," she admitted, "I've been here for a while."

"Care to tell me why you haven't gone inside?"

"Not really." She traded her unsettling thoughts for a smile. "One of the newspapers I applied to is interested in me."

"That's great, Annie."

"Deb and I were going to celebrate, but she's busy. I'm doing some commission work for Gary, so I thought I might take a drive out to Echo Canyon and catch a few shots of the river while the sun sets and do a little celebrating of my own." She stared at the champagne bottle on the seat next to her, then at him. "You want to come along?" The words were out before she could think better of them, not that she would have.

Annie was happy, and she wanted to share that happiness with someone. No, not just *someone*. Him.

He grinned, pocketed the keys of his Harley and rounded the nose of the pickup to climb into the passenger seat. "I thought you'd never ask."

WHEN THEY REACHED THE RIVER, Annie spent the next half hour snapping pictures of the waning sunlight and giving Tack a play-by-play description of what she was doing. She talked about everything from the speed of film she used, to adding texture to the photographs by capturing just the right amount of light and shadow.

Tack turned out to be much more interested than she'd ever imagined, and he even took a few pictures of his own. He clicked off some shots of the river, the sunset, her.

"That was great," she said breathlessly, when they finally collapsed on the tailgate of her pickup truck. Dusk settled around them. The radio filtered from the Chevy's cab, filling the growing darkness with a slow country tune.

Tack grabbed the champagne, worked the cork with his pocketknife until it popped. "Now to drink a toast."

Champagne spurted, wetting the front of Annie's blouse and skirt. She laughed and hooked her mouth on the opening to suck up the foaming bubbles. A long, sputtering drink and she passed the bottle to him.

He took a long swallow, his gaze riveted on her face.

Self-consciously, Annie wiped at the wetness on her chin, but Tack reached out and pulled her hand away.

The moment of contact sizzled across her nerve endings and she found herself trapped in the moment.

"Let me." Dark eyes drilled into hers as he waited for her permission, and something shifted deep inside her.

She nodded, expecting a gentle swipe of his fingers.

Instead, Tack leaned in, his tongue flicking out to lap at the champagne on her chin. He didn't kiss her, just licked her skin and nibbled at the corners of her mouth and stirred an ache so fierce she wanted to weep.

"You taste so good, Annie, so damn good."

"It's the champagne."

He pulled away from her to stare deeply into her eyes. "It's *you*."

The words slid into her ears, so soft and low and seductive, and her insides quivered. She fought to remember every reason why she shouldn't want him—that she'd once loved him with all her heart and was in imminent danger of falling hard and fast again. But this... this *heat* flaring between them didn't have anything to do with her heart, or so she told herself.

The truck creaked as Tack got to his feet, stood on the tailgate and reached for her.

"Let's dance, honey."

"Here?" She held out her hand.

"Here." He pulled her upright and drew her a few feet forward until they stood in the middle of the truck bed and faced each other. "Right here," he said, sliding an arm around her waist. "For old times' sake."

It was their first dance all over again. Swaying together in the flatbed of an old pickup truck, the music drifting from the cab. Moonlight filtered through the trees. Celestial shadows danced around them, moving with the faint breeze, lending a dreamy quality to the evening.

A dream. That's what it felt like. As if she were caught in one of her dreams, reliving those few precious hours after the homecoming game when she'd kissed him for the first time.

Her hands crept up the hard wall of his chest, arms twined around his neck and she pressed herself closer. His heart beat against her breasts. His warm breath sent shivers over her earlobe, the slope of her neck. His hands splayed at the base of her spine, his thumb rubbing lazy circles just above the swell of her bottom.

A dream. A sweet, intoxicating dream.

"I want you, Annie. I've never felt this way about any woman before." The words, raw and ragged, shattered the hazy pleasure fogging her senses and jerked her back to reality—to Tack and the all-important fact that he wasn't the young boy who'd swept her off her feet. He was a grown man, harder, hungrier, and Annie was this close to giving in to him.

She tore herself away. Putting her back to him, she stared at the play of moonlight on the water and tried to catch her breath and think. But she couldn't. Her thoughts were focused on the man so close behind her, his presence heating her blood, making the humid air seem hotter, steamier, stealing the air from her frantic lungs.

His words upped the temperature.

"Don't hide from me, Annie."

"I'm not hiding."

"Then look at me, honey, and see how much I want you."

She shook her head.

"Then listen to me," he said, his warm breath rushing against her earlobe as he leaned in just enough to send goose bumps dancing over her skin, "and hear it."

He took a deep, ragged breath. "You're all I think about, Annie. I close my eyes, and you're there. I open them, and you're there. I used to dream about you, but it goes way beyond that now."

"Don't—"

"I'm not breaking my promise by touching you, but

I damn sure won't hide what I feel. You're my fantasy, Annie," he went on. "The only trouble is, you're real. So damn real, and it's taking all I have not to reach for you, to peel your clothes away and see you naked and beautiful in the moonlight." The erotic words slid into her ears to tease her senses and heighten the expectancy pooling inside her. "Your blouse would be the first to go. Then your bra." His voice deepened even further, so husky and arousing. "You have the most incredible breasts. Soft and full with wine-colored nipples that pucker whenever I glance at them." Where he didn't reach out with his hands, he did so with his voice. "Are they puckered now, honey? Tight and hard and sensitive?"

She could barely manage a nod.

"Touch them to make sure."

She wasn't sure why she complied. Maybe it was the moonlight, the soft music, his erotic words or the sheer desperation that overrode the passion in his voice. It didn't matter. While she wouldn't cross the line with him, there seemed nothing wrong with inching toward it. Just a little.

Her fingertip found the tip of her breast. Sensation bolted through her and she gasped.

"So beautiful," he murmured, his lips close to the nape of her neck. Close but not quite there. "Touch the other one, Annie. See if it feels as tight. As needy."

She did. Her fingertips circled the ripe crest until she struggled to draw air into her lungs.

"Do you know what I would do next?"

She knew what she wanted him to do, and it was as

if he read her mind, knew her desire as well as he knew his own.

"I would glide my fingertips down your belly real soft and slow."

Her hand followed his instruction, fingertips sliding, searching.

"Like that, baby. Just like that."

Her breath caught when she reached the vee between her legs, her touch burning through the thin material of her skirt and panties.

"Do you like what I'd do to you, honey?" The question rumbled through her head, so deep and intimate, with an undertone of satisfaction and pure male possessiveness.

She nodded.

"Then let me." His voice came out a raw, pained whisper. "Let *me,* Annie. Admit that you feel something for me that you don't feel for any other man."

She was so close to saying the words. Too close.

"It's late." Her shaky voice shattered the spell between them. "I—I really need to get home."

He didn't say a word. He simply jumped down off the tailgate and held out a hand to help her down.

Annie didn't want to touch him. Her control was tentative and she knew a slow, sensuous slide down his hot body would send her over the edge.

She needn't have worried. Hands at her waist, he lifted her to the ground, and promptly let her go.

They drove to her house in silence, with only the wind whistling through the open window. It did little to ease the heat that still raged inside her. Sweat dampened Annie's forehead, slid down her temples. The truck jumped and jolted over bumps. Her sensitive nipples rasped against her bra, her bottom rubbed against the seat. It was only a short ride, but enough to keep her hormones buzzing.

"Just leave the keys under the seat." She practically jumped out of the truck before it rolled to a stop alongside her house. A fraction before she slammed the door, she heard his voice.

"Aren't you tired of fighting, Annie?"

The words followed her to the back door. She knew he wasn't talking about any verbal disagreement, but the need that raged between them. Hunger. She wanted him, and he'd made no secret that he wanted her.

Her hand closed around the doorknob and she paused.

What the hell was she doing?

Reality hit her hard and fast while she stood on her doorstep. Deb must have returned the pups because the twins were barking frantically on the other side of the porch door, while the truck's lights blazed in back of her as Tack waited for her to get safely inside.

He wanted her and she wanted him. *Want.*

It didn't have to go beyond that if she didn't let it, if she cut herself off emotionally from the physical lust and kept her emotions carefully in check.

Temporary.

It was only a little while. Annie could guard her heart for the next few days and enjoy herself in the process. Couldn't she?

She could.

She *would*.

She desperately wanted another memory to add to her

store, another sweet dream to comfort her in her lonely future, because she knew, no matter where her dreams led her, she would never find another man like Tack.

Her fingers abandoned the doorknob and she turned. The side of the house to her left blocked her from Mrs. Pope's prying eyes, while an endless field stretched to her right, the garage at her back. Plenty of seclusion for what she had in mind.

The headlights blazed, blinding her and obliterating everything beyond the beams, including the darkened cab where he sat, but Annie didn't care. He could see her and that was all that mattered.

Leaving her purse at the back door, she stepped down off the steps and stood in the shower of headlights.

Yes, she was tired of fighting.

Tired of losing.

For once, Annie wanted to taste victory, however brief.

She took a deep breath, gathered her courage and slid the first button of her blouse free. The material soon parted and slid down her arms. Trembling fingers worked at the catch of her bra, freeing her straining breasts. The scrap of lace landed at her feet. The gauzy material of her skirt joined the growing heap until Annie stood in nothing but her panties and a slick layer of perspiration. She hooked her thumbs at the waistband, slid them down and stepped free.

Her first instinct was to cover herself, but she fought it, determined to show Tack just how much she wanted him.

Tack.

She focused on the image of him in her mind, not the

boy from years past, but the man who smiled and teased and made her feel beautiful and wicked and wanted.

The warm night air whispered over her bare shoulders and breasts. Her nipples tightened, throbbed, but she touched herself just to be sure.

Just for him.

Her breath caught at the first swirl of fingertips at the aching tips. She wanted to close her eyes, but she forced them open, kept them trained straight ahead just at a point above one of the beams where she knew he sat. Watching.

Her hands moved lower, down the slick, quivering skin of her stomach, to the damp curls at the base of her thighs. The air seemed to stand still around her. Even the twins' harsh barks faded for a few heartbeats. Her breath caught, and she touched herself. One fingertip slid along the soft, wet folds between her legs, heat pulsed through her hot body and a shameless moan curled up her throat.

The engine died and the headlights flicked off, plunging Annie into a blinding darkness. A door slammed. Boots crunched across the gravel.

She barely managed to blink before he reached her. He stopped, paused, waiting for her to say the words and she did.

"You aren't any man, Tack. I want you. *You.* I have for the past ten years, and now it's even more intense because you aren't a figment of my dreams or wishful thinking. You're flesh and blood and you want me back."

Strong, muscled arms wrapped around her and drew her close as his mouth captured hers in a deep, thorough kiss that sucked the air from her lungs and made her legs tremble.

Annie clutched at his shoulders. Denim rasped her sensitive breasts and thighs in a delicious friction that made her quiver and pant and claw at the hard muscles of his arms.

Strong hands slid down her back, cupped her bottom and urged her legs up on either side of him. Then he lifted her, cradled and kneaded her buttocks as she wrapped her legs around his waist and settled over the straining bulge in his jeans.

"Please," she whimpered, rubbing herself against him.

As anxious as Tack was to be inside the warm, sweet woman in his arms, he'd waited too long to have it over with at the flick of a zipper and the hard thrust of his thighs, and that's all it would take.

He stilled her movements and rested his forehead against hers long enough to drag some air into his lungs and give his fogged brain a burst of much-needed oxygen.

"Not here, Annie. Not like this." He leaned behind her, opened the back door and manuevered his way across the fenced-in porch, Tex and Rex snapping at his heels. Blackness engulfed them as he stepped inside the kitchen and inched the door closed behind him, leaving the two excited puppies on the porch.

He carried her to the bedroom, stretched her out on the bed and flipped on the bedside lamp.

"Here," he said, leaning back to stare into her eyes for a long moment. "Like this."

And then he kissed her, long and slow and deep. His

tongue tangled with hers, stroking, coaxing until she whimpered and tugged at the waistband of his jeans.

He covered her hand and stilled his movements. "If I take them off, there's no way this is going to go slow, and I want it slow between us. The first time, your first time, I was an anxious kid..." He drew in a deep, shuddering breath. "And my first night back in town, I was drunk. Both times I was thinking about me, Annie. About how you made me feel, how desperate I was to be inside you. But I want to make you feel this time. That's all I've been thinking about. How I'd touch you, what I'd do..."

"So stop thinking and do it."

He grinned at her impatience and feathered his lips over hers, so light and teasing it drew a frustrated moan from her. Then he licked a path down her fragrant neck, the slope of her breast, before pulling back to stare at her. "You're so damn perfect, Annie." His tongue flicked out, lapped at the tight nipple like a cat tasting sweet cream.

Her fingers threaded through his hair and held him to her breast as he suckled her until she writhed beneath him, her hips moving, begging for more. For him.

The blood rushed through his veins, his erection pressed painfully against his jeans, desperate for release, but he held himself in check, determined to take his own pleasure by pleasuring her.

He nibbled a path down the warm skin of her belly to the damp curls between her legs. His fingertips trailed reverently over her slick feminine folds and she gasped.

"Ah, honey, you feel so good. So hot and wet… Just the way I want you."

His hands touched the insides of her soft thighs, spread her legs until she was wide-open for him. He cupped her bottom and tilted her closer. At the first glide of his tongue, she bucked. A strangled cry burst from her lips.

"Shhh," he murmured, fingers stroking, soothing.

"It's just—" she gulped for air "—no one's ever done that. I wasn't expecting…" The words tangled in a sob.

"Don't expect, Annie. Just relax and feel. That's all you have to do, baby. Just feel."

When he touched her with his mouth, she started, but gradually her muscles relaxed. Her legs spread wider, giving him better access to the sweetness deep inside. He feasted on her, his tongue rasping the tender flesh until she threaded her fingers through his hair, arched her hips and shuddered with the force of her release.

Several frantic breaths later, Tack slid up her sweat-dampened body and stretched out on his side to look at her.

Her silver hair lay spread out on the pillow, several damp strands clinging to her flushed face. Her eyes were closed, her full lips parted in breathless rapture. He'd never seen a woman look so beautiful, so sexy, so… *real.*

Tack didn't count on the sucker punch to his gut just the sight of her caused. Nor did he count on the way her soft sigh echoed in his head and made his blood thrum and his heart miss its next beat. And no way in hell did he count on the fierce wave of possessiveness that swept through him. The sudden, desperate urge to brand every inch of her as his and touch her in ways no man could.

Ways no man ever would because Annie Divine was his.

Whether she admitted it or not.

Then her green eyes opened, her hands reached out, stroked the rock-hard length of him through his jeans, and all thought fled. His eyes closed and he relished her touch all of five heartbeats before he caught her hand.

"If you don't stop, I'm liable to explode."

"That's the idea."

"Not yet. There are a few more things I want to do to you."

"Actually," she purred, "there are a few things *I* want to do to *you*. You aren't the only one who's been fantasizing."

Annie unbuttoned his jeans, slid the zipper down and he sprang hot and huge and throbbing into her hands. Her fingertips stroked the long, solid length of him and a pearl of liquid beaded on the plum-ripe head. Annie smiled, dipped her head and demonstrated one of her favorite fantasies.

She tasted his essence, loved him with her mouth as he splayed his fingers through her hair and cradled her head. She pleasured him until his chest pumped from his frantic breathing and his fingers clenched into fists.

"Stop!" he gasped, and she did, because as much as she wanted to please him, she wanted him deep, deep inside her even more.

He shed his jeans and settled between her legs, his weight pressing her back into the mattress. His erection slid along her damp flesh, making her shudder and moan and arch toward him, but he held back.

"Are you still on the Pill?" he asked, remembering what she'd told him the morning after his first night back.

"Yes." He pressed just a fraction into her and she trembled. "And—" she caught her bottom lip as he slid a fraction more "— there's no chance of your, um... *it* shriveling up and falling off—" The words caught on another tremble. "You asked me once before about past lovers, but I don't have any." Her gaze caught his. "There's only been you, Tack. Just you." She wasn't sure what prompted the admission, only that she wanted him to know. Tonight, she'd vowed to put her fears and doubts on hold and enjoy every moment in his arms.

Tonight.

His expression grew serious and his eyes brightened to a feverish blue. "There's never been anyone but you," he told her. When she started to protest, he slid just an inch into her and the words caught on her lips.

"In my head and my heart," he added, making her want him all the more for his honesty and the heartfelt sincerity gleaming in his eyes. "Only and always you, Annie."

And then he plunged fast and sure and deep, burying himself to the hilt in one luscious thrust that tore a joyful cry from her lungs.

"Wrap your legs around me, honey, and hold on."

She did, the motion lifting her body. He slid deeper, the sensation of being stretched, filled, consumed by the raw strength of him stealing her breath for several long moments.

He started to move, building the pressure, pushing them both higher, higher until they reached the top of the mountain and teetered on the edge. With one final thrust, he pumped into her and sent them both over.

Annie cried out his name, her nails digging into the hard muscles of his shoulders, her legs clamping tight as her body milked him of every hot, sweet drop of his release.

When he rolled over without breaking their intimate contact and cradled her on his chest, Annie felt such pure joy that it frightened her.

She fought the feeling back down, consoling herself with the fact that he would be gone soon. She didn't have to worry about making the same mistake as her mother and sacrificing her future for a man, because she and Tack had only tonight. Now.

Annie held the knowledge close and fixed her attention on the steady thud of his heart, the strong arms around her, the chest hairs tickling her cheek.

This moment.

CHAPTER TWELVE

"THIS HEAT IS KILLING ME." Moonlight filtered through the bedroom window along with a slight breeze that provided little relief to Annie's sweat-drenched body. She wiped the moisture from her face and took a long drink of the iced tea she'd retrieved from the kitchen.

She felt his smile even before she saw it, a warmth stealing through her insides followed by a slash of dazzling white as he loomed over her. His gaze locked with hers and the expression faded.

"Let's see what I can do to help." He took the glass from her hands, his fingertips brushing one already sensitive nipple. She caught her bottom lip as electricity tingled up her spine.

Condensation dripped onto her stomach, sliding over her feverish skin as Tack brought the glass to his lips. He took a long drink of tea and caught an ice cube between his teeth.

Annie's body arched toward him as he touched the ice to her throat. The mixture of hot, hungry lips surrounding shivering relief, sent a jolt of electricity through her and she gasped.

He worked his way down, sliding the ice over her feverish skin. At the first touch to her nipple, a sob caught in her throat. The touch was hot and cold, the sensation both pleasure and delicious pain as he circled the throbbing peak.

Then the sensation disappeared. Her eyes opened in time to see him tip the glass. Cold liquid dribbled onto her belly and she gasped.

"You'll get me all sticky and wet."

"Mmm," he murmured as he surveyed his handiwork. "Sticky and wet." His fingers slid down to probe the drenched flesh between her legs for emphasis. "Just the way I like you."

He pressed a finger deep, deep inside her and lapped at the sweet tea on her belly.

Annie gasped at the rasping heat of his tongue, the cold dribble of tea, the pressure of his wonderful fingers working her into a frenzy. The ripe smell of sweetness and sex and hungry male filled her nostrils, arousing her senses the way Tack aroused her body.

Another cold dribble and she caught her bottom lip to keep from screaming from the delicious sensation.

"I didn't realize I was so thirsty," he murmured against her quivering belly.

"You're going to ruin the sheets," she said in a shaky voice as he dribbled another trickle across her scorching skin.

"I'll buy you new ones." His movements stilled as he leaned up to stare at her. "If you say it's okay, Annie. Only if you say it's okay."

He would never know how much the words meant to her, how they slid into her ears and sent a sweet warmth spreading through her more fierce than the physical response his touch drew. Because she knew then that he respected her independence, her control.

A smile tugged at her lips as she traced the curve of his stubbled jaw. "Fast and wild," she said, reaching down his sweat-slick body to stroke his rigid sex. Her fingers wrapped around him and a fierce light flared in his eyes. "We had it slow and sweet, now I want it fast and wild." She rolled him over and straddled him.

Her stare never shifted from his as she impaled herself on his hard, hot length in one exquisite motion that took both their breaths away.

He gripped her hips to set the pace, but she caught his hands and urged them to the bed. As if he sensed her need to call the shots, to drive them both to the brink of madness and relish the feminine power she held over him, he followed her command. Tanned fingers gripped her sheets.

"Just sit back and enjoy the trip," she whispered before capturing his lips in a deep, erotic kiss that sent a shiver through his hard body.

And then she started to ride him, fast and wild, until she brought them both to a shattering climax and they collapsed together, hot and spent and sated.

For the moment.

ANNIE WOKE THE NEXT MORNING to find the sheets tangled and the bed empty. Panic gripped her, a sudden feeling of emptiness that made her heart pound faster, until she heard the slow drawl of his voice from outside. She climbed from the bed, pulled on a pair of shorts and a tank top, and walked out onto the front porch to see Tack standing in her front yard wearing nothing but his jeans and a grin.

"Walking around half-naked," Mrs. Pope huffed from her flower garden. "What's the neighborhood coming to?"

"Come on, now, Earline. You were catching a peek and checking me out when I bent over." He winked and Mrs. Pope turned a bright shade of pink. "Admit it, darlin'."

"I was doing no such thing. I'll have you know I'm a God-fearing Christian woman and I have better things to do with my time than stare at a half-dressed man who parades around with his pants unbuttoned without an ounce of decency."

He gave her a knowing smile. "And how would *you* know if you weren't checking my…*decency* out?"

Mrs. Pope fired an even brighter shade, and Annie couldn't help herself. Maybe it was the past night of wondrous lovemaking, but she was feeling charitable. "Tack, come back inside and stop bothering Mrs. Pope. She's got roses to tend."

Mrs. Pope's head snapped up and her gaze locked with Annie's. "It's all your fault." She jabbed her gardening spade in Annie's direction. "You're the heathen giving this neighborhood a bad name. Leaving your lights on at all hours, letting those mongrel pups run wild, bringing home half-naked men."

The words prodded old wounds and reminded her of so many similar scenes, only the accusations had been directed at her mother. While Cherry had been in love, she'd never been proud of being the other woman, and so she'd let people talk. She'd done her penance by hanging her head and shying away from confrontation because she'd felt deserving of the gossip.

Like mother, like daughter.

Annie summoned her courage, stepped down off the porch and walked over to Tack.

"Just one man," she told Mrs. Pope. "This man, not that it's any of your business. What I do, who I do it with—none of it is your business, Mrs. Pope." And then she kissed him, in front of God and Mrs. Pope and anyone who might have driven by.

"Are you all right?" he asked when Mrs. Pope had walked into her house and slammed the door.

She nodded and smiled. "A little tired and very hungry."

He slid an arm around her waist and steered her toward the house. "I'll make you breakfast. I cook great pancakes."

"Actually," she said, a wicked gleam in her eyes, "I had something a little different in mind. I've got a sudden craving for peaches."

IT WAS THE MOST TIRING WEEKEND of Annie's life, and the most incredible. She spent Saturday and Sunday working on the sales shots for Echo Canyon with Tack taking a break from the ranch to act as her assistant. He carried her equipment and followed her around, and made love to her. In the sweet grass with the sun shining down on them. In the cool river with the moonlight playing off the surface and the stars blazing overhead. In the hot, blistering heat of her bedroom.

It was incredible, unforgettable, and it was almost over.

Thankfully. The loving was too fierce, the joy too consuming, the need growing with every moment she spent with him.

She forced the thoughts away and concentrated on going over this week's schedule. Only a few more days. She could hold out until then, keep her emotions in check. She could.

"Somebody had a good weekend," Deb chimed as

she walked by Annie's desk. "My sources have it that you and Tack were seen together several times driving around town. Is it safe to assume you and this cowboy are an item?"

Annie smiled despite herself. "A temporary item."

Deb gave her a thumbs-up then sank onto the corner of the desk. She sighed. "It's good to know somebody's life is looking up. Mine stinks. The trial is today. Speaking of which," she glanced at her watch, "I need you to hold down the fort for a little while."

"I could hold down the fort," Wally grumbled from the corner. "If somebody around here would just give me a break."

Deb and Annie exchanged amused glances.

"So, can you?" Deb asked Annie.

"No problem. I don't have another assignment until after lunch..." Her words faded as a familiar sensation skittered over her senses.

She turned to find Tack standing in the doorway, looking tired and worn and happier than she'd ever seen him.

Just the way she felt.

"I came by to see if you're free for lunch?" he explained.

"I would love to, but I promised Deb—"

"She's definitely free," Deb cut in. She dropped a huge key ring on Wally's desk. "Heads up, Ace. You just got lucky." While the copy boy stared at the keys as if he were holding a winning lottery ticket, Deb turned to Annie. "Wally's in charge for the next few hours. Don't ever let it be said that Deb Strickland stood in the way of true lust!"

A HALF HOUR LATER, after following Tack out to the Big B, Annie stood in the wildflower field near her mother's headstone and stared at the newly erected stone bench.

"What is this?" she asked.

"It's a bench."

"I know that, but why?"

"I thought you might like to come out here and sit sometimes. Do you like it?"

"Yes." She blinked back the tears that threatened to overwhelm her.

A bribe. That's what she wanted to think, but this wasn't a dozen roses or a box of chocolates or an expensive trinket, or any of the other things Coop had used to win her mother's favor and bend her to his will.

This was...*different.*

"I was never really close to my mother," he went on in a quiet, strained voice, as if the words fought to get out just as he battled to hold them back. "In a lot of ways, she was like Coop—quiet, reserved, fixated on the ranch. That's why my father's affair never bothered her half as much as it bothered me. She married this ranch, not him."

"I still don't understand why you did this. You never liked my mother."

"I never liked that my father liked her. I never really knew her enough to say one way or another. Never even said hello."

"What are you trying to say?"

"That maybe I should have. Maybe I should have given her a chance. Given my father a chance... Hell, I don't know. It doesn't matter anyhow. What's past is past and I can't change anything. I just wanted you to know that I'm glad for you, Annie. I'm glad you made peace with her." His words rang with sincerity and a tremble echoed in Annie's heart. "I didn't want to be, but I am."

She sank onto the bench and trailed her hand over the smooth stone, but she didn't feel stone. She felt Tack. His pain. His peace. She *felt* him the way she had so long ago. Despite her best efforts, she was falling for him all over again.

"Truth or dare," she finally said. "I pick truth." She stared at the headstone glittering in the midmorning sun, keenly aware of him so close. His heat, his strength, the frantic *bam, bam* of her own heart. "I spent my whole life trying to prove to myself and everyone else that I was nothing like my mother. She was outgoing, beautiful, flirtatious, so I made sure I was just the opposite. Then you came along and I realized I was more like her than I ever thought."

"I don't understand."

"You made me feel things, Tack. You stirred a passion I'd convinced myself I didn't possess—a passion my mother was notorious for. When you left, I wanted to hate you, to forget you, but I couldn't. Just like my mother couldn't hate or forget your father or shut him out of her life. That's what changed our relationship and drew us together. Not her illness, but the fact that we cared about two men we could never, ever have."

"I didn't mean to hurt you, Annie. I had to leave."

"I know that, and I'm glad. I always knew that love between two people didn't guarantee a happy ending. My mother was living proof that love is more pain than pleasure. Some people aren't meant to be together. My mother and your father were two of them. You and me…

we weren't meant to be together either." She shook her head. "Your leaving was for the best. I realized then that loving someone else wasn't half as important as loving myself. I learned to make my own way and my own happiness."

"I'm signing the final sale papers today."

"That's great."

"I have to leave," he added, as if he meant to convince her, but Annie didn't need any more proof than the strange fluttering in her stomach, the sudden ache in her chest as her heart admitted what her mind wasn't yet prepared to accept.

There was no falling involved. Annie was in love with him.

"I *have* to…" His voice faded into a heated curse. Then Tack Brandon did what he did best.

He walked away.

He wasn't staying.

Tack headed back to the house to meet Gary and get on with things. The sale, and the Kawasaki contracts he'd been avoiding much too long.

No, he wasn't staying. No matter how much Tack had come to like the feel of a horse beneath him during the day, a clear blanket of stars overhead at night. No matter how fond he'd grown of Bones, or how he liked watching the sun set from Annie's front porch.

Or how much he liked watching Annie, talking to her, being with her. No matter how much he wanted to prove her wrong.

Love.

What did he really know about love?

He didn't. He'd grown up in a household devoid of

love, and while his mother had cared for him, she'd never been affectionate, and his father...

Tack didn't know anything about love.

He only knew that hearing the tears in Annie's voice had twisted a knife in his chest, listening to her confess she'd loved him once had sent a burst of joy through him, and seeing the gratitude in her eyes when she'd touched the bench so lovingly had filled him with satisfaction. Pride. Happiness.

Love.

Dammit, he couldn't stay. He was a motocross racer, not a cowboy. He lived for the thrill of the race, the wind rushing at his face during a good ride, the sweat gliding down his temples, the aches and pains from taking too many turns and a rough ride that made him feel tired and worn and sore and so damn good because he'd accomplished something very few people ever did.

"He's down!"

The cry cut into Tack's thoughts and he picked up his steps, aiming for the corral instead of the ranch house. He reached the fence just in time to see Fern rear up on her hind legs. Two cowboys desperately tried to anchor her with ropes, while a handful of men helped a wounded Eli from the corral.

"What the hell happened?" Tack met Eli at the gate.

"Tried to saddle her today. She kicked and snapped my arm clear in two."

"You boys get the truck and get him to the hospital," Tack ordered, sending two hands scurrying toward the garage and another to fetch Vera.

"Had to give it one last shot," Eli said, "for Coop's sake. Thought I had her, too." He groaned as Tack examined the foreman's twisted arm. "As smart as she is, you'd think she'd realize breaking's for her own good. She ain't no use like she is, wild as all get-out. No good to anybody."

The words rang in Tack's ears as Eli left with two cowboys and a worried Vera, headed for Grant County Hospital.

No good to anybody.

He watched as the cowboys loosened the ropes and hightailed it out of the corral before Fern could do some damage to them. The horse danced a few seconds, before settling down. Calm. As calm as the quarter horses in the adjoining stable. But it was just a front for the light that glittered in her eyes.

"Tack, you ready?" Gary shouted from the back porch of the house. "We're meeting Jimmy in a half hour."

"I'll be right there."

His gaze swiveled back to the animal, to the gleam in her eyes, the wildness.

He recognized it because he saw it in his own eyes when he looked in the mirror. Smelled it in the fine scent of leather and tobacco and fear when he sat in his father's study and tried to concentrate on the books— the walls and the memories closing in on him. Felt it deep in his bones when anybody—Eli or Annie or even Bones—got too close and made him think beyond racing and winning.

The truth hit him then as he stood there, staring at the horse. At himself. It wasn't the ranch he'd always hated, the cowboying, it was his father's pushing it on him. The way Eli had tried to push the saddle onto Fern's back.

Truthfully, Tack liked cowboying. He enjoyed the feel of the horse beneath him, the bone-tiring work that made him feel worn and sore and so damn good because he was doing something that mattered. Caring for the horses, the stock, the land.

Hell, he loved it. Not because he had to, because it was his duty or his legacy or his job, just *because*.

Things were different now. Tack had a choice.

And he was staying.

"DON'T TELL ME," DEB SAID as she watched Annie slide the phone into place. "It was the *Houston Chronicle*." At Annie's nod, she squealed, "You got it, didn't you?"

Annie replayed the phone conversation in her head and wondered why she didn't feel near the excitement she'd anticipated just a few days ago.

We want you, Miss Divine. Your work is good and we'd like to offer you a position on our staff.

"Yes."

"I knew it!" Deb clapped her hands. "Photographer?"

Annie nodded again. "They want me to start next Monday."

"Monday!" Deb squealed, before the news sank in and her smile disappeared. "Monday. But that's only a week away."

"I know it's short notice." She had eight days to pack up everything she owned and find a place in Houston. "I could call them back and ask for more time."

"You'll do no such thing. It's just…" She raised suddenly misty eyes to Annie. "I'm going to miss you."

"I know." Annie wrapped her arms around the woman and they hugged.

Wally walked in, Annie filled him in on the news, and he joined the hug.

Deb finally sniffled and pulled away. "I hope nobody sees this. It'll ruin my image."

"I've seen it," Wally informed her. "Prime blackmail material."

"You'd blackmail the woman giving you a promotion?"

"A promotion?" His eyes widened with excitement.

"I need somebody to help me fill Annie's shoes, not that you could even come close. But you're a hard worker."

"Yeeeee-hahhhhhhh!" He grabbed Deb around the waist and twirled her for a long moment, before she threatened bodily injury.

After he plopped her on her feet, Deb pulled and tugged at her red suit. "Now, if we've got all this emotional stuff over with, I say let's hit BJ's. We've got a lot to celebrate. Annie's job, Wally's new promotion and my new lease on life."

"Which is?" Annie asked.

"To make Jimmy Mission as miserable as is humanly possible. The slug won in court. I have to pay him damages."

"That seems fair considering you caused the damages," Annie said.

"And pain and suffering he endured while driving around with red paint smeared on his bumper."

"That's ridiculous."

"That's exactly what I said." At Annie's raised eyebrow, Deb shrugged. "Okay, I said that and a few more choice things that got me another nice, big fat fine for contempt." She blew out a deep breath. "Let's go, gang. I'm buying."

A HALF HOUR LATER, Deb was on her fourth drink while Annie worked on her second and Wally twirled Jenny Peters around a crowded dance floor.

"Monday," Deb mused. "Don't get me wrong. I'm thrilled for you, Annie. You know I am. It's just that I was kind of hoping you might end up staying here. Maybe freelance for magazines, open a photograpy studio, do calendars or brochures or anything that lets you showcase your work, and do it right here."

"I've got too much invested in my career to up and change now." Annie had spent too many years focusing herself, working toward a specific career goal, to suddenly switch courses. She had a journalism degree, after all. Years of experience in the field. Stay here and do straight photography? *No.*

No matter how appealing the idea or how much she'd been enjoying the landscape shots she'd been doing for Gary, or how many of the same thoughts she'd been having lately, especially since Tack had rolled back into town.

She had to finish what she'd set out to do.

She downed the last of her drink and steeled herself. "I knew there was someone out there who wanted me."

"Ditto on that, honey." Deb chuckled. "And he's walking this way."

Annie's gaze swiveled just in time to see a pair of worn jeans moving toward her. Her gaze slid higher, over trim thighs and a lean waist, to a faded denim shirt covering a broad chest... *Tack.* A straw Resistol sat atop his dark head, slanted at just the angle she remembered and making him look every bit the cowboy he was trying so hard not to be.

Boy? No, he was every bit a man, and Annie was all too aware of that fact, of the man's hunger that burned in his gaze when he looked at her the way he was right now.

"What brings you here?" she asked as he stopped next to her table, Jimmy Mission at his side.

"Celebrating," Jimmy replied, tipping his hat to Annie before flashing a grin at Deb, who scowled.

"You sold the ranch," Annie said.

"Actually—" Tack's gaze caught and held hers "—I didn't. That's what we're celebrating. That and Jimmy's win in court. Mind if we join you? There aren't many tables."

"No," Deb said, propping her feet on the chair next to her before Jimmy could sit down.

He frowned. She smirked. Then he leaned over, grabbed her ankles and plopped her feet on the floor, before sliding into the now-vacant seat.

"Pain and suffering for a little bumper scratch," Deb muttered. "That's the stupidest thing I've ever heard."

"No, the stupidest thing was you cussing out the judge," Jimmy replied.

"I hate you."

"Your lips say hate, but your eyes say you want me, darlin'."

"The day the devil starts dishing up snow cones..."

The verbal exchange faded as Annie stared up at Tack, his words echoing in her head like a broken record.

"You really didn't sell?"

He shook his head and the knowledge sank in. Tack was settling down. Staying at the Big B. Planting roots.

Joy erupted inside her, stirring a wave of panic that made her heart pound faster.

"B-but what about Kawasaki?"

"I tore up the contracts and told them no. I'm retiring."

Her gaze narrowed. "Just like that?"

"Actually, I've been thinking about it for a while, that's why I didn't sign with them right away. I'm tired of being on the road. I need something steady. Besides, Bones has kind of gotten attached to the place, and I've gotten attached to him, among other things." His gaze darkened. "I'm staying, Annie."

"And I'm leaving." Before he could reply, Annie bolted to her feet and fled through the crowd, fear pushing her faster when she heard Tack's shout.

"Annie, wait!"

But she couldn't. He was *staying.* The knowledge sent a wave of panic through her and she picked up her steps. She slammed her palms against the rear exit and stumbled out into the parking lot. Gravel crunched as her legs ate up the distance to her truck.

"Annie!" The name rang out a second before he caught her arm in a firm jerk that brought her whirling around to face him. "Annie, I—"

"Don't say it!" She shook her head, blinking back the tears that suddenly threatened to overwhelm her. "Please don't."

"I love you."

The tears spilled over and she shook her head,

fighting the truth of his words and the emotion in her heart. "Let me go. I—I have to get out of here."

"Annie?" Strong, warm hands cradled her face, his thumbs smoothing her tears. "What is it, baby? Didn't you hear me? I said I love—"

"Don't!" Pleasure rushed through her, so fierce it stirred the fear and the panic and made her fight harder. She pushed at his hands. "Don't make this any harder. Just let me go."

"If saying I love you makes it harder for you to go, then I love you, I love you, *I love you,* dammit!" His eyes took on a determined light. "Because I damn sure don't want you to go anywhere." He gripped her hands with his, ignoring her attempts to pull free. "I thought you felt the same way."

"You thought wrong."

"Did I?" Fierce blue eyes drilled into hers and she came so close to blurting out the truth.

Instead, she shook her head, clinging to her anger and her fear and the pain of hearing her mother cry herself to sleep at night because she'd been so miserable. Because she'd given up everything for the man she loved.

She'd risked it all and she'd gained nothing. Only a lot of pain and loneliness that a few moments of joy couldn't begin to ease.

"I'm leaving, Tack. The *Chronicle* called. I start Monday."

"Houston?" He looked as if she'd landed a punch to his gut. He shook his head. "You can't."

"I *can*. I can do anything I want."

"But I don't want you to go."

"That's just it. It's not about what you want. It's about

what *I* want. Don't you understand? I've worked my entire adult life for a chance like this. I can't forget about it now because you say you love me."

"How about because *you* love *me?*"

She shook her head. "It's not enough."

Truthfully, it was too much. The emotion gripping her heart made her want to throw it all to the wind, wrap her arms around him and forget the job, the past, the future—everything but this moment. Now. Him.

No!

"I'm not making the same mistake as my mother." She yanked free and rushed for her truck. Inside, she gunned the engine and took a deep, shaking breath.

Heaven help her, she'd done it. She'd traded Tack for her independence, her pride, her dreams, her sense of self, what her mother had never had the courage, or the desire, to do with Cooper Brandon. So why did it suddenly feel as if Annie had turned her back on the one thing that mattered the most?

Wiping frantically at a flood of hot tears, she chanced a glance in her mirror to see Tack standing where she'd left him, staring after her, fists clenched, his body taut, as if it took all his strength not to go after her.

It was an image that haunted her all through the night and the rest of the week as Annie packed up boxes, made phone calls and prepared for the rest of her life.

Without Tack Brandon.

CHAPTER THIRTEEN

ANNIE RANG MRS. POPE'S DOORBELL for the third time. She waited a few more seconds then left the envelope she'd been holding on the woman's front step. The drive to Houston was four hours and Annie still had one more stop.

She managed three steps toward her truck before a door opened behind her.

"What's this?"

She turned to find Mrs. Pope staring at the seven dollars stuffed into the envelope.

"The money I owe you."

A strange expression eased the woman's usually hard features. "You're really leaving?"

Annie nodded. "I start my new job first thing in the morning. But don't worry, Gary Tucker said he'll find a nice neighbor for you. He's handling the sale for me. Take care, Mrs. Pope." She turned to walk away, but the woman's voice stopped her.

"You're a good girl, Annie Divine."

Annie turned and stared at the old woman. "What did you say?"

"I said you're a good girl."

It shouldn't matter. It never had. Mrs. Pope had scowled and hollered for most of Annie's life, and it had never mattered. The woman disliked her, and she'd accepted it. Oddly enough, the words warmed Annie's heart anyway.

"I know I razzed you a lot," Mrs. Pope went on, "especially since I retired from the library. I want you to know, though, it isn't because I never liked you. It's just that an old woman like me needs something to keep her going. My Claire's tried to push me into that blasted nursing home over in Grant County for the past ten years. Said I'd have folks my own age to keep me company instead of puttering around here all by my lonesome. What she didn't understand was I had something to do, something pulling me out of bed besides my gardening and Jerry Springer." The old woman smiled. "You called me out on every dadblastit complaint, gave me tit for tat when I got too out of hand. I looked forward to buttin' heads with you, dear. Highlight of my day, and I'm going to miss it. And you. I'm surely enough going to miss you."

Annie wiped at her suddenly misty eyes. "I'm going to miss you, too, Mrs. Pope." And then she turned away because the last thing she wanted to do was cry again. She'd done too much of that over the past week. As she'd packed up the house and said goodbye to all of her friends, more than she'd ever realized she had. Somewhere over the past ten years, as Annie Divine had stopped trying so hard to fit in, she'd done just that. She'd become a part of the town, one of the folks. While there were plenty who didn't like her, there were even more who did.

Granny Baines had baked her farewell cookies and Bobby Jack had given her a goodbye party last night at BJ's. Half the town had come, including Tack. Not that he'd said more than a hello. He'd spent the evening nursing a beer and visiting, but all the while, his gaze had been trained on Annie. As if to say, *Here I am. I've laid my cards on the table. The next move is yours, honey.*

It had surprised her. She'd expected him to come at her like gangbusters, to order and demand and do exactly what his father had done to keep Cherry Divine in town and in his bed.

Tack had done none of that, proving he was less like his father than she'd initially thought.

Not that it mattered. Annie had to leave.

Had? There was no *had* about it. She wanted to leave, to make her own way, to live for herself and no one else for the first time in her life. To make her dreams come true.

If only fulfilling her dreams didn't hurt so damn much.

She steeled herself against the thought and climbed into her Chevy. The puppies sat on the seat next to her in their traveling cage. Annie gave the house one last glimpse, wiped at her watery eyes and pulled out of the driveway for the last time.

"LET HER LOOSE!" TACK YELLED, holding on to the reins for all he was worth. The two cowboys holding the ropes on Fern drew them back and she reared up, nearly throwing Tack, who sat firmly in the saddle, riding her for the first time.

He held on, his grip determined as she kicked and stomped and snorted against the feel of the saddle and the weight on her back. Seconds ticked by until she accepted the inevitable and started to calm beneath Tack's guidance.

Cheers went up a few minutes later as he climbed off after a brief, but exhilarating ride.

"That wasn't so bad now, was it, girl?" He stroked Fern's mane. "If only Eli could have been here." But at this moment, his foreman was pacing the hospital, his arm in a cast, waiting for Vera to give birth to their third child. He smiled as he remembered the excitment on Eli's face when one of the boys had come to fetch him from the corral just a few hours ago, yelling, "Daddy, Daddy! It's time!"

Daddy. A pang of envy shot through Tack. While he'd achieved so much in his life, he wanted more.

A home. Kids. *Annie.*

Tack soothed the lathered horseflesh a minute more, gave Fern a final pat and started to unhitch the saddle. He'd just unstrapped the cinch when he caught sight of a familiar white pickup pulling around the house, the truck bed packed full of boxes.

He swung the saddle over the fence post, exited the corral and started toward her. She climbed out of the truck and met him halfway between the house and the barn.

"You're here," he said, his heart revving faster than a primed cycle poised at the starting gate.

"I just wanted to give you something before I left." She handed him a box. "I made it for you. Something to remember me by."

As if he could forget her.

She'd lived and breathed in his memories for so long,

and now she'd taken up permanent residence in his heart, and there wasn't a damn thing he could do about it.

There was, a nagging voice whispered. He could hitch her over his shoulder, take her into the house and love her until she changed her mind. The heat burned so fierce between them, it would be hot enough to change her mind. For a little while anyway.

His fingers itched and he touched her hand. Her gaze met his and he read the fear in her eyes, the expectancy. That's exactly what she expected him to do. What a part of her wanted. That part she was trying so hard to ignore because she was afraid to give up her version of Austin and the Silver Spurs.

She wasn't her mother.

And Tack wasn't his father. He pulled his hand away even though every fiber of him wanted to crush her in his arms and kiss her.

He concentrated on opening the box.

A navy blue photo album lay inside, nestled in tissue paper. Tack pulled the album free and turned to the first page to see several of the panoramic shots Annie had taken of the Big B. He flipped through several more pages, saw more pictures of the ranch, old photos of Tack and his mother, and even one of Annie and Cherry.

"You liked the memory book I made of my mother," she explained. "So I thought I'd make one of Coop."

Tack simply stared and flipped, until he reached the last page that held a full glossy of himself astride a Yamaha race bike, his expression tense as he arched for a jump.

"This was his favorite," she said. "He wrote to your fan club and requested it. If you get lonely for him—"

"When," he cut in. "When I get lonely for him."

She smiled, a beautiful curve to her lips that warmed him even more than the hot Texas sun. "*When,* you can open up the album and you'll be surrounded by all the things he loved. By him."

He swallowed the baseball-size lump in his throat. "Thanks." With stiff fingers, he managed to close the book. His gaze captured hers. "Do you love me? Because if you do, I need to hear it."

Fear brightened her eyes, made her hands tremble and, for a split second he thought she was going to turn and run without ever admitting the truth. To him. To herself.

"Yes."

The word sang through his head, echoed through his heart. He wanted to hear her say it again and again, to feel the one syllable against his lips. "Then stay. We're not Cherry and Coop."

"Don't you see?" Tears filled her voice, betraying the calm she always tried so hard to maintain. "If I stay, we are, Tack. *We are.*"

"Then kiss me, honey. One last time. For old times' sake."

"I don't..." She shook her head, so close to refusing. Then her gaze caught and held his. "For old times' sake." She stepped toward him and touched her mouth to his.

The photo album thudded to the ground. Tack wrapped his arms around Annie and held her tight, as if he never meant to let go. He gave her a gentle, searing kiss that intensified the ache deep inside him and made him want to hold her forever.

She loved him, he loved her. This was crazy. They could have a life together starting now. *Today.*

A life filled with resentment. While Annie might return his feelings, he knew deep down inside she would always hate herself for not following her ambition, for buckling under the weight of her feelings just as she'd always done in her life.

Maybe she wouldn't. Maybe they'd live happily ever after.

It wasn't a chance he could take. She'd given up so much for the people she cared about, put them and her love for them before her own dreams. As much as Tack wanted her, he didn't want to be another sacrifice.

"I'm not my father, Annie," he murmured against her soft, sweet lips. "And I'm not making the same mistake either." While he knew with dead certainty they were meant for each other, Annie had to discover it for herself.

And if she didn't?

Tack shoved his greatest fear aside and did the hardest thing he'd ever had to do in his life. He let Annie Divine walk away.

"JUST GET THE SHOT AND come on, Annie!" David Bruce, the reporter Annie had been assigned to, motioned her toward a beige Infinity. She clicked off two shots of the charity golf tournament winners as they stepped off the podium and rushed to keep up with the man.

Rushed. That described the past three weeks of her

life since she'd moved to Houston and started her new job. She'd covered numerous stories and taken an obscene number of pictures, and she couldn't call to mind one single subject. She barely had time to look through her viewfinder before she was hustling off to the next assignment.

Deb had been right. Big-city reporting wasn't what it was cracked up to be, the focus on quantity rather than quality. The reporter told the stories with words while the pictures served only as reinforcement. Inconsequential. A second thought.

"Are you okay?" David asked as Annie climbed into the seat beside him and they swerved out into downtown traffic.

"Fine. A little winded."

"You'll get used to it. This is the major league. Pretty soon you'll thrive on the fast pace."

Annie wasn't placing any bets. While she'd remained true to herself and finished what she'd set out to do—taken the job of her dreams and made the move—her heart was no longer in it.

Her heart was back in Inspiration.

With Tack.

Funny that she'd had to travel hundreds of miles to find the courage to admit that to herself. For the first time in her life, Annie not only understood her mother's choices, she sympathized. Cherry had been caught in a catch-22 situation, stay and be miserable as Coop's mistress or go and be miserable without him.

But Annie's situation had been different.

Had it?

While Tack had mentioned love, he hadn't said anything about marriage or family or a future. Just *stay*.

Maybe he'd wanted nothing more than his father.

Maybe he had wanted more.

We're not Cherry and Coop. Annie forced aside the haunting questions, clipped on her press pass and climbed out when they reached their next stop—the Southwest Bridal Fest, a fashion show and formal-wear convention at Buffalo Bayou Park.

While David interviewed some of the designers, Annie snapped picture after picture of the latest bridal wear, cake creations and floral arrangements. David sought her out twenty minutes later and informed her she had a half hour to catch a bite before they headed over to the Harris County courthouse to cover a charity auction.

The opportunity was too tempting to resist. She left David scarfing down stuffed mushrooms at one of the catering booths and headed toward the trees that lined Buffalo Bayou. She'd been denied the simple pleasure of searching for the right shot, the perfect angle, for weeks now, and she was going into withdrawal.

Which was why she'd made up her mind to change things. She'd sent off a few pictures of the Big B to a Texas magazine and had landed her first freelance assignment.

Aiming her camera, she snapped off several landscape shots, then walked farther away from the crowd, along the grassy, tree-lined bank of the bayou.

She aimed for another picture and a strange awareness skittered over her skin, as if someone watched her.

As if…

She glanced around, her gaze searching the trees behind her. Noise rose in the distance, but Annie was out of eyesight of the festival crowd, with just the trees and the water for company.

It was just her imagination, she finally concluded, turning her attention back to her camera. Because no way in heaven, hell or even Texas could Tack Brandon actually be here—

The thought scattered the minute she sighted the familiar face in her viewfinder.

He'd stepped from behind a nearby tree. The bayou twinkled in the background. The overhead branches swayed with the slight breeze. Sunlight chased shadows across his heavily stubbled face. Her mind flashed back to a similar scene, to a man standing down by the creek bed, eating peaches.

But he wasn't standing. He was walking toward her. And he wasn't eating...

He raised a succulent peach to his mouth, took a bite, and Annie felt the sensation clear to her toes, along with a deep burst of joy in her heart.

"You look like hell," she said as he reached her and she noted the tight lines around his mouth, the shadows beneath his eyes, as if he hadn't slept in days. Weeks.

"And you look like pure heaven, sweetheart." He tossed what was left of his peach.

"What are you doing here?"

Two fingers dived into his jeans pocket and he pulled a familiar scrap of white and peach lace free. He grinned that Texas-heartbreaker grin that made her insides jump as he dangled her panties from one tanned finger. "I thought you might want these back."

A smile tugged at her lips despite her best efforts. "I'm wearing new ones."

Instead of saying, "I'll just keep these then," as he had when they'd played this same scene in the *In Touch* office, he said, "I know, honey. I want those, too."

"So you're here collecting women's lingerie?"

"Just yours, Annie." Desperation flared in his eyes, along with a determination that took her breath away. "Only yours. Always yours. I plan to add every damn pair you possess to my stash because I love you and I'm not letting you go."

She'd been fighting what she felt for him for so long, and her defenses automatically kicked in. "You can't force me to come back."

"I would never do that, and I won't ask you to give up your dreams, either. I've been keeping myself away to let you know I respect your decisions, your ambitions. But I'm here now because I'm following *my* dream. You," he said, his fingertips trailing along her cheek as if he couldn't quite believe she was real. "You're my dream, Annie. I want you. Here, or wherever you go."

"What about the ranch? It's your home."

"You're home." His hands cradled her face, his thumbs smoothing across her trembling bottom lip. "Wherever you are, that's where I'll hang my hat. Eli knows the Big B like the back of his hand, he'll take care of things as good as I ever could."

"You can't just leave it all, not now that you've made peace and settled things."

"I can, and I will. For you."

"And spend the rest of your life tagging along after me? I don't want that."

Anger flared deep in his eyes as his mouth drew in a grim line. "So you don't love me. Is that what you're trying to say?"

"No! I do love you. With all my heart. It's just…I don't want that." She shook her head and turned to stare at the shimmering creek. Just beyond, the freeway formed a frenzied maze. Cars zipped back and forth, rushing here and there…

This is what she'd traded sun-drenched fields of flowers and picturesque landscapes for. While the city had its own beauty, it didn't hold a permanent place in Annie's heart.

Not like Inspiration.

Home.

Tack.

"One person making all the sacrifices," Annie said. "That's not what love is all about. It's about give-and-take. An equal amount of both."

"Meaning?" He came up behind her, so close she could feel the heat from his body, hear his heart beating in her ears.

Just where Annie wanted him. Now, and forever.

"I proposed an idea called 'Wild About Texas' to *Texas Highways*," she told him. "The idea is for a collection of nature shots showcasing the untamed beauty of Texas. They bought the proposal and asked about making it a monthly feature." She turned and stared into his eyes. "The closest thing to untamed around here is my new next-door neighbor's Doberman. He went crazy when Tex and Rex moved in, and has been trying to have them for lunch ever since."

Hope fired in his deep blue gaze. "Are you saying what I think you're saying?"

"If you think I'm saying I love you and I want to be with you, then yes, I am. On one condition," she said when he started to reach for her. She caught his arms and held him off, determined to resolve the unanswered questions between them. "I'm not my mother. I won't settle for anything less than everything. Love, marriage, babies—*everything*." She swallowed, and forced herself to say the last two words. "Or nothing."

She'd given him the ultimatum, and as much as she wanted to take the words back and accept whatever he offered, she wouldn't. She wanted an equal relationship, mutual love.

He grinned, the sight easing the anxiety that had been coiling inside her. "*Lots* of babies," he declared as he drew her into his arms and hugged her fiercely. "Ten, at least."

"I was thinking two or three," she said, her heart swelling with the certainty that he loved her as much as she loved him.

"Six," he said.

"Four."

"Five and a half."

She drew away, laughter bubbling on her lips. "A half?"

He grinned. "We'll work something out." His expression went from happiness to serious desperation. "Marry me, Annie, and we'll make a home for ourselves at the Big B and have however many kids God blesses us with. You can take pictures to your heart's content and do anything that makes you happy, as long as we're together. I want you in my bed." He touched one nipple and brought the tip to throbbing awareness. "In my heart." His hand slid higher, over the pounding between her breasts. "In my life." His thumb came to rest over the frantic jump of her pulse. *"Everywhere."*

She smiled through a blurry haze of tears and pulled away from him to grab the hem of her sundress and run her hands up her bare legs.

His expression went from puzzled to hungry. "What are you doing?"

She sniffled and smiled wider. "Giving you a deposit."

She shimmied and wiggled until her peach-colored panties pooled at her ankles. Stepping free, she dangled the scrap of silk in front of him before stuffing the undies into his pocket along with the other pair already in his possession.

"And there will be many more to come. A future of them. *Forever.*" And then she kissed him, surrendering her body to his roaming hands, her heart to his and her soul to whatever the future held.

Love. Happiness. A lifetime of both.

* * * * *

If you enjoyed Tori Carrington's
PRIVATE INVESTIGATIONS,
you'll love her upcoming title,
UNDENIABLE PLEASURES,
available August 2011.

Security expert Jason Savage's next assignment—
protect government witness Jordan Cosby. In two weeks,
Jordan takes the witness stand—but until then, she's
confined to her apartment for her safety. Fortunately
for her, Jason is a substantial distraction, and since
Jordan always gets her way, this may prove to be
an assignment too tempting for him to resist....

Here's a sneak peek...

"This—you and me—shouldn't happen. And it isn't going
to. Not on my watch," Jason said.

Jordan's entire body throbbed with desire. "Are you kidding?"

He stared at her. "Honey, there are two things I never
joke about—sex and war."

She squinted at him. "And which category would you
classify this as?"

He considered her for a long moment. "Both."

He strode from the room as if he were ducking live fire.

Jordan remained on the counter, gaping at the empty air
he'd left in his wake, trying to wrap her head around what
had just happened.

Seriously? Had he really just left her hanging like that?
After nearly making love to her in her own kitchen?

She glanced down at her rumpled clothes. Pulling them
tighter around her, she headed for her bedroom.

As for Mr. Savage, well, he had another thing coming if

he expected her to continue pursuing him after tonight. She might have been desperate enough to try to seduce him this time, but not even she was stupid enough to invite another rejection.

A damn shame. The preview she'd been given told her they would have been very, very good together.

Will Jason be able to resist Jordan's temptation?
After all, the chemistry between them is potent,
*overwhelming…*undeniable!

Make sure to pick up this title!

UNDENIABLE PLEASURES

Available August 2011.

Only from Harlequin® Blaze™.

Harlequin® Blaze™
red-hot reads

If you enjoyed these stories by
Tori Carrington and Kimberly Raye,
you'll love their upcoming titles!

UNDENIABLE PLEASURES
By Tori Carrington

Things are about to get steamy when security expert Jason Savage
is assigned his next case: protecting hot and sexy Jordan Cosby.

THE BRADDOCK BOYS:
TRAVIS
By Kimberly Raye

After a series of bad relationships, Holly Simms is ready to go from
hopeless romantic to town hottie. And lucky for her, hunky cowboy
vampire Travis Braddock knows exactly how to revamp her image!

On Sale August 2011.

Celebrating

Blaze™
10 years of
red-hot reads

Featuring a special August author lineup of
six fan-favorite authors who have written
for Blaze™ from the beginning!

The Original Sexy Six:

Vicki Lewis Thompson
Tori Carrington
Kimberly Raye
Debbi Rawlins
Julie Leto
Jo Leigh

Pick up all six Blaze™
Special Collectors' Edition titles!

August 2011

Plus visit
HarlequinInsideRomance.com
and click on the Series Excitement Tab
for exclusive Blaze™ 10th Anniversary content!